Crime at Christmas

JACK ADRIAN has also edited:

E.F. Benson.
The Flint Knife: Further Spook Stories

Edgar Wallace
The Sooper — And Others
The Death-Room
The Road to London

Sapper
The Best Short Stories

Sexton Blake Wins

Crime at Christmas

A SEASONAL BOX OF MURDEROUS DELIGHTS

Selected and introduced by

JACK ADRIAN

Illustrated by Brian Denington

EQUATION

First published 1988

Crime at Christmas
1. Crime short stories in English, 1900-
—Anthologies
I. Adrian, Jack, *1945-*
823'.0872

ISBN 1-85336-031-7

Equation is an imprint of the
Thorsons Publishing Group,
Wellingborough, Northamptonshire, NN8 2RQ, England

Printed in Great Britain by The Bath Press, Bath, Avon
Typeset by MJL Typesetting, Hitchin, Hertfordshire

1 3 5 7 9 10 8 6 4 2

Contents

Introduction

DICKENS WAS to blame, to begin with. There is no doubt whatever about that. As far as Christmas jollifications go, he has a lot to answer for.

And as the annual flood-tide of festive good cheer threatens once more to engulf us all (as I write, at the beginning of November—seven whole weeks before the dreadful day itself), it's hard not to sympathize with the putative villain of the piece, Ebenezer Scrooge, who, before his unhappy transformation into putty-hearted old buffer, struck the right note exactly: 'Every idiot who goes about with "Merry Christmas" on his lips should be boiled with his own pudding, and buried with a stake of holly through his heart.'

Indeed. And bring back the Poor Laws, bring back the workhouse; especially, bring back the treadmill, and let anyone who so much as whispers 'Compliments of the Season' be sentenced to thirty days on it, without the option.

I have a dream of a perfect Christmas, during which barrel-organs, bedecked with holly and rolled out on Saturday mornings by grinning buffoons with jingling collectors' tins to catch the shopping precinct crowds, will be grenaded. Hot-potato men will have their wares mashed, the resulting sludge stuffed down their trousers; hot-chestnut sellers, especially those dressed in Dickensian garb, dumped in their own braziers; street-actors impersonating Tiny Tim their crutches kicked from under them.

Special task-forces brandishing furled umbrellas with needle-sharp points will be directed to the street-corner pitches of balloon-sellers, there to wreak noisy havoc. Turkeys stuffed with Chinese firecrackers will be sold at knock-down prices, thus spelling ruin for the country's poultry farmers as well as creating mayhem in the kitchen. Carol-singers will be offered LSD-spiked mulled wine, and just let them try getting through 'God Rest You Merry, Gentlemen' when the words start soaring up off the page at them. I see flying-columns of misanthropic midgets dressed as children harassing Santa's Grottos throughout the land. And as for Santa himself, it's the Lucky Dip barrel for him. Head-first.

Do I mean any of this?

Of course not.

Not really.

Well, not entirely. There's no getting away from the fact that Christmas—or at least its extended overture—can at times be an ordeal that tries the bravest heart, the strongest nerve, the mightiest patience.

Hence *Crime at Christmas*, a Box of Murderous (and other) Delights to take your mind off the rigours of the festive season. Here are eighteen short stories and no old sweats—absolutely no stories which, however excellent, you must have read a score or more times before. Most have never appeared in book-form and two, by British crime writer James Melville and American suspense-writer Bill Pronzini, have been written especially for this anthology.

There are tales of tension, tales of brain-racking ingenuity; grim tales, comic tales, atmospheric tales, undeniably acidic tales, tales with twists to their tails. There is a puzzle-story to ponder over, perhaps while cracking nuts beside the fire. There's even a recipe (and a very good one too; and from a surprising source). And all illustrated in fine style by Brian Denington.

All that remains for me now is to wish you, the readers, a downright Dickensian Christmas.

After all, Dickens may be guilty of first-degree assault and battery in the matter of popularizing roast turkey, plum pudding, holly-wreaths, six-foot spruces laden with glitter, and boisterous, back-slapping good cheer; but he had his good points too. Never forget what lay in store for Edwin Drood at the Festive Season . . .

TO OPEN the entertainment, a very special—and very seasonal—story by Nicholas Blake who, of course, wasn't really Nicholas Blake at all but the British poet (later Laureate) Cecil Day Lewis (1904–72), one of a small clutch of critics, academics, and donnish littérateurs who for one reason or another chose to cloak their sub-literary activities beneath a pseudonym.

Blake wrote twenty detective novels, many excellent, and most distinguished by acute observation, a lightly leftish perspective, and (not unnaturally) a sensitive use of language, although the earlier books are a bit over-ripe in literary allusion; at times a bit too larky for real comfort. His main detective was Nigel Strangeways (usefully, a nephew of one of Scotland Yard's assistant commissioners) who, in the early books, had more than a touch of Blake's friend the poet W. H. Auden about him. The best Blakes are those published during the 1940s and 1950s—*Minute For Murder* (1947), for instance, *Head of a Traveller* (1949), and *End of Chapter* (1957)—although his final book, the semi-autobiographical *The Private Wound* 1968, (*sans* Strangeways) is a fine novel which just happens to be a very good puzzle as well.

Blake did not write many short stories (too busy, as C. Day Lewis, attending to his various academic chores); on the evidence of those he did, he ought to have written more. 'A Problem In White' first appeared in 1949, in one of the final issues of the *Strand Magazine*—last and greatest of the grand old periodicals to survive from the Golden Age of fiction magazines that stretched from Edwardian times up to the Second World War, although now somewhat shrivelled in size and format. Still, even in those austere times its editor could spring a surprise or two—such as this ingenious puzzle story set against that most beguiling of backgrounds (at least for the reader, esconced in an armchair toasting toes in front of the fire): the night-express to Scotland trapped in a snowdrift on the Shap.

There are sub-plots, red herrings, and some very suspicious characters—and there is, of course, a murder. But who, of all the suspects, is the murderer? The answer is not at the end of the story because the end of the story has, as with its first appearance in the *Strand*, been shifted elsewhere. The clues are all laid out, just waiting to be spotted. But can you spot them?

1

A Problem in White

NICHOLAS BLAKE

'SEASONABLE weather for the time of year,' remarked the Expansive Man in a voice succulent as the breast of a roast goose.

The Deep Chap, sitting next to him in the railway compartment, glanced out at the snow swarming and swirling past the window-pane. He replied:

'You really like it? Oh well, it's an ill blizzard that blows nobody no good. Depends what you mean by seasonable, though. Statistics for the last fifty years would show—'

'Name of Joad, sir?' asked the Expansive Man, treating the compartment to a wholesale wink.

'No, Stansfield, Henry Stansfield.' The Deep Chap, a ruddy-faced man who sat with hands firmly planted on the knees of his brown tweed suit, might have been a prosperous farmer but for the long, steady meditative scrutiny which he now bent upon each of his fellow-travellers in turn.

What he saw was not particularly rewarding. On the opposite seat, from left to right, were a Forward Piece, who had taken the Expansive Man's wink wholly to herself and contrived to wriggle her tight skirt farther up from her knee; a desiccated, sandy, lawyerish little man who fumed and fussed like an angry kettle, consulting every five minutes his gold watch, then shaking out his *Times* with the crackle of a legal parchment, and a Flash Card, dressed up to the nines of spivdom, with the bold yet uneasy stare of the young delinquent.

'Mine's Percy Dukes,' said the Expansive Man. 'PD to my friends, General Dealer. At your service. Well, we'll be across the border in an hour and a half, and then hey for the bluebells of bonny Scotland!'

'Bluebells in January? You're hopeful,' remarked the Forward Piece.

'Are you Scots, master?' asked the Comfortable Body sitting on Stansfield's left.

'English outside'—Percy Dukes patted the front of his grey suit, slid a flask from its hip pocket, and took a swig—'and Scotch within.' His loud laugh, or the blizzard, shook the railway carriage. The Forward Piece giggled. The Flash Card covertly sneered.

'You'll need that if we run into a drift and get stuck for the night,' said Henry Stansfield.

'Name of Jonah, sir?' The compartment reverberated again.

'I do not apprehend such an eventuality,' said the Fusspot. 'The station-master at Lancaster assured me that the train would get through. We are scandalously late already, though.' Once again the gold watch was consulted.

'It's a curious thing,' remarked the Deep Chap meditatively, 'the way we imagine we can make Time amble withal or gallop withal, just by keeping an eye on the hands of a watch. You travel frequently by this train, Mr—?'

'Kilmington. Arthur J Kilmington. No, I've only used it once before.' The Fusspot spoke in a dry Edinburgh accent.

'Ah yes, that would have been on the 17th of last month. I remember seeing you on it.'

'No, sir, you are mistaken. It was the 20th.' Mr Kilmington's thin mouth snapped tight again, like a rubber band round a sheaf of legal documents.

'The 20th? Indeed? That was the day of the train robbery. A big haul they got, it seems. Off this very train. It was carrying some of the extra Christmas mail. Bags just disappeared, somewhere between Lancaster and Carlisle.'

'Och, deary me,' sighed the Comfortable Body. 'I don't know what we're coming to, really, nowadays.'

'We're coming to the scene of the crime, ma'am,' said the expansive Mr Dukes. The train, almost dead-beat, was panting up the last pitch towards Shap Summit.

'I didn't see anything in the papers about where the robbery took place,' Henry Stansfield murmured. Dukes fastened a somewhat bleary eye upon him.

'You read all the newspapers?'

'Yes.'

The atmosphere in the compartment had grown suddenly tense. Only the Flash Card, idly examining his fingernails, seemed unaffected by it.

'Which paper did you see it in?' pursued Stansfield.

'I didn't.' Dukes tapped Stansfield on the knee. 'But I can use my loaf. Stands to reason. You want to tip a mail-bag out of a train—get me? Train must be moving slowly, or the bag'll burst when it hits the ground. Only one place between Lancaster and Carlisle where you'd *know* the train would be crawling. Shap Bank. And it goes slowest on the last bit of the bank, just about where we are now. Follow?'

Henry Stansfield nodded.

'O.K. But you'd be balmy to tip it off just anywhere on this God-forsaken moorland,' went on Mr Dukes. 'Now, if you'd travelled this line as much as I have, you'd have noticed it goes over a bridge about a mile short of the summit. Under the bridge runs a road: a nice, lonely road, see? The only road hereabouts that touches the railway. You tip out the bag there. Your chums collect it, run down the embankment, dump it in the car they've got waiting by the bridge, and Bob's your uncle!'

'You oughta been a detective, mister,' exclaimed the Forward Piece languishingly.

Mr Dukes inserted his thumbs in his armpits, looking gratified. 'Maybe I am,' he said with a wheezy laugh. 'And maybe I'm just little old PD, who knows how to use his loaf.'

'Och, well now, the things people will do!' said the Comfortable Body. 'There's a terrible lot of dishonesty to-day.'

The Flash Card glanced up contemptuously from his fingernails. Mr Kilmington was heard to mutter that the system of surveillance on railways was disgraceful, and the Guard of the train should have been severely censured.

'The Guard can't be everywhere,' said Stansfield. 'Presumably he has to patrol the train from time to time, and—'

'Let him do so, then, and not lock himself up in his van and go to sleep,' interrupted Mr Kilmington, somewhat unreasonably.

'Are you speaking from personal experience, sir?' asked Stansfield.

The Flash Card lifted up his voice and said, in a Charing-Cross-Road American accent, 'Hey, fellas! If the gang was gonna tip out the mail-bags by the bridge, like this guy says—what I mean is, how could they rely on the Guard being out of his van just at that point?' He hitched up the trousers of his loud check suit.

'You've got something there,' said Percy Dukes. 'What I reckon is, there must have been two accomplices on the train—one to get the Guard out of his van on some pretext, and the other to chuck off the bags.' He turned to Mr Kilmington. 'You were saying something about the Guard locking himself up in his van. Now if I was of a suspicious turn of mind, if I was little old Sherlock H. in person'—he bestowed another prodigious wink upon Kilmington's fellow-travellers—'I'd begin to wonder about you, sir. You were travelling on this train when the robbery took place. You went to the Guard's van. You *say* you found him asleep. You didn't by any chance call the Guard out, so as to—?'

'Your suggestion is outrageous! I advise you to be very careful, sir, very careful indeed,' enunciated Mr Kilmington, his precise voice crackling with indignation, 'or you may find you have said something actionable. I would have you know that, when I—'

But what he would have them know was to remain undivulged. The train, which for some little time had been running cautiously down from Shap Summit, suddenly began to chatter and shudder, like a fever patient in high delirium, as the vacuum brakes were applied; then, with the dull impact of a fist driving into a feather pillow, the engine buried itself in a drift which had gathered just beyond the bend of a deep cutting. The time was five minutes past seven.

'What's this in aid of?' asked the Forward Piece, rather shrilly, as a hysterical outburst of huffing and puffing came from the engine.

'Run into a drift, I reckon.'

'He's trying to back us out. No good. The wheels are slipping every time. What a lark!' Percy Dukes had his head out of the window on the lee side of the train. 'Coom to Coomberland for your winter sports!'

'Guard! Guard, I say!' called Mr Kilmington. But the blue-clad figure, after one glance into the compartment, hurried on his way up the corridor. 'Really! I *shall* report that man.'

Henry Stansfield, going out into the corridor, opened a window. Though the coach was theoretically sheltered by the cutting on this windward side, the blizzard stunned his face like a knuckleduster of ice. He joined the herd of passengers who had climbed down and were stumbling towards the engine. As they reached it, the Guard emerged from its cab: no cause for alarm, he said; if they couldn't get through, there'd be a relief engine sent down to take the train back to Tebay; he was just off to set fog-signals on the line behind them.

The driver renewed his attempts to back the train out. But, what with its weight, the up-gradient in its rear, the icy rails, and the clinging grip of the drift on the engine, he could not budge her.

'We'll have to dig out the bogeys, mate,' he said to the fireman. 'Fetch them shovels from the forward van. It'll keep the perishers from freezing, any road.' He jerked his finger at the knot of passengers who, lit up by the glare of the furnace, were capering and beating their arms like savages amid the swirling snow-wreaths.

Percy Dukes, who had now joined them, quickly established himself as the life and soul of the party, referring to the grimy-faced fireman as 'Snowball,' adjuring his companions to 'Dig for Victory,' affecting to spy the approach of a herd of St Bernards, each with a keg of brandy slung round its neck. But, after ten minutes of hard digging, when the leading wheels of the bogey were cleared, it could be seen that they had been derailed by their impact with the drift.

'That's torn it, Charlie. You'll have to walk back to the box and get 'em to telephone through for help,' said the driver.

'*If* the wires aren't down already,' replied the fireman lugubriously. 'It's above a mile to that box, and uphill. Who d'you think I am? Captain Scott?'

'You'll have the wind behind you, mate, any road. So long.'

A buzz of dismay had risen from the passengers at this. One or two, who began to get querulous, were silenced by the driver's offering to take them anywhere they liked if they would just lift his engine back on to the metals first. When the rest had dispersed to their carriages, Henry Stansfield asked the driver's permission to go up into the cab for a few minutes and dry his coat.

'You're welcome.' The driver snorted: 'Would you believe it? "Must get to Glasgow tonight." Damn ridiculous! Now Bert—that's my Guard—it's different for him: he's entitled to fret a bit. Missus been very poorly. Thought she was going to peg out before Christmas; but he got the best surgeon in Glasgow to operate on her, and she's mending now, he says. He reckons to look in every night at the nursing home, when he goes off work.'

Stansfield chatted with the man for five minutes. Then the Guard returned, blowing upon his hands—a smallish, leathery-faced chap, with an anxious look in his eye.

'We'll not get through to-night, Bert. Charlie told you?'

'Aye. I doubt some of the passengers are going to create a rumpus,' said the Guard dolefully.

Henry Stansfield went back to his compartment. It was stuffy, but with a sinister hint of chilliness, too: he wondered how long the steam heating would last: depended upon the amount of water in the engine boiler, he supposed. Amongst the wide variety of fates he had imagined for himself, freezing to death in an English train was not included.

Arthur J Kilmington fidgeted more than ever. When the Guard came along the corridor, he asked him where the nearest village was, saying he must get a telephone call through to Edinburgh—most urgent appointment—must let his client know, if he was going to miss it. The Guard said there was a village two miles to the north-east; you could see the lights from the top of the cutting; but he warned Mr Kilmington against trying to get there in the teeth of this blizzard—better wait for the relief engine, which should reach them before 9 p.m.

Silence fell upon the compartment for a while; the incredulous silence of civilized people who find themselves in the predicament of castaways. Then the expansive Mr Dukes proposed that, since they were to be stuck here for an hour or two, they should get acquainted. The Comfortable Body now introduced herself as Mrs Grant, the Forward Piece as Inez Blake; the Flash Card, with the over-negligent air of one handing a dud half-crown over a counter, gave his name as Macdonald—I. Macdonald.

'A fine old Scots name,' said Mrs Grant.

'I for Ian,' said Mr Dukes. 'Or would it be Izzy?'

'Irving, if you want to know,' replied the young man. 'Any objection? You like to make something of it?'

'Keep your hair on, young shaver.'

'So I'm a Yid, am I? That's your idea, uh?'

'If you get steamed up any more,' said Mr Dukes, 'it'll ruin that permanent wave of yours.'

'It only remains for one of you to suggest a nice friendly game of cards, now we've had the preliminary patter,' said Henry Stansfield.

This reference to the technique of card-sharpers who work the trains silenced even Percy Dukes for a moment. However, he soon recovered.

'I see you weren't born yesterday, mister. We must've sounded a bit like that. You can always tell 'em a mile off, can't you? No offence meant to this young gent. Just P.D.'s little bit of fun.'

'I wish somebody would tell me what this is all about,' asked Inez Blake, pouting provocatively at Mr Dukes, who at once obliged.

'They must be awfu' clever,' remarked Mrs Grant, in her singsong Lowland accent, when he had finished.

'No criminals are clever, ma'am,' said Stansfield quietly. His ruminative eye passed, without haste, from Macdonald to Dukes. 'Neither the small fry nor the big operators. They're pretty well subhuman, the whole lot of 'em. A dash of cunning, a thick streak of cowardice, and the rest is made up of stupidity and boastfulness. They're too stupid for anything but crime, and so riddled with inferiority that they always give themselves away, sooner or later, by boasting about their crimes. They like to think of themselves as the wide boys, but they're as narrow as starved eels—why, they haven't even the wits to alter their professional methods: that's how the police pick 'em up.'

'I entirely agree, sir,' Mr Kilmington snapped. 'In my profession I see a good deal of the criminal classes. And I flatter myself none of them has ever got the better of me. They're transparent, sir, transparent.'

'No doubt you gentlemen are right,' said Percy Dukes comfortably. 'But the police haven't picked up the chaps who did this train robbery yet.'

'They will. And the Countess of Axminster's emerald bracelet. Bet the gang didn't reckon to find that in the mail-bag. Worth all of £25,000.'

Percy Duke's mouth fell open. The Flash Card whistled. Overcome, either by the stuffiness of the carriage or the thought of £25,000-worth of emeralds, Inez Blake gave a little moan and fainted all over Mr Kilmington's lap.

'Really! Upon my soul! My dear young lady!' exclaimed that worthy. There was a flutter of solicitude, shared by all except the cold-eyed young Macdonald who, after stooping over her a moment, his back to the others, said, 'Here you—stop pawing the young lady and let her stretch out on the seat. Yes, I'm talking to you, Kilmington.'

'How dare you! This is an outrage!' The little man stood up so abruptly that the girl was almost rolled on to the floor. 'I was merely trying to—'

'I know your sort. Nasty old men. Now, keep your hands off her! I'm telling you.'

In the shocked silence that ensued, Kilmington gobbled speechlessly at Macdonald for a moment; then, seeing razors in the youth's cold-steel eye, snatched his black hat and brief-case from the rack and bolted out of the compartment. Henry Stansfield made as if to stop him, then changed his mind. Mrs Grant followed the little man out, returning presently, her handkerchief soaked in water, to dab Miss Blake's forehead. The time was just on 8.30.

When things were restored to normal, Mr Dukes turned to Stansfield. 'You were saying this necklace of—who was it?—the Countess of Axminster, it's worth £25,000? Fancy sending a thing of that value through the post! Are you sure of it?'

'The value? Oh, yes.' Henry Stansfield spoke out of the corner of his mouth, in the manner of a stupid man imparting a confidence. 'Don't let this go any farther. But I've a friend who works in the Cosmopolitan—the Company where it's insured. That's another thing that didn't get into the papers. Silly woman. She wanted it for some big family do in Scotland at Christmas, forgot to bring it with her, and wrote home for it to be posted to her in a registered packet.'

'£25,000,' said Percy Dukes thoughtfully. 'Well, stone me down!'

'Yes. Some people don't know when they're lucky, do they?'

Dukes's fat face wobbled on his shoulders like a globe of lard. Young Macdonald polished his nails. Inez Blake read her magazine. After some while, Percy Dukes remarked that the blizzard was slackening; he'd take an airing and see if there was any sign of the relief engine yet. He left the compartment.

At the window, the snowflakes danced in their tens now, not their thousands. The time was 8.55. Shortly afterwards, Inez Blake went out; and ten minutes later, Mrs Grant remarked to Stansfield that it had stopped snowing altogether. Neither Inez nor Dukes had returned when, at 9.30, Henry Stansfield decided to ask what had happened about the relief. The Guard was not in his van, which adjoined Stansfield's coach, towards the rear of the train. So he turned back, walked up the corridor to the front coach, clambered out, and hailed the engine cab.

'She must have been held up,' said the Guard, leaning out. 'Charlie here got through from the box, and they promised her by nine o'clock. But it'll no' be long now, sir.'

'Have you seen anything of a Mr Kilmington—small, sandy chap—black hat and overcoat, blue suit—was in my compartment? I've walked right up the train and he doesn't seem to be on it.'

The Guard pondered a moment. 'Och aye, yon wee fellow? Him that asked me about telephoning from the village. Aye, he's awa' then.'

'He did set off to walk there, you mean?'

'Nae doot he did, if he's no' on the train. He spoke to me again—juist on nine, it'd be—and said he was awa' if the relief didna turn up in five minutes.'

'You've not seen him since?'

'No, sir. I've been talking to my mates here this half-hour, ever syne the wee fellow spoke to me.'

Henry Stansfield walked thoughtfully back down the permanent way. When he had passed out of the glare shed by the carriage lights on the snow, he switched on his electric torch. Just beyond the last coach, the eastern wall of the cutting sloped sharply down and merged into moorland level with the track. Although the snow had stopped altogether, an icy wind from the north-east still blew, raking and numbing his face. Twenty yards farther on, his torch lit up a track, already half filled in with snow, made by several pairs of feet, pointing away over the moor, towards the north-east. Several passengers, it seemed, had set off for the village, whose lights twinkled like frost in the far distance. Stansfield was about to follow this track when he heard footsteps scrunching the snow farther up the line. He switched off the torch; at once it was as if a sack had been thrown over his head, so close and blinding was the darkness. The steps came nearer. Stansfield switched on his torch, at the last minute, pinpointing the squab figure of Percy Dukes. The man gave a muffled oath.

'What the devil! Here, what's the idea, keeping me waiting half an hour in that blasted—?'

'Have you seen Kilmington?'

'Oh, it's you. No, how the hell should I have seen him? Isn't he on the train? I've been walking up the line, to look for the relief. No sign yet. Damn parky, it is—I'm moving on.'

Presently Stansfield moved on, too, but along the track towards the village. The circle of his torchlight wavered and bounced on the deep snow. The wind, right in his teeth, was killing. No wonder, he thought, as after a few hundred yards he approached the end of the trail, those passengers turned back. Then he realised they had not all turned back. What he had supposed to be a hummock of snow bearing a crude resemblance to a recumbent human figure, he now saw to be a human figure covered with snow. He scraped some of the snow off it, turned it gently over on its back.

Arthur J Kilmington would fuss no more in this world. His brief-case was buried beneath him: his black hat was lying where it had fallen, lightly covered with snow, near the head. There seemed, to Stansfield's cursory examination, no mark of violence on him. But the eyeballs started, the face was suffused with a pinkish-blue colour. So men look who have been strangled, thought Stansfield, or asphyxiated. Quickly he knelt down again, shining his torch in the dead face. A qualm of horror shook him. Mr Kilmington's nostrils were caked thick with snow, which had frozen solid in them, and snow had been rammed tight into his mouth also.

And here he would have stayed, reflected Stansfield, in this desolate spot, for days or weeks, perhaps, if the snow lay or deepened. And when the thaw at last came (as it did that year, in fact, only after two months), the snow would thaw out from his mouth and nostrils, too, and there would be no vestige of murder left—only the corpse of an impatient little lawyer who had tried to walk to the village in a blizzard and died for his pains. It might even be that no one would ask how such a precise, pernickety little chap had ventured the two-mile walk in thin shoes and without a torch to light his way through the pitchy blackness; for Stansfield, going through the man's pockets, had found the following articles—and nothing more: pocket-book, fountain-pen, handkerchief, cigarette-case, gold lighter, two letters and some loose change.

Stansfield started to return for help. But, only twenty yards back, he noticed another trail of footprints, leading off the main track to the left. This trail seemed a fresher one—the snow lay less thickly in the indentations—and to have been made by one pair of feet only. He followed it up, walking beside it. Whoever made this track had walked in a slight right-handed curve back to the railway line, joining it about 150 yards south of where the main trail came out. At this point there was a platelayers' shack. Finding the door unlocked, Stansfield entered. There was nothing inside but a coke-brazier, stone cold, and a smell of cigar-smoke . . .

Half an hour later, Stansfield returned to his compartment. In the meanwhile, he had helped the train crew to carry back the body of Kilmington, which was now locked in the Guard's van. He had also made an interesting discovery as to Kilmington's movements. It was to be presumed that, after the altercation with Macdonald, and the brief conversation already reported by the Guard, the lawyer must have gone to sit in another compartment. The last coach, to the rear of the Guard's van, was a first-class one, almost empty. But in one of its compartments, Stansfield found a passenger asleep. He woke him up, gave a description of Kilmington, and asked if he had seen him earlier.

The passenger grumpily informed Stansfield that a smallish man, in a dark overcoat, with the trousers of a blue suit showing beneath it, had come to the door and had a word with him. No, the passenger had not noticed his face particularly, because he'd been very drowsy himself, and

besides, the chap had politely taken off his black Homburg hat to address him, and the hat screened as much of the head as was not cut off from his view by the top of the door. No, the chap had not come into his compartment: he had just stood outside, inquired the time (the passenger had looked at his watch and told him it was 8.50); then the chap had said that, if the relief didn't turn up by nine, he intended to walk to the nearest village.

Stansfield had then walked along to the engine cab. The Guard, whom he found there, told him that he'd gone up the track about 8.45 to meet the fireman on his way back from the signal-box. He had gone as far as the place where he had put down his fog-signals earlier; here, just before nine, he and the fireman met, as the latter corroborated. Returning to the train, the Guard had climbed into the last coach, noticed Kilmington sitting alone in a first-class compartment (it was then that the lawyer announced to the Guard his intention of walking if the relief engine had not arrived within five minutes). The Guard then got out of the train again, and proceeded down the track to talk to his mates in the engine cab.

This evidence would seem to point incontrovertibly at Kilmington's having been murdered shortly after 9 p.m., Stansfield reflected as he went back to his own compartment. His other fellow-passengers were all present and correct now.

'Well, did you find him?' asked Percy Dukes.

'Kilmington? Oh yes, I found him. In the snow over there. He was dead.'

Inez Blake gave a little, affected scream. The permanent sneer was wiped, as if by magic, off young Macdonald's face, which turned a sickly white. Mr Dukes sucked in his fat lips.

'The puir wee man,' said Mrs Grant. 'He tried to walk it then? Died of exposure, was it?'

'No,' announced Stansfield flatly, 'he was murdered.'

This time, Inez Blake screamed in earnest; and, like an echo, a hooting shriek came from far up the line: the relief engine was approaching at last.

'The police will be awaiting us back at Tebay, so we'd better all have our stories ready.' Stansfield turned to Percy Dukes. 'You, for instance, sir. Where were you between 8.55, when you left the carriage, and 9.35 when I met you returning? Are you sure you didn't see Kilmington?'

Dukes, expansive no longer, his piggy eyes sunk deep in the fat of his face, asked Stansfield who the hell he thought he was.

'I am an inquiry agent, employed by the Cosmopolitan Insurance Company. Before that, I was a Detective Inspector in the C.I.D. Here is my card.'

Dukes barely glanced at it. 'That's all right, old man. Only wanted to make sure. Can't trust anyone nowadays.' His voice had taken on the ingratiating, oleaginous heartiness of the small businessman trying to clinch a deal with a bigger one. 'Just went for a stroll, y'know—stretch the old legs. Didn't see a soul.'

'Who were you expecting to see? Didn't you wait for someone in the platelayers' shack along there, and smoke a cigar while you were waiting? Who did you mistake me for when you said "What's the idea, keeping me waiting half an hour"?'

'Here, draw it mild, old man.' Percy Dukes sounded injured. 'I certainly looked in at the hut: smoked a cigar for a bit. Then

I toddled back to the train, and met up with your good self on the way. I didn't make no appointment to meet—'

'Oo! Well I *must* say,' interrupted Miss Blake virtuously. She could hardly wait to tell Stansfield that, on leaving the compartment shortly after Dukes, she'd overheard voices on the track below the lavatory window. 'I recognised this gentleman's voice,' she went on, tossing her head at Dukes. 'He said something like, "You're going to help us again, chum, so you'd better get used to the idea. You're in it up to the neck—can't back out now." And another voice, sort of mumbling, might have been Mr Kilmington's—I dunno—sounded Scotch anyway—said, "All right. Meet you in five minutes: platelayers' hut a few hundred yards up the line. Talk it over".'

'And what did you do then, young lady?' asked Stansfield. 'You didn't return to the compartment, I remember.'

'I happened to meet a gentleman friend, farther up the train, and sat with him for a bit.'

'Is that so?' remarked Macdonald menacingly. 'Why, you four-flushing little—!'

'Shut up!' commanded Stansfield.

'Honest I did,' the girl said, ignoring Macdonald. 'I'll introduce you to him, if you like. He'll tell you I was with him for, oh, half an hour or more.'

'And what about Mr Macdonald?'

'I'm not talking,' said the youth sullenly.

'Mr Macdonald isn't talking. Mrs Grant?'

'I've been in this compartment ever since, sir.'

'Ever since—?'

'Since I went out to damp my hankie for this young lady, when she'd fainted. Mr Kilmington was just before me, you'll mind. I saw him go through into the Guard's van.'

'Did you hear him say anything about walking to the village?'

'No, sir. He just hurried into the van, and then there was some havers about it's no' being lockit this time, and how he was going to report the Guard for it—I didna listen any more, wishing to get back to the young lady. I doubt the wee man would be for reporting everyone.'

'I see. And you've been sitting here with Mr Macdonald all the time?'

'Yes, sir. Except for ten minutes or so he was out of the compartment, just after you'd left.'

'What did you go out for?' Stansfield asked the young man.

'Just taking the air, brother, just taking the air.'

'You weren't taking Mr Kilmington's gold watch, as well as the air, by any chance?' Stansfield's keen eyes were fastened like a hook into Macdonald's, whose insolent expression visibly crumbled beneath them.

'I don't know what you mean,' he tried to bluster. 'You can't do this to me.'

'I mean that a man has been murdered: and, when the police search you, they will find his gold watch in your possession. Won't look too healthy for you, my young friend.'

'Naow! Give us a chance! It was only a joke, see?' The wretched Macdonald was whining now in his native cockney. 'He got me riled—the stuck-up way he said nobody'd ever got the better of him. So I thought I'd just show him—I'd have given it back, straight I would, only I couldn't find him afterwards. It was just a joke, I tell you. Anyway, it was Inez who lifted the ticker.'

'You dirty little rotter!' screeched the girl.

'Shut up, both of you! You can explain your joke to the police. Let's hope they don't die laughing.'

At this moment the train gave a lurch, and started back up the gradient. It halted at the signal-box, for Stansfield to telephone to Tebay, then clattered south again.

On Tebay platform, Stansfield was met by an Inspector and a Sergeant of the County Constabulary, with the Police Surgeon. No passengers were permitted to alight till he had had a few words with them. Then the four men boarded the train. After a brief pause in the Guard's van, where the Police Surgeon drew aside the Guard's black off-duty overcoat that had been laid over the body, and began his preliminary examination, they marched along to Stansfield's compartment. The Guard who, at his request, had locked this as the train was drawing up at the platform and was keeping an eye on its occupants, now unlocked it. The Inspector entered.

His first action was to search Macdonald. Finding the watch concealed on his person, he then charged Macdonald and Inez Blake with the theft. The Inspector next proceeded to make an arrest on the charge of wilful murder. . .

BUT WHO DID the Inspector arrest for the murder of the disagreeable Arthur J. Kilmington? And why? Nicholas Blake placed eight clues to the killer's identity in the text (two major clues; six minor ones); they cover motive as well as method.

Baffled? Read the story again—or meander through the rest of the stories in the book (there's never any hurry over Christmas) and then read it once more.

If you still can't identify the who, the how, and the why—turn to page 221 at the very end of the book, where all is revealed.

TODAY, ALAS, John Dickson Carr (1906–77, also wrote as Carter Dickson) is not perhaps so well thought of as once he was—at least judging by the number of books-in-print a decade or so after his death. Probably the sea-change in taste caused by the Second Coming of the Private Eye over the past four or five years has a lot to do with that, because in many ways (viewpoint, politics, ideals, general attitude) Carr is unashamedly pre-War—although he did have a curiously modern fondness for female characters who were by no means virtuous, and strive as he might to fall in with the popular conventions his murderesses (of whom there were not a few) come alive as his heroines often don't. But then you never looked to Carr for sharply drawn and realistic characters (his two main detectives, Dr Fell and Sir Henry Merrivale, though vastly entertaining, are wildly extravagant caricatures): you looked to him for dazzling virtuoso plots—and rarely were you disappointed. Carr could plot, in spades.

From 1930 to 1960, roughly, he virtually cornered the market in that toughest yet most alluring of sub-genres, the Impossible Crime, which of course takes in such knotty problems as the Locked-Room Murder, the Vanishing Corpse, the Disappearing Murderer, the Body-Surrounded-By-Unmarked-Sand, the Stiff-Found-In-A-House-Encircled-By-Virgin-Snow, and so on. Carr not only triumphantly rang the changes on all of these but also created a couple of score more brain-racking situations which (and here was the genius of the man) when explained were really as simple as ABC.

He was also (and this too goes against the current trend) a master of shuddery atmosphere, a genuine *frisson*-creator who preferred cold grue for his effects to bucketfuls of gore and eviscerated guts. Still my favourite Carr is *The Burning Court* (1937), a masterpiece not only for two Impossible Disappearances brilliantly explained but also for the aura of brooding horror that permeates its pages—and which, unsettlingly, lingers on after you've finished.

Carr wrote very good historical mysteries (one, *Fire, Burn!*, with a time-travel theme), quantities of chilling radio-plays for both CBS's *Suspense* series and the BBC's wonderful *Appointment With Fear*, and a host of short stories, many of which are now recognized classics.

'Detective's Day Off' is not a classic, but it is a model of its kind featuring, in its short space, not one but two astonishing vanishments from areas under police observation. It is also, as far as I know, the only John Dickson Carr short story never to have appeared in bookform anywhere in the world.

2

Detective's Day Off

JOHN DICKSON CARR

WITH Christmas only three days away, men and women throughout London were celebrating the season of joy and goodwill by elbowing and pushing each other ferociously through every shop and department store.

And at Omniums, the giant store in Oxford Street, it was worse than anywhere.

Outside, past lanes of lighted windows, festive snowflakes sifted from a darkening sky. A loudspeaker van blared 'Hark the Herald Angels Sing' to crowds struggling in slush.

Inside, frantic shoppers assailed the gift counters, and assaulted each other in the process.

Their noise was a shuffle and roar. Their aroma was a steam of wet overcoats.

And at the entrance to Toyland on the fifth floor stood a pretty, fair-haired girl. Her loving glance at the tall, handsome man beside her was clouded with annoyance. The little boy, clutching his hand, jumped up and down in a desperate attempt to break his far-away look of intense preoccupation.

The girl said: 'For heaven's sake, Bob, what is the matter with you?'

Detective Superintendent Robert Pollard for a moment did not reply. Officially off duty, he was still thinking hard about the case he had left for others to solve at New Scotland Yard—so that he could take his fiancée, Elsa Rawson, shopping at Omniums, and her six-year-old nephew, Tommy, to the toyfair.

'Bob,' said the girl again, in exasperation, 'do look as though you're enjoying yourself.'

'I've just thought,' said Bob, returning once again to the shopping battle. 'When I left the office, I didn't ring the Duty Room to say where I was going.'

'And that's all?' asked the astonished Elsa. 'That's all you're worried about?'

'Elsa, everybody has to phone the Duty Room when he leaves Scotland Yard . . .'

Young Tommy, saucer-eyed, leaped high in the air.

'Scotland Yard!' he cried in ecstasy. 'Scotland Yard . . . Yeepee!'

'Tommy, please do be quiet, said Elsa, 'or Uncle Bob won't take you to see Father Christmas.' Tommy writhed. Privately, he thought this Father Christmas business all a gag. But you couldn't be sure, and it was too close to Christmas to take any risks.

'Anyway, Bob, is it all that important?' she asked, searching his face closely for an endearing look.

From the moment they left for their shopping expedition, Elsa's suspicion grew—Bob did not have his mind on her. She wondered if perhaps Tommy's presence had annoyed him. Was he really more concerned about his precious crime work than pleasing her?

She couldn't restrain a petulant note when she asked:

'And how are all the little coppers at Scotland Yard? Are they having a happy Christmas?'

To Det. Supt. Pollard this was the last straw. He raised his powerful voice above a din which included the whiz of toy trains and a radio loudly blaring 'Hark the Herald Angels Sing'.

'If anybody at the Yard started singing about herald angels,' Pollard said. 'I hate to think what would happen to him. Anyway, they've got something else to think about right now, Elsa. It's a really big case. And we're all in a flap about it.'

'Is it a murder, Uncle Bob?' screamed Tommy.

'No, old chap, it's not a murder. And yet, in way, it's worse.'

'Crumbs,' said Tommy, and jumped so high that he seemed to be levitated from Pollard's hand.

'Bob, stop it!' snapped Elsa. 'You mustn't tease the child.'

'I am not teasing. This case isn't a teasing matter. It's not every day that we hear about two people, at exactly the same moment, but in completely different parts of London, both disappearing like soap-bubbles before the eyes of police witnesses.'

'Tommy, don't listen! He's joking!'

'Elsa, I'm not. A crook known as "The Colonel", and another crook known as "Shorty", both vanished off the face of the earth. Twenty thousand pounds' worth of uncut diamonds went with them. The point is *how did they vanish*?'

'Tommy, don't believe a word of this,' cried Elsa, gripping Tommy's other hand so that he was tugged between them. 'Uncle Bob never talks about police work. I can't make him talk about it!'

In fact, having just reached the howling

centre of Toyland, Bob couldn't make himself heard.

Tommy was yanked away between his captors to a place of comparative quiet. There, behind his counter, the conjuror was exhibiting a large skull which first made whistling noises and then talked like Marshal Wyatt Earp.

Elsa was shivering with excitement.

'Why do they call him The Colonel?'

'Because he looks like a colonel in a comic paper. Middle-aged; military bearing; usually wears an eyeglass. Even when he doesn't wear an eyeglass, he has a gesture he can't help making. He keeps dragging down the side of his left eye. Like this!'

'Darling, for heaven's sake, don't leer. You look horrible.'

'Well, so does The Colonel. But you can spot that gesture a mile away, and you can spot him. As a rule, he's a confidence man.'

'A confidence man? You mean he swindled somebody out of £20,000 worth of uncut diamonds?'

'No!' Pollard snapped. 'It's worse. For the first time in his life, the fool used violence.'

'Did he murder somebody?' shouted Elsa. 'Cut some poor man's throat?'

Tommy, who had been trying vainly to scream gave it up and writhed in an agony of fascination. But Pollard only shook his head.

'Elsa, don't be so infernally bloodthirsty! No'.

'Then what was it?'

'In Sykes Street, a little turning off Upper Regent Street, there's a diamond-merchant named Van Bele. For years, Van Bele's been carrying regularly a fortune in uncut stones in a little wash-leather bag in his pocket. Up to now he's got away with it; nobody's bothered him.'

'And now?'

'On Tuesday, about 10.15 a.m., Van Bele had a phone-call asking him to visit some clients. It was a fake call; The Colonel sent it. Van Bele walked downstairs from his office. The Colonel, in his best Savile Row suit and overcoat, was waiting in the entry. He just walloped Van Bele on the jaw, knocked him out, took the little leather bag, and ran for it.'

Elsa spluttered.

'But—my dear Bob! Wouldn't they have caught him straight away?'

'No. With all this Christmas rush, he could have got clean away. But he had bad luck. Two constables were coming along Sykes Street opposite the Regent Street end. They saw our friend grab the bag and run.

'The Colonel jumped aboard a bus crossing Oxford Circus and went along Oxford Street. One of the constables followed; the other phoned the Yard.

'Within a few minutes they had the whole area covered in a net. In just two minutes, one of the Sweeneys—sorry, I mean a Flying Squad car—pulled up beside the bus in Oxford Street. The Colonel was standing on the platform.

'He jumped down, and dodged across the street. Two of our men followed, keeping him in sight. The Colonel, believe it or not, ran into Omnium's. Our men still had him in sight when he ducked into a telephone box in the basement. And that's all.'

'All? What do you mean?'

'The Colonel just vanished.'

'In the telephone box?'

'Apparently, yes.'

'But he can't have done!'

'I know it's impossible. But it happened.'

Behind them, at the magician's counter, the talking skull left off gibbering and now loudly sang 'Silent Night' in competition to the radio's version of 'Silent Night'. But Elsa, Tommy, and Pollard himself had forgotten the pandemonium of Toyland.

'Remember,' Pollard insisted, 'that these diamonds were uncut. That's to say: they were only greyish lumps, like pebbles, and of no use to The Colonel until they were cut and polished.

'What's the first thing he would do? He'd get in touch with his diamond-cutter, of course. Naturally, Criminal Records knew who it was.'

'And this diamond-cutter was the other man you mentioned. . . Shorty?'

'Yes. Except that Shorty is a woman.'

'A woman?' said Elsa, yanking Tommy forward.

'Yes; why not?' retorted Pollard, yanking Tommy back. 'She's The Colonel's girlfriend. They live not far apart.

'After the first phone-call to the Yard, the division had orders to put a tail on Shorty. Not to arrest her—'

'Why ever not?'

'Dammit, Elsa, Shorty hadn't done anything—yet.

'But where was The Colonel meeting her to give her the diamonds? And how was he going to give her the diamonds? And when? That's what they had to know.'

'So . . .?'

'Two policewomen, in plain clothes, picked up Shorty outside her lodgings. Shorty was carrying a large parcel. She knew she was being followed. You'll have guessed she and The Colonel planned this before-hand, in case they were followed. Shorty's quite an attractive trick, by the way: brunette, smooth skin, in her early twenties. She walked faster. So did the policewomen. Shorty hurried into Ilkley's—that big women's dress shop not far from here. So did the policewomen. And in the shop, Shorty dodged into a telephone box. . .'

Here Pollard had to stop.

'You're not going to tell me,' said Elsa, who still thought that her beloved was spinning a fairy story, 'that *she* disappeared out of a 'phone box?'

'Apparently, yes. Parcel and all.'

Elsa's pretty face coloured pink with anger. She turned away abruptly.

'I don't believe it,' she said, violently jerking Tommy's left arm. 'It's silly! Look at the crowd here now. Just look!'

'Very well,' said Pollard, jerking Tommy's right arm. 'I'm looking. What about it?'

'Crowds and crowds and crowds,' said Elsa, 'all moving. Could you be certain somebody's disappeared out of a 'phone box, even if you were only ten feet away?'

'You could be pretty certain that two different people couldn't vanish out of two different shops under the conditions the police established. As soon as The Colonel entered Omnium's, and Shorty entered Ilkley's, both places were surrounded. Every possible entrance or exit was guarded. Every nook and cranny was searched. Every customer was stopped and questioned. . .'

'Wait! What about all the sales staff?'

'They were the first to be questioned. Both Omnium's and Ilkley's open at nine o'clock. The managers could tell from their time-sheets that every person was at his or her proper place. No employee could have been larking about with a pocket full of diamonds, or could have changed places afterwards with somebody who had. Face it, my dear! Shorty and The Colonel didn't leave the shops. And yet they weren't in the buildings either. They'd simply vanished.'

Elsa marched forward, dragging the others like a string of sausages.

'Come along, Tommy,' she said in exasperation.

'It's not very nice of Uncle Bob to enrage you like this. He's insufferable, and I'll never speak to him again.'

'Now wait a bit, Elsa!'

'This way, Tommy; mind where you're going. We'll take you to see Father Christmas.'

They had pushed through to a long grotto, a kind of mysterious and softly lighted cavern, where even in Toyland voices were hushed.

Here children walked slowly.

At the grotto pay box, over which large red letters said that Father Christmas would be in attendance from 11 a.m. to 6 p.m., Pollard bought three tickets.

The grotto was murmurous with 'Oh's!' and 'Ah's!' Brightly painted in cardboard or plaster, figures and backgrounds showed fairy stories. They were well along in the cavern when Pollard stopped. His mouth fell open. He stood rigid, staring straight ahead.

At the end of the cavern, on a platform festooned in holly where children could mount the two steps and whisper their wishes, sat Father Christmas himself.

At Father Christmas's right hand was a table piled with small gift-boxes wrapped in bright paper.

Even as Pollard stared, a little girl of possibly 12 years walked up the steps.

She was very dainty in white fur jacket and white cap. Her long yellow curls fell forward as she bent to whisper.

Father Christmas chuckled. He nodded. Selecting a gift-box from the table, he turned back in one vast beam to give this present to his small friend. And, as he did so, Father Christmas's large left eyebrow closed down as though he leered or held an eyeglass.

'Uncle Bob!' screamed Tommy. 'Did you see it? The funny eyes. You remember. You said The Colonel . . .'

Detective Superintendent Pollard, Criminal Investigation Department, quickly turned to the boy and hushed him.

Then, in a flash, he charged.

He was a big man. He avoided the children, but parents scattered before him like skittles. There was a crash as he jumped up on the platform.

'I don't think you'd like that one, my dear,' he said pleasantly to the little girl, and nodded towards the box held out in Father Christmas's hand.

In a low voice he added: 'Better give me the diamonds, Colonel. As for you, Shorty . . .'

The little girl lifted sweet and innocent eyes.

'Coppers!' she whispered, showing her teeth. 'He's a copper, Colonel; that's what the so-and-so is.'

'When a man is called Shorty,' said Pollard in the same low tone, 'it may not mean much. But when a woman is called that, as we ought to have realized, she must be almost a dwarf. I suppose your little-girl clothes, and the blonde wig, were in that parcel? And you changed in the dress-shop? Nobody would notice a 12-year-old; the

police weren't to blame for that mistake.

'But we were to be blamed about you, Colonel,' he added. 'Omnium's opens at nine; we thought everybody had to be on duty then. And yet, as you can see by a sign over the pay-box back there, this grotto doesn't open until eleven. You could slosh Van Bele and get back on time. Your Father Christmas suit was left in the phone-box and all you had to do was nip into it while the crowd barged around outside and our men were still trying to push their way through, and then simply step out of the booth. It was a risk, but it worked. In any case, when the police finally reached the phone-box they weren't looking for Santa Claus with all the trimmings, they were trying to spot The Colonel in smart suit and overcoat.'

In that paralysed scene, the bright-coloured box was still held out in Father Christmas's hand. 'Cut and run for it, Shorty!' he chuckled. 'I hate to spoil the kids' Christmas, but I'll get this copper before they get me.'

'Think so?' smiled Pollard. 'You haven't a chance against me and you know it. I can't help you. But it's Christmas—and I can help Shorty get away. Fair?'

'Turn it up, copper!' sneered the sweet-faced girl—and yet an edge of hope appeared in her face.

'Give me the box,' Pollard said. 'If the diamonds are inside, she hasn't officially received them. She can go now and take her chance of being picked up later. Fair?'

Father Christmas looked warily at Pollard before exchanging a knowing glance with the girl.

Then, without a word, he handed over the box to Pollard.

As he did so, he noticeably sagged with relief behind his beard.

Then his rich, soothing, cultured voice rang out.

'Ladies and gentlemen!' carolled Father Christmas. 'This gentleman is particularly anxious to have this box. I hope he finds in it what he's looking for.

'Personally, I'd rather give the little girl another box. Here it is. Now hurry down the steps, and out of this store. Others are waiting.'

At the sight of a monocled Father Christmas, a ripple of laughter spread out over the grotto, carrying with it the spirit of Christmas as children crowded forward.

Tommy, pushing forward, hardly noticed that Elsa was no longer watching Father Christmas.

She was looking at Pollard—and in her eyes shone admiration—and unconcealed adoration!

THE FIRST time I came across a book by James Melville (real name Peter Martin, b. 1931) I was reviewing crime fiction for one of the literary monthlies and had had it up to the back of my throat, and beyond, with oddball and/or exotically ethnic sleuths.

As each new parcel arrived I knew I was doomed yet again to deal with a fresh crop of antique-dealer detectives, pet-shop owner detectives, mortuary attendant detectives; a dreadful parade of Philippinos, Basques, Romanys, Liechtensteiners, and pure-bred Inuits—all of whom would (naturally) bring their own special talents or peculiar native wit to bear on the knotty and murderous problems posed by their creators (most of whom, you bet, would have had but a passing acquaintance with the profession or country of their choice, merely bowing to one of the unwritten rules of mystery fiction: make your manhunter *colourful*). So a Japanese detective—all those incomprehensible rituals, all that tedious inscrutability—was the last thing I needed.

But I was wrong. The book was Melville's third novel, *A Sort of Samurai* (1981), and from the first page I was entranced. So entranced that I didn't offload it on my usual bookshop (at the reviewer's perk of a third of the published price) but kept it, located the first two, and have bought each new Melville—on publication, with my own money (greater love hath no fan)—ever since.

Melville writes police procedurals, and a good deal of the charm of the series lies in the fact that the police, led by Superintendent Tetsuo Otani of the Hyogo Prefecture, with full supporting cast, proceed in an utterly alien manner. To the Occidental eye, anyhow.

If that were all, Melville's series would be just the same as any other foreign-cop series—often, merely irritatingly different. But James Melville is a fine writer with a dry sense of humour and a neat (as neat as a *netsuke*, to use the shorthand of my reviewing days) line in subtle characterization. And he loves Japan. As you read, you begin to, too.

There's precious little blood in an Otani story, few car-chases, and the level of violence is abysmally low. But who cares? All these ingredients may be had elsewhere, in abundance. The manners and mores of Japanese society are described so compellingly, the mysteries to be solved posed in such a delicate and ironical manner, the running cast of characters is brought so sharply to life (I'm currently fascinated by the relationship between the highly intelligent and attractive young policewoman Junko Migishima and her somewhat put-upon husband, who is experiencing at first-hand precisely what the phrase 'new women' means) that, in short, Otani is just the ticket for the palate bruised and brutalized by the crash and rush of the average modern detective novel.

When I asked James Melville to write an original Otani story for *Crime At Christmas* he was distinctly apprehensive. 'I've never written a short story before', he said. You'd never know it. He really ought to write more.

— 3 —

Santa-San Solves It

JAMES MELVILLE

'TRY IT just once more,' Inspector Kimura said encouragingly. 'Your "Jingle Bells" is fine.'

'Hardly surprising. Everybody knows *Jinguru Beru*; you can't get away from the wretched tune. Television, department stores, coffee shops. They've been playing it twenty-four hours a day since November.'

'True. So you've no worries on that account. All the children will join in at the top of their voices and you'll hardly be heard anyway. No, it's the "Ho! Ho! Ho!" you need to work on.'

Superintendent Tetsuo Otani glowered first at his trusted lieutenant and then at his shoes. 'Ho! Ho! Ho!', he said in an undertone, sounding like an embarrassed Englishman repeating the word 'whore'. 'It's no good, I can't and won't say it. It's not as if it means anything, anyway.'

'Of course you can, Chief, you can't let the Rotarians down. But do try to look a bit more cheerful. It's a Christmas party you're going to, not a funeral. And you'll only be centre stage for twenty minutes or so after all.'

'Half an hour at least, the chairman of

the social work sub-committee said. Dressed up like an idiot. All this Santa Claus business is a foreign idea anyway,' Otani complained. 'I don't see why they picked on me. There are two or three foreign Rotarians in other clubs in Kobe who'd probably have been only too glad to volunteer. And lots in Osaka. Ho Ho Ho indeed.'

Kimura sucked in his breath and shook his head. Nothing could be done with the superintendent when he had made up his mind to be mulish. 'Oh, well,' he said, 'I expect it'll be all right if you ring your bell while you say it. And the beard will cover up your expression, I suppose. Now, can I talk for a minute about Mrs Bencivenni?'

Otani sat back in his chair, his black look replaced by one of mild interest. 'I've heard that name somewhere recently,' he said. 'She's. . . yes, of course, isn't she the women who runs the place?'

'The children's home where your Rotary Club is paying for the Christmas party, yes, but she doesn't exactly run it, she's the president of the committee of management. Fund-raisers, in effect. There are several foreign ladies on it. Goes back to the origins of the place during the occupation, when most of the kids were mixed-blood.'

'Babies bar-girls had by American GI's, you mean. I always felt sorriest for the ones who were half black. Incredible to think some of them must be getting on for forty now. Can't be much of a life for them here, neither the one thing nor the other. We Japanese have a bad record with misfits, Kimura.'

Otani sighed and Kimura nodded briefly, still after years of close association capable of being surprised on occasion by subversive remarks from a man he usually thought of as being a thoroughly old-fashioned Japanese with predictable prejudices. 'Well, it's an odd coincidence that I should be going to this charity place of hers, I suppose, but worrying about foreigners is your job. Why do you want me to hear about this Bencivenni woman of yours?'

'Funny you should mention mixed-blood children, Chief. You must be psychic. Mrs Bencivenni was one of them herself, brought up in that self-same children's home. It was called the Nada Orphanage in those days. Her father couldn't have been black, though, she's fair skinned, looks quite European. Good-looking woman, in fact, speaks perfect Japanese. Middle to late thirties.'

'In that case be specially careful, Kimura. You know how susceptible you are. The lady has a husband, I presume?'

'She does indeed. Luciano Bencivenni, an American citizen, aged fifty-six, known as Luke. He's the problem.'

'Ah. Bigger than you, is he? Inclined to be jealous?'

Kimura cast an ostentatious glance heavenwards and pressed on, privately relieved that Otani seemed to be regaining his normal equable humour. 'Mr Bencivenni used to be a bank official, but has been in business on his own account for a number of years as a personal financial consultant. In practice he's a kind of all-round adviser to the western community here in the Kobe-Osaka area. Prepares tax returns for Americans, sells life insurance, arranges long-term investment plans for children's school and college fees and so forth. He's the agent for a number of American and British insurance companies. And Mrs Bencivenni thinks he's planning to kill her.' Kimura paused, wondering whether his chief's renowned poker face would be proof against such an artfully sprung surprise. It was.

'Does she indeed? How do you know?'

'She turned up downstairs here at headquarters yesterday and asked to speak to a senior officer in confidence about a matter involving the foreign community. I interviewed her and she told me herself.'

'Do you believe her?'

'Well, she's certainly not off her head, and she's obviously worried sick. What she told me was disturbing enough for me to organize a certain amount of digging, and I think you ought to know what we've come up with.'

'Stand *still*!' Hanae commanded, and Otani froze. She very seldom used that particular tone of voice, and when she did it was advisable to do her bidding. The Father Christmas outfit had been delivered to the house earlier that day, by Hanae's friend Mrs Hamada, who was also married to a Rotarian and who from time to time spoke vaguely of connections in show business. Hanae took it for granted that it was these which gave her access to such colourful fancy dress.

Over a cup of coffee they had unpacked the exotic garments, shaken out the folds, and agreed that the ensemble must have been made for a giant. They'd both giggled helplessly when Mrs Hamada tied a doubled-up *zabuton* cushion to her tummy and sportingly modelled the voluminous tunic, and after subsiding agreed that it would need a huge tuck in the back. The eighteen inches or so of excess length presented no problem: it could be hitched up as though the garment were a *kimono*.

Three safety-pins later, Hanae rose from her knees, stepped back and surveyed her husband. 'It won't take long to tack up,' she said, obviously having forgiven him for fidgeting.

'Why don't you just leave the safety-pins in? You won't be able to see them under that sash thing.'

Hanae decided to ignore such a heretical suggestion, and eased the ungainly garment off Otani's shoulders. 'Why didn't you tell me that some of the other Rotary wives are going to be helping on the day? I'd have been glad to take some cakes or something along.'

Something remarkably like a blush darkened Otani's naturally swarthy face. 'Because I shall feel quite enough of a fool as it is without you being there to watch,' he mumbled.

'Ah. I thought it might have been that you wanted the glamorous Mrs Bencivenni all to yourself.'

Otani gazed at her in amazement as he slowly lowered himself to the *tatami* matting, reached for the *sake* flask on the low lacquer table and refilled his cup. 'What on earth do *you* know about Mrs Bencivenni?' he enquired as Hanae looked down at him, her arch little smile fading rapidly. 'Have you met her?'

'No. Er, have you?'

'No. So there's no need to look so tragic. But I have been hearing quite a lot about her recently. From Kimura. Presumably you and Mrs Hamada have been discussing her too. What did she say? Sit down and have some *sake*.'

A little over two hours later Otani slid the *shoji* screen in the upstairs room to one side and gazed pensively through the glazed

panel behind it at his favourite night view, of the great sweep of Osaka Bay. It was crisp and clear outside, with only a few rags of cloud occasionally obscuring a moon almost at the full. The huddle of tiled roofs with their solar water-heating panels and the forest of television aerials on the houses lower down the foothills of Mount Rokko which offended his eye by day were effectively obliterated, while the navigation lights on ships a mile or so away from where he stood twinkled cheerfully and a distant glow to the left marked the coast of Wakayama Prefecture.

Nothing Hanae had passed on from the gossipy Mrs Hamada contradicted what Kimura had told him about Judy Bencivenni, but his mental picture of the lady was nevertheless now subtly different. Kimura's team had assembled an impressive file of papers about her and her husband. Mrs Bencivenni's real first name as registered by her Japanese mother was Midori, but by the time she won a scholarship to the élite Canadian Academy in Kobe she was Judy, and Judy she remained through its junior and senior high school departments. A Kobe Carnival Queen at eighteen, she had been photographed by the Kobe Shimbun newspaper, whose files yielded a print showing a startlingly pretty girl and a two-paragraph 'interview' in which she spoke touchingly of the loving care she had known at the Kobe Orphanage and her determination to do anything she could to help those less fortunate than herself.

The record showed that she had honoured that pledge. Judy had been a star student both academically and on the sports field, but the orphanage budget could not afford college fees for her and there are no scholarships for higher education in Japan. Her looks and talents stood her in good stead, though, and after graduation from the Canadian Academy she had landed a good job as a bilingual secretary with the American Consulate-General.

She maintained a continuing connection as a volunteer helper with what had by then become known as the International Children's Home. Being technically a stateless alien, at twenty-two she applied for Japanese nationality and was turned down; but strings must have been pulled by her American employers because within six months she had been able to obtain an American passport and move to the United States. During six years there she kept in touch by letter with the children's home, and indeed—according to Mrs Hamada, who was on the committee of management—was reputed to have donated two or three hundred dollars every Christmas to pay for presents for the children. Mrs Hamada thought that she was working at this time as a secretary for Japan Air Lines in Los Angeles, but wasn't sure.

Kimura's file showed that Mr Luke Bencivenni arrived in Japan as a member of the staff of an American bank in 1978, accompanied by his wife Arlene, who drowned while swimming in Lake Chuzenji near Nikko the following summer. After the tragedy Bencivenni returned briefly to America but remained with the bank, being transferred to its Osaka branch. That Christmas he went for a brief holiday to Hawaii, returning with a new bride, the former Judy Nakano.

Kobe Prefectural Police might not have picked up the connection had not the second Mrs Bencivenni almost at once plunged herself into a round of charitable activities which meant that she soon began to figure in the gossip columns of the English-language press (which was routinely scanned by Kimura's staff in the Foreign Residents' Liaison Section). The fact that she was beautiful and had excellent dress sense helped, as did her husband's early retirement from the bank and the rapid expansion of the consultancy business he started immediately afterwards. He did very well, and within a year or two the Bencivennis were leading figures in the western community in Kobe.

Inevitably, such a socially prominent alumna of the children's home as Judy was soon elected to its committee of management, and she had been its president for the past two years; by all accounts an effective manager of committee business and a tireless drummer-up of financial support. Mrs Hamada had told Hanae that it was Mrs Bencivenni's idea to approach the Kobe South Rotary Club to which Otani belonged for a contribution, and Mrs Hamada herself—confound her—who hit upon the idea of a lavish Christmas party financed and organized by the Rotarians.

Otani sighed, turned away from the window, dropped his *yukata* on the *tatami* and slid under the *futon*. Hanae was as usual tranquil and immobile, wearing her own *yukata* which if he knew her would still be mysteriously uncreased when she got up the next morning.

'And I'm stuck with the job of being Santa Claus,' he grumbled. Then he raised himself on one forearm. 'What I don't understand is why he should *want* to kill her. According to both Kimura and your Mrs Hamada they're successful and popular. Luxury apartment, no children—not of their own, anyway. I suppose Bencivenni might have had some by his previous marriage, but there's no note of any and even if he had they'd be adults by now. And he's got this very attractive wife.' A thought struck him. 'Ha-chan, he's a good bit older than her. I wonder, did Mrs Hamada hint that she might be having an affair?'

Hanae had been so still that she might have been asleep, but in the bar of moonlight which lay across their bedding he saw her eyes blink open. 'No. Quite the reverse, if anything. It seems that several of the men in their circle have tried to start something, but she's never given any of them the least encouragement. And of course, a woman in her position, it would be all over town in five minutes if she did. Even Mrs Hamada's obviously a bit jealous of her looks, so I expect the foreign ladies on the committee are too. They're all older, I believe. So they'd pounce on the least suggestion of scandal.'

Otani didn't quite follow, but rolled on to his back and made himself comfortable. 'Sorry to keep you awake. I'm afraid I'm not a bit sleepy. Want a cup of tea or anything?'

'Not really. I don't mind talking anyway, it's interesting. Surely she must have given Mr Kimura some reason for saying such an extraordinary thing about her husband?'

'Oh, she did, but it doesn't impress me. She said she'd discovered that he recently took out a huge insurance policy on her life. A husband can do that, you know. And that he's let slip that he had collected a substantial sum by way of insurance when his former wife drowned. Putting two and two together, Mrs Bencivenni thinks her death might not in fact have been an accident.'

'What an awful thing to suggest! But... but why *now*?'

'Well, Bencivenni handles investments for a lot of Americans living here. And you know what happened on the New York stock exchange recently. Here too, of course. She told Kimura she thinks he might have over-committed himself financially and be in urgent need of funds to avoid bankruptcy.'

Hanae reflected in silence for a long time. 'I'm so glad we keep our savings in the bank, dear,' she then said thoughtfully. 'What are you going to do?'

Otani sighed. 'Well, I suppose the least we can do is check the local police report on that drowning in Chuzenji years ago. It might help me sort out my ideas.'

The party at the children's home was a great success. Safely concealed behind an enormous white beard and moustache and with his floppy red hat well down on his forehead, Otani rang his bell with gusto and was delighted to discover what he should have realized from the first, that all the children not only spoke Japanese but that nearly all *were* Japanese.

The extent of the munificence of the Kobe South Rotarians revealed when Otani opened his sack and handed out the presents brought squeals of delight from the children and approving nods from the staff of the home; and afterwards when he had divested himself of his finery Otani was drawn aside by a senior member of his club and gravely thanked for his outstanding contribution to the festivities.

'Such a pity Mrs Bencivenni couldn't be here after all, though. I know she would have wished to thank you personally, but I understand she was unavoidably detained.'

'I can't follow your reasoning, Chief,' Kimura said for the second time. 'All right, so central immigration records indicate that she was in Japan as a tourist at the time the first Mrs Bencivenni was drowned, and the only so-called witness the local police managed to find did have a vague recollection that there had been one other woman swimming in that part of the lake before Arlene Bencivenni went under. But he was a long way away and it proves nothing, even granted that Judy Nakano was an all-round athlete at school. Surely the husband remains the obvious suspect if she really was murdered...and that isn't by any means established.'

'I'm not looking forward to it, but I'm going to talk to the poor woman myself,' Otani said. 'I think that with careful handling she'll confess that she accused her husband of planning her murder because she intended to kill him... so that when she eventually did so she could claim it was in self-defence. Why otherwise come to the Japanese police with such a tale? What were we supposed to do? Why not simply leave him? She'd proved beyond question that she could earn her own living both in Japan and in America.'

'But there's still no *reason* for it. Remember, he insured her life, not the other way round.'

'Oh, there's a reason. She hates him, you see. With a deep, consistent, murderous hatred that at first sustained her, then fed on itself and brought her to crisis point. When you first described Mrs Bencivenni to me you said she wasn't off her head. Not obviously, perhaps, but in my opinion hopelessly unhinged. More to the point, hopelessly obsessed.'

Otani paused, rubbed his eyes and

blinked. 'A victim of circumstance, some would say. I don't know. Anyway, I propose to suggest to her that her years of—not dedicated exactly, calculated perhaps—her years of service to the orphanage where she'd been brought up gave her such a position of trust there that the time came when she could delve into their confidential records more or less at will and turn up a name or names. Have you got a cigarette on you?'

Kimura gave him one and lit it for him. Otani looked tired, but soon began to speak again. 'I'll point out that either when she was working in the Consulate-General here in Kobe or when she went to the United States she was able to check US Army records or hire an enquiry agent to do it for her. I'll suggest that these confirmed—as we can find out for ourselves easily enough—that a certain young GI was serving with the Occupation forces in Japan in 1949 and 1950. And I shall explain that we think her next step was to discover his current whereabouts and circumstances and use her beauty and intelligence to entrap him. Ah, I see it's beginning to dawn on you too, Kimura.'

'I don't believe it, Chief!'

'I don't want to myself, but I do, and I can't help feeling sorry for her. It's a terrible burden she's borne for most of her life, Kimura. Bottling up all that dark hatred from childhood onwards so successfully . . . then living with the knowledge that she seduced her own father, murdered his wife and married him with the intention of one day killing him too. A man who still probably has no idea he even has a daughter, much less who she is.'

'PETER TODD' was just one of the twenty-five or more pseudonyms employed by Charles Hamilton (1876–1961) in a writing career that spanned nearly seven decades, during which he banged out (mostly on a 1900s' Remington) upwards of an awesome 70 million words. That's roughly 950 average-length novels. Or, to put it another way, fourteen books a year, *every* year, for nearly seventy years. Except Hamilton didn't much write books.

His forte was schoolboy fiction for weekly papers such as *Pluck*, *Boys' Friend*, *Boys' Realm*, *Boys' Herald*, *Popular*, *Modern Boy*, *Gem* and, especially, *Magnet*. There were 1,683 issues of the *Magnet*; Hamilton, under his best-known pen-name Frank Richards—the name he used when writing about his most famous creation Billy Bunter, the Fat Owl of Greyfriars School—wrote nearly 1,400 of them. At the peak of his creative powers (roughly, the 1920s) he was producing two 20,000-word stories a week as well as an assortment of shorter material. He once wrote an 18,000-word story in a single day. At a time when the average income was £180 a year, Hamilton was earning well over £3,000. One could, if asked, continue to pile up Ripleyesque one-liners about Charles Harold St John Hamilton till the cows come home.

But perhaps the most striking fact of all is that he was a very good writer. To be sure, when reading his stories belief must to a great extent be suspended (Hamilton wrote of great public schools, but had never been to one); even so he had a fine grasp of character and an unusual understanding of the darker, less agreeable side of a boy's nature; his dialogue was generally excellent (read it aloud and it works), and he had the natural yarn-spinner's priceless gift of being thumpingly readable. Too, having a short way with humbug and a sharp eye for the absurdities of adult life he could at times be an inspired comic writer (and only a man with a highly developed sense of humour, after all, could have translated 'Won't You Come Home, Bill Bailey' into Latin). His school stories are full of mordant asides on politicians, retired military men, elderly pedagogues, faddists, pettifogging bureaucrats, tax inspectors (especially tax inspectors).

Hamilton used the 'Peter Todd' pseudonym mainly for his Sherlock Holmes parodies, of which (here's another It's-A-Fact) he wrote well over sixty, all—with their pawky jokes, nimble puns, satirical stings—uniformly delightful. In 1975 the Mysterious Press published a selection in *The Adventures of Herlock Sholmes*: highly recommended. Here's one that's never made it between hard covers before.

— 4 —

Herlock Sholmes's Christmas Case

PETER TODD

I

CHRISTMAS tomorrow!' Herlock Sholmes remarked thoughtfully.

I started.

'My dear Sholmes!' I murmured.

Herlock Sholmes smiled.

'You are surprised, Jotson, to hear me make that statement with such positiveness,' he remarked. 'Yet, I assure you that such is the case.'

'I acknowledge, Sholmes, that I ought no longer to be surprised at anything you may say or do. But from what grounds do you infer——'

'Quite simple, my dear Jotson. Look from the window upon the slushy streets and the hurrying crowds, all indicative of the approach of Christmas!'

'True! But why tomorrow precisely?'

'Ah, there we go a little deeper, Jotson. I deduce that Christmas occurs tomorrow from a study of the calendar!'

'The calendar!' I exclaimed, in astonishment.

'Exactly!'

'As you know, Sholmes, I have endeavoured to study your methods, in my humbler way, yet I confess that I do not see the connection——'

'Probably not, Jotson. But to the trained, professional mind it presents no difficulties. Christmas, you are aware, falls upon the twenty-fifth day of the month!'

'True!'

'Look at the calendar, Jotson!'

I obeyed.

'It tells you nothing?'

'Nothing!' I confessed.

Sholmes smiled again, a somewhat bored smile.

'My dear fellow, the calendar indicates that today is the twenty-fourth!'

'Quite so. But——'

'And as Christmas falls upon the twenty-fifth, it follows—to an acute mind accustomed to rapid deductions—that tomorrow is Christmas!'

I could only gaze at my amazing friend in silent admiration.

'But there will be no holiday for us tomorrow, my dear Jotson' resumed Herlock Sholmes. 'I have received a wire from the Duke of Hookeywalker, who—— Ah, his Grace has arrived!'

Even as Sholmes spoke the Duke of Hookeywalker was shown into our sitting-room.

Herlock Sholmes removed his feet from the mantelpiece with the graceful courtesy so natural to him.

'Pray be seated,' said Sholmes. 'You may speak quite freely before my friend, Dr Jotson!'

'Mr Sholmes, I have sustained a terrible loss!'

Sholmes smiled.

'Your Grace has lost the pawnticket?' he inquired.

'Mr Sholmes, you must be a wizard! How did you guess——'

'I never guess,' said Herlock Sholmes quietly. 'My business is to deal with facts. Pray let me have some details.'

'It is true, Mr Sholmes, that the pawn-ticket is missing,' said the duke in an agitated voice. 'You are aware that the house of Hookeywalker has a great reputation for hospitality, which must be kept up even in these days of stress. It was necessary for me to give a large Christmas party at Hookey Castle, and, to obtain the necessary funds, the family jewels were pledged with Mr Ikey Solomons, of Houndsditch. The ticket was in my own keeping—it never left me. I kept it in my own card-case. The card-case never left my person. Yet now, Mr Sholmes, the ticket is missing!'

'And the card-case?'

'Still in my pocket!'

'When were the Hookeywalker jewels placed with Mr Solomons?'

'Yesterday morning!'

'And the ticket was missing——'.

'Last night,' faltered the duke. 'I looked in my card-case to make sure that it was still safe, and it was gone. How it had been purloined, Mr Sholmes, is a mystery —an unfathomable mystery!'

'No mystery is unfathomable to a trained mind' said Sholmes calmly. 'I have every hope of recovering the missing pawnticket.'

'Mr Sholmes, you give me new life. But how——'

Sholmes interrupted.

'After leaving Mr Solomons' establishment, where did your Grace go?'

'I had to make a call at the Chinwag Department of the War Office, and from there I returned to Hookey Castle.'

'You made no other call?'

'None.'

'It is scarcely possible that a skilled pickpocket is to be found in the Chinwag Department,' said Sholmes thoughtfully.

'Impossible, Mr Sholmes! Every official of that great Department is far above suspicion of being skilled in any manner whatsoever!'

'True!'

'There is no clue!' said the duke in despairing tones. 'But unless the missing ticket is recovered, Mr Sholmes, the famous Hookeywalker jewels are lost!'

'You may leave the case in my hands,' said Herlock Sholmes carelessly. 'I may call at Hookey Castle with news for you tomorrow.'

'Bless you, Mr Sholmes!'

And the duke took his leave.

Herlock Sholmes lighted a couple of pipes, a habit of his when a particularly knotty problem required great concentration of thought. I did not venture to interrupt the meditations of that mighty intellect.

Sholmes spoke at last, with a smile.

'A very interesting little problem, Jotson. I can see that you are puzzled by my deduction that the pawnticket was lost before his Grace had mentioned it.'

'I am astounded, Sholmes.'

'Yet it was simple. I had heard of the great social gathering at Hookey Castle,' explained Sholmes. 'I deduced that his Grace could only meet the bills by hypothecating the family jewels. His hurried visit to me and his agitation could have had but one meaning—I deduced that the pawnticket was lost or stolen. Quite elementary my dear Jotson! But the recovery of the missing ticket——'

'That will not be so simple, Sholmes.'

'Who knows, Jotson?' Sholmes rose to his feet and drew his celebrated dressing-gown about him. 'I must leave you for a short time, Jotson. You may go and see your patients, my dear fellow.'

'One question, Sholmes. You are going——'

'To the Chinwag Department.'

'But——'

But Herlock Sholmes was gone.

II

I confess that Sholmes' behaviour perplexed me. He had declared that the pickpocket could not be found in the Chinwag Department, yet he had gone there to commence his investigations. When he returned to Shaker Street, he made no remark upon the case, and I did not venture to question him. The next morning he greeted me with a smile as I came down into the sitting-room.

'You are ready for a little run this morning, Jotson?' he asked.

'I am always at your service, Sholmes.'

'Good! Then call a taxi.'

A few minutes later a taxicab was bearing us away. Sholmes had given the direction to the driver—'Hookey Castle.'

'We are going to see the duke, Sholmes?' I asked.

He nodded.

'But the missing pawnticket?'

'Wait and see!'

This reply, worthy of a great statesman, was all I could elicit from Sholmes on the journey.

The taxi drove up the stately approach to Hookey Castle. A gorgeous footman admitted us to the great mansion, and we were shown into the presence of the duke.

His Grace had left his guests to see us.

There was a slight impatience in his manner.

'My dear Mr Sholmes,' he said, 'I supposed I had given you the fullest particulars yesterday. You have called me away from a shove-ha'penny party.'

'I am sorry,' said Sholmes calmly. 'Return to the shove-ha'penny party, by all means your Grace, and I will call another time with the pawnticket.'

The duke bounded to his feet.

'Mr Sholmes! You have recovered it?'

Sholmes smiled. He delighted in these dramatic surprises.

The duke gazed with startled eyes at the slip of pasteboard my amazing friend presented to him.

'The missing pawnticket!' he ejaculated.

'The same!' said Sholmes.

'Sholmes!' I murmured. I could say no more.

The Duke of Hookeywalker took the ticket with trembling fingers.

'Mr Sholmes' he said in tones of deep emotion, 'you have saved the honour of the name of Hookeywalker! You will stay to dinner, Mr Sholmes. Come, I insist—there will be tripe and onions!' he added.

'I cannot resist the tripe and onions,' said Sholmes, with a smile.

And we stayed.

III

It was not till the taxi was whirling us homeward to Shaker Street that Herlock Sholmes relieved my curiosity.

'Sholmes!' I exclaimed as the taxi rolled out of the stately gates of Hookey Castle. 'How, in the name of wonder——'

Sholmes laughed.

'You are astounded, as usual, Jotson?'

'As usual, Sholmes.'

'Yet it is very simple. The duke carried the pawnticket in his card-case,' said Sholmes. 'He called only at the Chinwag Department of the War Office before returning home. Only a particularly clever pickpocket could have extracted the ticket without the cardcase, and, as his Grace himself remarked, it was useless to assume the existence of any particularly clever

individual in a Government department. That theory, therefore, was excluded—the ticket had not been taken.'

'Sholmes!'

'It had not been taken, Jotson' said Sholmes calmly. 'Yet it had left the duke's possession. The question was—how?'

'I confess it is quite dark to me, Sholmes.'

'Naturally,' said Sholmes drily. 'But my mental powers, my dear Jotson, are of quite a different calibre.'

'Most true.'

'As the ticket had not been taken from the duke, I deduced that he had parted with it unintentionally.'

'But is that possible, Sholmes?'

'Quite! Consider, my dear Jotson. His Grace kept the pawnticket, for safety, in his card-case. On calling at the Chinwag Department he sent in his card, naturally. By accident, Jotson, he handed over the pawnticket instead of his own card——'

'Sholmes!'

'And that ticket, Jotson, was taken in instead. That was the only theory to be deduced from the known facts. I proceeded to the Chinwag Department, and interviewed the official upon whom the duke called. There was a little difficulty in obtaining an interview; but he was awakened at last, and I questioned him. As I had deduced, the missing pawnticket was discovered on the salver, where it had lain unnoticed since the duke's call.'

'Wonderful!' I exclaimed.

Sholmes smiled in a bored way.

'Elementary, my dear Jotson. But here we are at Shaker Street.'

SOMEONE should swiftly slap a protection order on Edward D. Hoch (b. 1930). He's one of a kind. At least, I don't know of any other writer who these days makes a serious living out of writing short stories, and only short stories.

And not just any old short stories, either, for Ed Hoch has a most peculiar mind. A hefty proportion of his vast output is in the toughest mystery sub-genre of them all: the Impossible Crime.

Ed Hoch is very good at the Impossible Crime. Here's one. A man staggers from out of a small curtained voting-booth mortally wounded from a dagger-thrust to the heart. He dies within seconds. He was alone in the booth; there were eight people in the room outside, none of whom killed him; the knife is nowhere to be found. And what about this one. An armed policeman is alone with a woman in a locked room. A shot crashes out, the woman lurches backwards, blood spurting from her chest. The cop didn't kill her, although his gun—which he drew only after the shot—has been fired. Yet no one outside the room killed her either. Ed Hoch is *awfully* good at the Impossible Crime.

And not simply because he can think up wild and way-out situations time after time (and he can), but because the wildest, most way-out situations invariably have neat and logical and perfectly fair solutions. The kind of solutions that make you strike your forehead with the palm of your hand and mutter, through gritted teeth, 'Of *course*!'

He's awfully good too at coming up with fresh and original, not to say bizarre, series-characters. There's Ben Snow, a cowboy detective who is possibly the reincarnation of Billy the Kid; Simon Ark, who pursues Ancient Evil inexorably, and who might, just might, be 2000 years old; Dr Sam Hawthorne, whose home-village of Northmont certainly contains more screwball murderers than the rest of New England put together (I'm tempted to say the rest of the United States); Nick Velvet, the thief who hires himself out to steal worthless items only (a toy mouse, the water from a swimming-pool, the dust from an empty room) for 20,000 bucks a time—and gets plenty of takers.

Ed has been other things than a writer, but not many. He was in the army in the early 1950s, worked as a researcher in a public library, did a stint at a paperback publisher's, ground out copy for an ad agency. But mostly, since his first sale in 1955, he's written, and what he's written has mostly been mystery fiction, rarely less than three thousands words long, rarely more than eight.

I don't know how many stories there have been (I often wonder if

Ed himself knows), but the total, as I type these words, will be about thirty or forty less than the total when these words are actually printed, fifty or sixty less than when they're finally read. It can't be too long before he reaches that magic figure of 1000 short stories.

It might be thought that any writer with that total under his belt must have repeated himself, and to be sure Ed has his favourite themes, his old dependables (he's quite fond of fishing-rods, I've noticed; it had never really occurred to me how invaluable a fishing-rod can be when you have murder on your mind). Yet again, and again, and again, and seemingly effortlessly, he comes up with the new twist, the fresh slant, the novel approach (the late John Dickson Carr once said of him, 'Satan himself could be proud of his ingenuity').

Who else but Ed Hoch, when faced with the prospect of an importunate editor and a Christmas-issue deadline coming up fast, would reject footprints in the snow, dead Santa Clauses, exploding parcels, killer Christmas trees, and present a tale that on the face of it doesn't seem to have a lot to do with the Festive Season at all.

The Three Travellers

EDWARD D. HOCH

'NOW the three had journeyed several days when at last they came upon the Oasis of Ziza, and Gaspar who was the wisest of them said, 'We will rest our horses here this night. It will be safe.'

'Safe for horses and men,' Melchior agreed. 'But what of the gold?'

'Safe for the gold also. No one knows we carry it.'

The sun was low in the western sky as they approached, and Gaspar held up a hand to shield his eyes. It would be night soon.

A young herdsman came out to meet them and take their horses. And he said, 'Welcome to the Oasis of Ziza. Have you ridden far?'

'A full moon's journey,' Gaspar replied, speaking in the nomadic tongue. 'What is your name?'

And the herdsman answered, 'They call me Ramoth, sire.'

'Here is a gold coin for you, Ramoth. Feed and water our mounts for the journey and another will be yours on the morrow.'

'Which way do you travel, sire?'

'Towards the west,' Gaspar said, purposely vague.

When the young herdsman had departed with the horses, fat Balthazar said, 'I am not pleased, Gaspar. You lead us, it is true, but the keeping of the gold is my responsibility. And travellers guided by the heavens would do well to journey by night.'

'The desert is cold by night, my friend. Let us cease this bickering and settle ourselves here till the dawn.'

Then Melchior and Balthazar went off to put up their tent, and Gaspar was much relieved. It had been a long journey, not yet ended, and he treasured these moments alone. Presently he set off to inspect the oasis where they would spend the night, and he came upon a stranger who wore a sword at his waist.

'Greetings, traveller,' the man said. 'I am Nevar, of the northern tribe. Do you journey this route often?'

'Not often, no. My name is Gaspar and I come with my two companions from the east.'

Nevar nodded, and stroked his great growth of beard. 'Later, when the sun is gone, there are games of chance—and women for those who have the gold to pay.'

'That does not interest me,' Gaspar said.

'You will find the companionship warming,' Nevar said. 'Come to the fire near the well. That is where we will be.'

Gaspar went on, pausing to look at the beads and trinkets the nomad traders offered. When he reached the well at the far end of the oasis, he saw a woman lifting a great earthen jar to her shoulder. She was little more than a child, and as he watched, the jar slipped from her grasp and shattered against the stones, splashing her with water. She burst into tears.

'Come, child,' Gaspar said, comforting her. 'There is always another jar to be had.'

And she turned her wide brown eyes to him, revealing a beauty he had not seen before. 'My father will beat me,' she said.

'Here is a gold coin for him. Tell him a stranger named Gaspar bumped you and made the jar break.'

'That would not be true.'

'But it is true that I am Gaspar. Who are you?'

'Thantia, daughter of Nevar.'

'Yes, I have met your father. You are very lovely, my child.'

But his words seemed to frighten her, and she ran from him.

Then he returned to the place where Melchior had erected their tent. They had learned from past encampments to leave nothing of value with the horses, and Gaspar immediately asked the location of the gold.

'It is safe,' Balthazar told him. 'Hidden in the bottom of this grain bag.'

'Good. And the perfume?'

'With our regular supplies. No one would steal that.'

Melchior chuckled. 'If they did, we could smell out the culprits quickly enough!'

And then Balthazar said, 'There is gaming tonight, near the well.'

'I know,' Gaspar replied. 'But it is not for us.'

The fat man held out his hands in a gesture of innocence. 'We could but look,' he said.

And Gaspar reluctantly agreed. 'Very well.'

Later, when the fire had been kindled and the people of Ziza came forth from their tents to mingle, the three travellers joined them. Almost at once Gaspar was sought out by a village elder, a man with wrinkled skin and rotting teeth. 'I am Dibon,' he said, choosing a seat next to Gaspar. 'Do you come from the east?'

'Yes, from Persia.'

'A long journey. What brings you this far?'

Gaspar did not wish to answer. Instead, he motioned towards a group of men with small smooth stones before them. 'What manner of sport is this?'

'It is learned from the Egyptians, as are most things sinful.' Then the old man leaned closer, and Gaspar could smell the foul odour of his breath. 'Some say you are a magus.'

'I have studied the teachings of Zoroaster, as have my companions. In truth some would consider me a magus.'

'Then you journey in search of Mazda?'

'In search of truth,' Gaspar replied.

Then he felt the presence of someone towering over him, and saw it was the figure of Nevar. His right hand rested on the sword at his waist. 'I would have words with you, Gaspar.'

'What troubles you?'

'My only daughter Thantia, a virgin not yet twenty, tells me you gave her a gold coin today.'

'Only because I feared the broken water jug was my fault.'

'No stranger approaches Thantia! You will leave Ziza this night!'

'We leave in the morning,' Gaspar said quietly.

Nevar drew his sword, and Gaspar waited no longer. He flung himself at the big man and they tumbled towards the fire as the game-players scattered. Gaspar pulled Nevar's sword from his grip.

Then Thantia broke from the crowd, running to her father.

'This stranger did me no harm!' she cried out.

'Silence, daughter!' Nevar reached for a piece of burning firewood and hurled it at Gaspar, but it went wide of its mark and landed on a low straw roof nearby.

'The stable!' someone shouted, and Gaspar saw it was the herdsman Ramoth hurrying to rescue the horses. The others helped to quench the flames with water from the well, but not before a quantity of feed and supplies had been destroyed.

Then Gaspar and Melchior went in search of fat Balthazar, who had disappeared during the commotion. They found him behind the row of tents, playing the Egyptian stone game with a half dozen desert riders. He had a small pile of gold coins before him.

'This must cease!' Gaspar commanded.

The nomads ran at his words, and Balthazar struggled to his feet. 'It was merely a game.'

'Our task is far more important than mere gaming,' Gaspar reminded him, and the fat man looked sheepish. 'While you idled I was near killed by the swordsman Nevar.'

'A trouble-maker,' Balthazar agreed. 'I will not rest easy until Ziza is behind us on our journey.'

Then as they passed the burned stable on the way to their tent, old Dibon approached them saying, 'This ruin is your fault, Gaspar. Yours and Nevar's.'

'That is true, old man. We will stay here tomorrow and help rebuild the stable.'

Dibon bowed his head. 'A generous offer. We thank you.'

But when they were alone, Balthazar complained, 'This will delay us an entire day!'

'We will travel a distance by night, as you wished.'

Now another surprise was waiting at their tent. As Melchior raised the flap to enter, there was a whimper from within. Gaspar pushed past his hesitating companion and lit the oil lamp. By its glow they saw the girl Thantia crouched behind a pile of robes.

'Please!' she gasped. 'Please hide me. My father has beaten me and I fear for my life!'

'I fear for ours if he finds you here,' Melchior said.

Gaspar held the oil lamp closer and saw the bruises on her face and arms. 'We cannot send you back to him. Remain here with Melchior and Balthazar. I will return shortly.'

Then he made his way to the place where old Dibon rested, and he told the elder what had happened. Dibon nodded and said, 'My daughter and her husband will find room for Thantia until Nevar regains his senses. You were wise to come to me.'

Gaspar and his companions delivered the girl to Dibon, and went with them to the dwelling place of Dibon's daughter. Later, in their tent, Balthazar grumbled again about the delayed departure. But they settled down at last to sleep, as the fires of the encampment burned low around them.

In the morning, by the first rays of the rising sun, Gaspar was awakened by Balthazar's panic-filled voice. 'Wake quickly, Gaspar!' he pleaded, shaking him. 'Someone has stolen our gold!'

Gaspar saw at once that the words were true.

The leather sack of grain contained only grain now. Though the tent showed no sign of forced entry, and though their regular supplies were untouched, the gold had vanished.

'I cannot believe it!' Melchior gasped. 'How could a thief have entered while we slept?'

Gaspar agreed such a thing was impossible. 'The gold was stolen before we retired last night,' he reasoned. 'We were away from the tent during the gaming and fire, and again while escorting Thantia. A thief could have entered at either time.'

'What of the perfume and incense?' Melchior asked.

'Untouched,' Balthazar said. 'My special knot is still in place on the other bags.'

'Only the gold,' Gaspar mused.

'It is truly as if someone knew where to look.'

'The girl!' Balthazar exclaimed. 'We found her in here! She could have searched for the gold and found it.'

'Possible,' Gaspar admitted. 'But I cannot bring myself to believe it'.

'We cannot leave Ziza without the gold,' Melchior said.

'Let us put our minds to the problem while we work at the stable,' Gaspar said.

Now when they reached the stable Nevar was already there, toiling with the others. He paused in his labours when he saw the three, and shot an accusing finger at Gaspar. 'You have stolen away my daughter. I will revenge myself!'

'Your daughter is safe, in the care of Dibon and his family.'

His words quieted Nevar, but Melchior asked, 'If he was so concerned, why did he not come after us in the night?'

Balthazar agreed. 'Or did he come, and steal our gold away?'

Then presently old Dibon appeared, with the girl Thantia at his side. She cast not a glance in her father's direction, and he went about his work ignoring her. Gaspar laboured diligently through the morning, instructing Dibon and the others in Persian building techniques. He too ignored Nevar, not wanting more trouble.

Once, while Balthazar was off to the well for water, Melchior whispered, 'Is it possible that our companion betrays us, Gaspar? Might he have stolen the gold himself to cover his losses at the stone game?'

But Gaspar would hear none of it. 'We must never doubt each other, Melchior. In my heart I know Balthazar is innocent, as I know you are innocent. And I remember the scene at the stone game. There were gold coins in front of him. He was winning, not losing.'

'How will we recover the gold, Gaspar?'

'Through the power of our minds, Melchior. We are wise men, and we must use our minds to determine the thief's identity.'

'But there is no clue to his identity!'

'Sometimes the lack of a clue can be one.'

Balthazar returned with the water and they drank eagerly. Later as they ate of their supplies, Thantia came to them. 'I thank you for helping me,' she said. 'The elders have spoken to my father and he has promised never again to beat me. I will return to him now.'

'We need no thanks,' Gaspar assured her.

Then old Dibon came to join them. 'How may we repay you for your work on the stable?'

'You may recover our stolen gold,' Balthazar blurted out.

'Gold? Stolen gold?'

'It was stolen from our tent,' Balthazar hurried on, before Gaspar could silence him.

'There are no thieves in Ziza!'

'There is one.'

'I will summon the elders. We will search for your gold.'

'No, no,' said Gaspar. 'We will recover it.'

'But how?'

'By finding the thief. It is best to say nothing and catch him off guard.'

Old Dibon bowed his head. 'I will do as you suggest.'

'One favour. Could you ask that our horses be brought to us? We must appear to be leaving.'

Then, as they waited, Balthazar gathered their supplies. And Melchior said, 'I have put my mind to the problem, Gaspar. But there are too many possibilities. The girl Thantia could be the thief, or her father Nevar. Or any of the game players.'

'Or old Dibon himself,' Balthazar added. 'There are too many to suspect.'

Gaspar nodded. 'What is needed is an oracle.'

'You mean to kill a beast as the Romans do?'

Gaspar shook his head. 'My oracle will be a living animal.' He saw the herdsman Ramoth leading their horses. 'My steed will tell me who has our gold.'

'Your horse?' fat Balthazar laughed. 'Who learns anything from a dumb animal?'

Gaspar held out some grain for the horse. 'You see how he eats? He is hungry.'

'What does that tell us?' Melchior asked.

'That our gold was stolen by Ramoth!'

It was after Dibon spoke to Ramoth that the young herdsman confessed his crime and begged forgiveness. When the missing gold had been returned to Gaspar's hands, the others questioned him.

'How did you know it was Ramoth?' Melchior asked. 'We barely spoke to the youth.'

'My horse told me, as I told you he would. The horse was hungry, so had not been fed. You see, the thief never touched our other supplies, never unfastened Balthazar's special knot. How could he have found the gold so easily, without searching for it? But the gold was hidden in a sack of grain, and after the fire destroyed the stable, Ramoth came in search of feed for our horses. He came while we were away, and looked in only one place—the grain bag. Feeling the weight of it, his fingers reached through the grain and came upon the gold. He stole it, but then could not take the grain lest we realize he was the thief. So the horses went hungry.'

'You are a wise man, Gaspar,' Balthazar conceded.

'As we all are. Come, let us mount.'

'It will be dark soon,' Melchior said.

Gaspar nodded. 'We will get bearings from the star.'

Dibon was by the well to wish them farewell. 'Ramoth will be punished,' he promised.

'Show mercy,' Gaspar said.

'Do you ride west with your gold?'

'West with gifts for a King. Gold and frankincense and myrrh.'

'Good journey,' Dibon said.

He watched them for a long time, until the three vanished from sight over the desert wastes.

PETER LOVESEY (b. 1936) made his name with a series of mystoricals (eight in all) set in Victorian times and featuring the down-to-earth Sergeant Cribb.

The first Cribb case, *Wobble To Death* (1970), won the Macmillan best first novel contest and has much to answer for, since it was almost certainly responsible for the positive plague of Victorian sleuths with which the 1970s, in retrospect, seem infested (although Arthur Swinson's popular Sergeant Cork television series and subsequent books did precede). There were times during that decade when it seemed that no one was writing a detective story not set sometime during the nineteenth century (and if writers weren't busy doing that they were dashing off Sherlock Holmes pastiches, which I suppose comes to the same thing). Some were good, some were not so good; some were downright dangerous to the blood pressure because their authors went to such insane lengths to get their dialogue exactly right for the period that, unless you happened to have a slang dictionary at your elbow, they might just as well have been writing in Martian.

Lovesey didn't go to those extremes and his Sergeant Cribb books are enjoyable enough without ever reaching the heights of ingenuity and gamey realism of Francis Selwyn's (i.e. Donald Thomas's) Sergeant Verity novels or the hilariously bawdy and inventive depths plumbed in the Jeremy Sturrock (a.k.a. Ben Healey) saga.

Lovesey's 1978 Cribb offering *Waxwork* gained the British CWA Silver Dagger and probably he thought that was a decent note to end on because there's been no Cribb since. Cribb fans doubtless mourned and the smart money was probably on the old writer's saw that if you have a good thing going, stick at it, else disaster will inevitably befall. But I think Lovesey did well to throw off his shackles. I'll reword that. I *know* Lovesey did well to throw off his shackles. His post-Cribb novels, without exception, are wonderfully imaginative, wonderfully readable, wonderfully *eccentric*.

In *The False Inspector Dew* (1982) an errant dentist who fails to kill his wife is mistaken for the man who collared Crippen and forced to solve a murder on the *Mauretania*. This delightful *tour de force* quite rightly went one better than his previous book and won the CWA Golden Dagger. In *Keystone* (1983) a failed, destitute, stubbornly sobersided British music-hall comedian is grudgingly taken on as an extra by Mack Sennett and becomes embroiled in the desperate schemes of a murderous Mr X who kidnaps the worst actress in Hollywood. In *Rough Cider* (1986) a crippled college lecturer is mercilessly badgered by an appalling American female student into trying to unravel a 25-year-old murder in which he was unwittingly involved.

Lovesey's short stories are just as entertaining, just as inventive, just as twisty. *Butchers* (1985) was as dazzling a box of tricks as I've been fooled by in a long time. Here's a neat little tale with a snap to it that will surely appear in his next collection.

6

Murder in Store

PETER LOVESEY

AMONG all the children hanging around the department, this one was definitely the most persistently bothersome. Even now, she was tugging at Pauline's sleeve.

'Hey, miss.'

'What is it now?'

'Something's up with Santa.'

'That's quite enough from you, young lady,' Pauline said sharply—unseasonably sharply for Christmas week in an Oxford Street department store.

The Toy Fair was a bedlam of electric trains, robots, talking dolls, and whining infants, but the counter staff, however hard-pressed they might be feeling, weren't expected to threaten the kids.

The day had got off to a distinctly trying start when a boy with mischief in mind had pulled a panda off the shelf and started an avalanche of soft toys. Pauline had found herself wading knee-deep in teddies, rabbits, and hippos.

Now she was desperately trying to reassemble the display, between attending to customers and coping with little nuisances like this one, dumped in the department while their parents went off and shopped elsewhere in the store.

'Take a butcher's in the grotto, miss.'

Pauline glared at the girl, a six-year-old by the size of her, with gaps between her teeth and a dark fringe like a helmet. A green anorak, white corduroy trousers, and red wellies. She'd been a regular visitor since the school term ended. Her quick, sticky hands were a threat to every toy within reach. But she had shining brown eyes and a way with words that could be amusing at times less stressful than this.

'I think Santa's snuffed it, miss.'

'For the last time . . .'

A man held out a green felt crocodile, and Pauline rolled her eyes upwards and exchanged a smile. She rang up the sale, locked her till, and stepped around the counter to look for Mark Daventry, the head of the toy department. The child had a point. It was 10:05 and Santa's grotto should have opened at 10:00. A queue had started to form. There was no sign of Zena, the 'gnome' who sold the tickets.

It was shamefully unfair. Mark hadn't been near the department this morning. No doubt he was treating Zena to coffee in the staff canteen. When blonde Zena had first appeared three weeks ago in her pointed hat, short tunic, and red tights, Mark had lingered around the grotto entrance like a six-foot kid lining up for his Christmas present. Soon he'd persuaded her to join him for coffee breaks: the Mark Daventry routine familiar to Pauline and sundry other ex-girlfriends in the store.

However, Zena wasn't merely the latest Christmas casual in the toy department. She wasn't merely an attractive blonde. She happened to be the wife of Santa Claus.

Big Ben, as he was known outside the grotto, was a ready-made Santa, a mountainous man who needed no padding under the crimson suit, and whose beard was his own, requiring only a dusting of talc. On Saturday nights, he could be seen in a pair of silver trunks in the wrestling-ring at Streatham. This time, Mark was flirting dangerously.

'Coming, miss?'

Pauline felt her fingers clutched by a small, warm hand. She allowed herself to be led to the curtain at the far end of the grotto.

The child dived through the curtain and Pauline followed. Surprisingly, the interior was unlit. The winking lights hadn't been switched on and the mechanical figures of Santa's helpers were immobile. There was no sign of Ben and Zena. They generally came up by the service lift that was cunningly enclosed in the grotto, behind Santa's workshop. They used the workshop as a changing room.

'See what I mean, miss?'

Pauline saw where the child was pointing, and caught her breath. In the gloom, the motionless figure of Santa Claus was slumped on the throne where he usually sat to receive the children. His head and shoulders hung ominously over to one side.

It was difficult not to scream. Only the presence of the child kept Pauline from panicking.

'Stay here. Don't come any closer.'

She knew what she had to do: check whether his pulse was beating. He might have suffered a heart attack. Ben was not much over thirty, but anyone so obviously over-weight was at risk. She took a deep breath and stepped forward.

She discovered he wasn't actually wearing the costume. It was draped over him. Somehow, she had to find the courage to look. She reached out and lifted the furry trim of the hood. She gave a start. She was looking into a pair of eyes without a flicker of life. But it wasn't Ben.

It was Mark Daventry. And there was something embedded in his chest—a bolt from a crossbow.

Pauline rushed the child out of the grotto and dashed to the phone.

She called Mr Beckington, the store manager, but got through to Sylvia, his secretary. Even suave Sylvia, equal to every emergency, gave a cry of horror at the news. 'Mark? Oh my God! Are you sure!'

'Is Mr Beckington there?'

'Mr Beckington? Yes.'

'Ask him to come down at once. I'll make sure no one goes in.'

When she came off the phone, Pauline looked around for the small girl. She'd wandered off, probably to spread the news. Soon the whole store would know that Santa was dead in his grotto. Pauline shook her head and went to stand guard.

She told the queue that Santa was going to be late, and someone made a joke about reindeer in the rush hour.

This is totally bizzare, Pauline thought, standing here under the glitter with these smiling people and their children, and 'Jingle Bells' belting out from the public address, while a man lies murdered a few yards away. Her nerves were stretched to snapping point.

Fully ten minutes went by before Mr Beckington appeared, smoking his usual cigar, giving a convincing impression of the unflappable executive in a crisis. He liked customers to be aware that he managed the store, so he always wore a rosebud on his pin-striped lapel. He nodded sociably to the queue and then murmured to Pauline. 'What's all this, Miss Fothergill?' as if she were the cause of it.

She took him to the grotto.

They stopped and stared.

The winking lights were on. The model figures were in motion, wielding their little hammers. Santa was alive and on his throne, dressed for work. Zena the gnome was powdering his beard.

'Ho-ho,' Ben greeted them in his jocular voice, 'and what do you want in your Christmas stockings?'

Mr Beckington turned to Pauline, his eyes blazing behind his glasses. 'If this is some kind of joke, it's in lamentably bad taste.'

She reddened and repeated what she'd seen. Ben and Zena insisted that everything had been in its usual place when they'd arrived in the lift a few minutes late. They certainly hadn't seen a dead body.

She gaped at them in disbelief.

Mr Beckington said, 'We're all under stress at this time of the year, Miss Fothergill. The best construction I can put upon this incident is that you had some kind of hallucination brought on by overwork. You'd better go home and rest.'

She said, trying to stay calm, 'I'm perfectly well, thank you. I don't need to go home. And if it's all my imagination, where's Mark Daventry?'

Mr Beckington told her: 'He's down with flu. We had a message.'

'Darling, I think some meany played a trick on you,' Zena suggested. 'That kid with the teeth missing is a right little scamp. Some joker must have put her up to it.'

Pauline shook her head and frowned, unwilling to accept the explanation, but trying to fathom how it could have been done.

'If you're not going home, you'd better get back to your position,' Mr Beckington told her. 'And let's get this blasted grotto open.'

She spent the rest of the morning in a stunned state, going through the motions of selling toys and answering inquiries while her mind tried to account for what had happened. If only the small girl had returned, she'd have got the truth from her by some means, but, just when the kid was wanted, she'd vanished.

About 12:30, there was a quiet period. Pauline asked Zena to keep an eye on her counter for five minutes.

'I want to check the stocklists in the sports department.'

'Whatever for?'

'To see if a crossbow is missing.'

The sports department was located next to the toys on the same floor. Disappointingly, Pauline found that every crossbow was accounted for. She told herself that if the murderer was on the staff, he could easily have borrowed the weapon and replaced it later. But what about the bolt?

She examined the crossbow kits. Six bolts were supplied with each. She checked the boxes and found one with only five. She *hadn't* been hallucinating.

'What are you going to do about it?' Zena asked, when Pauline told her.

'I've got some more checking to do.'

'Proper Miss Marple, aren't you? You're wasting your time, darling.'

'Coming from you, that's good.'

Zena said without a hint of embarrassment, 'Jealous of my coffee breaks, are you? That's all water under the bridge. Look, I still say this is someone playing silly games. It could even be Mark himself.'

Pauline shook her head. 'Zena, he's dead, and I'm going to find out why. Tell me, did you and Ben arrive together this morning?'

Zena smiled. 'You bet we did.'

'What's funny?'

'He guards me like a harem girl since he found out Mark was after me. We had a monumental row last week, and I told Ben straight out that he shouldn't take me for granted. Now he watches me all the time.' She adjusted her pointed hat. 'I find it rather a turn-on.'

'But you definitely finished with Mark last week?'

'Absolutely. I wouldn't say he was heartbroken. You know how he is. Adaptable.'

'That isn't the word I'd use,' said Pauline, thinking of all the women Mark had chatted up.

During her lunch hour, she went downstairs and talked to the security man on the staff entrance, a solemn Scot who'd made himself unpopular with everyone but the management by noting daily who was in, and at what time. Pauline asked if Mr Mark Daventry was in.

'Yes, he's here. He arrived early this morning, just after 8:15.'

She said, 'Are you sure?'

To prove his point, the security man showed her Mark's overcoat in the staff locker-room. There was no question now that what she had seen was true.

She asked the security man about Ben and Zena. They'd arrived together at their usual time, 9:50—which was odd, not to say suspicious, considering how late the grotto had opened.

She decided to have it out with them. The grotto closed between 1:00 and 2:00, so she found them in the staff canteen. They'd

finished lunch and Ben had his arm around Zena. They looked like two innocent choirboys on a Christmas card.

She warned them that she'd been checking downstairs.

'I want a straight answer. Why weren't you ready to open the grotto at ten this morning?'

'There's no mystery, darling,' answered Zena. 'We had to wait ages for the lift.'

A reasonable explanation. The lift was their only means of access to the grotto. Pauline had to accept it for the moment. She said, 'I'm going to search the grotto.'

Ben said affably, 'Fine. Let's all make a search.'

They had twenty minutes. Pauline had hoped to find bloodstains on Santa's throne, but it was painted red. She went behind the scenery, where it was supported on wood and chicken wire. 'There's something under here.'

It was a wooden packing case. Ben dragged it out and pulled off the lid. There was a layer of the small, white chips of polystyrene used in packing. Ben dug into them with his large hands.

Zena screamed as a tuft of dark hair was revealed. It didn't take long to confirm that Mark's body had been crammed into the packing case.

'We'd better report it,' said Ben in a shocked voice. Reassuringly, he and Zena seemed genuinely surprised at the discovery.

'Before we do,' said Pauline, 'look in his pockets.'

In an inside pocket Ben discovered the note Pauline hoped to find. *Something* must have lured Mark to his death in the grotto.

It was a short, typed message: 'See what Santa has for you, darling. Tuesday morning, 8:45.'

'I've seen that typestyle recently,' said Ben.

'On our letter of appointment,' said Zena.

'Sylvia?' said Ben, frowning, 'Mr Beckington's secretary?'

Pauline and Zena exchanged a long, uncomprehending look.

They covered the body and took the lift to the management floor above. On the way up, Pauline said, 'I've thought of something terribly important. Did you find out why you had to wait so long for the lift this morning?'

'It's usually because a storeman's delivering goods,' Ben answered.

Pauline said, 'I believe it was the murderer jamming the lift door open at our floor so that no one would interrupt the killing. When it finally arrived, did you see a storeman?'

'No,' said Zena, 'it was empty.' She hesitated. 'But we smelled cigar smoke.'

There wasn't time to reflect on that, because the lift doors opened at the top floor and Mr Beckington was waiting there, a cigar jutting from his mouth. At the sight of the three of them together, his features twisted in alarm. He turned and made a dash for the stairs.

'Ben!' shouted Zena.

The commotion brought people from their offices, among them Sylvia. Pauline grabbed her arm and drew her into the lift. Zena pressed the ground floor button and the three women started downward.

'Mr Beckington,' Zena blurted out. 'He murdered Mark.'

Sylvia's hand went to her mouth.

'But why?' said Pauline.

Sylvia said in a small, shocked voice, 'He

was jealous. Silly man. He was forever trying to start something with me, but I wasn't interested. I mean, he's married, with a daughter my age. Then last week Mark started taking an interest in me. I always thought him dishy, and . . . well, on Friday evening we spent a little time in the grotto.'

'By arrangement?'

Sylvia nodded. 'When everyone else was gone.' Pauline showed her the note they'd found in Mark's pocket. 'I didn't type this?' said Sylvia.

'Mr Beckington did,' Pauline explained, 'on your typewriter, to make sure Mark turned up this morning. He killed Mark in the grotto and he must have still been in there when the child sneaked in. He must have been hiding behind the scenery when I came in. I raised the alarm, and while I was standing outside like a lemon, he hid the body in a packing case. I just hope Ben catches him.'

The lift gave a shudder as they reached the ground floor. When the doors opened, a police sergeant was waiting. Two constables were nearby, standing at the foot of the stairs.

'All right, girls,' said the sergeant. 'Just stand over there, well out of the way.'

In a moment, there was the clatter of footsteps on the stairs, then Mr Beckington ran straight into the arms of the waiting policemen. He offered no resistance.

Pauline felt a tug on her skirt and looked down at the small girl. 'You?' she said. 'You called the police?'

The child smiled smugly and nodded.

'And you believed her?' Pauline asked the sergeant.

'She's my daughter, miss. The way I see it, if my little girl tells me Santa's snuffed it, I've got to be very, very concerned.'

NOT MUCH seems to be known about Ethel Lina White (1887–1944). I know; I've looked. The odd mention here and there, one or two references in the older standard works, a brief essay in the first edition of Reilly's mammoth *20th Century Crime And Mystery Writers*, which was ruthlessly chopped out of the second. And that's about it.

Astonishing, really, when you think that two of her books were transformed into classic movies: *Some Must Watch* (1933) as *Spiral Staircase*; *The Wheel Spins* (1936) as Hitchcock's British masterpiece *The Lady Vanishes* (that moment when Margaret Lockwood discovers that the bandaged figure in the compartment *isn't* Dame May Whitty. . . the running cricket cross-talk act between Naunton Wayne and Basil Radford. . . the gun-battle in the forest when Cecil Parker, at his most stutteringly craven, gets his. . . the moment when Michael Redgrave and Margaret Lockwood are desperately trying to recall that crucial tune, and *then*—but enough, enough).

In Reilly, White's life is summed up thus: 'British. Born in Abergavenny, Monmouthshire, in 1887. Worked in the Ministry of Pensions. Died in 1944.' Only the excellent—and, come to think of it, even more mysterious— Thurman Warriner gets shorter shrift, but there's nothing in his *c.v.* to compare with 'Worked in the Ministry of Pensions. Died. . .'

Chilling stuff. As chilling as some of Miss (Mrs?) White's own books. She wrote seventeen in all, in between 1927 and 1944, but you may have to stump round secondhand bookshops for years before you catch sight of even one, apart from *The Lady Vanishes* in tattered paperback. But it'll be worth the effort. Ethel Lina White wrote some of the most atmospheric thrillers of the 1930s.

None of her early books was a mystery. Her first, *The Wishbone*, judging by a review which talks of her 'keen sense of humour', appears to have been a comedy; her second, judging by the title, *'Twill Soon Be Dark* (a pretty cheerless line from Emerson on the transcience of human life), a tragedy; her third, *The Eternal Journey*, was very strong on reincarnation.

But after that, more often than not she wrote of imperilled and friendless females bending under intolerable emotional (even unearthly) pressures. Her heroines are invariably young, alone in the world, not quite pretty (the Jane Eyre touch), struggling at a dead-end job; and whatever sinister entanglements they fall into. . . *no one believes a word they say*. Still, they may bend but they never crack, although at the end of the story, when all has been sorted out, the menace defied and vanquished, they usually feel as though they've been shoved backwards through a wringer.

Even when she was not telling of some put-upon heroine struggling in the toils—the excellent *She Faded Into Air* (1941), for instance, is relatively un-doomladen, although it's a cracking tale of an Impossible Vanishment—Ethel Lina White could certainly pile on the atmospherics. One of my own favourites is *Wax* (1935), a story of murder and sudden, shocking *appearances* (as opposed to disappearances) in that most eerie of settings, an old, rundown waxworks.

Which, of course, brings us to 'Waxworks', the story on which the novel is only very loosely based. Not quite a murder story, not quite a ghost story—but certainly a tale of nerve-jangling tension...

— 7 —

Waxworks

ETHEL LINA WHITE

SONIA made her first entry in her notebook:

Eleven o'clock. The lights are out. The porter has just locked the door. I can hear his footsteps echoing down the corridor. They grow fainter. Now there is silence. I am alone.

She stopped writing to glance at her company. Seen in the light from the street-lamp, which streamed in through the high window, the room seemed to be full of people. Their faces were those of men and women of character and intelligence. They stood in groups, as though in conversation, or sat apart, in solitary reverie.

But they neither moved nor spoke.

When Sonia had last seen them in the glare of the electric globes, they had been a collection of ordinary waxworks, some of which were the worse for wear. The black velvet which lined the walls of the Gallery was alike tawdry and filmed with dust.

The side opposite to the window was built into alcoves, which held highly moral tableaux, depicting contrasting scenes in the career of Vice and Virtue. Sonia had slipped into one of these recesses, just before closing-time, in order to hide for her vigil.

It had been a simple affair. The porter had merely rung his bell, and the few courting-couples which represented the Public had taken his hint and hurried towards the exit.

No one was likely to risk being locked in, for the Waxwork Collection of Oldhampton, had lately acquired a sinister reputation. The foundation for this lay in the fate of a stranger to the town—a commercial traveller—who had cut his throat in the Hall of Horrors.

Since then, two persons had, separately, spent the night in the Gallery and, in the morning, each had been found dead.

In both cases the verdict had been 'Natural death, due to heart failure.' The first victim—a local alderman—had been addicted to alcoholism, and was in very bad shape. The second—his great friend—was a delicate little man, a martyr to asthma, and slightly unhinged through unwise absorption in spiritualism.

While the coincidence of the tragedies stirred up a considerable amount of local superstition, the general belief was that both deaths were due to the power of suggestion, in conjunction with macabre surroundings. The victims had let themselves be frightened to death by the Waxworks.

Sonia was there, in the Gallery, to test its truth.

She was the latest addition to the staff of the *Oldhampton Gazette*. Bubbling with enthusiasm, she made no secret of her literary ambitions, and it was difficult to feed her with enough work. Her colleagues listened to her with mingled amusement and boredom, but they liked her as a refreshing novelty. As for her fine future, they looked to young Wells—the Sporting Editor—to effect her speedy and painless removal from the sphere of journalism.

On Christmas Eve, Sonia took them all into her confidence over her intention to spend a night in the Waxworks, on the last night of the old year.

'Copy there,' she declared. 'I'm not timid and I have fairly sensitive perceptions, so I ought to be able to write up the effect of imagination on the nervous system. I mean to record my impressions, every hour, while they're piping-hot.'

Looking up suddenly, she had surprised a green glare in the eyes of Hubert Poke.

When Sonia came to work on the *Gazette*, she had a secret fear of unwelcome amorous attentions, since she was the only woman on the staff. But the first passion she awoke was hatred.

Poke hated her impersonally, as the representative of a Force, numerically superior to his own sex, which was on the opposing side in the battle for existence. He feared her, too, because she was the unknown element, and possessed the unfair weapon of charm.

Before she came, he had been the star turn on the *Gazette*. His own position on the staff gratified his vanity and entirely satisfied his narrow ambition. But Sonia had stolen some of his thunder. On more than one occasion she had written up a story he had failed to cover, and he had to admit that her success was due to a quicker wit.

For some time past he had been playing with the idea of spending a night in the Waxworks, but was deterred by the knowledge that his brain was not sufficiently temperate for the experiment. Lately he had been subject to sudden red rages, when he had felt a thick hot taste in his throat, as though of blood. He knew that his jealousy of Sonia was accountable. It had almost reached the stage of mania, and trembled on the brink of homicidal urge.

While his brain was still creaking with the idea of first-hand experience in the ill-omened Gallery, Sonia had nipped in with her ready-made plan.

Controlling himself with an effort, he listened while the sub-editor issued a warning to Sonia.

'Bon idea, young woman, but you will find the experience a bit raw. You've no notion how uncanny these big deserted buildings can be.'

'That's so,' nodded young Wells, 'I once spent a night in a haunted house.'

Sonia looked at him with her habitual interest. He was short and thick-set, with a three-cornered smile which appealed to her.

'Did you see anything?' she asked.

'No, I cleared out before the show came on. Windy. After a bit, one can imagine *anything*.'

It was then that Poke introduced a new note into the discussion by his own theory of the mystery deaths.

Sitting alone in the deserted Gallery, Sonia preferred to forget his words. She resolutely drove them from her mind while she began to settle down for the night.

Her first action was to cross to the figure of Cardinal Wolsey and unceremoniously raise his heavy scarlet robe. From under its voluminous folds, she drew out her cushion and attaché-case, which she had hidden earlier in the evening.

Mindful of the fact that it would grow chilly at dawn, she carried on her arm her thick white tennis-coat. Slipping it on, she placed her cushion in the angle of the wall, and sat down to await developments.

The Gallery was far more mysterious now that the lights were out. At either end, it seemed to stretch away into impenetrable black tunnels. But there was nothing uncanny about it, or about the figures, which were a tame and conventional collection of historical personages. Even the adjoining Hall of Horrors contained no horrors, only a selection of respectable-looking poisoners.

Sonia grinned cheerfully at the row of waxworks which were visible in the lamplight from the street.

'So you are the villains of the piece,' she murmured. 'Later on, if the office is right, you will assume unpleasant mannerisms to try to cheat me into believing you are alive. I warn you, old sports, you'll have your work cut out for you . . . And now I think I'll get better acquainted with you. Familiarity breeds contempt.'

She went the round of the figures, greeting each with flippancy or criticism. Presently she returned to her corner and opened her note-book ready to record her impressions.

Twelve o'clock. The first hour has passed almost too quickly. I've drawn a complete blank. Not a blessed thing to record. Not a vestige of reaction. The waxworks seem a commonplace lot, without a scrap of hypnotic force. In fact, they're altogether too matey.

Sonia had left her corner, to write her entry in the light which streamed through the window. Smoking was prohibited in the building, and, lest she should yield to temptation, she had left both her cigarettes and matches behind her, on the office table.

At this stage she regretted the matches. A little extra light would be a boon. It was true she carried an electric torch, but she was saving it, in case of emergency.

It was a loan from young Wells. As they were leaving the office together, he spoke to her confidentially.

'Did you notice how Poke glared at you? Don't get up against him. He's a nasty piece of work. He's so mean he'd sell his mother's shroud for old rags. And he's a cruel little devil, too. He turned out his miserable pup, to starve in the streets, rather than cough up for the licence.'

Sonia grew hot with indignation.

'What he needs to cure his complaint is a strong dose of rat-poison,' she declared. 'What became of the poor little dog?'

'Oh, he's all right. He was a matey chap, and he soon chummed up with a mongrel of his own class.'

'You?' asked Sonia, her eyes suddenly soft.

'A mongrel, am I?' grinned Wells. 'Well, anyway, the pup will get a better Christmas than his first, when Poke went away and left him on the chain . . . We're both of us going to over-eat and over-drink. You're on your own, too. Won't you join us?'

'I'd love to.'

Although the evening was warm and muggy the invitation suffused Sonia with the spirit of Christmas. The shade of Dickens seemed to be hovering over the parade of the streets. A red-nosed Santa Claus presided over a spangled Christmas-tree outside a toy-shop. Windows were hung with tinselled balls and coloured paper festoons. Pedestrians, laden with parcels, called out seasonable greetings.

'Merry Christmas.'

Young Wells' three-cornered smile was his tribute to the joyous feeling of festival. His eyes were eager as he turned to Sonia.

'I've an idea. Don't wait until after the holidays to write up the Waxworks. Make it a Christmas stunt, and go there tonight.'

'I will,' declared Sonia.

It was then that he slipped the torch into her hand.

'I know you belong to the stronger sex,' he said. 'But even your nerve might crash. If it does, just flash this torch under the window. Stretch out your arm above your head, and the light will be seen from the street.'

'And what will happen then?' asked Sonia.

'I shall knock up the miserable porter and let you out.'

'But how will *you* see the light?'

'I shall be in the street.'

'All night?'

'Yes; I sleep there' Young Wells grinned. 'Understand,' he added loftily, 'that this is a matter of principle. I could not let any woman—even one so aged and unattractive as yourself—feel beyond the reach of help.'

He cut into her thanks as he turned away with a parting warning.

'Don't use the torch for light, or the juice may give out. It's about due for a new battery.'

As Sonia looked at the torch, lying by her side, it seemed a link with young Wells. At this moment he was patrolling the street, a sturdy figure in old tweed overcoat, with his cap pulled down over his eyes.

As she tried to pick out his footsteps from among those of the other passers-by, it struck her that there was plenty of traffic, considering that it was past twelve o'clock.

'The witching hour of midnight is another lost illusion,' she reflected. 'Killed by night-clubs, I suppose.'

It was cheerful to know that so many citizens were abroad, to keep her company. Some optimists were still singing carols. She faintly heard the strains of 'Good King Wenceslas.' It was in a tranquil frame of mind that she unpacked her sandwiches and thermos.

'It's Christmas Day,' she thought, as she drank hot coffee. 'And I'm spending it with Don and the pup.'

At that moment her career grew misty, and the flame of her literary ambition dipped as the future glowed with the warm firelight of home. In sudden elation, she held up her flask and toasted the waxworks.

'Merry Christmas to you all! And many of them.'

The faces of the illuminated figures remained stolid, but she could almost swear that a low murmur of acknowledgment seemed to swell from the rest of her company—invisible in the darkness.

She spun out her meal to its limit, stifling her craving for a cigarette. Then, growing bored, she counted the visible waxworks, and tried to memorise them.

'Twenty-one, twenty-two . . . Wolsey. Queen Elizabeth, Guy Fawkes, Napoleon ought to go on a diet. Ever heard of eighteen days, Nap? Poor old Julius Cæsar looks as though he'd been sun-bathing on the Lido. He's about due for the melting-pot.'

In her eyes they were a second-rate set of dummies. The local theory that they could terrorise a human being to death or madness seemed a fantastic notion.

'No,' concluded Sonia. 'There's really more in Poke's bright idea.'

Again she saw the sun-smitten office—for the big unshielded window faced south—with its blistered paint, faded wall-paper, ink-stained desks, typewriters, telephones, and a huge fire in the untidy grate. Young Wells smoked his big pipe, while the sub-editor—a ginger, pig-headed young man—laid down the law about the mystery deaths.

And then she heard Poke's toneless dead-man's voice.

'You may be right about the spiritualist. He died of fright—but not of the waxworks. My belief is that he established contact with the spirit of his dead friend, the alderman, and so learned his real fate.'

'What fate?' snapped the sub-editor.

'I believe that the alderman was murdered,' replied Poke.

He clung to his point like a limpet in the face of all counter-arguments.

'The alderman had enemies,' he said. 'Nothing would be easier than for one of them to lie in wait for him. In the present circumstances, *I* could commit a murder in the Waxworks, and get away with it.'

'How?' demanded young Wells.

'How? To begin with, the Gallery is a one-man show and the porter's a bonehead. Anyone could enter, and leave, the Gallery without his being wise to it.'

'And the murder?' plugged young Wells.

With a shudder Sonia remembered how Poke had glanced at his long knotted fingers.

'If I could not achieve my object by fright, which is the foolproof way,' he replied, 'I should try a little artistic strangulation.'

'And leave your marks?'

'Not necessarily. Every expert knows that there are methods which show no trace.'

Sonia fumbled in her bag for the

cigarettes which were not there.

'Why did I let myself think of that, just now?' she thought. 'Really too stupid.'

As she reproached herself for her morbidity, she broke off to stare at the door which led to the Hall of Horrors.

When she had last looked at it, she could have sworn that it was tightly closed . . . But now it gaped open by an inch.

She looked at the black cavity, recognizing the first test of her nerves. Later on, there would be others. She realized the fact that, within her cool, practical self, she carried a hysterical, neurotic passenger, who would doubtless give her a lot of trouble through officious suggestions and uncomfortable reminders.

She resolved to give her second self a taste of her quality, and so quell her at the start.

'That door was merely closed,' she remarked as, with a firm step, she crossed to the Hall of Horrors and shut the door.

One o'clock. I begin to realize that there is more in this than I thought. Perhaps I'm missing my sleep. But I'm keyed up and horribly expectant. Of what? I don't know. But I seem to be waiting for—something. I find myself listening—listening. The place is full of mysterious noises. I know they're my fancy . . . And things appear to move. I can distinguish footsteps and whispers, as though those waxworks which I cannot see in the darkness are beginning to stir to life.

Sonia dropped her pencil at the sound of a low chuckle. It seemed to come from the end of the Gallery which was blacked out by shadows.

As her imagination galloped away with her, she reproached herself sharply.

'Steady, don't be a fool. There must be a cloak-room here. That chuckle is the air escaping in a pipe—or something. I'm betrayed by my own ignorance of hydraulics.'

In spite of her brave words, she returned rather quickly to her corner.

With her back against the wall she felt less apprehensive. But she recognized her cowardice as an ominous sign.

She was desperately afraid of someone—or something—creeping up behind her and touching her.

'I've struck the bad patch,' she told herself. 'It will be worse at three o'clock and work up to a climax. But when I make my entry, at three, I shall have reached the peak. After that every minute will be bringing the dawn nearer.'

But of one fact she was ignorant. There would be no recorded impression at three o'clock.

Happily unconscious, she began to think of her copy. When she returned to the office—sunken-eyed, and looking like nothing on earth—she would then rejoice over every symptom of groundless fear.

'It's a story all right,' she gloated, looking at Hamlet. His gnarled, pallid features and dark smouldering eyes were strangely familiar to her.

Suddenly she realized that he reminded her of Hubert Poke.

Against her will, her thoughts again turned to him. She told herself that he was exactly like a waxwork. His yellow face—symptomatic of heart-trouble—had the same cheesy hue, and his eyes were like dull black glass. He wore a denture which was too large for him, and which forced his lips apart in a mirthless grin.

He always seemed to smile—even over the episode of the lift—which had been no joke.

It happened two days before. Sonia had rushed into the office in a state of molten excitement because she had extracted an interview from a Personage who had just received the Freedom of the City. This distinguished freeman had the reputation of shunning newspaper publicity, and Poke had tried his luck, only to be sent away with a flea in his ear.

At the back of her mind, Sonia knew that she had not fought level, for she was conscious of the effect of violet-blue eyes and a dimple upon a reserved but very human gentleman. But in her elation she had been rather blatant about her score.

She transcribed her notes, rattling away at her typewriter in a tremendous hurry, because she had a dinner-engagement. In the same breathless speed she had rushed towards the automatic lift.

She was just about to step into it when young Wells had leaped the length of the passage and dragged her back.

'Look, where you're going,' he shouted.

Sonia looked—and saw only the well of the shaft. The lift was not waiting in its accustomed place.

'Out of order,' explained Wells before he turned to blast Hubert Poke, who stood by.

'You almighty chump, why didn't you grab Miss Fraser, instead of standing by like a stuck pig?'

At the time Sonia had vaguely remarked how Poke had stammered and sweated, and she accepted the fact that he had been petrified by shock and had lost his head.

For the first time, she realized that his inaction had been deliberate. She remembered the flame of terrible excitement in his eyes and his stretched ghastly grin.

'He *hates* me,' she thought. 'It's my fault. I've been tactless and cocksure.'

Then a flood of horror swept over her.

'But he wanted to see me crash. It's almost *murder*.'

As she began to tremble, the jumpy passenger she carried reminded her of Poke's remark about the alderman.

'He had enemies.'

Sonia shook away the suggestion angrily.

'My memory's uncanny,' she thought. 'I'm stimulated and all strung up. It must be the atmosphere. . . Perhaps there's some gas in the air that accounts for these brainstorms. It's hopeless to be so utterly unscientific. Poke would have made a better job of this.'

She was back again to Hubert Poke. He had become an obsession.

Her head began to throb and a tiny gong started to beat in her temples. This time, she recognized the signs without any mental ferment.

'Atmospherics. A storm's coming up. It might make things rather thrilling. I must concentrate on my story. Really, my luck's in.'

She sat for some time, forcing herself to think of pleasant subjects—of arguments with young Wells and the Tennis Tournament. But there was always a point when her thoughts gave a twist and led her back to Poke.

Presently she grew cramped and got up to pace the illuminated aisle in front of the window. She tried again to talk to the waxworks, but, this time, it was not a success.

They seemed to have grown remote and secretive, as though they were removed to another plane, where they possessed a hidden life.

Suddenly she gave a faint scream. Someone—or something—had crept up behind her, for she felt the touch of cold fingers upon her arm.

Two o'clock. They're only wax. They shall not frighten me. But they're trying to. One by one they're coming to life. . . Charles the Second no longer looks sour dough. He is beginning to leer at me. His eyes remind me of Hubert Poke.

Sonia stopped writing, to glance uneasily at the image of the Stuart monarch. His black velveteen suit appeared to have a richer pile. The swart curls which fell over his lace collar looked less like horse-hair. There really seemed a gleam of amorous interest lurking at the back of his glass optics.

Absurdly, Sonia spoke to him, in order to reassure herself.

'Did *you* touch me? At the first hint of a liberty, Charles Stuart, I'll smack your face. You'll learn a modern journalist has not the manners of an orange-girl.'

Instantly the satyr reverted to a dummy in a moth-eaten historical costume.

Sonia stood, listening for young Wells' footsteps. But she could not hear them, although the street now was perfectly still. She tried to picture him, propping up the opposite building, solid and immovable as the Rock of Gibraltar.

But it was no good. Doubts began to obtrude.

'I don't believe he's there. After all, why should he stay? He only pretended, just to give me confidence. He's gone.'

She shrank back to her corner, drawing her tennis-coat closer, for warmth. It was growing colder, causing her to think of tempting things—of a hot-water bottle and a steaming tea-pot.

Presently she realized that she was growing drowsy. Her lids felt as though weighted with lead, so that it required an effort to keep them open.

This was a complication which she had not foreseen. Although she longed to drop off to sleep, she sternly resisted the temptation.

'No. It's not fair. I've set myself the job of recording a night spent in the Waxworks. It *must* be the genuine thing.'

She blinked more vigorously, staring across to where Byron drooped iike a sooty flamingo.

'Mercy, how he yearns! He reminds me of—— No, I won't think of *him*. . . I must keep awake. . . Bed. . . blankets, pillows. . . No.'

Her head fell forward, and for a minute she dozed. In that space of time, she had a vivid dream.

She thought that she was still in her corner in the Gallery, watching the dead alderman as he paced to and fro, before the window. She had never seen him, so he conformed to her own idea of an alderman—stout, pompous, and wearing the dark-blue, fur-trimmed robe of his office.

'He's got a face like a sleepy pear,' she decided. 'Nice old thing, but brainless.'

And then, suddenly, her tolerant derision turned to acute apprehension on his account, as she saw that he was being followed. A shape was stalking him as a cat stalks a bird.

Sonia tried to warn him of his peril, but, after the fashion of nightmares, she found herself voiceless. Even as she struggled to scream, a grotesquely long arm shot out and monstrous fingers gripped the alderman's throat.

In the same moment, she saw the face of the killer. It was Hubert Poke.

She awoke with a start, glad to find that it was but a dream. As she looked around her with dazed eyes, she saw a faint flicker of light. The mutter of very faint thunder, together with a patter of rain, told her that the storm had broken.

It was still a long way off, for Oldhampton seemed to be having merely a reflection and an echo.

'It'll clear the air.' thought Sonia.

Then her heart gave a violent leap. One of the waxworks had come to life. She distinctly saw it move, before it disappeared into the darkness at the end of the Gallery.

She kept her head, realizing that it was time to give up.

'My nerve's crashed,' she thought. 'That figure was only my fancy. I'm just like the others. Defeated by wax.'

Instinctively, she paid the figures her homage. It was the cumulative effect of their grim company, with their simulated life and sinister associations, that had rushed her defences.

Although it was bitter to fail, she comforted herself with the reminder that she had enough copy for her article. She could even make capital out of her own capitulation to the force of suggestion.

With a slight grimace, she picked up her note-book. There would be no more on-the-spot impressions. But young Wells, if he was still there, would be grateful for the end of his vigil, whatever the state of mind of the porter.

She groped in the darkness for her signal-lamp. But her fingers only scraped bare polished boards.

The torch had disappeared.

In a panic, she dropped down on her knees, and searched for yards around the spot where she was positive it had lain.

It was the instinct of self-preservation which caused her to give up her vain search.

'I'm in danger,' she thought. 'And I've no one to help me now. I must see this through myself.'

She pushed back her hair from a brow which had grown damp.

'There's a brain working against mine. When I was asleep, someone—or something—stole my torch.'

Something? The waxworks became instinct with terrible possibility as she stared at them. Some were merely blurred shapes—their faces opaque oblongs or ovals. But others—illuminated from the street—were beginning to reveal themselves in a new guise.

Queen Elizabeth, with peaked chin and fiery hair, seemed to regard her with intelligent malice. The countenance of Napoleon was heavy with brooding power, as though he were willing her to submit. Cardinal Wolsey held her with a glittering eye.

Sonia realized that she was letting herself be hypnotised by creatures of wax—so many pounds of candles moulded to human form.

'This is what happened to those others,' she thought. '*Nothing happened*. But I'm afraid of them. I'm terribly afraid... There's only one thing to do. I must count them again.'

She knew that she must find out whether her torch had been stolen through human agency; but she shrank from the experiment, not knowing which she feared more—a tangible enemy or the unknown.

As she began to count, the chilly air inside

the building seemed to throb with each thud of her heart.

'Seventeen, eighteen.' She was scarcely conscious of the numerals she murmured. 'Twenty-two, twenty-three.'

She stopped. Twenty-three? If her tally were correct, there was an extra waxwork in the Gallery.

On the shock of the discovery came a blinding flash of light, which veined the sky with fire. It seemed to run down the figure of Joan of Arc like a flaming torch. By a freak of atmospherics, the storm, which had been a starved, whimpering affair of flicker and murmur, culminated, and ended, in what was apparently a thunderbolt.

The explosion which followed was stunning; but Sonia scarcely noticed it, in her terror.

The unearthly violet glare had revealed to her a figure which she had previously overlooked.

It was seated in a chair, its hand supporting its peaked chin, and its pallid, clean-shaven features nearly hidden by a familiar broad-brimmed felt hat, which—together with the black cape—gave her the clue to its identity.

It was Hubert Poke.

Three o'clock.

Sonia heard it strike, as her memory began to reproduce, with horrible fidelity, every word of Poke's conversation on murder.

'Artistic strangulation.' She pictured the cruel agony of life leaking—bubble by bubble, gasp by gasp. It would be slow—for he had boasted of a method which left no tell-tale marks.

'Another death,' she thought dully. 'If it happens everyone will say that the Waxworks have killed me. What a story... Only, I shall not write it up.'

The tramp of feet rang out on the pavement below. It might have been the policeman on his beat; but Sonia wanted to feel that young Wells was still faithful to his post.

She looked up at the window, set high in the wall, and, for a moment, was tempted to shout. But the idea was too desperate. If she failed to attract outside attention, she would seal her own fate, for Poke would be prompted to hasten her extinction.

'Awful to feel he's so near, and yet I cannot reach him,' she thought. 'It makes it so much worse.'

She crouched there, starting and sweating at every faint sound in the darkness. The rain, which still pattered on the sky-light, mimicked footsteps and whispers. She remembered her dream and the nightmare spring and clutch.

It was an omen. At any moment it would come...

Her fear jolted her brain. For the first time she had a glimmer of hope.

'I didn't see him before the flash, because he looked exactly like one of the waxworks. Could I hide among them, too?' she wondered.

She knew that her white coat alone revealed her position to him. Holding her breath, she wriggled out of it, and hung it on the effigy of Charles II. In her black coat, with her handkerchief-scarf tied over her face, burglar fashion, she hoped that she was invisible against the sable-draped walls.

Her knees shook as she crept from her shelter. When she had stolen a few yards, she stopped to listen...In the darkness, someone was astir. She heard a soft padding of feet, moving with the certainty of one who sees his goal.

Her coat glimmered in her deserted corner.

In a sudden panic, she increased her pace, straining her ears for other sounds. She had reached the far end of the Gallery where no gleam from the window penetrated the gloom. Blindfolded and muffled, she groped her way towards the alcoves which held the tableaux.

Suddenly she stopped, every nerve in her body quivering. She had heard a thud, like rubbered soles alighting after a spring.

'He knows now.' Swift on the trail of her thought flashed another. 'He will look for me. Oh, *quick*!'

She tried to move, but her muscles were bound, and she stood as though rooted to the spot, listening. It was impossible to locate the footsteps. They seemed to come from every quarter of the Gallery. Sometimes they sounded remote, but, whenever she drew a freer breath, a sudden creak of the boards close to where she stood made her heart leap.

At last she reached the limit of endurance. Unable to bear the suspense of waiting, she moved on.

Her pursuer followed her at a distance. He gained on her, but still withheld his spring. She had the feeling that he held her at the end of an invisible string.

'He's playing with me, like a cat with a mouse,' she thought.

If he had seen her, he let her creep forward until the darkness was no longer absolute. There were gradations in its density, so that she was able to recognize the first alcove. Straining her eyes, she could distinguish the outlines of the bed where the Virtuous Man made his triumphant exit from life, surrounded by a flock of his sorrowing family and their progeny.

Slipping inside the circle, she added one more mourner to the tableau.

The minutes passed, but nothing happened. There seemed no sound save the tiny gong beating inside her temples. Even the raindrops had ceased to patter on the sky-light.

Sonia began to find the silence more deadly than noise. It was like the lull before the storm. Question after question came rolling into her mind.

'Where is he? What will he do next? Why doesn't he strike a light?'

As though someone were listening-in to her thoughts, she suddenly heard a faint splutter as of an ignited match. Or it might have been the click of an exhausted electric torch.

With her back turned to the room, she could see no light. She heard the half-hour strike, with a faint wonder that she was still alive.

'What will have happened before the next quarter?' she asked.

Presently she began to feel the strain of her pose, which she held as rigidly as any artist's model. For the time—if her presence were not already detected—her life depended on her immobility.

As an overpowering weariness began to steal over her a whisper stirred in her brain:

'The alderman was found dead on a bed.'

The newspaper account had not specified which especial tableau had been the scene of the tragedy, but she could not remember another alcove which held a bed. As she stared at the white dimness of the quilt she seemed to see it blotched with a dark, sprawling form, writhing under the grip of long fingers.

To shut out the suggestion of her fancy, she closed her eyes. The cold, dead air in the alcove was sapping her exhausted vitality, so that once again she began to nod. She dozed as she stood, rocking to and fro on her feet.

Her surroundings grew shadowy. Sometimes she knew that she was in the alcove, but at others she strayed momentarily over strange borders...She was back in the summer, walking in a garden with young Wells. Roses and sunshine...

She awoke with a start at the sound of heavy breathing. It sounded close to her—almost by her side. The figure of a mourner kneeling by the bed seemed to change its posture slightly.

Instantly maddened thoughts began to flock and flutter wildly inside her brain.

'Who was it? Was it Hubert Poke? Would history be repeated? Was she doomed also to be strangled inside the alcove? Had Fate led her there?'

She waited, but nothing happened. Again she had the sensation of being played with by a master mind—dangled at the end of his invisible string.

Presently she was emboldened to steal from the alcove, to seek another shelter. But though she held on to the last flicker of her will, she had reached the limit of endurance. Worn out with the violence of her emotions and physically spent from the strain of long periods of standing, she staggered as she walked.

She blundered round the Gallery, without any sense of direction, colliding blindly with the groups of waxwork figures. When she reached the window her knees shook under her and she sank to the ground—dropping immediately into a sleep of utter exhaustion.

She awoke with a start as the first grey gleam of dawn was stealing into the Gallery. It fell on the row of waxworks, imparting a sickly hue to their features, as though they were creatures stricken with plague.

It seemed to Sonia that they were waiting for her to wake. Their peaked faces were intelligent and their eyes held interest, as though they were keeping some secret.

She pushed back her hair, her brain still thick with clouded memories. Disconnected thoughts began to stir, to slide about... Then suddenly her mind cleared, and she sprang up—staring at a figure wearing a familiar black cape.

Hubert Poke was also waiting for her to wake.

He sat in the same chair, and in the same posture, as when she had first seen him, in the flash of lightning. He looked as though he had never moved from his place—as though he could not move. His face had not the appearance of flesh.

As Sonia stared at him, with the feeling of a bird hypnotised by a snake, a doubt began to gather in her mind. Growing bolder, she crept closer to the figure.

It was a waxwork—a libellous representation of the actor—Kean.

Her laugh rang joyously through the Gallery as she realized that she had passed a night of baseless terrors, cheated by the power of imagination. In her relief she turned impulsively to the waxworks.

'My congratulations,' she said. 'You are my masters.'

They did not seem entirely satisfied by her homage, for they continued to watch her with an expression half-benevolent and half-sinister.

'*Wait!*' they seemed to say.

Sonia turned from them and opened her bag to get out her mirror and comb. There, among a jumble of notes, letters, lipsticks and powder-compresses, she saw the electric torch.

'*Of course!*' she cried. 'I remember now, I put it there. I was too windy to think properly. . . Well, I have my story. I'd better get my coat.'

The Gallery seemed smaller in the returning light. As she approached Charles Stuart, who looked like an umpire in her white coat, she glanced down the far end of the room, where she had groped in its shadows before the pursuit of imaginary footsteps.

A waxwork was lying prone on the floor. For the second time she stood and gazed down upon a familiar black cape—a broad—brimmed conspirator's hat. Then she nerved herself to turn the figure so that its face was visible.

She gave a scream. There was no mistaking the glazed eyes and ghastly grin. She was looking down on the face of a dead man.

It was Hubert Poke.

The shock was too much for Sonia. She heard a singing in her ears, while a black mist gathered before her eyes. For the first time in her life she fainted.

When she recovered consciousness she forced herself to kneel beside the body and cover it with its black cape. The pallid face resembled a death-mask, which revealed only too plainly the lines of egotism and cruelty in which it had been moulded by a gross spirit.

Yet Sonia felt no repulsion—only pity. It was Christmas morning, and he was dead, while her own portion was life triumphant. Closing her eyes, she whispered a prayer of supplication for his warped soul.

Presently, as she grew calmer, her mind began to work on the problem of his presence. His motive seemed obvious. Not knowing that she had changed her plan, he had concealed himself in the Gallery, in order to poach her story.

'He was in the Hall of Horrors at first,' she thought, remembering the opened door. 'When he came out he hid at this end. We never saw each other, because of the waxworks between us; but we heard each other.'

She realized that the sounds which had terrified her had not all been due to imagination, while it was her agency which had converted the room into a whispering gallery of strange murmurs and voices. The clue to the cause of death was revealed by his wrist-watch, which had smashed when he fell. Its hands had stopped at three minutes to three, proving that the flash and explosion of the thunderbolt had been too much for his diseased heart—already overstrained by superstitious fears.

Sonia shuddered at a mental vision of his face, distraught with terror and pulped by raw primal impulses, after a night spent in a madman's world of phantasy.

She turned to look at the waxworks. At last she understood what they seemed to say.

'But for Us, you should have met—at dawn.'

'Your share shall be acknowledged, I promise you,' she said, as she opened her notebook.

Eight o'clock. The Christmas bells are ringing and it is wonderful just to be alive. I'm through the night, and none the worse for the experience,

although I cracked badly after three o'clock. A colleague who, unknown to me, was also concealed in the Gallery has met with a tragic fate, caused, I am sure, by the force of suggestion. Although his death is due to heart-failure, the superstitious will certainly claim it is another victory for the Waxworks.

JOSEPH COMMINGS (b. 1913) is the forgotten man of detective fiction. Thirty-odd years ago he toiled mightily in the field, tapping out story after story about one of the most colourful characters in the genre—that grizzled old Washington bison in the dusty frock-coat and saggy, baggy britches held up by bourbon-bottle-width scarlet suspenders, US Senator Brooks U. Banner, whose awesome girth gave birth to the Foggy Bottom canard that his shirts must all have been run up by Omar the Tentmaker.

Banner is a wonderfully rambunctuous creation, who rumbles crackerbarrel frontiersman philosophy round the disgusting Pittsburgh stogies he continually chaws, usually unlit, clears his throat with a tremendous '*Haak-haak*!' (sometimes in the direction of an adjacent spitoon, sometimes not), galumphs his raintub-sized figure around with all the grace of a bull elephant on the rampage, and dispenses his own unique brand of lumberingly coy gallantry to gals pretty, not so pretty, and downright back-end-of-a-bus.

He also solves baffling Impossible Crimes—for the very simple reason that it was the sub-genre that Commings, heavily influenced by John Dickson Carr (although Banner himself is not at all a cardboard copy of Dr Fell or Sir Henry Merivale), delighted in and was, moreover, extremely ingenious at.

Commings, as a boy, attended first grade at High School but thereafter educated himself. He jobbed around variously before the War, wrote bits and pieces for the newspapers, began writing detective fiction in a pup-tent in Sardinia within the sound of battle and for the amusement of his comrades. After the War he began to crack the pulp market, his first published story, 'Murder Under Glass', appearing in *10-Story Detective* in 1947. That featured Banner, as did most of his published output (and unpublished—there's a Banner novel in typescript still floating around somewhere). He wrote for *10-Story, Ten Detective Aces, Hollywood Detective*; he even wrote Impossible Crimes with a blazing-sixguns background for *Western Trails*.

But the majority of Joe Commings's stories were written for one of the most bizarre magazines of the 1950s, *Mystery Digest*, run by the decidedly eccentric Rolfe Passer (whose good right arm, at one stage, was a young tyro, just out of the USAF, called Donald E. Westlake). Passer never quite seemed able to make up his mind whether *Mystery Digest* should run mystery stories, or sex stories, or pieces about UFOs, 'mind-power', and the activities of the more lunatic-fringe cultists. The Contents page was invariably a strange stew of oddball items, written by people whose names positively scream 'pseudonym' at you (even Commings became 'Monte Craven' for a while). Passer didn't mind wasting space, either: whole pages of *Mystery Digest* would be devoted to single gnomic utterances such as 'The best doctor is the one you run for and can't find.'

When, with the inevitability of the sun going down, *Mystery Digest* folded, Joe took to knocking out paperback smut with titles like *All The Men She Had*, *Sailors' Nympho*, *Man-Eater*, and *Lesbian Heaven*. Well, some writers have done worse, and at least it kept the wolf from the door. Eighteen years ago Joe Commings was felled by a massive stroke, and hasn't written since. It's certainly time someone collected the Banner stories into volume form.

Some of them are masterpieces of the plotter's craft. Time and again Joe would come up with an outrageous (no other word for it) plot-premise—and then proceed, deftly and gleefully, to show you how the Impossible gimmick was actually as easy as winking. Surely his best was 'The X-Street Murders', in which the victim is shot in a closed room and the still-smoking gun is produced only seconds later, from a sealed envelope next-door.

Unfortunately, 'The X-Street Murders' didn't take place at Christmas time. But this one does...

8

Serenade to a Killer

JOSEPH COMMINGS

MURDER and Christmas are usually poles apart. But this Yuletide Senator Brooks U. Banner had the crazy killing at Falconridge dumped into his over-sized elastic stocking.

At the Cobleskill Orphanage, he stood among the re-painted toys like a clean-shaven Kris Kringle. He was telling the kids how he'd begun his career as a parentless tyke—just as they—with a loaf of Bohemian rye under one arm and six bits in his patched jeans. He followed that revelation with a fruity true crime story about a lonely hearts blonde who killed six mail-order husbands and how he'd helped the police to catch her. The two old maids who ran the orphanage paused to listen and were scandalized, but the kids loved him. He was six feet three inches tall and weighed 280 pounds, and he looked so quaint in his greasy black string tie, dusty frock-coat, baggy grey britches, and the huge storm rubbers with the red ridged soles.

Presenting the toys, he made little comic speeches and ruffled up the kids' hair. While this was going on a young man came in and stood in the bare, draughty dining-hall with its shrivelled brown holly wreaths. He was sallow-skinned and slight, with a faint moustache and large lustrous eyes.

He waited impatiently until Banner was done, then he approached.

'Senator, my name is Verl Griffon. I'm a reporter for my father who owns the local paper, *The Griffon*.'

Banner beamed. 'And you wanna interview me!' He stabbed a fresh corona cigar in his mouth. 'Yass, yass! Wal, my lad, if you'd come in a li'l earlier, you'd've heard me telling the young-timers that—'

'No, this isn't merely an interview, Senator.' Verl's luminous eyes zigzagged nervously. 'Where can I see you privately?'

Frowning, Banner led the way into a gloomy office that had a cold radiator and a two-dimensional red-cardboard Christmas bell on the window. They looked dubiously at the rickety ladder-backed chairs and remained standing.

Verl chewed his knuckles. 'Senator, I've read a lot about the way you handle things. Things like murders. And I was at the trial of Jack Horner in New York.'

Banner grunted from his top pants-button. 'Izzat so? Then you saw how I made that poisoner holler uncle.'

'Indeed I did. Now I need your help. You've heard of Caspar Woolfolk, the famous pianist, haven't you?'

Banner grinned. 'Lad, when it comes to music, I lissen to a jook-box every Saturday night.'

Verl plunged on regardless. 'Early this morning Woolfolk was murdered!'

'No!'

'And a woman I know very well says she killed him—but the facts are all against it!' His eyes, peering into the middle distance, were stunned with bewilderment.

Banner shifted ponderously. 'Tell it to me from A to Izzard. Pin the donkey on the tail.'

Verl talked rapidly, gravely. 'Woolfolk owned Falconridge, a manor outside town. On the grounds is a little octagonal house he called the Music Box. He kept his piano and music library there. This morning I found him in there dead. He was killed and no one knows how the murderer could have done it. . . You see, I went to the manor after breakfast to wish everybody a happy holiday. Ora met me at the door. She had the jitters.'

'Who's Ora?'

'Ora Spires. That's the woman I referred to. She's governess to little Beryl, Woolfolk's ten-year-old daughter. Woolfolk was a widower. Ora, as I said, greeted me with a look of panic. All she could tell me was that something terrible must have happened to Woolfolk inside the Music Box. She hadn't dared go look for herself . . . It snowed during the night. There's over an inch of it on the ground. The snow on the lawns hadn't been disturbed, save where Woolfolk had walked out in it toward the Music Box. I could see by the single line of clear-cut footprints that Woolfolk hadn't come back. I walked alongside his tracks. The door opened to my touch. This morning was so gloomy that I switched on the light. Woolfolk was at the grand piano, sitting on the bench, the upper part of his body lying across the music. He was stone cold dead—shot through the centre of the forehead.'

Cold as the room was, Banner could see a sheen of sweat on Verl's puckered forehead.

'Remembering that I'd seen only Woolfolk's tracks,' continued Verl, 'the first thought that struck me was: *If he's been murdered, the murderer is still here*! I searched the place. There was no one else there. Even the weapon that'd killed Woolfolk was missing—proving beyond a doubt that it wasn't suicide. How can a thing like that be. It stopped snowing around midnight. Woolfolk walked out there after that time. Then somebody killed him. And whoever it was got away *without leaving a trace anywhere in the snow*!'

'How far from the main house is the Music Box?'

'A good hundred yards.'

'A sharpshooter might've plugged Woolfolk through an open window while standing a hundred yards or more away.'

'No,' said Verl. 'The doors and windows were closed. Woolfolk was shot at close range. The murderer stood on the other side of the piano.'

Ruminating, Banner finally said: 'Wal, sir. You can take your pick of three possible answers.'

'Three! said Verl with a bounce of surprise.

Banner held up a thick blunt thumb. 'One. The murderer went out there *before* it'd stopped snowing. The snow that fell after he walked through it covered up his tracks. When Woolfolk came later, he killed Woolfolk and managed to conceal himself so cleverly in the Music Box that you failed to see him.'

Verl looked annoyed—and disappointed. 'That's out of the question. No one was there, I tell you.'

Banner, undismayed, stuck up his forefinger. 'Two. Both the murderer *and* Woolfolk went out there before it'd stopped snowing. *Both* their tracks were covered up by the falling snow. After killing Woolfolk, the murderer put on Woolfolk's shoes and walked backwards toward the main house.'

Verl shook his head sourly. 'Woolfolk was wearing his own shoes when I found him. The police, who came later, went over all that. There's absolutely no trickery about the footprints. They were made by a man walking forward. Made by Woolfolk. That's certain!'

Banner lifted his middle finger. He stared at it thoughtfully and with hesitation. 'Three. Again, the murderer got out there before Woolfolk did—'

He paused so long that Verl said: 'And how did he get back?'

'*He knows a way of crossing a hundred yards of snow without leaving a mark on it*!'

Verl's mouth dropped open. He snapped it shut again. 'Ora Spires,' he said, jittery, 'has part of an answer. She thinks she killed Woolfolk. She keeps saying that.' He paused. 'But she doesn't know how she got out there and back.'

Quizzically Banner raised his black furry eyebrows. 'Right now,' he said, reaching for the doorknob, 'I'm so fulla curiosity that Ora has more lure for me than a sarong gal.'

Verl took a step toward the held-open door and then he said: 'Something else, Senator. She walks in her sleep.'

The great Spanish shawl that covered the whole top of the grand piano in the Music Box was clotted with blood. Woolfolk's body had been removed. Banner walked behind the piano bench. On the piano-rack was the sheet music for Bellini's *La Sonnambula*.

'Was this electric lamp tipped over when you found him?' asked Banner.

Verl nodded.

Ten paces beyond the piano stood a grandfather's clock. The wall shelves were stuffed with music albums.

Verl said: 'Doesn't that music on the

piano strike you as being particularly significant, Senator? *La Somnambula*. The Sleep Walker!'

'Uh-huh.' Banner bobbed his grizzled mop of hair.

Verl rattled on as if he couldn't restrain himself. 'Woolfolk was a funny one. Peculiar. His talk wasn't all music. He was full of weird theories about the power of suggestion, mind over matter, that sort of thing. He sometimes mentioned a lot of grotesque characters and objects, like: Abbé Faria, Carl Saxtus's zinc button, Baron du Potet's magic mirror, and Father Hell's magnet. He thought all that esoteric knowledge would help him to rule women. But I don't think it helped very much. Women,' he added regretfully, 'know intuitively how to get the best of men.'

Banner didn't answer. He lumbered to both windows. He opened each. Thirty feet to the east of the small house stood a pole with insulated cross-arms. Nowhere was the snow on the ground disturbed. There was no snow on either of the window-sills. The over-hanging eaves had sheltered them. He looked up at the eaves.

Verl said in a tired voice: 'The snow on the roof hasn't been disturbed either.

Banner closed the windows and they both trudged across the white lawn to the manor house.

Ora Spires was a thirty-one-year-old spinster. She wore horn-rimmed eyeglasses and her hair was drawn back from a worried brow and knotted into a tight black bun. Her slack dress left you guessing about her figure. Her mouth had a pinched-in look as if she were trying to cork up all her feelings with her lips. Yet with some attention to her features she wouldn't have been half bad looking. Banner wondered if she deliberately made herself unattractive or if she didn't know any better.

'The police have gone,' she said in a cracked whisper to Verl. 'They've taken him to Hostetler's.' She looked at Verl as if he had just come in to have her try on the glass slipper.

Verl said to Banner: 'Ora means Woolfolk's body. Hostetler is the town undertaker. . . Ora, you haven't told the police what you told—'

'Oh no,' she said.

Banner got impatient. 'I'm Senator Banner. Verl thinks I can help you.'

'Oh, yes,' she said quickly. 'I voted for you once.'

'Mighty fine. Tickled to meetcha.' He pumped her limp hand. 'Come sit down. We'll iron this out.'

When they sat down in the parlor she said fretfully: 'This morning I thought I'd dreamed I'd killed Mr Woolfolk, but the whole nightmare has turned out to be real.'

Banner was deep in the waffle-back armchair. 'Tell me everything.'

Her eyes were cloudy behind the glasses. She would tell him everything. Banner was the kind of man you told your troubles to. 'I've lived in Cobleskill all my life. My parents are dead and my sister Caroline helped bring me up. She's four years older than I am. About three years ago I came to work for Mr Woolfolk taking care of his little daughter. Have you told him much about Beryl, Verl?'

Verl shuffled his feet on the bird-of-paradise pattern rug. 'Only just mentioned her.'

Ora smiled sadly. 'Beryl's ten now, she's very hard to manage.'

'That's putting it mildly,' groaned Verl.

'But I stuck it out, Senator. Mr Woolfolk

was always going away on concert tours, leaving me alone with Beryl.' She was thatching her long, white, sensitive fingers nervously. 'I keep a diary. It's locked up secretly in my bureau drawer and I wear the key around my neck. One night, about two weeks ago, I took it out of the drawer to make my day's entry. I was stunned to see that the last words I had written were: *I hate Mr Woolfolk*!' She stiffened. 'I never remember writing those words!'

'Clever forgery?' suggested Banner.

She shook her head. 'How could it be? It was positively my handwriting. Besides, how could the forger have gotten to where I hide my diary? The lock on the bureau drawer wasn't forced . . . All that night I lay sleepless thinking about it. I realized there were a lot of things I didn't like about Mr Woolfolk, things that could make me hate him. Things that had never entered my conscious mind before.'

'What were they?' said Banner when she paused to draw a shuddery breath.

'Why, little habits I detested. The way he dressed—one shoe always used to squeak when he walked. The way he put extra spoonfuls of sugar on his morning cereal. The way he coughed irritatingly after he'd smoked a cigarette too many. The—the thin whistle of the breath in his nose whenever he breathed too near me. And the way he would drop little hints to me about what a devil he was with the ladies, trying to get it across to me that—Yes, all that night an inner voice kept saying to me: *I hate Mr Woolfolk*!'

'During this last week he got on my nerves more than I can say. Yesterday was Christmas Eve. After supper he left for town to visit my sister Caroline. She's been deathly sick lately. I tried to amuse Beryl, but she was extra unruly and I finally had to pack her off to bed as punishment. Mr Woolfolk returned about ten o'clock. There was snow on his coat. He said, "It's snowing out." And I thought that was a perfectly hateful. I *knew* it was snowing. I could see it on him. It was a perfectly exasperating remark and I hated his false teeth when he grinned at me. He hung his coat up and came over to me. He reached out and felt my hand. It was the first time he'd ever touched me like that. Inwardly I squirmed. I tried to draw my hand back without offending him. He said suggestively, 'I'm going out to the Music Box afterwards. Come out where you hear me playing.'

'I answered with as much sarcasm as I dared. "Christmas carols?" He was still grinning. "No," he said. "Not exactly Christmas carols." I didn't answer him. I walked away from him.' She paused to straighten her eyeglasses primly on her narrow nose. 'Oh, I knew what he meant. But he didn't press me about it. I worked on the Christmas tree and spread presents around it until I noticed the clock striking in the hall. It was twelve midnight. I felt he was down here in the parlor and went up the stairs. On the first landing I stopped for a moment and looked out the window. The snow had stopped falling. The moon was out. Everything was beautiful and white. I hurried up the rest of the stairs to my bedroom. I locked the door. I felt too tired to open my diary last night, but something kept drawing me to it. At last I decided: A few words. When I opened it and saw what was in it, it fell out of my hands. The last words written in it were: *Tonight I'm going to kill Mr Woolfolk.*'

She swallowed painfully. 'I thought I must have gone insane. Why should I have written such a terrible thing? It couldn't have been me. Yet it was in my own handwriting. I flung the book back into the drawer and crawled into bed, trembling, sick at my thoughts. It was as if some evil thing had come into the house and taken possession of me during the past two weeks. I knew I walked in my sleep. Beryl told me that she'd seen me. Once I found some silverware in my room where I'd hidden it while I was asleep. I was afraid I'd do something horrible when I had no conscious control of myself. I didn't want to go to sleep, ever. I lay awake, fighting it, for as long a time as I could. I kept listening. The house was still. But I couldn't keep awake. I couldn't. I did fall asleep—and I dreamed . . .'

Her face was the color of ashes. 'Somewhere in a dim corner of my mind I remembered Mr Woolfolk saying, "Come where you hear me playing." My actions were all of a dreamlike floating quality. In the distance I could hear Mr Woolfolk playing a part of *La Somnambula* score. I don't know how I got there, but I was eventually facing him across the Spanish shawl on the piano. The music had stopped. He was rising to his feet, grinning. I hated him more than I ever did. There was a gun in my hand. I don't know how it got there. He kept repeating, "Shoot me! Go ahead! Shoot me! If you hate me so much, why don't you shoot?" I heard the shots stabbing into my brain. Then it all faded out again.

'When I woke up it was morning and I was in bed. I thought: Thank God, it's all been a horrible dream. I dressed, woke Beryl up, and went down to make breakfast. Mr Woolfolk wasn't anywhere in the house and when I looked outside for him I saw those footprints that led to the Music Box. That's where he was. He wouldn't have stayed out here all night, unless—I *knew* what had happened, but I was too terrified to go and look. And then Verl came . . .'

Banner frowned. 'When did Woolfolk die?'

Verl answered: 'The police say about four o'clock in the morning—four hours after it'd stopped snowing.'

'And the weapon used?'

'The old horse pistol that was kept in the stable.'

'Have they found it?'

'They searched the house from top to bottom first, before they did find it. The murderer had laid a stick across the chimney stack and the gun was hanging halfway down on the inside tied to a string.'

Banner heard a thin voice pipe up behind his chair. 'You should see the dog now. I painted him blue.'

Banner swiveled his big head. The child was staring at him with blank green eyes as if they were painted on a wooden face. Two rat-tails of carroty hair hung down over her scrawny shoulders. The pale-skinned arms had freckles sprinkled on them and her bloodless lips were chapped.

Ora had reached the limit of her endurance. She lifted her voice shrilly. 'Beryl! I told you to stay in bed!'

'I won't. I tore up the bed. You'll have to make it over.' She stared steadily at Banner. 'I don't like you. You're fat and filthy and you can't play the piano.'

Banner said sweetly to Ora: 'Does Snookums know about Daddy?'

'Yes, we told her,' said Ora.

'She doesn't seem very grieved,' said Verl.

'Let her stay up if she wants to.' Banner plowed his hand into one of the roomy kangaroo pockets of his coat and took out a paper-wrapped candy bar. He held it up. 'Butterscotch,' he said. 'It melts in your mouth. I would've given it to you, tadpole, if you'd wiggled off to bed. But since you'd rather stay up—' He gave a titanic shrug.

She watched sullenly while he returned the butterscotch to his pocket. Then she sat on a footstool and appeared to be reconsidering the situation.

Verl's mind was tinkering with something. He said: 'Ora, has the radio aerial been fixed yet?'

'No,' said Ora listlessly.

'What happened to it?' siad Banner.

Beryl squirmed on the footstool. 'I broke it yesterday,' she confessed.

'*You* broke it!' said Banner.

Beryl shrugged her thin shoulders. 'Sure. I was up on the roof, breaking off shingles, when I thought I'd climb the aerial. Is it any business of yours?'

Banner scowled. 'Yep. I investigate that under the head of monkey business.'

Ora was sitting looking wide-eyed at Verl. 'How did you know the aerial was broken? I never told—'

'Yes, you did. You told me about it when you saw me yesterday in town.'

'I never saw you yesterday!' she said strongly.

'Why, Ora, you most certainly did. You dropped into *The Griffon* editorial office and asked me if I wanted to go with you to the all-Tschaikowsky afternoon concert at the school hall. And we went. And you liked the *Nutcracker Suite.*'

'Verl! Stop ragging me! I was right here all afternoon. I stayed in and cleaned the house.'

'See here, Ora. You spent at least two full hours with me.'

'That's a lie!'

Verl checked an angry retort. 'Ora,' he said tightly, 'I can prove it. Several other people saw you too, my father among them. Why should we all lie about it?'

She was near frantic tears. 'But, Verl, I never left the house. I remember what I did all afternoon. I never went out!'

'Someone was masquerading as you, I suppose?' Verl shook his head. 'No, it was you. We've grown up together. Nobody could pull off a deception like that.'

Beryl perked up accusingly. 'You walk in your sleep.'

'People don't act that wide-awake in their sleep,' argued Verl. 'I tell you, Ora, you were awake and you were with me.'

'I won't listen to any more.' Ora stood up. 'Beryl, for the last time, are you going to lie down?'

Beryl looked questioningly at Banner's pocket. 'I might go if—'

Banner chuckled. 'Hunky-dory.' He put the butterscotch in her hand. 'Off to blanket class.'

Beryl, pacified, left with Ora.

Banner said sternly: 'What snicklefritz needs is to get the tar whaled outta her.'

Verl flung out his arms and snapped: 'Why should she deny being with me? I know I'm not lying.'

'Mebbe she ain't either,' said Banner cryptically. 'Does anybody like Beryl?'

'Her father did. God knows why. She's a heller. She spies on people and tells nothing but lies. Breaking the aerial was just another one of those things. She takes showers with all her clothes on. She rings the dinner bell before time. She lets all the horses out of the stable. She floods the garden. She puts heavy books in her pillow-slip when she wants a pillow fight. She says Ora is loony.'

Verl broke off suddenly.

Banner glanced sideways at a slight sound and saw a strange woman standing in the doorway. It was Caroline Spires. Caroline was totally different from her dowdy sister. The figure was thickening (fat with sin, as Banner liked to put it), but it was dressed in the latest of fashions. She had strawy blonde hair, fresh from a cold perm-wave and a little too much pancake makeup on. Banner had a feeling that in spite of her placid exterior she could be a vixen when aroused.

'Hello, Caroline,' said Verl, with some surprise. 'I want you to meet Senator Banner.'

Caroline teetered in on very high heels and used the properly sorrowful smile for the occasion as she shook his hand. 'How do you do?' she enunciated.

'Meetcha,' said Banner.

'Seeing you standing there, Caroline,' went on Verl, 'gave me a turn. Ora said that last night you weren't able to lift a finger. You've made a very rapid recovery.'

A crease of annoyance came and went between her penciled brows. 'Oh, no matter how I felt, I couldn't stay away at a time like this.' She took a package wrapped in holiday tissue from her handbag. 'I know that Caspar would have wanted me to bring this.' She let her lower lip tremble. 'Who knows? In another few weeks I might have been Mrs Woolfolk.'

Banner thought: *Nice acting, baby.*

He said: 'You felt that Beryl needed you for a mother.'

'I should say not,' said Caroline forcefully. 'She's ungovernable. I wouldn't feel safe living in the same house with that brat. I wanted her sent away to a school. I told him so. I wouldn't marry him under any other condition.'

'Woolfolk visited you at your sick-bed last night. He left near ten. Didja get up any time after that?'

She smiled archly. 'I hardly dared. My nurse looked in every half hour to see if I was asleep. Surely you don't think *I* did it. I'm not one that's likely to kill a goose with golden eggs.' She twisted the wrapped gift over in her manicured hands. 'Excuse me. I want to put this under the tree.' Before she turned away she added: 'What a horrible Christmas!'

They listened to her heels tap away in the hall.

Verl said: 'If she'd had her way with Woolfolk, she'd be mistress of Falconridge now. Lately she's been afraid that Woolfolk might get too interested in Ora. There's a rivalry between those two sisters, but it doesn't show on the surface. I don't think she was sick for one minute. This sudden recovery proves it. She did it to keep Woolfolk at her bedside morning and night. Finally he would have married her out of sheer sympathy.'

Banner studied him with his shrewd baby-blue eyes. 'Are you in love with Ora? Or vice versa?'

Verl looked genuinely surprised, then he grinned. 'That's funny. I never thought of that before.' He shook his head. 'I'm afraid not, Senator. We've known each other all our lives. We're good friends. But I doubt that Ora will ever marry anyone. She's a born and bred spinster. Since she was a tot, Caroline put the fear of men in her.' He paused. 'There's that interesting sidelight on Woolfolk that I was telling you about. Come into the library. I'll show you.'

Banner followed him in.

Three of the room's four walls were banked with heavy books.

Verl waved his hand at them. 'Abnormal psychology—every last one of them.' He handled a volume. 'Most of these subjects are old familiars with me. I majored in psych at Holy Cross.'

Banner ran his eye over the titles: Paranoia. Mania. Melancholy. Hallucination. Hypochondria. Sadism. Masochism. Lycanthropy.

There was a volume lying closed on a square table. Banner leafed through it and stopped at a chapter headed *Schizophrenia*. There was a marginal note in a fine masculine hand: *There's no doubt she has a split personality*.

Banner snapped the book shut. To whom had Woolfolk referred? Ora? Beryl? Caroline? Or someone else?

Banner trotted across the library and laid the book on a victrola top. 'What kinda gun did the police find hanging down the chimney?'

'I told you. The old horse pistol. A single loader.'

'When the police searched the house, they didn't find another gun?'

'Another one? No. Why should they? It was the horse pistol that killed Woolfolk.'

Without answering, Banner galumphed across the carpet and out of the library. He went into the dining room. Verl followed.

The Christmas fir was there. The gifts underneath its tinseled boughs were undisturbed. Beryl, the little brat, had hung some of her soiled underwear on the tree. Caroline was nowhere in sight.

Banner plumped down on his well-padded knees and sorted out all the packages meant for Woolfolk. He ripped open the smaller ones like a ghoulish vandal. It wasn't until he reached the fifth package. When he tore it open a small black automatic fell out and clattered on the parquet floor.

'The devil!' cried Verl. 'How'd that get there?'

Banner's head shot around, his eyes probing. 'You've seen it before?'

'Yes. It's Woolfolk's.'

'Tell Ora and Caroline to come to the library.'

'But, Senator, what's the gun doing there?'

'That's where Ora hid it and that's the one place the police neglected to look.'

'Ora!'

'Find her and Caroline! Skeedaddle!'

Verl ran upstairs.

Banner stuck a pencil into the pistol-barrel and picked it up. He pranced into the library and looked thoughtfully at the victrola. Then he opened the records cabinet and hunted. Finally he held up a record to the dull light from the window. He chuckled. The label said: *Selections from La Somnambula. Pianist, Caspar Woolfolk*.

He heard the other three coming.

'Ora,' he said to her in his bullfrog voice as she came faltering in, 'Your story didn't fuse. If you'd walked out to the li'l house on the lawn in your sleep, you'd've left tracks in the snow. And when you told me how you killed Woolfolk you used the word *shots*.'

'I did,' she said frantically. 'I kept shooting over and over. I don't know how many times.'

'Woolfolk was shot only once. He was killed with a single loader. You can't fire the horse pistol more than once without jamming in another round.'

Ora stared. 'You mean *I* didn't shoot—'

Banner held up the black automatic. 'This's the gun you shot at him with.'

'Then I killed him after all,' she cried in

bewildered despair.

Banner chuckled. 'With *blanks*!'

'Blanks!' exploded Verl. 'What kind of games were they playing last night?'

'Mighty deep ones,' said Banner seriously. 'Woolfolk was hipped on psychology. What started him off we'll go into later. Woolfolk tried an ignoble experiment on Ora. Would she—hypnotized—be compelled to commit murder!'

'Hypnotism!' Verl snapped his fingers with elation.

'Sure,' said Banner. 'Woolfolk babbled about the magic mirror, Carl Saxtus's zinc button, and Father Hell's magnet. It's all hypnotism!'

'I was hypnotized?' said Ora dully. 'Oh no. No. Mr Woolfolk never hypnotized me. He couldn't do that against my will. Nobody can.'

'You walk in your sleep, duck,' said Banner. 'Somnambulism's the nearest thing to a hypnotic trance. Woolfolk would meet you and gently suggest—'

'He saw me—he saw me in my night clothes!' She was mortified. This was worse than being accused of murder.

Banner grinned and continued: 'Bug doctors call it post-hypnotic suggestion. You tell a person to do something the next day and to forget they've done it.'

'That's why she didn't remember being with me in town yesterday afternoon,' said Verl.

'Yass. At his suggestion, Ora, you put notations in your diary. He was experimenting with you, as I said. He was conditioning your mind for a pseudo murder. He wanted to see how far a gentle-natured woman, like yourself, would go. And he'd selected himself as the victim. Finally Woolfolk was ready for the experiment. He told you to come where you could hear him playing.'

'I remember that,' she said.

Caroline Spires, in the background, was drinking it all in greedily, not making a sound.

Banner said: 'Last night, Ora you woke up about 3.30, under post-hypnotic compulsion. The little black automatic, loaded with blanks, had been laid on your night table by your bed by Woolfolk himself. You couldn't help but see it when you woke. You took the gun in your hand and started downstairs. You could hear Woolfolk's arrangement of *La Somnambula*. But the music wasn't coming from outside the house. It came from right here in the library. Woolfolk had considered the cold and the snow and your scanty nightdress. So he duplicated the Music Box here in the library. All he needed was piano music and a piano. He built up this square table with books and threw the large Spanish shawl over all of it. You *thought* it was the piano, cuz the shawl always covered the piano. The music you heard was from one of Woolfolk's own recordings being played on the victrola.' He jabbed a dynamic forefinger at it. 'He turned it off when he heard you coming. He rose up, then goaded you till you fired the harmless automatic at him. That's how you *murdered* Woolfolk.'

She sobbed with relief.

'But somebody *did* kill Woolfolk in the Music Box!' cried Verl.

'I'm coming to that. After Ora fled back to her room, he put the record and books away—probably with mixed emotions over what'd just occurred—and threw the Spanish shawl over his arm. He went to the door. It was nearly four o'clock. It'd stopped snowing some time before. Carrying the shawl, he walked across the snow to the

Music Box, leaving the only tracks.'

The others were breathlessly silent.

'The murderer was waiting in the little house—had been waiting there for hours . . .'

'Ah,' said Verl. It was as soft as a prayer.

Caroline cleared her throat raspingly. 'How did the murderer know that Caspar was going out there at all?'

'Cuz,' said Banner, 'the murderer overheard Woolfolk telling Ora *to come where he would be playing*. And where else would that be but the Music Box where the piano is?' There was a light dawning in Verl's eyes, but Banner went on evenly: 'Woolfolk came in and arranged the shawl and sheet music on the piano, putting everything back in its proper place, y'see. The murderer was hiding behind the grandfather's clock, the horse pistol cocked, the fingers that held it stiff from waiting. As Woolfolk sat down on the bench to run his fingers over the keys, the murderer stepped out into view and fired. Woolfolk, a bullet in his skull, fell forward onto the piano.'

'My God,' breathed Ora, her hand fluttering at her white throat.

Verl was excited. 'But now you've got the murderer trapped out there!'

'For the moment. To walk back across the snow would leave distinctive, incriminating footprints. There had to be another way.' Banner looked into Verl's luminous eyes. 'You told me the answer at the orphanage, in your first recital of your discovery of the crime. There's only one way out.'

'*I*?' said Verl incredulously. '*I* know?'

Banner nodded grimly. 'You said that when you came into the little house the day was so gloomy that you had to switch on the light. Later I also called attention to the tipped-over table lamp. That means *electricity*!'

'No, I can't—' puzzled Verl.

'And electricity means *wires*!'

'Oh,' said Verl, like a deflated balloon.

'The insulated wire runs at a long slant up from under the eaves to the cross-armed pole thirty feet away. You can reach the wire from one of the windows. It ain't slippy. It hasn't been cold enough for ice. More poles carry the wire across the snow to the trampled road, where all footprints're lost.' Banner shrugged. 'That's all there is to know.'

Caroline whispered: 'Then the murderer is someone who would have no trouble climbing. Like a little monkey.'

'Yass,' said Banner gloomily. 'Someone who can climb things like radio aerials. That should've given you an idea. A tomboy—'

Ora had her hands up to her mouth in shocked horror.

Someone screamed in the hall and dashed in furiously to spit and tear at Banner.

'He was going to send me away!' Beryl screeched at him. 'I heard him tell Caroline! He wanted to marry her and send me away! And he liked Ora even better than me!'

Ora sat horrified listening to a child's confession of murder.

Later a psychiatrist said to Banner: 'So Woolfolk took up psychology to study his own child's case. His layman's diagnosis was correct. She is schizophrenic.'

Another psychiatrist interrupted: 'I think, in this particular case, that dementia praecox is the more precise term.'

Banner waggled his big speckled hand at both of them and grunted: 'Gentlemen, she was just plain nuts.'

PROWL through the Christmas issues of the English monthly popular fiction magazines of the third decade of this century and you'll find, far more often than not, Edgar Wallace (1875-1932). Come to think of it, prowl through *any* issue of the newspapers and periodicals from that period and chances are you'll stumble across something by him, even if it's only a quickie racing piece. He was, after all, immensely prolific and didn't mind a scrap what or who he wrote for, from the prestigious *Strand Magazine* down to its junkier, all-fiction stablemate the *Grand*, from *Competitors' Journal* (incorporating *Everybody's Weekly*) up to the lordly *Morning Post*.

But the Christmas issue was special. Once a year editors could cheerfully afford to be reckless with the office chequebook, the better to tempt star writers to pull out all the stops and help provide (as they used to say) a Big Bumper Budget Bursting With Festive Fun And Fiction. And during the 1920s Wallace certainly qualified as a star, whose name on a front cover, in bold upper-case, was guaranteed to cause a highly satisfactory leap in copies sold.

Wallace wasn't, as is still popularly supposed, the most prolific writer this century has seen; he wasn't even the most prolific mystery-writer. Even E. Phillips Oppenheim and William le Queux beat him in the matter of thrillers published; and as far as sheer wordage goes, any number of American pulp-writers were hundreds of thousands—some were millions—of words ahead. But for a good long while he was surely the most celebrated writer; certainly the best loved.

When he died in Hollywood, working on the script of *King Kong* (and it's now been established that he contributed far more to *Kong* than he's ever been given credit for), his body was shipped back in state on the *Berengaria* and in Southampton flags were at half-mast, ships' sirens boomed, and bare-headed crowds silently watched the coffin come ashore. In Fleet Street, his spiritual home, the bells tolled and the death itself was announced in front-page banner headlines. I can think of no other author—let alone a scribbler of hectically-paced thrillers — whose passing was so mourned. But then I can think of no other author whose books sold so prodigiously. During the 1920s, the peak of his fame, one in every four books sold in England was, astonishingly, an Edgar Wallace.

Typically, he loved Christmas. He loved all the sentimental paraphernalia of the very British and very Dickensian Festive Season—the fairy lights, the family gathered together, mysterious packages wrapped in gaily-coloured paper and, especially, snow. Wallace was fond of snow. Which is why he usually spent Christmas in Switzerland, well away from the rigours and wretchedness of the English winter, when London in particular was more likely to be muggy, drizzly, and fog-sodden than snowbound.

Just as typically, these annual pilgrimages to Caux, overlooking Lake Lucerne, were in the nature of a royal progress, a minor Grand Tour, no expense spared. A boisterous party of family and friends, mainly subsidised by Wallace and equipped as though for a siege (even down to boxes of tea because Wallace swore you couldn't find a decent brew in Switzerland), would dump itself in his favourite hotel above the lake, there to spend three weeks skiing, skating, bobbing, and tobogganing, while Wallace himself dictated a stream of articles and short stories in his centrally-heated suite, watching the snow float down.

To be sure, there's not much snow in 'Stuffing', but there is a rich old skinflint, two poverty-stricken newly-weds, a Christmas dinner that looks as though it'll consist of sausages— and a happy ending. What more could anyone want?

Stuffing

EDGAR WALLACE

THERE are several people concerned in this story whom it is impossible within a limited space to describe. If you are on friendly terms with the great men of Scotland Yard you may inspect the photographs and finger-prints of two—Harry the Valet and Joe the Runner.

Lord Carfane's picture you can see at intervals in the best of the illustrated weeklies. He was once plain Ferdie Gooberry, before he became a contractor and supplied the army with odds and ends and himself with a fortune and a barony.

In no newspaper, illustrated or otherwise, do the names of John and Angela Willett appear. Their marriage at a small registrar's office had excited no public comment, although he was a BA of Cambridge and she was the grand-niece of Peter Elmer, the shipping magnate, who had acknowledged his relationship by dictating to her a very polite letter wishing her every happiness.

They lived in one furnished room in Pimlico, this good-looking couple, and they had the use of the kitchen. He was confident that he would one day be a great engineer. She also believed in miracles.

Three days before Christmas they sat

down calmly to consider the problem of the great annual festival and how it might best be spent. Jack Willett scratched his cheek and did a lightning calculation.

'Really, we ought not to spend an unnecessary penny,' he said dolefully. 'We may be a week in Montreal before I start work, and we shall need a little money for the voyage.'

They were leaving on Boxing Day for Canada; their berths had been taken. In Montreal a job was awaiting Jack in the office of an old college friend: and although twenty-five dollars per did not exactly represent luxury, it was a start.

Angela looked at him thoughtfully.

'I am quite sure Uncle Peter is going to do something awfully nice for us,' she said stoutly.

Jack's hollow laugh was not encouraging.

There was a tap at the door, and the unpleasant but smiling face of Joe the Runner appeared. He occupied an attic bedroom, and was a source of worry to his landlady. Once he had been in the newspaper business, running evening editions, and the name stuck to him. He had long ceased to be associated with the Press, save as a subject for its crime reporters, but this the Willetts did not know.

'Just thought I'd pop in and see you before I went, miss,' he said. 'I'm going off into the country to do a bit of work for a gentleman. About that dollar, miss, that you lent me last week.'

Angela looked uncomfortable.

'Oh, please don't mention it,' she said hastily.

'I haven't forgotten it,' said Joe, nodding solemnly. 'The minute I come back, I'll bring it to you.' And with a large and sinister grin he vanished.

'I lent him the money because he couldn't pay his rent,' said Angela penitently, but her husband waved her extravagance away.

'Let's talk about Christmas dinner. What about sausages . . . !'

'If Uncle Peter——' she began.

'Let's talk about sausages,' said Jack gently.

Foodstuffs were also the topic of conversation between Lord Carfane and Prince Riminoff as they sat at lunch at the Ritz-Carlton. Lord Carfane emphasized his remarks with a very long cigar.

'I always keep up the old English custom of distributing food to the poor,' he said. 'Every family on my estate on Christmas Eve has a turkey from my farm. All my workers,' he corrected himself carefully, 'except old Timmins. Old Timmins has been very rude to me, and I have had to sack him. All the tenants assemble in the great hall . . . But you'll see that for yourself, Prince.'

Prince Riminoff nodded gravely and tugged at his short beard. That beard had taken Harry the Valet five months to grow, and it was so creditable a production that he had passed Chief Inspector Malling in the vestibule of the Ritz-Carlton and had not been recognised.

Very skilfully he switched the conversation into more profitable channels.

'I do hope, my dear Lord Carfane, that you have not betrayed my identity to your guests?'

Ferdie smiled.

'I am not quite a fool,' he said, and meant it.

'A great deal of the jewellery that I am disposing of, and of which you have seen specimens, is not mine. I think I have made that clear. I am acting for several of my unfortunate compatriots, and frankly it would be embarrassing for me if it leaked out that I was the vendor.'

Ferdie nodded. He suspected that a great deal of the property which he was to acquire had been secured by underhand means. He more than suspected that, for all his princely origin, his companion was not too honest.

'That is why I have asked that the money you pay should be in American currency. By the way, have you made that provision?' Lord Carfane nodded. 'And, of course, I shall not ask you to pay a single dollar until you are satisfied that the property is worth what I ask. It is in fact worth three times as much.'

Lord Carfane was nothing if not frank.

'Now, I'm going to tell you, my dear chap,' he said, 'there will only be one person at Carfane Hall who will know anything whatever about this little transaction of ours. He's an expert jeweller. He is an authority, and he will examine every piece and price it before I part with a single bob!'

His Highness heartily, but gravely, approved of this act of precaution.

Lord Carfane had met his companion a few weeks before in a highly respectable night club, the introduction having been effected through the medium of a very beautiful lady who had accidentally spilt a glass of champagne over his lordship's dress trousers. She was so lovely a personage that Lord Carfane did no more than smile graciously, and a few minutes later was introduced to her sedate and imposing presence.

Harry the Valet invariably secured his introductions by this method. Usually he worked with Molly Kien, and paid her a hundred pounds for every introduction.

He spoke no more of jewels smuggled from Russia and offered at ridiculous prices, but talked sorrowfully of the misfortunes of his country; spoke easily of his estates in the Crimea and his mines in the Urals, now, alas! in Bolshevik hands. Lord Carfane was immensely entertained.

On the following evening, Harry drove down in Lord Carfane's limousine to Berkshire, and was introduced to the glories of Carfane Hall; to the great banqueting chamber with its high raftered roof; to the white-tiled larder where petrified turkeys hung in rows, each grisly corpse decorated with a gay rosette . . .

'My tenants come in on Christmas Eve,' explained Lord Carfane,' and my butler presents each one with a turkey and a small bag of groceries—'

'An old feudal custom?' suggested the Prince gravely.

Lord Carfane agreed with equal gravity.

The Prince had brought with him a large, heavily locked and strapped handbag, which had been deposited in the safe, which was the most conspicuous feature of Ferdie's library. The expert jeweller was arriving on the morrow, and his lordship looked forward, with a sense of pleasurable anticipation, to a day which would yield him 400 per cent profit on a considerable outlay.

'Yes,' said Ferdie at dinner that night, 'I prefer a combination safe. One can lose keys, but not if they're here'—he tapped his narrow forehead and smiled.

Harry the Valet agreed. One of his greatest charms was his complete agreement with anything anybody said or did or thought.

Whilst he dwelt in luxury in the halls of the great, his unhappy confederate had a more painful task. Joe the Runner had collected from a garage a small, light trolley. It was not beautiful to look upon, but it was fast, and under its covered tilt, beneath sacks and amidst baskets, a man making a swift getaway might lie concealed and be carried to London without exciting attention.

Joe made a leisurely way into Berkshire and came to the rendezvous at the precise minute he had been ordered. It was a narrow lane at the termination of a footpath leading across the Carfane estate to the house. It was a cold, blue-fingered, red-nosed job, and for three hours he sat and shivered. And then, coming across the field in the blue dusk, he saw an old man staggering, carrying a rush basket in one hand and an indescribable something in the other. He was evidently in a hurry, this ancient. From time to time he looked back over his shoulder as though he expected pursuit. Breathlessly, he mounted the stile and fell over rather than surmounted it.

Stumbling to his feet, he saw Joe sitting at the wheel of the van, and gaped at him toothlessly, his eyes wide with horror. Joe the Runner recognised the signs.

'What have you been doin'?' he demanded sternly.

For a few minutes the breathless old man could not speak; blinked fearfully at his interrogator; and then:

'He's fired me,' he croaked. 'Wouldn't give me no turkey or nothin, so I went up to the 'All and pinched one.'

'Oh!' said Joe judiciously.

It was not an unpleasant sensation, sitting in judgment on a fellow creature.

'There was such a bother and a fuss and shouting going on . . . what with the safe bein' found broke open, and that foreign man being caught, that nobody seed me,' whimpered the elderly Mr Timmins.

'Eh?' said Joe. 'What's that—safe broken open?'

The old man nodded.

'I heered 'em when I was hiding in the pantry. His lordship found that the safe had been opened an' money took. He sent for the constable, and they've got the prince locked up in a room, with the under-gardener and the butler on guard outside the door——'

He looked down at the frozen turkey in his red, numbed hand; and his lips twitched pathetically.

'His lordship promised me a turkey and his lordship said I shouldn't have——'

Joe Runner was a quick thinker. 'Jump up in the truck,' he commanded roughly. 'Where do you live?'

'About three miles from here,' began Mr Timmins.

Joe leaned over, and pulled him up, parcel, bag and turkey.

'Get through into the back, and keep quiet.'

He leapt down, cranked up the engine with some difficulty, and sent the little trolley lumbering on to the main road. When he passed three officers in a police car speeding towards Carfane Hall his heart was in his mouth, but he was not challenged. Presently, at the urgent desire of the old man, he stopped at the end of a row of cottages.

'Gawd bless you, mister!' whimpered Mr Timmins. 'I'll never do a thing like this again——'

'Hi!' said Joe sternly. 'What do I get out of this?'

And then, as the recollection of a debt came to him:

'Leave the turkey—and hop!'

Mr Timmins hopped.

It was nine o'clock on Christmas morning, and Angela Willett had just finished her packing.

Outside the skies were dark and cheerless, snow and rain were falling together, so that this tiny furnished room had almost a palatial atmosphere in comparison with the drear world outside.

'I suppose it's too early to cook the sausages—by the way, our train leaves at ten tonight, so we needn't invent ways of spending the evening—come in.'

It was Joe the Runner, rather wet but smiling. He carried under his arm something wrapped in an old newspaper.

'Excuse me, miss,' he said, as he removed the covering, 'but a gent I met in the street asked me to give you this.'

'A turkey!' gasped Angela. 'How wonderful. . . who was it?'

'I don't know, miss—an old gentleman,' said Joe vaguely. 'He said "Be sure an' give it to the young lady herself—wishin' her a happy Christmas".'

They gazed on the carcase in awe and ecstasy. As the front door slammed, announcing Joe's hasty departure:

'An old gentleman,' said Angela slowly. 'Uncle Peter!'

'Uncle grandmother!' smiled John. 'I believe he stole it!'

'How uncharitable you are!' she reproached him. 'It's the sort of thing Uncle Peter would do. He always had that Haroun al Raschid complex—I wrote and told him we were leaving for Canada tonight. I'm sure it was he.'

Half-convinced, John Willett prodded at the bird. It seemed a little tough.

'Anyway, it's turkey,' he said, 'And, darling, I adore turkey stuffed with chestnuts. I wonder if there are any shops open——'

There was a large cavity at one end of the bird, and as he lifted the turkey up by the neck, the better to examine it, something dropped to the table with a flop. It was a tight roll of paper. He shook the bird again and a second fell from its unoffending body.

'Good God!' gasped John.

With trembling hands he cut the string that bound the roll——

'It's money!' she whispered.

John nodded.

'Hundred dollar bills. . . five hundred of them at least!' he said hollowly.

Their eyes met.

'Uncle Peter!' she breathed. 'The darling!'

Mr Peter Elmer, the eminent shipowner, received the following day a telegram which was entirely meaningless:

Thank you a thousand times for your thought and generosity. You have given us a wonderful start and we shall be worthy of your splendid kindness.

It was signed 'Angela'. Mr Peter Elmer scratched his head.

And at that moment Inspector Malling was interrogating Harry the Valet in the little police station at Carfane.

'Now come across, Harry,' he said kindly. 'We know you got the money out of the safe. Where did you plant it? You couldn't have taken it far, because the butler saw you leaving the room. Just tell us where the money is, and I'll make it all right for you when you come up in front of the old man.'

'I don't know what you're talking about,' said Harry the Valet, game to the last.

BILL PRONZINI (b. 1943) is a writer to his fingertips, a pro of the first water. This does not mean to say he particularly enjoys writing; he doesn't. Particularly. Show me the writer who leaps out of bed every morning, bright-eyed and bushy tailed, just raring to tackle that ol' typewriter, and I'll show you a nitwit. Writing's fine when the burn is on and every word's a gem, every paragraph seems fresh-minted, but otherwise what we're talking is mostly hard graft, and since the late 1960s Bill Pronzini has certainly done his share of that.

Thus far, he must have had a hand in well over eighty books, over half of which have been detective stories or novels of suspense, either under his own name or one or two pseudonyms, either solo or in collaboration (Pronzini is known as one of the most *simpatico* collabs in the business). He's edited (again, alone or with others) quantities of anthologies in the mystery, horror, SF and Western genres, often rescuing fine old-time writers from an oblivion they didn't deserve. He's written maybe 180 short stories, maybe more (and there are some real twist-ending stunners amongst them). He even did a stint producing torrid paperbacks for the sex market, but that was long ago and far away, and in any case his sense of the absurd kept getting in the way of the action.

Bill's main series detective has no name. This was not deliberate. He just didn't bother to fix a handle on his PI narrator in the first couple of books and then (for probably the only time in his career) couldn't figure out a way of dropping a name into the narrative without it appearing crass. So nameless he was and 'Nameless' he's become.

'Nameless' is terribly real. He's gruff, he's intelligent, he gets depressed, he has a mordant sense of humour, he panics about his health, he does stupid things and he does smart things; he has his highs and his lows. I do sometimes think that a capricious Fate slaps the poor so-and-so around just a little too much, but otherwise 'Nameless' seems to me to be one of the most flesh-and-blood fictional characters around.

But what I really admire are Pronzini's novels of suspense—such as *Games* (1977), *Night Screams* (1979, with Barry Malzberg), *Masques* (1981) and *The Lighthouse* (1987, with Marcia Muller)—which are just that: chilling exercises in pure wired-up tension. The kind of books where you're gritting your teeth so hard over the last fifty-odd pages that 'The End' brings little immediate relief, especially as he usually has some savage and unforeseen (but always fairly, if subliminally, signalled) twist all ready and waiting for you, the final sucker-punch that leaves you twitching. Sheer class.

Bill also writes a nifty Western. Secretly, he's hooked on oaters and has been since devouring copies of *Dime Western*, *Thrilling Western*, *Texas Rangers*, *.44 Western* and a slew of other titles as a kid. So to tempt him to do an original story for this anthology, it seemed wisest to hit him where he's weakest.

A Western? In *Crime At Christmas*? Ah, but its hero, John Quincannon, is a fully-fledged, no-nonsense *detective*—who has already appeared, incidentally, in *Quincannon* (1985) and the ingeniously-plotted *Beyond The Grave* (1986, with Marcia Muller). And it all happens on a wild night in the Sierra Nevada—the night of 24 December 1894...

10

No Room at the Inn

BILL PRONZINI

WHEN the snowstorm started, Quincannon was high up in a sparsely populated section of the Sierra Nevada—alone except for his rented horse, with not much idea of where he was and no idea at all of where Slick Henry Garber was.

And as if all of that wasn't enough, it was almost nightfall on Christmas Eve.

The storm had caught him by surprise. The winter sky had been clear when he'd set out from Big Creek in mid-morning, and it had stayed clear until two hours ago; then the clouds had commenced piling up rapidly, the way they sometimes did in this high-mountain country, getting thicker and darker-veined until the whole sky was the colour of moiling coal smoke. The wind had sharpened to an icy breath that buffeted both him and the ewe-necked strawberry roan. And now, at dusk, the snow flurries had begun—thick flakes driven and agitated by the wind so that the pine and spruce forests through which the trail climbed were a misty blur and he could see no more than forty or fifty feet ahead.

He rode huddled inside his fleece-lined long coat and rabbit-fur mittens and cap, feeling sorry for himself and at the same time cursing himself for a rattlepate. If he had paid more mind to that build-up of clouds, he would have realized the need to find shelter much sooner than he had. As it was, he had begun looking too late. So far no cabin or mine-shaft or cave or suitable geographical configuration had presented itself—not one place in all this vast wooded emptiness where he and the roan could escape the snapping teeth of the storm.

A man had no sense wandering around an unfamiliar mountain wilderness on the night before Christmas, even if he *was* a manhunter by trade and a greedy glory-hound by inclination. He ought to be home in front of a blazing fire, raosting chestnuts in the company of a good woman. Sabina, for instance. Dear, sweet Sabina, waiting for him back in San Francisco. Not by his hearth or in his bed, curse the luck, but at least in the Market Street offices of Carpenter and Quincannon, Professional Detective Services.

Well, it was his own fault that he was alone up here, freezing to death in a snow-storm. In the first place he could have refused the job of tracking down Slick Henry Garber when it was offered to him by the West Coast Banking Association two weeks ago. In the second place he could have decided not to come to Big Creek to investigate a report that Slick Henry and his satchel full of counterfeit mining stock were in the vicinity. And in the third place he could have remained in Big Creek this morning when Slick Henry managed to elude his clutches and flee even higher into these blasted mountains.

But no, Rattlepate John Quincannon had done none of those sensible things. Instead he had accepted the Banking Association's fat fee, thinking only of that *and* of the additional $5000 reward for Slick Henry's apprehension or demise being offered by a mining coalition in Colorado *and* of the glory of nabbing the most notorious—and the most dangerous—confidence trickster operating west of the Rockies in this year of 1894. Then, after tracing his quarry to Big Creek, he had not only bungled the arrest but made a second mistake in setting out on Slick Henry's trail with the sublime confidence of an unrepentant sinner looking for the Promised Land—only to lose that trail two hours ago, at a road fork, just before he made his *third* mistake of the day by underestimating the weather.

Christmas, he thought. 'Tis the season to be jolly. Bah. Humbug.

Ice particles now clung to his beard, his eyebrows; kept trying to freeze his eyelids shut. He had continually to rub his eyes clear in order to see where he was going. Which, now, in full darkness, was along the rim of a snow-skinned meadow that had opened up on his left. The wind was even fiercer here, without a single tree to deflect its force. Quincannon shivered and huddled and cursed, and felt sorrier for himself by the minute.

He should never have decided to join forces with Sabina and open a detective agency. She had been happy with her position as a female operative with the Pinkerton Agency's Denver office; he had been more or less content working in the San Francisco office of the United States Secret Service. What had possessed him to suggest, not long after their first professional meeting, that they pool their talents? Well, he knew the answer to that well enough. *Sabina* had possessed him. Dear, sweet, unseduceable, infuriating Sabina...

Was that light ahead?

He scrubbed at his eyes and leaned forward in the saddle, squinting. Yes, light—lamplight. He had just come around a jog in the trail, away from the open meadow, and there it was, ahead on his right: a faint glowing rectangle in the night's churning white-and-black. He could just make out the shapes of buildings, too, in what appeared to be a clearing before a sheer rock face.

The lamplight and the buildings changed Quincannon's bleak remonstrations into murmurs of thanksgiving. He urged the stiff-legged and balky roan into a quicker pace. The buildings took on shape and definition as he approached. There were three of them, grouped in a loose triangle; two appeared to be cabins, fashioned of rough-hewn logs and planks, each with a sloping roof, while the bulkiest structure had the look of a barn. The larger cabin, the one with the lighted window, was set between the other two and farther back near the base of the rock wall.

A lane led off the trail to the buildings. Quincannon couldn't see it under its covering of snow, but he knew it was there by a painted board sign nailed to one of the trees at the intersection. TRAVELLER'S REST, the sign said, and below that, in smaller letters, *Meals and Lodging*. One of the tiny roadhouses, then, that dotted the Sierras and catered to prospectors, hunters, and foolish wilderness wayfarers such as himself.

It was possible, he thought as he turned past the sign, that Slick Henry Garber had come this way and likewise been drawn to the Traveller's Rest. Which would allow Quincannon to make amends today, after all, for his earlier bungling, and perhaps even permit him to spend Christmas Day in the relative comfort of the Big Creek Hotel. Given his recent run of foul luck, however, such a serendipitous turnabout was as likely to happen as Sabina presenting him, on his return to San Francisco, with the holiday gift he most desired.

Nevertheless, caution here was indicated. So despite the warmth promised by the lamplit window, he rode at an off-angle toward the barn. There was also the roan's welfare to consider. He would have to pay for the animal if it froze to death while in his charge.

If he was being observed from within the lighted cabin, it was covertly: no one came out and no one showed himself in the window. At the barn he dismounted, took himself and the roan inside, struggled to reshut the doors against the howling thrust of the wind. Blackness surrounded him, heavy with the smells of animals and hay and oiled leather. He stripped off both mittens, found a lucifer in one of his pockets and scraped it alight. The barn lantern hung from a hook near the doors; he reached up to light the wick. Now he could see that there were eight stalls, half of which were occupied: three saddle horses and one work horse, each nibbling a pile of hay. He didn't bother to examine the saddle horses because he had no idea what type of animal Slick Henry had been riding. He hadn't got close enough to his quarry all day to get a look at him or his transportation.

He led the roan into an empty stall, unsaddled it, left it there munching a hay supper of its own. Later, he would ask the owner of Traveller's Rest to come out and give the beast a proper rubdown. With his hands mittened again he braved the storm on foot, slogging through calf-deep snow to the lighted cabin.

Still no one came out or appeared at the window. He moved along the front wall, stopped to peer through the rimed window glass. What he could see of the big parlour inside was uninhabited. He plowed ahead to the door.

It was against his nature to walk unannounced into the home of a stranger, mainly because it was a fine way to get shot, but in this case he had no choice. He could have shouted himself hoarse in competition with the storm before anyone heard him. Thumping on the door would be just as futile; the wind was already doing that. Again he stripped off his right mitten, opened his coat for easy access to the Remington Navy revolver he carried at his waist, unlatched the door with his left hand, and cautiously let the wind push him inside.

The entire parlour was deserted. He leaned back hard against the door to get it closed again and then called out, 'Hello the house! Company!' No one answered.

He stood scraping snowcake off his face, slapping it off his clothing. The room was warm: a log fire crackled merrily on the hearth, banking somewhat because it hadn't been fed in a while. Two lamps were lit in here, another in what looked to be a dining room adjacent. Near the hearth, a cut spruce reached almost to the raftered ceiling; it was festooned with Christmas decorations—strung popcorn and bright-coloured beads, stubs of tallow candles in bent can tops, snippets of fleece from some old garment sprinkled on the branches to resemble snow, a five-pointed star atop the uppermost branch.

All very cozy and inviting, but where were the occupants? He called out again, and again received no response. He cocked his head to listen. Heard only the plaint of the storm and the snicking of flung snow against the windowpane—no sound at all within the cabin.

He crossed the parlour, entered the dining room. The puncheon table was set for two, and in fact two people had been eating there not so long ago. A clay pot of venison stew sat in the centre of the table; when he touched it he found it and its contents still slightly warm. Ladlings of stew and slices of bread were on each of the two plates.

The hair began to pull along the nape of his neck, as it always did when he sensed a wrongness to things. Slick Henry? Or something else? With his hand now gripping the butt of his Navy, he eased his way through a doorway at the rear of the dining room.

Kitchen and larder. Stove still warm, a kettle atop it blackening smokily because all the water it had contained had boiled away. Quincannon transferred the kettle to the sink drainboard. Moved then to another closed door that must lead to a bedroom, the last of the cabin's rooms. He depressed the latch and pushed the door wide.

Bedroom, indeed. And as empty as the other three rooms. But there were two odd things here: the sash of a window in the far wall was raised a few inches; and on the floor was the base of a lamp that had been dropped or knocked off the bedside table. Snow coated the window sill and there was a sifting of it on the floor and on the lamp base.

Quincannon stood puzzled and scowling in the icy draft. No room at the inn?, he thought ironically. On the contrary, there was plenty of room at this inn on Christmas Eve. It didn't seem to have *any* people in it.

On a table near the bed he spied a well-

worn family Bible. Impulse took him to it; he opened it at the front, where such vital statistics as marriages, births, and deaths were customarily recorded. Two names were written there in a fine woman's hand: Martha and Adam Keene. And a wedding date: July 17, 1893. That was all.

Well, now he knew the identity of the missing occupants. But what had happened to them? He hadn't seen them in the barn. And the other, smaller cabin—guest accommodations, he judged—had also been in darkness upon his arrival. It made no sense that a man and his wife would suddenly quit the warmth of their home in the middle of a Christmas Eve supper, to lurk about in a darkened out-building. It also made no sense that they would voluntarily decide to rush off into a snowstorm on foot or on horseback. Forced out of here, then? By Slick Henry Garber or someone else? If so, *why*?

Quincannon returned to the parlour. He had no desire to go out again into the wind and swirling snow, but he was not the sort of man who could allow a confounding mystery to go uninvestigated—particularly a mystery that might involve a criminal with a handsome price on his head. So, grumbling a little, his unmittened hands deep in the pockets of his coat, he bent his body into what was swiftly becoming a full-scale blizzard.

He fought his way to the barn first, because it was closer and to satisfy himself that it really *was* occupied only by horses. The wind had blown out the lantern when he'd left earlier; he relighted it, but not until he had first drawn his revolver. One of the animals—not the rented roan—moved restlessly in its stall as he walked toward the far end. There were good-sized piles of hay in each of the empty stalls as well, he noticed. He leaned into those stalls with the lantern. If anyone were hiding in a haypile it would have to be close to the surface to avoid the risk of suffocation; he poked at each pile in turn with the Navy's barrel. Hay and nothing but hay.

In one corner of the back wall was an enclosure that he took to be a harness room. Carefully he opened the door with his gun hand. Buckles and bit chains gleamed in the narrow space within; he saw the shapes of saddles, bridles, hackamores. Something made a scurrying noise among the floor shadows and he lowered the lantern in time to see the tail end of a packrat disappear behind a loose board. Dust was the only other thing on the floor.

He went back toward the front, stopped again when he was abreast of the loft ladder. He climbed it with the lantern lifted above his head. But the loft contained nothing more than several tightly stacked bales of hay and a thin scattering of straw that wouldn't have concealed a packrat, much less a man or a woman.

No one in the main cabin, no one in the barn. That left only the guest cabin. And if that, too, was deserted? Well then, he thought irascibly, he would sit down in the main cabin and gorge himself on venison stew while he waited for somebody—the Keenes, Slick Henry, the Ghost of Christmas Past—to put in an appearance. He was cold and tired and hungry, and mystery or no mystery he was not about to wander around in a blizzard hunting for clues.

Out once more into the white fury. By the time he worked his way through what were now thigh-deep drifts to the door of the guest cabin, his legs and arms were stiff and his beard was caked with frozen snow. He wasted no time getting the door open, but he didn't enter right away. Instead he let the wind hurl the door inward, so that it cracked audibly against the wall, while he hung back and to one side with his revolver drawn.

Nothing happened inside.

He waited another few seconds, but already the icebound night was beginning to numb his bare hand; another minute or two of exposure and the skin would freeze to the gunmetal. He entered the cabin in a sideways crouch, caught hold of the door and crowded it shut until it latched. Chill, clotted black encased him now, so thick that he was virtually blind. Should he risk lighting a match? Well, if he wanted to see who or what this cabin might contain, he would have to risk it. Floundering around in the dark would no doubt mean a broken limb, his luck being what it was these days.

He fumbled in his pocket for another lucifer, struck it on his left thumbnail, ducked down and away from the flare of light. Still nothing happened. But the light revealed that this cabin was divided into two sparsely furnished bedrooms with an open door in the dividing wall; and it also revealed some sort of huddled mass on the floor of the rear bedroom.

In slow strides, holding the match up and away from his body, he moved toward the doorway. The flame died just as he reached it—just as he recognized the huddled mass as the motionless body of a man. He thumbed another match alight, went through the doorway, leaned down for a closer look. The man lay drawn up on his back, and on one temple blood from a bullet furrow glistened blackly in the wavering flame. Young man, sandy-haired, wearing an old vicuna cloth suit and a clean white shirt now spotted with blood. A man Quincannon had never seen before...

Something moved behind him.

Something else slashed the air, grazed the side of Quincannon's head as he started to turn and dodge, drove him sideways to the floor.

The lucifer went out as he was struck; he lost his grip on the Navy and it went clattering away into blackness as thick as the inside of Old Scratch's fundament. The blow had been sharp enough to set up a ringing in his ears, but the thick rabbit-fur cap had cushioned it enough so that he wasn't stunned. He pulled around on to his knees, lunged back toward the doorway with both hands reaching. Above him he heard again that slashing of the air, only this time the swung object missed him entirely. Which threw the man who had swung off-balance, at the same instant that Quincannon's right hand found a grip on sheepskin material not unlike that of his own coat. He yanked hard, heard a grunt, and then the heavy weight of his assailant came squirming and cursing down on top of him.

The floor of an unfamiliar, black-dark room was the last place Quincannon would have chosen for hand-to-hand combat. But he was a veteran of any number of skirmishes, and had learned ways to do grievous damage to an opponent that would have shocked the Marquis of Queensbury. (Sabina, too, no doubt. Or maybe not.) Besides which, this particular opponent, whoever he was, was labouring under the same disadvantages as he was.

There were a few seconds of scrambling and bumping about, some close-quarters pummelling on both sides, a blow that split Quincannon's lip and made his Scot's blood boil even more furiously, a brief and violent struggle for possession of what felt like a long-barrelled revolver, and then, finally, an opportunity for Quincannon to use a mean and scurrilous trick he had learned in a free-for-all on the Baltimore docks. His assailant screamed, quit fighting, began to twitch instead; and to groan and wail and curse feebly. This vocal combination made Quincannon's head hurt all the more, and led him, since he now had possession of the long-barrelled revolver, to thump the man on top of the head with the weapon. The groaning and wailing and cursing ceased abruptly. So did the twitching.

Quincannon got to his feet, stood shakily wiping blood from his torn lip. He made the mistake then of taking a blind step and almost fell over one or other of the two men now lying motionless on the floor. He produced another lucifer from his dwindling supply. In its flare he spied a lamp, and managed to get to it in time to light the wick before the flame died. He located his Navy, holstered it, then carried the lamp to where the men lay and peered at the face of the one who had tried to brain him.

'Well, well,' he said aloud, with considerable relish. 'A serendipitous turnabout after all. Just what I wanted for Christmas—Slick Henry Garber.'

Slick Henry Garber said nothing, nor would he be able to for a good while.

The young, sandy-haired lad—Adam Keene, no doubt—was also unconscious. The bullet wound on his head didn't seem to be serious, but he would need attention. *He* wouldn't be saying anything, either, for a good while. Quincannon would just have to wait for the full story of what had happened here before his arrival. Unless, of course, he got it from Adam Keene's wife...

Where *was* Adam Keene's wife?

Carrying the lamp, he searched the two bedrooms. No sign of Martha Keene. He did find Slick Henry's leather satchel, in a corner of the rear room; it contained several thousand shares of bogus mining stock and nine thousand dollars in greenbacks. He also found evidence of a struggle, and not one but two bullet holes in the back wall.

These things, plus a few others, plus a belated application of imagination and logic, allowed him to make a reasonably accurate guess as to tonight's sequence of events. Slick Henry had arrived just before the snowstorm and just as the Keenes were sitting down to supper. He had either put his horse in the barn himself or Adam Keene had done it; that explained why there had been *three* saddle horses present when only *two* people lived at Traveller's Rest. Most likely Slick Henry had then thrown down on the Keenes: he must have been aware that Quincannon was still close behind him, even if Quincannon hadn't known it, and must have realized that with the impending storm it was a good bet his pursuer would also stop at Traveller's Rest. And what better place for an ambush than one of these three buildings? Perhaps he'd chosen the guest cabin on the theory that Quincannon would be less on his guard there than at the other two. To ensure that, Slick Henry had taken Adam Keene with him at gunpoint, leaving Mrs Keene in the main cabin with instructions to tell Quincannon that no other travellers had appeared today, and to then send him to the guest cabin.

But while the two men were in that cabin Adam Keene had heroically attempted to disarm Slick Henry, there had been a struggle, and Keene had unheroically received a bullet wound for his efforts. Martha Keene must have heard at least one of the shots, and fearing the worst she had left the main cabin through the bedroom window and hidden herself somewhere. Had Slick Henry found her? Not likely. But it seemed reasonable to suppose he had been out hunting for her when Quincannon came. The violence of the storm had kept him from springing his trap at that point; he had decided instead to return to the guest cabin as per his original plan. And this was where he had been ever since, waiting in the dark for his nemesis to walk in like a damned fool—which was just what Quincannon had done.

This day's business, Quincannon thought ruefully, had been one long, grim comedy of errors on all sides. Slick Henry's actions were at least half-doltish and so were his own. Especially his own—blundering in half a dozen different ways, including not even once considering the possibility of a planned ambush. Relentless manhunter, intrepid detective. Hah. It was a wonder he hadn't been shot dead. Sabina would chide him mercilessly if he told her the entire story of his capture of Slick Henry Garber. Which, of course, he had no intention of doing.

Well, he could redeem himself somewhat by finding Martha Keene. Almost certainly she had to be in one of the three buildings. She wouldn't have remained in the open, exposed, in a raging mountain storm. She would not have come anywhere near the guest cabin because of Slick Henry. And she hadn't stayed in the main cabin; the open bedroom window proved that. Ergo, she was in the barn. But he had searched the barn, even gone up into the hayloft. No place to hide up there, or in the harness enclosure, or in one of the stalls, or . . .

The lamp base on the bedroom floor, he thought.

No room at the inn, he thought.

'Well, of course, you blasted rattlepate,' he said aloud. 'It's the only place she *can* be.'

Out once more into the whipping snow and freezing wind (after first taking the precaution of binding Slick Henry's hands with the man's own belt). Slog, slog, slog, and finally into the darkened barn. He lighted the lantern, took it to the approximate middle of the building, and then called out, 'Mrs Keene! My name is John Quincannon, I am a detective from San Francisco, and I have just cracked the skull of the man who terrorized you and your husband tonight. You have nothing more to fear.'

No response.

'I know you're here, and approximately where. Won't you save both of us the embarrassment of my poking around with a pitchfork?'

Silence.

'Mrs Keene, your husband is unconscious with a head wound and he needs you. Please believe me.'

More silence. Then, just as he was about to issue another plea, there was a rustling and stirring in one of the empty stalls to his left. He moved over that way in time to see Martha Keene rise up slowly from her hiding place deep under the pile of hay.

She was young, attractive, as fair-haired as her husband, and wrapped warmly in a heavy fleece-lined coat. She was also, Quincannon noted with surprise, quite obviously with child.

What didn't surprise him was the length of round, hollow glass she held in one hand—the chimney that belonged to the lamp base on the bedroom floor. She had had the presence of mind to snatch it up before climbing out the window, in her haste dislodging the base from the bedside table. The chimney was the reason neither he nor Slick Henry had found her; by using it as a breathing tube, she had been able to burrow deep enough into the haypile to escape a superficial search.

For a space she stared at Quincannon out of wide, anxious eyes. What she saw seemed to reassure her. She released a thin, sighing breath and said tremulously, 'My husband—you're sure he's not. . . ?'

'No, no. Wounded I said and wounded I meant. He'll soon be good as new.'

'Thank God!'

'And you, my dear? Are you all right?'

'Yes, I. . . yes. Just frightened. I've been lying here imagining all sorts of dreadful things.' Mrs Keene sighed again, plucked clinging straw from her face and hair. 'I didn't *want* to run and hide, but I thought Adam must be dead and I was afraid for my baby. . . oh!' She winced as if with a sudden sharp pain, dropped the lamp chimney and placed both hands over the swell of her abdomen. 'All the excitement. . . I believe the baby will arrive sooner than expected.'

Quincannon gave her a horrified look. 'Right here? *Now*?'

'No, not that soon.' A wan smile. 'Tomorrow. . .'

It was his turn to put forth a relieved sigh as he moved into the stall to help her up.

Tomorrow. Christmas Day. Appropriate that she should have her baby then. But it wasn't the only thing about this situation that was appropriate to the season. This was a stable, and what was the stall where she had lain with her unborn child but a manger? There were animals in attendance, too. And at least one wise man (wise in *some* things, surely) who had come bearing a gift without even knowing it, a gift of a third—no, a half—of the $5000 reward for the capture of Slick Henry Garber.

Peace on earth, good will to men.

Quincannon smiled; of a sudden he felt very jolly and very much in a holiday spirit. This was, he thought, going to be a fine Christmas after all.

CYRIL HARE (real name Alfred Alexander Gordon Clark, 1900—58) only wrote nine detective novels. Double that would still have been too few. Out of those nine books, four—*Tragedy At Law* (1942), *With A Bare Bodkin* (1946), *When The Wind Blows* (1949), and *An English Murder* (1951)—constitute a quartet of peculiarly English masterpieces of the murder-writer's art.

Not that the rest of his slim output is that far behind (one book not included is *The Magic Bottle*, a wholly delightful fantasy for children which begs to be reprinted). I have a particular fondness for *Suicide Excepted* (1939), a fine novel, much underrated, with a nicely contrived shock at the end. Cyril Hare was good at shocks. Even his last book, *He Should Have Died Hereafter* (1958), though plotline-slim, manages effortlessly to surprise the reader, even though there's a strong nudge in the direction of the solution in its own title. But then he never seemed to mind taking risks. *Tragedy At Law* has 284 text pages; the only murder takes place on page 253. On the face of it that's not just a risk, it's an act of madness. Yet since it was first published half a century ago the book has achieved classic status. Judge Henry Leon (who, as Henry Ceceil, wrote quantities of legal farces as well as some entertaining and characterful near-mysteries) praised it immoderately; Julian Symons included it amongst his list of 'best, anywhere, ever'.

For most of his working life—apart from a brief wartime stint at the Ministry of Economic Warfare, and a longer spell under the Director of Public Prosecutions—Cyril Hare was at the hard end of the law, a working barrister whose career reached its peak when he was appointed a County Court judge. By all accounts he was a congenial man, urbane, dryly amusing, a lawyer to his fingertips yet one who had a gratifyingly short way with life's little problems. His friend Michael Gilbert recalls an occasion when the gasfire in the Detection Club died and no one had a shilling for the meter; it was Cyril Hare who gently pointed out that an Italian one-lira coin worked just as well. All things considered, if I'd been up before the beak on the Surrey circuit circa 1950-58, I rather think I wouldn't have minded that beak being Judge Gordon Clark.

His short stories are little gems. I've yet to come across a real dud. Even his earliest efforts—those written in his twenties for the popular weeklies and glossy magazines of the day: the *Novel Magazine*, *Pearson's Weekly*, *Passing Show*, the *Bystander*—exhibit an enviable deftness of touch, narrational and plotting skills well above average, and a natural bent towards jurisprudence, however oddball ('The Devil and Mr Tosher', a very early story and never reprinted, hinges on a slackly drawn-up infernal contract). He had a lively sense of irony which he never lost, and was one of those rare souls— Leslie Charteris was another—capable of keeping a joke going throughout a full-length novel (there's a priceless last line to *That Yew Tree's Shade* which has clearly been biding its time for most of the book's 70,000 words).

Mind you, on occasion—like that other great detective story writer and meter-out of the law, Henry Wade—Cyril Hare's irony could take on a decidedly darker tinge . . .

11

Sister Bessie

CYRIL HARE

At Christmas-time we gladly greet
   Each old familiar face.
At Christmas time we hope to meet
   At th' old familiar place.
Five hundred loving greetings, dear,
   From you to me
To welcome in the glad New Year
   I look to see!

HILDA TRENT turned the Christmas card over with her carefully manicured fingers as she read the idiotic lines aloud.

'Did you ever hear anything so completely palsied?' she asked her husband. 'I wonder who on earth they can get to write the stuff. Timothy, do you know anybody called Leech?'

'Leech?'

'Yes—that's what it says: 'From your old Leech.' Must be a friend of yours. The only Leach I ever knew spelt her name with an a and this one has two e's.' She looked at the envelope. 'Yes, it was addressed to you. Who is the old Leech?' She flicked the card across the breakfast-table.

Timothy stared hard at the rhyme and the scrawled message beneath it.

'I haven't the least idea,' he said slowly.

As he spoke he was taking in, with a sense of cold misery, the fact that the printed message on the card had been neatly altered by hand. The word 'Five' was in ink. The original, poet no doubt, had been content with 'A hundred loving greetings'.

'Put it on the mantelpiece with the others,' said his wife. 'There's a nice paunchy robin on the outside.'

'Damn it, no!' In a sudden access of rage he tore the card in two and flung the pieces into the fire.

It was silly of him, he reflected as he travelled up to the City half an hour later, to break out in that way in front of Hilda; but she would put it down to the nervous strain about which she was always pestering him to take medical advice. Not for all the gold in the Bank of England could he have stood the sight of that damnable jingle on his dining-room mantelpiece. The insolence of it! The cool, calculated devilry! All the way to London the train wheels beat out the maddening rhythm:

At Christmas-time we gladly greet...

And he had thought that the last payment had seen the end of it. He had returned from James's funeral triumphant in the certain belief that he had attended the burial of the blood-sucker who called himself 'Leech'. But he was wrong, it seemed.

Five hundred loving greetings, dear...

Five hundred! Last year it had been three, and that had been bad enough. It had meant selling out some holdings at an awkward moment. And now five hundred, with the market in its present state! How in the name of all that was horrible was he going to raise the money?

He would raise it, of course. He would have to. The sickening, familiar routine would be gone through again. The cash in Treasury notes would be packed in an unobstrusive parcel and left in the cloakroom at Waterloo. Next day he would park his car as usual in the railway yard at his local station. Beneath the windscreen wiper — 'the old familiar place'—would be tucked the cloakroom ticket. When he came down again from work in the evening the ticket would be gone. And that would be that—till next time. It was the way that Leech preferred it and he had no option but to comply.

The one certain thing that Trent knew about the identity of his blackmailer was that he—or could it be she?—was a member of his family. His family! Thank heaven, they were no true kindred of his. So far as he knew he had no blood relation alive. But 'his' family they had been, ever since, when he was a tiny, ailing boy, his father had married the gentle, ineffective Mary Grigson, with her long trail of soft, useless children. And when the influenza epidemic of 1919 carried off John Trent he had been left to be brought up as one of that clinging, grasping clan. He had got on in the world, made money, married money, but he had never got away from the 'Grigsons'. Save for his stepmother, to whom he grudgingly acknowledged that he owed his start in life, how he loathed them all! But 'his' family they remained, expecting to be treated with brotherly affection, demanding his presence at family reunions, especially at Christmas-time.

At Christmas-time we hope to meet...

He put down his paper unread and stared forlornly out of the carriage window. It was at Christmas-time, four years before, that the whole thing started—at his stepmother's Christmas Eve party, just such a boring family function as the one he would have to attend in a few days' time. There had been some silly games to amuse the children—Blind Man's Buff and Musical Chairs—and in the course of them his wallet must have slipped fom his pocket. He discovered the loss next morning, went round to the house and retrieved it. But when it came into his hands again there was one item missing from its contents. Just one. A letter, quite short and explicit, signed in a name that had about then become fairly notorious in connection with an unsavoury enquiry into certain large-scale dealings in government securities. How he could have been fool enough to keep it a moment longer than was necessary!...but it was no good going back on that.

And then the messages from Leech had begun. Leech had the letter. Leech considered it his duty to send it to the principal of Trent's firm, who was also Trent's father-in-law. But, meanwhile, Leech was a trifle short of money, and for a small consideration...So it had begun, and so, year in and year out, it had gone on.

He had been so sure that it was James! That seedy, unsuccessful stock-jobber, with his gambling debts and his inordinate thirst for whisky, had seemed the very stuff of which blackmailers are made. But he had got rid of James last February, and here was Leech again, hungrier than ever. Trent shifted uneasily in his seat. 'Got rid of him' was hardly the right way to put it. One must be fair to oneself. He had merely assisted James to get rid of his worthless self. He had done no more than ask James to dinner at his club, fill him up with whisky and leave him to drive home on a foggy night with the roads treacherous with frost. There had been an unfortunate incident on the Kingston bypass, and that was the end of James—and, incidentally, of two perfect strangers who had happened to be on the road at the same time. Forget it! The point was that the dinner—and the whisky—had been a dead loss. He would not make the same mistake again. This Christmas Eve he intended to make sure who his persecutor was. Once he knew, there would be no half measures.

Revelation came at him midway through Mrs John Trent's party—at the very moment, in fact, when the presents were being distributed from the Christmas tree, when the room was bathed in the soft radiance of coloured candles and noisy with the 'Oohs!' and 'Ahs!' of excited children and with the rustle of hastily unfolded paper parcels. It was so simple, and so unexpected, that he could have laughed aloud. Appropriately enough, it was his own contribution to the party that was responsible. For some time past it had been his unwritten duty, as the prosperous member of the family, to present his stepmother with some delicacy to help out the straitened resources of her house in providing a feast worthy of the occasion. This year, his gift had taken the form of half a dozen bottles of champagne—part of a consignment which he suspected of being corked. That champagne, acting on a head unused to anything stronger than lemonade, was enough to loosen Bessie's tongue for one fatal instant.

Bessie! Of all people, faded, spinsterish Bessie! Bessie, with her woolwork and her charities—Bessie with her large, stupid, appealing eyes and her air of frustration, that put you in mind of a bud frosted just before it could come into flower! And yet, when you came to think of it, it was natural enough. Probably, of all the Grigson tribe, he disliked her the most. He felt for her all the loathing one must naturally feel for a person one has treated badly; and he had been simple enough to believe that she did not resent it.

She was just his own age, and from the moment that he had been introduced into the family had constituted herself his protector against the unkindness of his elder step-brother. She had been, in her revoltingly sentimental phrase, his 'own special sister'. As they grew up, the roles were reversed, and she became his protégée, the admiring spectator of early struggles. Then it had become pretty clear that she and everybody else expected him to marry her. He had considered the idea quite seriously for some time. She was pretty enough in those days, and, as the phrase went, worshipped the ground he trod on. But he had had the good sense to see in time that he must look elsewhere if he wanted to make his way in the world. His engagement to Hilda had been a blow to Bessie. Her old-maidish look and her absorption in good works dated from then. But she had been sweetly forgiving—to all appearances. Now, as he stood there under the mistletoe, with a ridiculous paper cap on his head, he marvelled how he could have been so easily deceived. As though, after all, anyone could have written that Christmas card but a woman!

Bessie was smiling at him still—smiling with the confidential air of the mildly tipsy, her upturned shiny nose glowing pink in the candle-light. She had assumed a slightly puzzled expression, as though trying to recollect what she had said. Timothy smiled back and raised his glass to her. He was stone-cold sober, and he could remind her of her words when the occasion arose.

'My present for you, Timothy, is in the post. You'll get it tomorrow, I expect. I thought you'd like a change from those horrid Christmas cards!'

And the words had been accompanied with an unmistakable wink.

'Uncle Timothy!' One of James's bouncing girls jumped up at him and gave him a smacking kiss. He put her down with a grin and tickled her ribs as he did so. He suddenly felt light-hearted and on good terms with all the world—one woman excepted. He moved away from the mistletoe and strolled round the room, exchanging pleasantries with all the family. He could look them in the face now without a qualm. He clicked glasses with Roger, the prematurely aged, overworked GP.No need to worry now whether his money was going in that direction! He slapped Peter on the back and endured patiently five minutes' confidential chat on the difficulties of the motor-car business in these days. To Marjorie, James's window, looking wan and ever so brave in her made-over black frock, he spoke just the right words of blended sympathy and cheer. He even found in his pockets some half-crowns for his great, hulking step-nephews. Then he was standing by his stepmother near the fireplace, whence she presided quietly over the noisy, cheerful scene, beaming gentle good nature from her faded blue eyes.

'A delightful evening,' he said, and meant it.

'Thanks to you, Timothy, in great part,' she replied. 'You have always been so good to us.'

Wonderful what a little doubtful champagne would do! He would have given a lot to see her face if he were to say: 'I suppose you are not aware that your youngest daughter, who is just now pulling a cracker with that ugly little boy of Peter's, is blackmailing me and that I shortly intend to stop her mouth for good?'

He turned away. What a gang they all were! What a shabby, out-at-elbows gang! Not a decently cut suit or a well-turned-out woman among the lot of them! And he had imagined that his money had been going to support some of them! Why, they all simply reeked of honest poverty! He could dee it now. Bessie explained everything. It was typical of her twisted mind to wring cash from him by threats and give it all away in charities.

'You have always been so good to us.' Come to think of it, his stepmother was worth the whole of the rest put together. She must be hard put to it, keeping up Father's old house, with precious little coming in from her children. Perhaps one day, when his money was really his own again, he might see his way to do something for her. . . But there was a lot to do before he could indulge in extravagant fancies like that.

Hilda was coming across the room towards him. Her elegance made an agreeable contrast to the get-up of the Grigson women. She looked tired and rather bored, which was not unusual for her at parties at this house.

'Timothy,' she murmured, 'can't we get out of here? My head feels like a ton of bricks, and if I'm going to be fit for anything tomorrow morning——'

Timothy cut her short.

'You go home straight away, darling,' he said. 'I can see that it's high time you were in bed. Take the car. I can walk—it's a fine evening. Don't wait up for me.'

'You're not coming? I thought you said——'

'No. I shall have to stay and see the party through. There's a little matter of family business I'd better dispose of while I have the chance.'

Hilda looked at him in slightly amused surprise.

'Well, if you feel that way,' she said. 'You seem to be very devoted to your family all of a sudden. You'd better keep an eye on Bessie while you are about it. She's had about as much as she can carry.'

Hilda was right. Bessie was decidedly merry. And Timothy continued to keep an eye on her. Thanks to his attentions, by the end of the evening, when Christmas Day had been seen in and the guests were fumbling for their wraps, she had reached a stage when she could barely stand. 'Another glass,' thought Timothy from the depths of his experience, 'and she'll pass right out.'

'I'll give you a lift home, Bessie,' said Roger, looking at her with a professional eye. 'We can just squeeze you in.'

'Oh, nonsense, Roger!' Bessie giggled. 'I can manage perfectly well. As if I couldn't walk as far as the end of the drive!'

'I'll look after her,' said Timothy heartily. 'I'm walking myself, and we can guide each other's wandering footsteps home. Where's your coat, Bessie? Are you sure you've got all your precious presents?'

He prolonged his leave-taking until all the rest had gone, then helped Bessie into her worn fur coat and stepped out of the house, supporting her with an affectionate right arm. It was all going to be too deliciously simple.

Bessie lived in the lodge of the old house. She preferred to be independent, and the arrangement suited everyone, especially since James after one of his reverses on the turf had brought his family to live with his mother to save expense. It suited Timothy admirably now. Tenderly he escorted her to the end of the drive, tenderly he assisted her to insert her latchkey in the door, tenderly he supported her into the little sitting-room that gave out of the hall.

There Bessie considerately saved him an enormous amount of trouble and a possibly unpleasant scene. As he put her down upon the sofa she finally succumbed to the champagne. Her eyes closed, her mouth opened and she lay like a log where he had placed her.

Timothy was genuinely relieved. He was prepared to go to any lengths to rid himself from the menace of blackmail, but if he could lay his hands on the damning letter without physical violence he would be well satisfied. It would be open to him to take it out of Bessie in other ways later on. He looked quickly round the room. He knew its contents by heart. It had hardly changed at all since the day when Bessie first furnished her own room when she left school. The same old battered desk stood in the corner, where from the earliest days she had kept her treasures. He flung it open, and a flood of bills, receipts, charitable appeals and yet more charitable appeals came cascading out. One after another, he went through the drawers with ever increasing urgency, but still failed to find what he sought. Finally he came upon a small inner drawer which resisted his attempts to open it. He tugged at it in vain, and then seized the poker from the fireplace and burst the flimsy lock by main force. Then he dragged the drawer from its place and settled himself to examine its contents.

It was crammed as full as it could hold with papers. At the very top was the programme of a May Week Ball for his last year at Cambridge. Then there were snapshots, press-cuttings—an account of his own wedding among them—and, for the rest, piles of letters, all in his hand-writing. The wretched woman seemed to have hoarded every scrap he had ever written to her. As he turned them over, some of the phrases he had used in them floated into this mind, and he began to apprehend for the first time what the depth of her resentment must have been when he threw her over.

But where the devil did she keep the only letter that mattered?

As he straightened himself from the desk he heard close behind him a hideous, choking sound. He spun round quickly. Bessie was standing behind him, her face a mask of horror. Her mouth was wide open in dismay. She drew a long shuddering breath. In another moment she was going to scream at the top of her voice...

Timothy's pent-up fury could be contained no longer. With all his force he drove his fist full into that gaping, foolish face. Bessie went down as though she had been shot and her head struck the leg of a table with the crack of a dry stick broken in two. She did not move again.

Although it was quiet enough in the room after that, he never heard his stepmother come in. Perhaps it was the sound of his own pulses drumming in his ears that had deafened him. He did not even know how long she had been there. Certainly it was

long enough for her to take in everything that was to be seen there, for her voice, when she spoke, was perfectly under control.

'You have killed Bessie,' she said. It was a calm statement of fact rather than an accusation.

He nodded, speechless.

'But you have not found the letter.'

He shook his head.

'Didn't you understand what she told you this evening? The letter is in the post. It was her Christmas present to you. Poor, simple, loving Bessie!'

He stared at her, aghast.

'It was only just now that I found that it was missing from my jewel-case,' she went on, still in the same flat, quiet voice. 'I don't know how she found out about it, but love—even a crazy love like hers—gives people a strange insight sometimes.'

He licked his dry lips.

'Then you were Leech?' he faltered.

'Of course. Who else? How otherwise do you think I could have kept the house open and my children out of debt on my income? No, Timothy, don't come any nearer. You are not going to commit two murders tonight. I don't think you have the nerve in any case, but to be on the safe side I have brought the little pistol your father gave me when he came out of the army in 1918. Sit down.'

He found himself crouching on the sofa, looking helplessly up into her pitiless old face. The body that had been Bessie lay in between them.

'Bessie's heart was very weak,' she said reflectively. 'Roger had been worried about it for some time. If I have a word with him, I daresay he will see his way to issue a death certificate. It will, of course, be a little expensive. Shall we say a thousand pounds this year instead of five hundred? You would prefer that, Timothy, I dare say, to—the alternative?'

Once more Timothy nodded in silence.

'Very well. I shall speak to Roger in the morning—after you have returned me Bessie's Christmas present. I shall require that for future use. You can go now, Timothy.'

MARGERY ALLINGHAM (1904-66) couldn't help becoming a writer, although it wasn't so much Fate that pushed her to it as blood (an ichor later to feature fairly strongly in her work).

Her grandfather, William Allingham, was owner-editor of the *Christian Globe* back in the 1860s; her great-uncle, John Allingham, the black sheep of the family, spurned writing tracts for his brother and became a prolific hack for the bloods and penny-dreadfuls of the 1880s, immersing himself so deeply in the persona of his chief character, Ralph Rollington, that he later took on his name. Her mother, Emily Allingham (*née* Hughes), was a journalist who also wrote weepies and Had-I-But-Knowners, and her father was the great H.J. of his ilk, something of a legend in his own lifetime who wrote prodigiously for dozens of boys' weekly papers from the 1890s to the year of his death (1935), and at one time was earning a princely £2.10*s*.6*d*. (just over £2.50) per thousand words, a whole guinea more than the drudges who banged out adult serials for the newspapers.

Margery Allingham herself left school at fifteen to work in the Amalgamated Press's vast fiction factory in London's Farringdon Street (aided and abetted by her father, then still one of the AP's chief scribblers), had a play, *Dido And Aeneas*, produced at the age of 18 (she once considered taking to the boards professionally, but wisely thought better of it), her first book, an energetic smuggling romp *Blakkerchief Dick*, published at 19 (actually written a couple of years before), and another play, *Water In A Sieve*, at 21.

What ought to have happened after that was another thirty-odd years hard labour grinding out saleable trash for the cheaper end of the market. What actually happened was that she began to write breezy and entertaining detective stories (some under the absurd pseudonym 'Maxwell March') which gradually, through the 1930s, became very good and sharply characterized detective novels, and then, during the 1940s and 1950s, superlative and skilful novels of crime.

She also wrote masterly short stories. Here is a late offering, in which her very human sleuth Albert Campion helps the excitable Superintendent Stanislaus Oates (Allingham was always very inventive with her names) clear his desk as retirement looms.

— 12 —

Murder Under the Mistletoe

MARGERY ALLINGHAM

MURDER under the Mistletoe—and the man who must have done it couldn't have done it. That's my Christmas and I don't feel merry thank you very much all the same.' Superintendent Stanislaus Oates favoured his old friend Mr Albert Campion with a pained smile and sat down in the chair indicated.

It was the afternoon of Christmas Day and Mr Campion, only a trifle more owlish than usual behind his horn rims, had been fetched down from the children's party which he was attending at his brother-in-law's house in Knightsbridge to meet the Superintendent, who had moved heaven and earth to find him.

'What do you want?' Mr Campion inquired facetiously. 'A little armchair miracle?'

'I don't care if you do it swinging from a trapeze. I just want a reasonable explanation.' Oates was rattled. His dyspeptic face with the perpetually sad expression was slightly flushed and not with festivity. He plunged into his story.

'About eleven last night a crook called Sampson was found shot dead in the back of a car in a garage under a small drinking club in Alcatraz Mews—the club is named The Humdinger. A large bunch of mistletoe which had been lying on the front seat ready to be driven home had been placed on top of the body partially hiding it—which was why it hadn't been found before. The gun, fitted with a silencer, but wiped of prints, was found under the front seat. The dead man was recognized at once by the owner of the car who is also the owner of the club. He was the owner's current boy friend. She is quite a well-known West End character called 'Girlski'. What did you say?'

'I said 'Oo-er,' murmured Mr Campion. 'One of the Eumenides, no doubt?'

'No.' Oates spoke innocently. 'She's not a Greek. Don't worry about her. Just keep your mind on the facts. She knows, as we do, that the only person who wanted to kill Sampson is a nasty little snake called Kroll. He has been out of circulation for the best of reasons. Sampson turned Queen's evidence against him in a matter concerning a conspiracy to rob Her Majesty's mails and when he was released last Tuesday Kroll came out breathing retribution.'

'Not the Christmas spirit,' said Mr Campion inanely.

'That is exactly what *we* thought,' Oates agreed. 'So about five o'clock yesterday afternoon two of our chaps, hearing that Kroll was at The Humdinger, where he might have been expected to make trouble, dropped along there and brought him in for questioning and he's been in custody ever since.

'Well, now. We have at least a dozen reasonably sober witnesses to prove that Kroll did not meet Sampson at the Club. Sampson had been there earlier in the afternoon but he left about a quarter to four saying he'd got to do some Christmas shopping but promising to return. Fifteen minutes or so later Kroll came in and stayed there in full view of Girlski and the customers until our men turned up and collected him. *Now* what do you say?'

'Too easy!' Mr Campion was suspicious. 'Kroll killed Sampson just before he came in himself. The two met in the dusk outside the club. Kroll forced Sampson into the garage and possibly into the car and shot him. With the way the traffic has been lately, he'd hardly have attracted attention had he used a mortat, let alone a gun with a silencer. He wiped the weapon, chucked it in the car, threw the mistletoe over the corpse, and went up to Girlski to renew old acquaintance and establish an alibi. Your chaps, arriving when they did, must have appeared welcome.'

Oates nodded. 'We thought that. *That is what happened*. That is why this morning's development has set me gibbering. We now have two unimpeachable witnesses who swear that the dead man was in Chipperwood West at six last evening delivering some Christmas purchases he had made on behalf of a neighbour. That is *a whole hour* after Kroll was pulled in.

'The assumption is that Sampson returned to Alcatraz Mews sometime later in the evening and was killed by someone else—which we know is not true. Unfortunately the Chipperwood West witnesses are not the kind of people we are going to shake. One of them is a friend of yours. She asked our Inspector if he knew you because you were "so good at crime and all that nonsense".'

'Good Heavens!' Mr Campion spoke piously as the explanation of the Superintendent's unlikely visitation was made plain to him. 'I don't think I know Chipperwood West.'

'It's a suburb which is becoming fashionable. Have you ever heard of Lady Larradine?'

'Old Lady 'ell?' Mr Campion let the joke of his salad days escape without its being noticed by either of them. 'I don't believe it. She must be dead by this time!'

'There's a type of woman who never dies before you do,' said Oates with apparent sincerity. 'She's quite a dragon, I understand from our Inspector. However, she isn't the actual witness. There are two of them. Brigadier Brose is one. Ever heard of *him*?'

'I don't think I have.'

'My information is that you'd remember him if you'd met him. Well, we'll find out. I'm taking you with me, Campion. I hope you don't mind?'

'My sister will hate it. I'm due to be Santa Claus in about an hour.'

'I can't help that.' Oates was adamant. 'If a bunch of silly crooks want to get spiteful at the festive season, someone must do the homework. Come and play Santa Claus with me. It's your last chance. I'm retiring in the summer.'

Oates continued in the same vein as he and Mr Campion sat in the back of a police car threading their way through the deserted Christmas streets where the lamps were growing bright in the dusk.

'I've had bad luck lately,' the Superintendent said seriously. 'Too much. It won't help my memoirs if I go out in a blaze of no-enthusiasm.'

'You're thinking of the Phaeton Robbery,' Mr Campion suggested. 'What are you calling the memoirs? *Man-eaters of the Yard*?'

Oates's mild old eyes brightened, but not greatly.

'Something of the kind,' he admitted. 'But no one could be blamed for not solving that blessed Phaeton business. Everyone concerned was bonkers. A silly old musical star, for thirty years the widow of an eccentric Duke, steps out into her London garden one autumn morning leaving the street door wide open and all her most valuable jewellery collected from strongrooms all over the country lying in a brown paper parcel on her bureau in the first room off the hall. Her excuse was that she was just going to take it to the Bond Street auctioneers and was carrying it herself for safety! The thief was equally mental to lift it.'

'It wasn't saleable?'

'Saleable! It couldn't even be broken up. The stuff is just about as well-known as the Crown Jewels. Great big enamels which the old Duke had collected at great expense. No fence would stay in the same room with them, yet, of course, they are worth the Earth as every newspaper has told us at length ever since they were pinched!'

'He didn't get anything else either, did he?'

'He was a madman.' Oates dismissed him with contempt. 'All he gained was the old lady's house-keeping money for a couple of months which was in her handbag—about a hundred and fifty quid—and the other two items which were on the same shelf, a soapstone monkey and plated paperknife. He simply wandered in, took the first things he happened to see and wandered out again. Any sneak thief, tramp, or casual snapper-upper could have done it and who gets blamed? *Me*!'

He looked so woebegone that Mr Campion hastily changed the subject. 'Where are we going?' he inquired. 'To call on her ladyship? Do I understand that at the age of one hundred and forty-six or whatever it is she is cohabiting with a Brig? Which war?'

'I can't tell you.' Oates was literal as usual. 'It could be the South African. They're all in a nice residential hotel—the sort of place that is very popular with the older members of the landed gentry just now.'

'When you say landed, you mean as in fish?'

'Roughly, yes. Elderly people living on capital. About forty of them. This place used to be called *The Haven* and has now been taken over by two ex-society widows and renamed *The CCraven*—with two Cs. It's a select hotel-cum-Old-Duck's Home for Mother's Friends. You know the sort of place?'

'I can envisage it. Don't say your murdered chum from The Humdinger lived there too?'

'No, he lived in a more modest place whose garden backs on *The CCraven*'s grounds. The Brigadier and one of the other residents, a Mr Charlie Taunton, who has become a bosom friend of his, were in the habit of talking to Sampson over the wall. Taunton is a lazy man who seldom goes out and has little money but he very much wanted to get some gifts for his fellow guests—something in the nature of little jokes from the chain stores, I understand; but he dreaded the exertion of shopping for them and Sampson appears to have offered to get him some little items wholesale and to deliver them by six o'clock on Christmas Eve-in time for him to package them up and hand them to Lady Larradine who was dressing the tree at seven.'

'And you say Sampson actually did this?' Mr Champion sounded bewildered.

'Both old gentlemen—the Brigadier and Taunton—swear to it. They insist they went down to the wall at six and Sampson handed the parcel over as arranged. My Inspector is an experienced man and he doesn't think we'll be able to shake either of them.'

'That leaves Kroll with a complete alibi. How did these Chipperwood witnesses hear of Sampson's death?'

'Routine. The local police called at Sampson's home address this morning to report the death, only to discover the place closed. The land-lady and her family are away for the holiday and Sampson himself was due to spend it with Girlski. The police stamped about a bit, making sure of all this, and in the course of their investigations they were seen and hailed by the two old boys in the adjoining garden. The two were shocked to hear that their kind acquaintance was dead and volunteered the information that he had been with them at six.'

Mr Campion looked blank. 'Perhaps they don't keep the same hours as anybody else,' he suggested. 'Old people can be highly eccentric.'

Oates shook his head. 'We thought of that. My Inspector, who came down the moment the local police reported, insists that they are perfectly normal and quite positive. Moreover, they had the purchases. He saw the packages already on the tree. Lady Larradine pointed them out to him when she asked after you. She'll be delighted to see you, Campion.'

'I can hardly wait!'

'You don't have to,' said Oates grimly as they pulled up before a huge Edwardian villa. 'It's all yours.'

'My dear Boy! You haven't aged any more than I have!'

Lady Larradine's tremendous voice-one of her chief terrors, Mr Campion recollected-echoed over the crowded first-floor room where she received them. There she stood in an outmoded but glittering evening gown looking, as always, exactly like a spray-flecked seal.

'I *knew* you'd come,' she bellowed. 'As soon as you got my oblique little S.O.S. How do you like our little hideout? Isn't it *fun*! Moira Spryg-Fysher and Janice Poole-Poole wanted something to do, so we all put our pennies in it and here we are!'

'Almost too marvellous,' murmured Mr Campion in all sincerity. 'We really want a word with Brigadier Brose and Mr Taunton.'

'Of course you do and so you shall! We're all waiting for the Christmas tree. Everybody will be there for that in about ten minutes in the drawing room. My dear, when *we* came they were calling it the Residents' Lounge!'

Superintendent Oates remained grave. He was startled to discover that the dragon was not only fierce but also wily. The news that her apparently casual mention of Mr Campion to the Inspector had been a ruse to get hold of him shocked the innocent Superintendent. He retaliated by insisting that he must see the witnesses at once.

Lady Larradine silenced him with a friendly roar. 'My dear man, you can't! They've gone for a walk. I always turn men out of the house after Christmas luncheon. They'll soon be back. The Brigadier won't miss his Tree! Ah. Here's Fiona. This is Janice Poole-Poole's daughter, Albert. Isn't she a pretty girl?'

Mr Campion saw Miss Poole-Poole with relief, knowing of old that Oates was susceptible to the type. The newcomer was young and lovely and even her beehive hair and the fact that she appeared to have painted herself with two black eyes failed to spoil the exquisite smile she bestowed on the helpless officer.

'Fabulous to have you really here,' she said and sounded as if she meant it. While he was still recovering, Lady Larradine led Oates to the window.

'You can't see it because it's pitch-dark,' she said, 'but out there, down in the garden, there's a wall and it was over it that the Brigadier and Mr Taunton spoke to Mr Sampson at six o'clock last night. No one liked the man Sampson-I think Mr Taunton was almost afraid of him. Certainly he seems to have died very untidily!'

'But he *did* buy Mr Taunton's Christmas gifts for him?'

The dragon lifted a webby eyelid.

'You have already been told that. At six last night Mr Taunton and the Brigadier went to meet him to get the box. I got them into their mufflers so I know! I had the packing paper ready, too, for Mr Taunton to take up to his room. . . Rather a small one on the third floor.'

She lowered her voice to reduce it to the volume of distant traffic. 'Not many pennies, but a dear little man!'

'Did you *see* these presents, Ma'am?'

'Not before they were wrapped! That would have spoiled the surprise!'

'I shall have to see them.' There was a mulish note in the Superintendent's voice

which the lady was too experienced to ignore.

'I've thought how to do that without upsetting anybody,' she said briskly. 'The Brigadier and I will cut the presents from the Tree and Fiona will be handing them round. All Mr Taunton's little gifts are in the very distinctive black and gold paper I bought from Millie's Boutique and so, Fiona, you must give every package in black and gold paper not to the person to whom it is addressed but to the Superintendent. Can you do that, dear?'

Miss Poole-Poole seemed to feel the task difficult but not impossible and the trusting smile she gave Oates cut short his objections like the sun melting frost.

'Splendid!' The dragon's roar was hearty. 'Give me your arm, Superintendent. You shall take me down.'

As the procession reached the hall, it ran into the Brigadier himself. He was a large, pink man, affable enough, but of a martial type and he bristled at the Superintendent. 'Extraordinary time to do your business—middle of Christmas Day!' he said after acknowledging the introductions.

Oates inquired if he had enjoyed his walk.

'Talk?' said the Brigadier. 'I've not been talking. I've been asleep in the card room. Where's old Taunton?'

'He went for a walk, Athole dear,' bellowed the dragon gaily.

'So he did. You sent him! Poor feller.'

As the old soldier led the way to the open door of the drawing room, it occurred to both the Superintendent and Mr Campion that the secret of Lady Larradine's undoubted attraction for the Brigadier lay in the fact that he could hear *her* if no one else. The discovery cast a new light altogether on the story of the encounter with Sampson in the garden.

Meanwhile, they had entered the drawing room and the party had begun. As Mr Campion glanced at the company, ranged in a full circle round a magnificent tree loaded with gifts and sparkling like a waterfall, he saw face after familiar face. They were elder acquaintances of the dizzy 1930s whom he had mourned as gone forever, when he thought of them at all. Yet here they all were, not only alive but released by great age from many of the restraints of convention.

He noticed that every type of headgear from night-cap to tiara was being sported with fine individualistic enthusiasm. But Lady Larradine gave him little time to look about. She proceeded with her task immediately.

Each guest had been provided with a small invalid table beside his armchair, and Oates, reluctant but wax in Fiona's hands, was no exception. The Superintendent found himself seated between a mountain in flannel and a wraith in mauve mink, waiting his turn with the same beady-eyed avidity.

Christmas Tree procedure at *The CCraven* proved to be well organized. The dragon did little work herself. Armed with a swagger stick, she merely prodded parcel after parcel hanging amid the boughs while the task of detaching them was performed by the Brigadier who handed them to Fiona.

Either to add to the excitement or perhaps to muffle any unfortunate comment on gifts received by the uninhibited company, jolly Christmas music was played throughout, and under cover of the noise Mr Campion was able to tackle his hostess.

'Where is Taunton!' he whispered.

'Such a nice little man. Most presentable, but just a little teeny-weeny bit dishonest.'

Lady Larradine ignored the question in his eyes and continued to put him in the picture at great speed, while supervising the Tree at the same time. 'Fifty-seven convictions, I believe, but only small ones. I only got it all out of him last week. Shattering! He'd been so *useful*, amusing the Brigadier. When he came, he looked like a lost soul with no luggage, but after no time at all he settled in perfectly.'

She paused and stabbed at a ball of coloured cellophane with her stick before returning to her startled guest.

'Albert, I am terribly afraid that it was poor Mr Taunton who took that dreadful jewelry of Maisie Phaeton's. It appears to have been entirely her fault. He was merely wandering past her house, feeling in need of care and attention. The door was wide open and Mr Taunton suddenly found himself inside, picking up a few odds and ends. When he discovered from all that fuss in the newspapers what he had got hold of—how well-known it was, I mean—he was quite horrified and had to hide. And where better place than here with us where he never had to go out?'

'Where indeed!' Mr Campion dared not glance across the room at the Superintendent unwrapping his black and gold parcels. 'Where is he now? Poor Mr Taunton, I mean.'

'Of course I hadn't the faintest idea what was worrying the man until he confessed,' the dragon went on stonily. 'Then I realized that something would have to be done at once to protect everybody. The wretch had hidden all that frightful stuff in our toolshed for three months, not daring to keep it in the house; and to make matters worse, the impossible person at the end of the garden, Mr Sampson, had recognized him and *would* keep speaking. Apparently people in the—er—underworld all know each other just like those of us in—er—other closed circles do.'

Mr Campion, whose hair was standing on end, had a moment of inspiration. 'This absurd rigmarole about Taunton getting Sampson to buy him some Christmas gifts wholesale was *your* idea!' he said accusingly.

The dragon stared. 'It seemed the best way of getting Maisie's jewelry back to her without any *one* person being involved,' she said frankly. 'I knew we should all recognize the things the moment we saw them and I was certain that after a lot of argument we should decide to pack them up and send them round to her. But, if there *were* any repercussions, we should *all* be in it—quite a formidable array, dear Boy—and the blame could be traced to Mr Sampson if absolutely necessary. You see, the Brigadier is convinced that Sampson *was* there last night. Mr Taunton very cleverly left him on the lawn and went behind the toolshed and came back with the box.'

'How completely immoral!' Mr Campion couldn't restrain himself.

The dragon had the grace to look embarrassed.

'I don't think the Sampson angle would ever have arisen,' she said. 'But if it had, Sampson was quite a terrible person. Almost a black-mailer. Utterly dishonest and inconsiderate. Think how he has spoiled everything and endangered us all by getting himself killed on the *one* afternoon when we said he was here, so that the police were brought in. Just the *one* thing I was trying to avoid. When the Inspector appeared this morning I was so upset I thought of you!'

In his not unnatural alarm Mr Campion so far forgot himself as to touch her sleeve. 'Where is Taunton now?'

The dragon threshed her train. 'Really, Boy! What a fidget you are! If you must know, I gave him his Christmas present—every penny I had in cash for he was broke again, he told me—and sent him for a nice long walk after lunch. Having seen the Inspector here this morning he was glad to go.'

She paused and a granite gleam came into her hooded eyes. 'If that Superintendent friend of yours has the stupidity to try to find him once Maisie has her monstrosities back, none of us will be able to identify him, I'm afraid. And there's another thing. If the Brigadier should be *forced* to give evidence, I am sure he will stick to his guns about Mr Sampson being down in the garden here at six o'clock last night. That would mean that the man Kroll would have to go unpunished for his revenge murder, wouldn't it? Sampson was a terrible person—but *no one* should have killed him.'

Mr Campion was silenced. He glanced fearfully across the room.

The Superintendent was seated at his table wearing the strained yet slap-happy expression of a man with concussion. On his left was a pile of black and gilt wrappings, on his right a rajah's ransom in somewhat specialized form.

From where he stood, Mr Campion could see two examples amid the rest- a breastplate in gold, pearl, and enamel in the shape of a unicorn and an item which looked like a plover's egg in tourmaline encased in a ducal coronet. There was also

a soapstone monkey and a solid-silver paperknife.

Much later that evening Mr Campion and the Superintendent drove quietly back to headquarters. Oates had a large cardboard box on his knee. He clasped it tenderly.

He had been silent for a long time when a thought occurred to him. 'Why did they take him into the house in the first place?' he said. 'An elderly crook looking lost! And no luggage!'

Mr Campion's pale eyes flickered behind his spectacles.

'Don't forget the Duchess' house-keeping money,' he murmured. 'I should think he offered one of the widows who really run that place the first three months' payment in cash, wouldn't you? That must be an impressive phenomenon in that sort of business, I fancy.'

Oates caught his breath and fell silent once more. Presently he burst out again.

'Those people! That woman!' he exploded. 'When they were younger they led me a pretty dance—losing things or getting themselves swindled. But now they're old they take the blessed biscuit! Do you see how she's tied my hands, Campion?'

Mr Campion tried not to grin.

'Snapdragons are just permissible at Christmas,' he said. 'Handled with extreme caution they burn very few fingers, it seems to me.'

Mr Campion tapped the cardboard box. 'And some of them provide a few plums for retiring coppers, don't they, Superintendent?'

THE LATE Will Scott was a humorist who flourished during the 1920s and 1930s; one of a number of second line dependables who rarely, if ever, made it into *Punch*, and were actually not too bothered that they didn't. Apart from anything else, *Punch* payments weren't all that marvellous (times haven't changed), it was something of a closed shop (times haven't changed), and in any case there were, in those golden inter-War years—golden for writers, anyhow—dozens of other humorous weeklies, as well as fortnightlies and monthlies (times definitely have changed, alas), whose editors were desperate to fill the gaps between the cartoons and the adverts. Scott and his brethren were more than happy to inject into those spaces a little light relief.

Browse through the yellowing pages of the old magazines—*Passing Show*, *The Humorist*, *Everybody's Weekly*, the *Sunny Mag*, the *Jolly Mag*, the *Happy Mag* (home of Richmal Crompton's exuberantly scruffy William), *John Bull*—and there they all are, yesterday's mirth-merchants (listed here to give them some slight, if posthumous, glory): Ashley Sterne, K. R. G. Browne, A. B. Cox, H. F. Maltby, A. A. Thomson, Herbert Farjeon, C. Hedley Barker, F. W. Thomas, H. M. Raleigh, W. Hodgson Burnett, A. M. Burrage, M. O. Sale, *et al.* All masters at the art of getting over a joke or a wry comment or a little fantastical farce into a piece no shorter than 500 words, no longer than a thousand.

No one got fat on it, but if you were quick and inventive you could place four or five pieces a week and that netted a darn sight more than the three-quid wage on which suburbia depended.

Most kept at their humorous hackwork until fingers or brain gave out. Some broke away, at least from the awful weekly grind: There was a time when F. W. Thomas, who wrote a daily column for the *Star* newspaper as well as a weekly one for *Tit-Bits*, was producing two or three books a year of his collected trifles. Herbert Farjeon—just one member of an extraordinary family: Eleanor produced quantities of light verse and children's books; J. Jefferson over seventy not at all bad thrillers—wrote or contributed to scores of theatrical revues. The scandalously neglected A. M. Burrage wrote one of the finest novels to come out of the 1914-18 conflict, *War Is War* (1930), as well as around a hundred ghost stories in the classic English tradition. And if anyone reading this does not know who A. B. Cox was, why on earth *are* you reading this? (Try 'Berkeley, Anthony' or 'Iles, Francis' in any of the standard works to gauge Mr Cox's contribution to the art of the detective story.)

Will Scott turned to crime. He wrote three novels concerning his offbeat detective Disher; another book featured the exploits of the even more eccentric 'Giglamps', a sort of tramp who kept on stumbling into sort of criminous situations, sometimes solving them, often profiting from them. Sort of.

One hero Scott created never made it between hard or soft covers, which is a pity. Jeremiah Jones, *alias* the Laughing Crook, was a kind of updated Raffles without the boring bits. Like the rather more swashbuckling Simon Templar, the Laughing Crook came straight out of Edgar Wallace's the Brigand and the Mixer and is none the worse for that. He's certainly more stylish than Berkeley Gray's gruesome Norman Conquest, more fun than John Creasey's plodding Toff.

Scott wrote a long series of Laughing Crook tales for the weekly *Passing Show*. Jones's Scotland Yard nemesis was the bulky Inspector Beecham, whom he invariably, and amusingly, led up the garden path. As here.

13

Christmas Train

WILL SCOTT

'YOU'RE sure of your facts, Maxwell?' Mr Jeremiah Jones inquired.

'Positive, sir,' replied the sober Maxwell. 'Mr Hadlow Cribb landed this morning at Southampton. He has the jewels with him. Forty thousand pounds' worth. The trouble is, you can't get that lot through the Customs without somebody getting to know. And I got to know. It cost a bit!'

'Luxuries,' reflected Mr Jones, with a grin, 'are always expensive. But go on.'

'Mr Hadlow Cribb leaves Liverpool Street tonight for his country home at Friars Topliss where he intends to spend Christmas,' Maxwell proceeded. 'The jewels, of course, go with him. The train is due out at fourteen minutes past six.'

'Four hours,' murmured Mr Jones, with a glance at his watch. 'Busy train. It won't be too easy. Still, nothing ventured, nothing gained. I wish I'd had a little experience of this kind of work.'

'I ought to add,' Maxwell resumed, 'that Mr Hadlow Cribb was accompanied up from Southampton by Marks.'

'Marks?' Mr Jeremiah Jones' eyebrows lifted quickly. 'The new fellow in

Beecham's office?'

'Exactly,' said Maxwell with a sigh.

'Scotland Yard protection! No, it isn't going to be too easy,' Mr Jones repeated. 'Can you get word to Dawlish,' he added as he reached for the telephone.

'Dawlish?'

Mr Jones nodded.

'You mean—as it were—put him wise?'

'Very wise, in a tactful way.'

'I might,' said Maxwell doubtfully.

'Aren't you sure?'

'I'm positive,' said Maxwell.

'Right. Then go and do it. Meet me here at five-thirty. Have everything ready—most important—mind you've got a bag that's as near as blow it to the one Mr Hadlow Cribb will carry his jewels in.'

'It shall be done,' Maxwell promised. And away he went.

Mr Jones unhooked the receiver.

'That Scotland Yard?' he was saying presently. 'Inspector Beecham? Say Mr Jones—an old friend!'

A minute passed and then a sly smile spread across Mr Jones' cheerful face.

'That you, Beecham? How are you? Merry Christmas! Well, why not? Peace on earth, goodwill to all men, and that kind of thing.

'Listen, Beecham, my own—I've a Christmas box for you. You remember I promised you, if I could get it, the—er—inside dope, as it's called—crude expression, I know, but it *is* called that, isn't it? I thought you'd know . . . My dear fellow, I *am* getting on with it; do let me finish . . .

'About that hold-up at Clapham the other week, when the girl was knocked out. You know how I hate brutality. I mean, he could have drugged her quite as easily, couldn't he? . . . But I'm telling you! I've got your man, address and everything.

'Listen, I shall be in the Baltic at four . . . No, no, Beecham, dear, I'd much rather see you personally . . . It's your face. It brightens my day. Baltic at four. Better write it down. You're *so* forgetful!'

After which Mr Jones, with a happy chuckle, hooked the receiver, went to Liverpool Street, bought a couple of first-class train tickets, and proceeded to his accustomed corner in the dim saloon of the Baltic Hotel, off Piccadilly.

Promptly at four o'clock the stolid face of Detective-Inspector Beecham of Scotland Yard appeared in sight, and the Scotland Yard man took a seat beside Mr Jones without a word.

'Compliments of the season!' said the latter brightly.

Beecham grunted.

'Cheer up!' Mr Jones beamed.

'You owe me some information,' Beecham reminded him.

'I have it here,' said Mr Jones, producing a pocket-book, which he placed on the table.

'When I say *owe* I mean owe,' Beecham added. 'Don't imagine you're paying off a debt. You're merely paying off arrears. You've slipped through my fingers so often that I take this without hesitation. I've a right to it. But it wipes nothing off. If I can get you tomorrow, I'll get you!'

'Why not tonight?' Mr Jones smiled.

'The first chance I get,' Beecham growled.

Mr Jones pulled a slip of paper from his pocket-book and began to unfold it. If he heard the suppressed gasp at his side he took no notice of it. He proceeded to unfold the little slip. But it wasn't the slip that had caused the Scotland Yard man to gasp. It was the sight of the two railway tickets. First class. To Friars Topliss.

'Here's the address,' said Mr Jones, passing the slip to the detective. You'll find your man there. You'll find the evidence too. And he richly deserves what's coming to him. You can tell him I said so, if you like, when you explain I obtained the information against him and so did your job for you.'

'Anything else?' asked Beecham.

'Nothing,' said Mr Jones, 'unless you'll let me call the waiter again, so that we can toast each other in the true festive——'

'I'll be going,' said Beecham curtly as he rose.

'You have a heart of stone, dear Beecham,' sighed Mr Jones. 'And yet, on Christmas Eve, when you see your stocking and the chimney shaft—who knows?'

But Detective-Inspector Beecham was already on his way to the door—and Scotland Yard.

Back in his office the big man rang a bell and summoned his new assistant Marks to his side.

'Ah, Marks,' he said crisply. 'About Mr Hadlow Cribb. He's being accompanied tonight on the train?'

'I'm going myself, sir,' said Marks.

'You needn't trouble,' Beecham grunted.

'Not trouble, sir?'

'*I'm* going, myself!'

And as Beecham pecked the end off a big cigar he almost smiled his self-satisfaction.

The six-fourteen out of Liverpool Street faced the snow before it started. The snow blew in through the open end of the great building, covering the front of the engine and the sides of the passengers and the friends who were seeing them off. It was agreed by the majority that the weather was seasonable, but the vote was unanimous that the journey was certain to be long and uncomfortable.

In the laughing, grumbling, cheerful and anxious holiday crowds a small greyish man passed unnoticed. The cheerful ones were too cheerful to take the slightest interest in a figure so small and grey; the anxious ones too anxious. He passed through to the train as though he and the inconspicuous black bag he carried did not in fact exist, and when he sank wheezily into the corner of a first-class compartment that compartment still seemed empty.

Whereas everybody, cheerful or anxious, had at least one glance to spare for the tall and handsome Mr Jeremiah Jones, who, with the grave and dignified Maxwell at his heels, strode along the platform with an assurance which implied that if he had not bought the station at least he had a ten-day option upon it.

But since nobody had noticed the first greyish man, nobody noticed now that the inconspicuous black bag which Maxwell carried in the wake of Mr Jones was the very twin brother of the inconspicuous black bag which the greyish man had carried a few moments before.

Except, that is, just one eager watcher with a black half-moon moustache, who now moved out of the obscurity of a dark corner and passed through the barrier not twenty feet behind Mr Jones and Maxwell.

Mr Jones and Maxwell passed the first-class compartment in which the greyish Mr Hadlow Cribb sat with his forty thousand pounds' worth of jewels, walked on until they were beyond the dining car and then selected a first-class compartment of their own.

But the eagerly watchful Detective-Inspector Beecham had a few quiet words with the guard at the other end of the train and sank back into obscurity once more, this time in the shadows of the guard's van.

The train moved out of the station and Detective-Inspector Beecham moved out of the guard's van together. The train moved out into the unfriendliness of the winter night, but Beecham moved out into the comparative cosiness of the corridor. This he traversed as far as the second coach where, having satisfied himself that Mr Hadlow Cribb was still alone and his shabby case unmolested, he took up his stand round the angle of the passage at the end of the coach and watched.

Mile succeeded mile, minute succeeded minute. Detective-Inspector Beecham began to grow restless. The corridor windows were coated with snow. There was nothing to see and as little to do. Cheerful Christmasy shouts reached his ears from the ends of the train. He began to feel out of it. He began to feel bored. He shook himself and set out to walk the length of the train.

He passed through the dining car. He passed through two coaches beyond the dining car—satisfied that neither Mr Jones nor Maxwell had seen him do so—before he pulled up, again round the angle of a passage at the end of a coach.

Again he had perforce to play a waiting game. Again he began to feel out of it and bored. But at last, about an hour out of Liverpool Street he was pleased to hear a door slide down the corridor and thrilled to see that the two men who came out of the first-class compartment and made off in the direction of the rear of the train were Mr Jones and Maxwell. And Maxwell carried the second shabby little bag.

'Ah!' said Beecham softly to himself.

He let them get round the angle at the end of the coach; then he followed. He followed them through the next coach. He gave them three-quarters of a minute, then he plunged into the dining car prepared for the interesting bit in the rear section of the train.

But there he stopped.

And there Mr Jones stopped, too. Stopped ordering turkey and Christmas pudding to stare up at Detective-Inspector Beecham and exclaim:

'Why, look who's here! Who could have thought it? Maxwell—wish the gentleman a Merry Christmas!'

'A Merry Christmas to you, sir,' said Maxwell, with a respectful dip of the head to the detective.

'Sit down and join us,' Mr Jones invited. 'After all, it only comes once a year and you can mutter "Without prejudice" under your breath as you drink my beer. Or shall it be port?'

Beecham sank wearily into the comfortable chair opposite the pair of them.

'I—' he stopped.

'Yes, dear fellow?' Mr Jones prompted.

'Nothing,' the detective mumbled.

'Don't tell me you're going away for Christmas,' said Mr Jones. 'I understand you don't believe in such tosh. Or am I wrong? Does that hard face of yours hide a heart that weeps after three glasses of rum punch and the sight of a holly berry?'

'The point is where are *you* going?' Beecham demanded.

'I don't see that's the point at all,' Mr Jones smiled. 'Waiter—or should it be steward? I travel so little—bring my friend

Detective-Inspector Beecham, of Scotland Yard, turkey and plum pudding and all things seasonable to eat and drink. Beecham, I don't think you know the steward, do you? The steward—Detective-Inspector Beecham. Of Scotland Yard, you know. My very good friend.'

The attendant departed smiling, while the detective, with a neck going steadily pinker, attempted the futility of looking out of the window.

'When I want to advertise . . .' he said fiercely.

'You never will' Mr Jones assured him. 'Too well known to need it. Too deeply established in the affections of the multitude to require such a cheap device. Advertise? You? When you have to civilization will have perished. What about the skating prospects for the holidays? I'd like your opinion.'

'What I'm never sure about,' said Beecham, turning a fierce glare on Mr Jones, 'is whether you're a crafty fool or just a fool.'

'Shall we say a lucky fool?' suggested Mr Jones.

'Luck, yes!' snapped Beecham.

'That shows,' said Mr Jones, 'how little you know me. You must get to know me better. Call round some time. Second Thursdays, you know. Tea. *And* cakes.'

To give the grim old man of Scotland Yard his due he almost enjoyed the turkey and plum pudding and the port that followed.

Despite his company he would have enjoyed the unusual even entirely had it not been for the business which found him there. As it was he said little. Nor did he do more than listen occasionally to the ceaseless flow of light-hearted chatter which poured from the lips of Mr Jones.

He gave himself up to a waiting game and tried to calculate the number of miles that had pounded themselves out under the wheels of the train.

Mr Jones glanced at his watch.

'Eight o'clock? The snow's keeping us back. We were due in at Friars Topliss at five minutes to, surely?'

Beecham looked up at the mention of Friars Topliss, but still he said nothing. Mr Jones offered a cigar, which was refused, and then lit one himself.

Ten minutes later the train began to slow down.

'Now where are we?' said Mr Jones.

All down the dining car there was much rubbing of steamed windows, which answered no questions. An attendant, laden with Christmas fare on a tray passed quickly.

'Tell me, steward, where are we?' Mr Jones inquired.

'Running into Etching Vale, sir,' replied the attendant. 'Friars Topliss in twenty-five minutes.'

'Thank you,' said Mr Jones, and turned to Maxwell.

'This is where we get off,' he said. 'Got everything, Maxwell?'

'Everything, sir,' Maxwell answered.

'Don't forget the bag.'

Maxwell stopped and picked up the shabby bag.

'Here it is, sir.'

Mr Jones rose. Maxwell rose too. Beecham stared, dissatisfied with he knew not what.

Maxwell helped Mr Jones into his big overcoat, pulled on his own and waited. Mr Jones pulled his hat down over his ears and turned up the collar of his coat.

The train stopped.

'Well, good-bye, Beecham, dear fellow,' Mr Jones said breezily. 'And, if I don't see you before, a Happy New Year.'

And out to the snow-covered platform he went, with Maxwell and the shabby little bag after him.

Beecham blinked. That little bag . . . Was it possible? Even before Hadlow Cribb reached the train? Or, by some trick, while he, Beecham, had been waiting his chance in the guard's van?

'Crafty, but I wonder if he's *really* a fool?' he thought solemnly.

The driving wind covered Mr Jones and the faithful Maxwell with snow in the twinkling of an eye. They dashed across the bleak platform of Etching Vale to the shelter of the station wall. And under this shelter they hurried to the barriers. Here Mr Jones offered two tickets.

The collector peered at the tickets in the doubtful lamplight.

'Pardon, sir,' he said, 'but this is Etching Vale.'

'Remarkable how you can tell, with all this snow on it,' remarked Mr Jones.

'These tickets are for Friars Topliss, sir,' said the collector.

'I know,' said Mr Jones, 'but I've changed my mind. I thought I'd get off here. It sort of called to me.'

'Not allowed to break the journey, sir,' the collector reminded him. 'I'm afraid you'll have to pay again.'

Mr Jones thrust a note into the collector's hand.

'Take it out of that,' he said, 'and buy your wife something for Christmas out of the balance.'

'No wife, sir,' the collector grinned.

'Soon will have,' Mr Jones assured him, 'with such charm as yours.'

He passed out into the snow-covered station square of Little Etching Vale, the soft footfalls of Maxwell on his left and, as he soon realized, other soft footfalls on his right. He turned and there once more was the stolid figure of Detective-Inpsector Beecham.

'Not again!' he exclaimed. 'But, my dear Beecham, I thought you were going on?'

'I thought you might be, too,' said Beecham.

'I changed my mind,' Mr Jones informed him.

'I changed my mind,' retorted Beecham.

'A costly process, I found it,' said Mr Jones.

'I didn't!' said Beecham.

'Oh, well, of course, you're known to the police,' said Mr Jones, 'which makes a difference!'

He smiled and waited, but Beecham waited too.

'Where now?' he asked.

'Where would you like to go?' said Beecham.

'You don't mean, do you, that the drinks are now on you?' said Mr Jones. 'But Beecham, my own, this is too touching! Very well—there's a decent-looking, old fashioned hostel over there. Shall we?'

'Anywhere,' growled Beecham.

They crossed the square to the old-fashioned hostel where, to Mr Jones' surprise, the Scotland Yard man immediately booked a private room and ordered the drinks to be sent up there.

'If you'll join me,' he said to Mr Jones.

'Delighted,' Mr Jones agreed. 'Does Maxwell remain in the weather and hold the horses' heads?'

'There'll be room for the three of us

upstairs,' said Beecham.

'What could be better?' said Mr Jones.

And upstairs they went, with a waiter and tray to follow them.

'Cosy,' remarked Mr Jones, when the waiter had left them and closed the door. 'Shall you be staying here long?'

'About as long as it will take me to go through that little bag of yours,' Beecham answered.

'Beecham!' Mr Jones gasped. 'I don't understand you.'

'You will,' said Beecham. 'I always thought you'd be too clever. You let me see your train tickets this afternoon. After that, I just had to take this trip with you. Hand over the bag.'

'You know, Beecham, my sweet,' said Mr Jones, 'really I don't think you have the right.'

'I can soon get that,' said Beecham. 'Please yourself, if you want to waste time. You'll waste it in my presence, that's all.'

Mr Jones sighed.

'Maxwell,' he said, 'nobody trusts us. It's a suspicious world. Pass the little bag to the gentleman.'

Maxwell passed the little bag to the gentleman, and the gentleman, frowning, promptly dragged it open. Out fell pyjamas, combs, and toothbrushes. Nothing else. Beecham clicked his teeth and looked up.

'Pockets, probably?' he said.

'No friendliness at all, observed Mr Jones with a fresh sigh. 'Your pockets, Maxwell.'

Maxwell emptied his pockets. Mr Jones emptied his. The detective's complexion darkened. He turned once more to the little bag, fumbled inside it, threw it on the floor. His hands passed swiftly, but certainly, down the attire of the other two men; then, with a muttered exclamation, he picked up a telephone that stood on a corner table.

'Friars Topliss police, quick!' he shouted.

'You might tell me, sweet Beecham, Mr Jones put in, 'what *is* on your mind.'

But Beecham didn't. He sat glaring at the instrument in front of his nose until there was a faint tinkle.

'Yes?' he roared. 'This is Detective-Inspector Beecham of Scotland Yard. Is the six-fourteen from Liverpool Street—what? Good Lord! Battered up? But I saw him—the jewels? Gone! I'll come along!'

He dropped the receiver and spun round.

'Without having the faintest idea as to what is on your mind,' said Mr Jones, 'I think you must admit that I never batter them up. I may have many failings, but *never* that.'

'I don't exactly know where you come into this,' snapped Beecham, 'but bear this in mind. I'll land you.'

'I doubt it,' Mr Jones smiled. 'You'd like to, I fear, but it's such a disappointing world.'

Beecham strode to the door.

'Say good-bye to the gentleman, Maxwell,' said Mr Jones.

And Maxwell said good-bye to the gentleman.

'Dapper' Dawlish, expert but unlikeable, let himself into his Baker Street flat and snapped on the lights. He was satisfied with himself and the world in general. Or, at least, he was until he snapped on the lights.

Then he found himself looking down the barrel of an automatic, and he changed his opinion of the world at once.

'Good evening,' said Mr Jones. 'Or morning. Or what is it? Travelling about the world in a snowstorm makes one lose one's sense of time.'

'Who are you?' snarled Dawlish.

'Doesn't matter in the least,' said Mr Jones.

'What do you want?'

'The jewels you stole from Mr Hadlow Cribb on the Friars Topliss train,' said Mr Jones. 'And I want them now. I've been waiting two hours without a fire. I'm depressed. And when I'm depressed I'm nasty. That bulge in your right pocket, I believe. Come on! One—two——'

Which was where 'Dapper' Dawlish threw in.

'I'm hanged if I see how you knew,' he grumbled.

'But, of course, I knew,' said Mr Jones. 'It was I who had you put wise this afternoon that the stuff would be on the train.'

'You?'

'Mind, you wouldn't have stood an earthly if I hadn't been on the train to take their attention away,' Mr Jones added. 'They watched dear old Cribb and you'd never have got near him. Brains, my lad. That's what gets you to the top.

'Mind, *I couldn't* have got the things. I'm too popular with the C.I.D. They won't let me out of their sight. Which is why I sometimes have to leave the labouring to others. Which reminds me.'

He opened the parcel of gems, separated one from the rest, and tossed it on the table.

'The labourer is worthy of his hire,' he said, with a smile. 'You'd have got two—or even three—if you hadn't battered him up. Battering-up is a thing I detest. Or, at least, I've always thought so. I may change my mind one day. Even this day. Try following me and see! Good-bye, Mr—Dawlish the name is, I believe. Charmed to have met you. And a Merry Christmas.'

WHY IS Robert Arthur (real name Robert Arthur Feder, 1909-69) so neglected? This is not a rhetorical question. I have no real idea of the answer. As a writer of short stories from the 1930s to the 1960s he was certainly as imaginative as Frederic Brown; on occasion as caustic (though by no means as obsessive) as Cornell Woolrich. Brown and Woolrich posthumously flourish (and rightly so); mention Robert Arthur's name to both mystery and fantasy enthusiasts and the response is likely to be 'Who?'

Well, very briefly, here's who. Born in the Phillippines into a typically peripatetic army family; first job in oil. That lasted seven years, from 1929 to 1936, though even then he was working at cracking the pulp, later the slick, markets and playing the field: mysteries, weirds, Westerns, science fiction. Joined MGM as a writer in 1937; from then on sat behind a typewriter, either as freelance or editor.

Maybe that's got something to do with his lack of profile. Arthur did a good many editing chores in his lifetime and a good many of the editing chores he did were uncredited. Of the score or more hugely popular anthologies quote-edited-unquote by Alfred Hitchcock, Arthur did all the hard graft on at least a third, possibly nearly half—that's to say, he chose the stories, copy-edited them, dickered with authors and agents, prowled through the proofs; it may well be that he wrote Alf's Intros as well. For not, I suspect, an awful lot of money. And for absolutely no kudos.

He veered off to a certain extent from the mainstream of writing by doing film work, TV work, and (probably more to his taste) a good deal of radio work, both as writer and producer. For radio he hammered out scripts for *The Mysterious Traveller* (as well as editing the excellent spin-off digest magazine) and *Murder By Experts*. Yet he was still a prodigious wordsmith for the pulps even when he was doing other things and was particularly proficient at producing the short-sharp-shock story (one, 'Change Of Address', is really one of the neatest little murderer-exposed-due-to-the-malice-of-Fate tales of the past forty years).

In the writing business, reputations still largely rest on books—objects that are not, like periodicals, instantly ephemeral; objects that you can get your hands round, that rest on shelves, that last. Robert Arthur had three books published, so I supoose he did slightly better than that other forgotten master of the short story, Arthur Porges. Even so, it's always seemed to me that Arthur was singularly unlucky, either with his agent or his publishers. Or both.

His only novel, *Somebody's Walking Over My Grave* (1961), proves that his true metier was the short story and is notable only for the most specious, not to say lunatic, editorial blurb I've ever come across while his two volumes of shorts—*Ghosts And More Ghosts* (1963) and *Mystery And More Mystery* (1966)—were, insanely, packaged for the juvenile market, sank without a trace pretty soon after they appeared, and are now almost impossible to find. But well worth paying out large sums for if you do stumble across copies. A hefty and representative collection of his stories is (American editorial directors, please note) long, long, long overdue.

Robert Arthur could be extremely damn funny (some of the stories he sold to *Unknown* magazine are gems). He could also be extremely not so damn funny. Here is a bleak little Christmas tale guaranteed to bring a wry twist to the mouth.

A Present For Christmas

ROBERT ARTHUR

YOUR name is Purvis—Edward Purvis. You're in your late thirties—a solid man, with a cold solid face and small, unwinking eyes. Just now you're crouching in the darkness beside a massive chimney on the broad, flat roof of an old building in the city slums. From time to time you stamp your feet in the light snow. It's Christmas Eve, and it's cold, and you've been waiting for an hour. But you know you won't have to wait much longer.

The children on the floor below have begun to sing Christmas carols, and the thin, high sweetness of their voices rises into the wintry night, reaching you with sharp clarity except when the roar of a passing elevated train, rushing by in the street well below the roof level, drowns them out. Yes, it can't be long; the children are on their third carol now . . .

Silent Night, holy night,
All is calm, all is bright . . .

Purvis shifted impatiently. He was warm and sweating inside the heavy sweater that he wore beneath his suit coat. He wore no overcoat. He didn't have one, and if he had, it wouldn't have been suitable to cat-footed creeping across roof tops. But though the wind, when it came, was raw, and the night was crystal sharp with the snap of a real Christmas Eve, he was sweating. Sweating with impatience, maybe, because the blood was running so hot in this veins.

Round yon Virgin mother and Child. . .

Below him was a gymnasium. Though he could not see through the snow-covered gravelled roof under his feet, he knew it. Because this was the building of the St Francis Foundling Home, and Ed Purvis had been a St Francis orphan.

Holy Infant, so tender and mild. . .

But that had been a long time ago, before Purvis had become a member of a teen gang, then a youthful mugger, then a dope peddler, and finally a killer.

Now it was only important because it meant he knew the building thoroughly. Knew the shabby gymnasium below where a hundred parentless children were singing, joyously, as they waited for Santa Claus. Knew the fire escape that angled down the side of the building next to the 'El' tracks, past the long frosted glass windows.

And especially because it meant he knew how to reach this roof from the roof of a building three numbers away—exactly how to reach it unseen and unsuspected, so that he could crouch in the shadows with a loaded gun in his pocket, and a tape-wrapped length of pipe in his gloved hand, waiting, like the kids below, for Santa Claus to come.

Sleep in heavenly peace,
Sleep in heavenly peace!

That needs explaining, doesn't it? Yes, of course it does. Because it's a somewhat complex series of events that has brought you here to the roof to St Francis Foundling Home on Christmas Eve, Ed.

So let us shift time and space about a bit. Let's turn the calendar back to early December. And now the scene is the State Penitentiary, a hundred miles to the north. It's Visitor's Day. And you, Ed, have a visitor. You're a convict, you're not free and you don't expect to be. But you have a visitor. A girl. Here name is Red. Just Red. Your girl. It's foolish of her to love you as desperately as she does. But that's how girls are. . .

They sat at one of those long tables with the little fence down the middle and stared at each other hungrily. Purvis' square, brutal face was set and tight. Red's face was white and pinched with too much rouge on her cheeks to cover the pallor and too much lipstick on her lips. But her eyes were dark and sunken, needing no eyeshadow, a look in them of fierce yearning.

'Ed, honey,' she whispered. 'Ed, honest, I'm doing everything I can. You known Ed, I want you out of here just as much as you want to be out. You know how I miss you.'

Her eyes, as she spoke, proclaimed her desperate sincerity. He was a killer, but she was his girl, and she wanted him back.

'Money!' Purvis rasped. 'That's all it takes to get a wiseguy out of this joint. Four or five grand. Nothing else! If the boys—'

Red shook her head, her lips tight. 'Ed,' she said huskily, 'the boys can't. McElroy got them. He killed Willie Rand and wounded Nick and Gander Johnson. They're waiting for sentence now. They'll get ten to twenty.'

Purvis's face darkened. 'McElroy!' he whispered. 'Smiling Jim McElroy! That copper! Some day I'll—'

'Ssh!' Red warned sharply. 'The guard will hear you. What I wanted to tell you was this. Lippy's left. Lippy and me. We managed to raise a thousand dollars. That's all.

'I took it last night to you-know-who on the Parole Board. I told him it was all I could raise. He wanted four grand. But I promised him more after you're out. He said he'd do what he could.

'I don't know if he means it or not, but it was the best I could do,' she added desperately. 'Oh, Ed, I want you back so much—'

There were tears in her eyes, winking bright as she leaned as close as the little fence would let her. 'Ed, the Board meets tomorrow. You'll go up before them. You've been here three years now. Surely they'll let you go! I got to have you back, Ed. I'll die if you don't come back to me soon!'

Purvis drummed softly with thick knuckles on the wooden table. His face was still dark with the congested blood of anger.

'Okay, Red,' he said, 'if that's the best you can do, that's the best. Even if it works out, it'll mean I'm here another thirty days at least. But when I do get out, there'll be one cop less who wants to see me fry. McElroy!

His voice lowered, but in a whisper it was still savage. 'I'm going to kill him, see, Red? I'm going to choke him with my own hands! I'll strangle him until his eyes bulge, and his tongue sticks out of his mouth and he wants to beg for mercy but can't! I'm going to kill that copper if it's the last thing I ever do!'

Red shook her head frantically, so that the cheap permanent came loose and her hair straggled down her face.

'No, Ed, no,' she begged, brushing it back. 'Don't say that. Don't even think it! They'll get you if you do it, Ed, and they'll send you to the chair. They'll take you away from me, not for just a few years, but forever! Forever, Ed! And that'd kill me. That'd—'

'Aaaaahhh!' Purvish said, and it was like a long strangled curse deep in his throat. 'Not me, they won't. If I could only get loose from here. Red, only get loose from here before Christmas, I'd show them.'

From his pocket he extracted a folded newspaper clipping, raggedly cut from a newspaper with a thumb nail.

'Look at this,' he said.

He raised a hand, and the attendant guard ambled over. Suddenly Purvis' voice was mild.

'Can I show this to the lady just for a minute?' he asked. 'Its only a newspaper clipping about a friend of ours.'

The Guard scanned the clipping and grunted. 'Okay,' he said. 'Against the rules, but there ain't anything harmful in it, I guess.'

He passed the clipping to Red, and the girl spread it flat and read it. It was just a headline and a few inches of text.

SANTA TO VISIT ORPHANS

Santa Claus will visit without fail this year the St Francis Foundling Home, on Melton Street. Not always has he stopped there on his annual visits, but from now on his yuletide presence will be assured thanks to Sergeant James McElroy, of the local police department, who took an interest in the institution when he and his wife adopted a child from it recently.

Smiling Jim McElroy, as he is called, is the most popular man in the department, and among the most courageous, as was evidenced by his recent exploit of apprehending two furloft thieves and killing a third. So the response of the department when he took up a collection to buy toys for kiddies who might otherwise go unremembered was generous.

Thanks to Smiling Jim, no kiddie in the St Francis Home will be neglected on Christmas Eve. Santa will be there on schedule, and will even come in through a real fireplace, and leave by the same route. Under Sergeant McElroy's expert direction, a large imitation fireplace has been erected in the gymnasium, in front of a window that leads to a fire escape.

Dressed as Saint Nick, Sergeant McElroy, some time before midnight on Christmas Eve, will descend the fire escape from the roof, emerge through the fireplace, and delight the hearts of a hundred parentless tots with presents from the pack on his back. Needless to say, the pack will be of ample dimensions.

There was more to it, and a picture of a large man with a square chin, level gray eyes, and a wide generous mouth that seemed made to grin good-naturedly. The girl read it quickly. Then the guard handed the clipping back to Purvis and moved away again to his post.

'I don't understand,' she said. 'What—'

'Don't be dumb,' Purvis exclaimed impatiently. 'Don't you remember—I'm a St Francis orphan myself. I didn't have any Santa Claus bringing *me* presents down a fake chimney, like those dirty-nosed brats will. I got thrown out on my ear when I was twelve, and thrown right in again—into the reformatory. But that isn't what I mean.

'What I mean is, I known the St Francis home like I know the back of my hand. And if I was on the outside, I'd be there waiting for McElroy when he came out on the roof dressed as Santa Claus and started down the fire escape. I'd be waiting, and I'd wipe the smile from his face and escape, and nobody would ever know who did it. If you custom-tailored a bump-off, you couldn't arrange one that would be any easier. Catch on?'

Red nodded. 'Yes, Ed,' she said pleadingly. 'But please, Ed, please don't think about it. I know McElroy sent you up, I know he broke up the gang. But think how lucky you were he only got you for concealed weapons. If he'd ever found that witness he was looking for, the one who saw you kill the watchman, you'd have gone to the chair. Think how lucky you were, Ed, and forget about hating McElroy. Forget him, *please*!

'Tell me what you'd like for Christmas instead. Tell me what you'd like, and I'll send it to you. We'll just think about each other this Christmas and pretend we're together like we will be when you get out.'

'He's still looking for that witness,' Purvis said implacably. 'Some day he'll find him. And so he has to die. If you want to know what I want for Christmas, I want McElroy's life. That's what I want.'

'Oh, Ed, Ed,' the girl cried, the tears wetting her thin cheeks, 'you'll get out and kill him and they'll catch you and take you away from me forever—'

'Time!' the guard said curtly. 'Time's up. You gotta go, lady.'

Red went, still weeping, and Purvis put the clipping back in his pocket and opened and shut his hands softly, thinking of what he'd do if only he were free to do it.

Well, now you're free, Purvis. Free to hide on a snow-covered roof on Christmas Eve, and stare at the crimson reflection of neon signs in the uptown sky or at the glassless window of the tenement across the street where, from time to time, a cigarette tip glows in one of the empty upper windows. Free to crouch there waiting for Santa Claus, a St Nick who will be Jim McElroy dressed up in crimson pants and false whiskers.

And when he comes you'll be able to give McElroy the present you've brought him—the present of death. . .

It had been completely unexpected when the guard had come for him only that morning and said the warden wanted to see him. Purvis had stood scowling in the warden's office, wanting to be insolent, but not quite daring to speak his mind, while the little man behind the big desk stared at him with level, frosty eyes.

'Purvis,' the warden said, tapping the desk with a pencil, 'You're surprised to be here. And I'm just as surprised to see you before me.'

He smiled bleakly. Purvis waited, wondering.

'We're both surprised. And frankly, for me the surprise is unpleasant. But the Parole Board has granted your request, and ordered me to turn you loose. You may regard it, if you wish, as a Christmas present from the state.'

Purvis' heart leaped. The thought of parole had dominated him night and day. But he had hardly expected to get it, for the Parole Board had been none too friendly. But Red had known; she'd been tipped off. That was what she had meant, then, by the letter she'd sent, the letter in his cell now.

Dear Ed:

Just to wish you a merry Xmas and to say that we're preparing a swell present for you, something you want very much. Can't tell you now, but you'll know soon and you'll be tickled. I know you will.

Love,
Red

She'd meant the parole, of course. The thousand bucks to the crooked Board member had turned the trick, and he must have told her so. Naturally, she couldn't pass the news along to Ed in a letter. No one was supposed to know the decisions of the Parole Board until they were announced, and it wouldn't look good for a prisoner to hear in a letter something he wasn't supposed to find out for a month.

But she'd wanted him to know he'd be free soon, though she could hardly have guessed it would be this soon.

'You see, Purvis,' the warden said, 'it was the thought of the Parole Board that since you were going to go free, it would be a nice gesture to free you in time for the Christmas festivities. Well, you know and I know how much you deserve freedom. But I have my orders, and I have to obey them. Remember, though—'

There was a lot more—guff about parole regulations, working, reporting monthly, and being subject to re-imprisonment for association with former companions.

It went in one ear and out the other. In an hour formalities having been expedited by the unexpected order, Purvis and half a dozen others were on their way to the city.

Once there, he had wasted no time in issuing stern injunctions to himself. A room, rented in a good neighborhood, first. Then hole up there until after dark. Don't even try to get in touch with Red. Don't risk being seen by newspaper reporters who might follow for a story, or dicks who might think it a good idea to tail a parolee on general principles.

No, he'd hole up in a respectable room until dark. Then he'd make a cautious sally to a certain number where a guy could rent a gun for the ten bucks, which the state had given him as a goodbye present.

After that a catlike approach to Melton

Street, through back alleys and backyards. An unseen entrance into an empty loft building. From the roof of that across the roof of the Saint Francis Foundling Home. Then nothing to do but wait.

Peace on earth, and mercy mild,
God and sinners reconciled!

Purvis cursed under his breath as the cold bit at his nose and ears. But he could wait. He'd waited a long time, and as his revenge came closer and closer, it tasted better and better. McElroy would be along any minute now, all tangled up in red pants and loaded down with a sack of toys. He'd come right past this chimney, never dreaming of what was waiting behind it for him. He'd come by, and Purvis would raise the taped pipe, bring it down—

He straightened. Was that a footstep? As he strained his ears the 'El' thundered by in the street and drowned out any noise he might have heard. When it had gone, leaving his ears ringing, he listened again.

This time it was clear. Footsteps, muffled by the snow, where unmistakably coming toward him.

Hark the herald angels sing. . .

Purvis tensed. Then the figure he had been waiting for appeared beyond the obscuring bulk of the chimney. Santa himself, with his bulbous stomach, baggy pants, fluttering beard, and tassled cap. Santa, with a lumpy pack on his back, stepping jauntily across the roof, shaking a little string of sleigh bells in his hands to make the kids below think he was stabling his reindeer.

Glory to the new-born King!

Purvis' lips twisted. The pipe descended. A sound like a customer thumping a ripe watermelon was lost in the night, and with a little surprised jangle of sleigh bells Santa stopped, his knees buckled, and he slid silently faced downward on the flat stone roof.

Purvis loosened the pack of toys and set it to one side. Then he rolled the unconscious figure over and ripped loose the false whiskers. From his coat pocket he took the flashlight he'd brought, and, muffling the beam with his hand, shined it on the unconscious man's face.

'Now, McElroy—' he began and stopped.

The man on the roof was not Smiling Jim McElroy.

Hideous disappointment rose in Purvis, so acute he could taste it. Disappointment and rage. He clicked the flashlight on again for a moment. But the beam of light still showed a face he did not know. It was a round face, a red, jolly face, but it was not the face of McElroy.

Purvis thrust pipe and flashlight back into his pocket.

Kneeling, he savagely slapped snow into the face until the eyes fluttered and opened. Then his features hidden by an upturned collar, his voice muffled, he snarled a question.

The open eyes fluttered vaguely.

'McElroy?' the man in Santa Claus costume said in a gasping voice. 'He's downstairs. Asked me to come along—play Santa—fool the kids. Thought they'd know *him*. Wanted it to seem real.''

The eyes closed. The voice stopped. The man he had hit was unconscious again, breathing with thick, stertorous gasps.

God rest ye merry gentlemen...

Purvis knelt there beside him and cursed. McElroy had made a last minute change in plans. So the kids would belive Santa was real! He'd be down there now, safe and in the brightly lighted gymnasium, surrounded by half a dozen women and a hundred brats—there were no men connected with St Francis, except the janitor—helping 'em sing the carols Purvis had been hearing for the last half hour.

Let nothing you dismay...

And then Purvis was suddenly calm again.

McElroy was down there, surrounded by dames and kids. Unsuspecting, unarmed. Suppose Purvis slipped down the fire escape Santa had been about to descend. Suppose he came out from that fireplace into a room full of startled kids and before McElroy could even—

No, wait! Suppose Santa himself came out from the fireplace, as everyone expected him to? Suppose that Santa, pack on his back and everything, came out and walked over to McElroy and said: 'Here's a present for you, copper, that I've been waiting a long time to give you!'

Then the thing in Santa's hand would smoke and flame, and McElroy would go down with a bullet in his heart and death eating at all his stalwart strength. And Santa Claus would scram—right back to the North Pole itself, as far as anybody would ever know.

For Jesus Christ our Saviour...

Back through the fireplace, out the window, down the fire escape. At the bottom a weighted length of ladder swung about a dark alley. Down that length, down into the alley. Rip off the Santa Claus suit, stuff it into an ash can, and be gone into the darkness before the dames and the kids stopped screaming. Be back in his room all the way across town, perhaps, before they even had the sense to call the cops.

What would be easier? He could kill McElroy that way in view of a hundred witnesses, and the Santa Claus outfit would be a perfect disguise.

Was born on Christmas Day!

Quickly he set to work to strip the costume off the unconscious man at his feet. The guy had a suit on underneath. He wouldn't freeze. Not that Purvis cared. He got the coat, the pants, the beard, and the cap, letting the boots go, and in the darkness hurriedly slipped into them.

His heavy build fitted the garments well enough. Attired, he took the unconscious man's handkerchief, necktie, a torn-off shirt tail, and with these bound his wrists, his ankles, and gagged him. They'd find him soon enough. Purvis could have killed him but it wasn't worth his time. He hadn't seen his attacker. And bigger game was below, down that fire escape and the dames and kids couldn't stop him.

Purvis shouldered the pack, got it steady on his back, and made sure his gun was ready. Then he picked up the little string of sleigh bells and jangled them. At the shrill tintinnabulation they gave off he grinned, and stepped over the roof coping onto the fire escape.

'Reindeer, huh?' he said aloud. 'But the

guy who drives them carries a scythe, not a pack of gifts.'

Lippy, a little man with a large, loose mouth and ferret eyes, crouching at the glassless window of the building across the 'El' tracks from the St Francis Home, heard the childish voices of the singing orphans rise on the night air and grinned.

It came upon a midnight clear...

'The kids are a little early,' he remarked. 'It ain't hardly nine-thirty. But they're right about its coming. Any minute now.'

He coughed. The room smelled of paint and plaster, and since there was no window in the frame, it was bitterly cold.

'Hasn't he come yet?' the girl asked tensely. She ground a cigarette beneath her shoe and tossed it out the window. 'Oh, I wish he'd come. I want to get this over with.'

That glorious song of old...

'We don't have to do it if you don't wana,' Lippy said, and pulled his coat tighter about his throat.

'Yes, we do!' the girl whispered shrilly. 'We have to do it. We have to!'

'Well, if we have to, we have to,' Lippy said, 'Personally, if it's got to be done, we couldn't think of no better way. Here we are in a building no one else is in, not thirty yards away. Nobody to hear us, nobody to see us come or go.

'Then there's the "El." A train's bound to go by the right time. We couldn't want a sweeter setup.'

'Oh, I don't want to do it,' the girl half-sobbed. Then her voice stiffened with desperate resolution. 'But we have to Lippy! We have to, don't we?'

'Yeah, I guess we do,' Lippy agreed, and turned his attention again to the building across the street where the fire escape cut a black spidery line past tall lighted windows.

From angels bending near the earth...

'Hey!' he said suddenly. 'Listen!'

They both heard it plainly—the little jingle of sleigh bells. Then they both saw the figure that appeared above the roof coping across the street, silhouetted for a moment against the sky—the bulbous-stomached figure with the beard, the tasseled cap, and the pack on his back, starting carefully down the spidery black fire escape toward the lighted windows below.

'Here comes a train,' the girl whispered shakily.

'I hear it.' Lippy flung away a cigarette and kneeled at the window. 'He'll get opposite the first window just as it comes by,' he announced.

To pluck their harps of gold...

Then the downtown 'El' train came roaring along, and suddenly it was opposite them, filling the canyon of the narrow street with thundering sound. And at the same moment the bulky figure on the fire escape opposite became silhouetted clearly against the first lighted window.

Red leaned forward, her throat so tight she could hardly breathe. Unhurriedly, Lippy lifted the rifle in his hand to his shoulder, gave a little *mmm*, and tightened his finger. A tiny pencil of flame leaped outward and was gone. The noise of the

shot was sucked away by the roaring elevated express.

But across the street the figure on the fire escape was swaying, tottering. Then it fell. It fell headlong down the iron steps, the pack on its back splitting open and tumbling small white packages into the air like a flurry of monster snow flakes.

The somersaulting figure rocketed against the guard rail of the fire escape and went over, plummeting downward.

From the street below came a solid crunching sound. Then, with eerie macabreness, a startled jingling of sleigh bells as the little strip of bells fell beside the dark spot in the snow in the alley far beneath.

Then—nothing.

Lippy took the gun apart swiftly, put it in a gayly wrapped package that looked like a Christmas present and moved toward the door.

'Come on, Red,' he said. 'That does it. There's our Christmas present to Ed. Just what he asked for—that damned McElroy's life.'

Red followed him. 'We had to do it,' she half-laughed and half-cried hysterically. 'We had to. Ed himself told me how easy it would be to do tonight, and we had to do it. Because we'd never get another chance. And because if we didn't kill him, Ed would, when he gets out.

'But now he won't have to. Now he won't have to kill McElroy. And so they won't take him away from me. Because we did it, and now Ed will be with me always and they won't take him away. We'll just be happy together, like I've always wanted to be, and I'll have him forever—'

Then her sobbing voice was gone too. Only the children's voices were left, singing in the stillness of the night.

Peace on the earth, goodwill to men,
From heaven's all gracious King;
The world in golden stillness lay
To hear the angels sing.

LITERARY critic, social historian, biographer, and poet, Julian Symons (b. 1912) is also one of detective fiction's most distinguished practitioners, although his first crime novel, *The Immaterial Murder Case* (1945), was conceived as a joke (with his friend and fellow-poet Ruthven Todd, who was himself to write several mildly eccentric detective stories as 'R.T. Campbell').

Perhaps some of Symons's early work is a bit larky, and there are times when jarring thriller-elements intrude—*The Paper Chase* (1956) in particular is a bizarre mix of Edgar Wallace plot (criminal's fortune hidden in old house) with strong traces of Dashiell Hammett (blazing shoot-outs; a Gutman/Wilmer relationship). He didn't mind occasionally taking on oddball projects like 'The What's My Line Murder', with British tele-personality Gilbert Harding as a distinctly grouchy sleuth, and 'Cup Final Kidnap', featuring Bolton Wanderers' wizard Nat Lofthouse in a central role (although oddball or not, both were ingeniously plotted and entertainingly presented).

But by the late-1950s Symons had pretty well served his apprenticeship and settled down to chart 'Subtopia' (neither town nor country, a territory he was to make his own) and explore the strange and at times horrific other-lives led by the outwardly respectable: sometimes to really chilling effect, as in *The Players And The Game* (1972), loosely based on the British Moors Murders.

Quite often his plots derive from real events, real people. The captain of industry who is by no means a man of probity—notably Johnny Bogue in *The Paper Chase*; Ocky Gaye in *The Killing of Francie Lake* (1962)—is clearly modelled on the notorious swindler Horatio Bottomley (Symons wrote an excellent biography of him in 1955); *The Belting Inheritance* (1965) has strong echoes of the Tichbourne Claimant case; the Thomas Wise literary forgeries are utilized in *Bland Beginning* (1949).

Not that Symons merely rehashes ancient history. He uses it to point up his most persistent theme: how tenuous the link between illusion and reality, how easily it snaps; how catastrophic the results. Symons specializes in dark secrets, disquieting secrets; revelations that shock and disturb (and for this reason, although for others as well, *The Blackheath Poisonings* is still one of my own Top Ten detective novels published since the War). Rub away the veneer and there are some pretty odd coves out there. Or perhaps not so odd, Symons implies. Perhaps the really odd ones are those with *no* mental blemishes, *no* emotional scars, *no* dark thoughts bubbling away under a bland mask of flesh. And perhaps there aren't too many of those around.

His short stories—especially those written in the more liberated climate of the past twenty-odd years—are often as unsettling as his novels, and sometimes have been used as jumping-off points for full-length books (like 'The Main Chance': later expanded into one of his most darkly ironical novels, *The Man Whose Dreams Came True*). For those who enjoy the fresh approach Symons's *The Great Detectives* (1981) is essential reading (beg, buy, or steal it). A *tour de force* by anybody's standards, it features Symons himself investigating, sometimes interviewing, characters as diverse as Holmes, Maigret, Archie Goodwin, and Philip Marlowe.

In England, the Second World War killed off most of the markets for short fiction, but during the 1950s there were still one or two outlets—magazines like *John Bull* and *Argosy*, newspapers like the London *Evening Standard*—and writers made the most of them. Dig deep and you find gold, some of it collected in bookform much later, a good deal of it still unreprinted.

Series characters abounded (a hangover from pre-War days). Michael Gilbert had a small host of heroes: Chief Inspector Hazlerigg; lawyers Nap Rumbold and Henry Bohun; Sergeant, later Inspector, Patrick Petrella. Edmund Crispin had Gervase Fen. John Appleby had Inspector Innes; Michael Innes had Sir John Appleby (one wonders what each thought of the other). All were likable characters. Julian Symon's sleuth was Francis Quarles.

The real Francis Quarles was a pamphleteer, pedant, and prosy poet who had a mind, according to the Worthy Dr Fuller, 'biased to devotion' (a lowering phrase if ever I heard one), and whose *Emblems* (1635) is a work of unspeakable tedium. The fictional Quarles (nice touch) is a donnish know-it-all whose superior manner, in real life, would invite a good kick in the ankles.

But he's a very good detective. . .

15

The Santa Claus Club

JULIAN SYMONS

IT IS not often, in real life, that letters are written recording implacable hatred nursed over the years, or that private detectives are invited by peers to select dining clubs, or that murders occur at such dining clubs, or that they are solved on the spot by a process of deduction. The case of the Santa Claus Club provided an example of all these rarities.

The case began one day a week before Christmas, when Francis Quarles went to see Lord Acrise. He was a rich man, Lord Acrise, and an important one, the chairman of this big building concern and director of that and the other insurance company, and consultant to the Government on half a dozen matters. He had been a harsh, intolerant man in his prime, and was still hard enough in his early seventies, Quarles guessed, as he looked at the beaky nose, jutting chin and stony blue eyes.

They sat in the study of Acrise's house just off the Brompton Road.

'Just tell me what you think of these,' Lord Acrise said.

These were three letters, badly typed on a machine with a worn ribbon. They were all signed with the name James Gliddon. The first two contained vague references to some wrong done to Gliddon by Acrise in the past. They were written in language that was wild but unmistakably threatening. *You have been a whited sepulchre for too long, but now your time has come. . . You don't know what I'm going to do, now I've come back, but you won't be able to help wondering and worrying. . . The mills of God grind slowly, but they're going to grind you into little bits for what you've done to me.*

The third letter was more specific. *So the thief is going to play Santa Claus. That will be your last evening alive. I shall be there, Joe Acrise, and I shall watch with pleasure as you squirm in agony.*

Quarles looked at the envelopes. They were plain and cheap. The address was typed, and the word *Personal* was on top of each envelope.

'Who is James Gliddon?' he asked.

The stony eyes glared at him. 'I'm told you're to be trusted. Gliddon was a school friend of mine. We grew up together in the slums of Nottingham. We started a building company together. It did well for a time, then went bust. There was a lot of money missing. Gliddon kept the books. He got five years for fraud.'

'Have you heard from him since then? I see all these letters are recent.'

'He's written half a dozen letters, I suppose, over the years. The last one came—oh, seven years ago, I should think. From the Argentine.' Acrise stopped, then added abruptly, 'Snewin tried to find him for me, but he'd disappeared.'

'Snewin?'

'My secretary. Been with me twelve years.'

He pressed a bell. An obsequious, fattish man, whose appearance somehow put Quarles in mind of an enormous mouse, scurried in.

'Snewin—did we keep any of those old letters from Gliddon?'

'No sir. You told me to destroy them.'

'The last ones came from the Argentine, right?'

'From Buenos Aires, to be exact, sir.'

Acrise nodded, and Snewin scurried out.

Quarles said, 'Who else knows this story about Gliddon?'

'Just my wife.'

'And what does this mean about you playing Santa Claus?'

'I'm this year's chairman of the Santa Claus Club. We hold our raffle and dinner next Monday.'

Then Quarles remembered. The Santa Claus Club had been formed by ten rich men. Each year they met, every one of them dressed up as Santa Claus, and held a raffle. The members took it in turn to provide the prize that was raffled—it might be a case of Napoleon brandy, a modest cottage with some exclusive salmon fishing rights attached to it, or a Constable painting. Each Santa Claus bought one ticket for the raffle, at a cost of one thousand guineas. The total of ten thousand guineas was given to a Christmas charity. After the raffle the assembled Santa Clauses, each accompanied by one guest, ate a traditional English Christmas dinner.

The whole thing was a combination of various English characteristics: enjoyment of dressing up; a wish to help charities; and the desire also that the help given should not go unrecorded.

'I want you to find Gliddon,' Lord Acrise said. 'Don't mistake me, Mr Quarles. I don't want to take action against him, I want to help him. I wasn't to blame, don't think I admit that, but it was hard that Jimmy Gliddon should go to jail. I'm a hard man, have been all my life, but I don't think my worst enemies would call me mean. Those who've helped me know that when I die they'll find they're not forgotten. Jimmy Gliddon must be an old man now. I'd like to set him up for the rest of his life.'

'To find him by next Monday is a tall order,' Quarles said. 'But I'll try.'

He was at the door when Acrise said, 'By the way, I'd like you to be my guest at the Club dinner on Monday night . . .'

There were two ways of trying to find Gliddon; by investigation of his career after leaving prison, and through the typewritten letters. Quarles took the job of tracing the past, leaving the letters to his secretary, Molly Player.

From Scotland Yard he found out that Gliddon had spent nearly four years in prison, from 1913 to late 1916. He had joined a Nottinghamshire regiment when he came out, and the records of this regiment showed that he had been demobilised in August, 1919, with the rank of Sergeant. In 1923 he had been given a sentence of three years for an attempt to smuggle diamonds. Thereafter all trace of him in Britain vanished.

Quarles made some expensive telephone calls to Buenos Aires, where the letters had come from seven years earlier. He learned that Gliddon had lived in that city from a time just after the Second World War until 1955. He ran an import-export business, and was thought to have been living in other South American Republics during the war. His business was said to have been a cloak for smuggling, both of drugs and of suspected Nazis, whom he got out of Europe into the Argentine. In 1955 a newspaper had accused Gliddon of arranging the entry into the Argentine of a Nazi war criminal named Hermann Breit. Gliddon disappeared. A couple of weeks later a battered body was washed up just outside the city.

'It was identified as Señor Gliddon,' the liquid voice said over the telephone. 'But you know, Señor Quarles, in such matters the police are sometimes unhappy to close their files.'

'There was still some doubt?''

'Yes. Not very much, perhaps. But in these cases there is often a measure of doubt.'

Molly Player found out nothing useful about the paper and envelopes. They were of the sort that could be bought in a thousand stores and shops in London and elsewhere. She had no more luck with the typewriter.

Lord Acrise made no comment on Quarles' recital of failure. 'See you on Monday evening, seven-thirty, black tie,' he said, and barked with laughter. 'Your host will be Santa Claus. '

'I'd like to be there earlier.'

'Good idea. Any time you like. You know where it is? Robert the Devil Restaurant . . .'

The Robert the Devil Restaurant is situated inconspicuously in Mayfair. It is not a restaurant in the ordinary sense of the word, for there is no public dining-room, but simply several private rooms accommodating any number of guests from two to thirty. Perhaps the food is not quite the best in London, but it is certainly the most expensive.

It was here that Quarles arrived at half-past six, a big, suave man, rather too conspicuously elegant perhaps in a midnight-blue dinner jacket. He talked to Albert, the *maître d'hotel*, whom he had known for some years, took an unobtrusive look at the waiters, went into and admired the sparkling kitchens.

Albert observed his activities with tolerant amusement.

'You are here on some sort of business, Mr Quarles?'

'I am a guest, Albert. I am also a kind of bodyguard. Tell me, how many of your waiters have joined you in the past twelve months?'

'Perhaps half a dozen. They come, they go.'

'Is there anybody at all on your staff—waiters, kitchen staff, anybody—who has joined you in the past year, and who is over sixty years old?'

'No. There is not such a one.'

The first of the guests came just after a quarter-past seven. This was the brain surgeon Sir James Erdington, with a guest whom Quarles recognized as the Arctic explorer, Norman Endell. After that they came at intervals of a minute or two: a junior minister in the Government; one of the three most important men in the motor industry; a general elevated to the peerage to celebrate his retirement; a theatrical producer named Roddy Davis, who had successfully combined commerce and culture.

As they arrived, the hosts went into a special robing room to put on their Santa Claus clothes, while the guests drank sherry.

At seven-twenty-five Snewin scurried in, gasped, 'Excuse me, place names, got to put them out,' and went into the dining-room. Through the open door Quarles glimpsed a large oval table, gleaming with silver, bright with roses.

After Snewin came Lord Acrise, jutting-nosed and fearsome-eyed. 'Sorry to have kept you waiting,' he barked, and asked conspiratorially, 'Well?'

'No sign.'

'False alarm. Lot of nonsense. Got to dress up now.'

He went into the robing room with his box—each of the hosts had a similar box, labelled 'Santa Claus'—and came out again bewigged, bearded and robed. 'Better get the business over, and then we can enjoy ourselves. You can tell 'em to come in,' he said to Albert.

This referred to the photographers, who had been clustered outside, and now came into the room specially provided for holding the raffle. In the centre of the room was a table, and on the table stood this year's prize, two exquisite T'ang horses. On the other side of the table were ten chairs arranged in a semi-circle, and on these sat the Santa Clauses. Their guests stood inconspicuously at the side.

The raffle was conducted with the utmost seriousness. Each Santa Claus had a numbered slip. These slips were put into a tombola, and Acrise put in his hand and drew out one of them. Flash bulbs exploded.

'The number drawn is eight,' Acrise announced, and Roddy Davis waved the counterfoil in his hand.

'Isn't that *wonderful?* It's my ticket.' He went over to the horses, picked up one. 'I'm bound to say that they couldn't have gone to *anybody* who'd have appreciated them more.'

Quarles, standing near the general, whose face was as red as his robe, heard him mutter something uncomplimentary. Charity, he reflected, was not universal, even in a gathering of Santa Clauses. Then there were more flashes, the photographers disappeared, and Quarles' views about the nature of charity were reinforced when, as they were about to go into the dining-room, Sir James Erdington said, 'Forgotten something, haven't you, Acrise?'

With what seemed dangerous quietness Acrise answered, 'Have I? I don't think so.'

'It's customary for the Club and guests to sing "Noel" before we go in to dinner.'

'You didn't come to last year's dinner. It was agreed then that we should give it up. Carols after dinner, much better.'

'I must say I thought that was just for last year, because we were late,' Roddy Davis fluted.

'Suggest we put it to the vote,' Erdington said sharply.

Half a dozen of the Santas now stood looking at each other with subdued hostility. Then suddenly the Arctic explorer, Endell, began to sing 'Noel, Noel' in a rich bass. There was the faintest flicker of hesitation, and then the guests and their hosts joined in. The situation was saved.

At dinner Quarles found himself with Acrise on one side of him and Roddy Davis on the other. Endell sat at Acrise's other side, and beyond him was Erdington. Turtle soup was followed by grilled sole, and then three great turkeys were brought in. The helpings of turkey were enormous. With the soup they drank a light, dry sherry, with the sole Chassagne Montrachet, with the turkey an Aloxe Corton.

'And who are *you*?' Roddy Davis peered at Quarles' card and said, 'Of course, I know your name.'

'I am a criminologist.' This sounded better, Quarles thought, than 'private detective.'

'I remember your monograph on criminal calligraphy. Quite fascinating.'

So Davis *did* know who he was. It would be easy, Quarles thought, to underrate the intelligence of this man.

'These beards really do get in the way rather,' Davis said. 'But there, one must suffer for tradition. Have you known Acrise long?'

'Not very. I'm greatly privileged to be here.'

Quarles had been watching, as closely as he could, the pouring of the wine, the serving of the food. He had seen nothing suspicious. Now, to get away from Davis' questions, he turned to his host.

'Damned awkward business before dinner,' Acrise said. 'Might have been, at least. Can't let well alone, Erdington.'

He picked up his turkey leg, attacked it with Elizabethan gusto, wiped his mouth and fingers with his napkin. 'Like this wine?'

'It's excellent.'

'Chose it myself. They've got some good Burgundies here.' Acrise's speech was slightly slurred, and it seemed to Quarles that he was rapidly getting drunk.

'Do you have any speeches?'

'No speeches. Just sing carols. But I've got a little surprise for 'em.'

'What sort of surprise?'

'Very much in the spirit of Christmas, and a good joke too. But if I told you, it wouldn't be a surprise, would it?'

There was a general cry of pleasure as

Albert himself brought in the great plum pudding, topped with holly and blazing with brandy.

'That's the most wonderful pudding I've ever seen in my life,' Endell said. 'Are we really going to eat it?'

'Of course,' Acrise said irritably. He stood up, swaying a little, and picked up the knife beside the pudding.

'I don't like to be critical, but our Chairman is really not cutting the pudding very well,' Roddy Davis whispered to Quarles. And indeed, it was more of a stab than a cut that Acrise made at the pudding. Albert took over, and cut it quickly and efficiently. Bowls of brandy butter were circulated.

Quarles leaned towards Acrise. 'Are you all right?'

'Of course I'm all right.'

The slurring was very noticeable now. Acrise ate no pudding, but he drank some more wine, and dabbed at his lips. When the pudding was finished, he got slowly to his feet again and toasted the Queen. Cigars were lighted. Acrise was not smoking. He whispered something to the waiter, who nodded and left the room. Acrise got up again, leaning heavily on the table.

'A little surprise,' he said. 'In the spirit of Christmas.'

Quarles had thought that he was beyond being surprised by the activities of the Santa Claus Club, but he was astonished at the sight of the three figures who entered the room.

They were led by Snewin, somehow more mouselike than ever, wearing a long, white smock and a red nightcap with a tassel. He was followed by an older man dressed in a kind of grey sackcloth, with a face so white that it might have been covered in plaster of Paris. This man carried chains, which he shook. At the rear came a young-middle-aged lady who seemed to be completely hung with tinsel.

'I am Scrooge,' said Snewin.

'I am Marley,' wailed grey sackcloth, clanking his chains vigorously.

'And I,' said the young-middle-aged lady, with abominable sprightliness, 'am the ghost of Christmas past.'

There was a ripple of laughter.

'We have come,' said Snewin in a thin, mouse voice, 'to perform for you our own interpretation of *A Christmas Carol*...Oh, sir, what's the matter?'

Lord Acrise stood up in his robes, tore off his wig, pulled at his beard, tried to say something. Then he clutched at the side of his chair and fell sideways, so that he leaned heavily against Endell and slipped slowly to the floor.

There ensued a minute of confused, important activity. Endell made some sort of exclamation and rose from his chair, slightly obstructing Quarles. Erdington was first beside the body, holding the wrist in his hand, listening for the heart. Then they were all crowding round. Snewin, at Quarles' left shoulder, was babbling something, and at his right were Roddy Davis and Endell.

'Stand back,' Erdington snapped. He stayed on his knees for another few moments, looking curiously at Acrise's puffed, distorted face, bluish around the mouth. Then he stood up.

'He's dead.'

There was a murmur of surprise and horror, and now they all drew back, as men do instinctively from the presence of death.

'Heart attack?' somebody said.

Quarles moved to his side. 'I'm a private detective, Sir James. Lord Acrise feared an attempt on his life, and asked me to come along here.'

'You seem to have done well so far,' Erdington said drily.

'May I look at the body?'

'If you wish'.

As Quarles bent down, he caught the smell of bitter almonds. 'There's a smell like prussic acid, but the way he died precludes cyanide, I think. He seemed to become very drunk during dinner, and his speech was blurred. Does that suggest anything to you?'

'I'm a brain surgeon, not a physician.' Erdington stared at the floor. 'Nitro benzene?'

'That's what I thought. We shall have to notify the police.'

Quarles went to the door and spoke to a disturbed Albert. Then he returned to the room and clapped his hands.

'Gentlemen. My name is Francis Quarles, and I am a private detective. Lord Acrise asked me to come here tonight because he had received a threat that this would be his last evening alive. The threat said, "I shall be there, and I shall watch with pleasure as you squirm in agony". Lord Acrise has been poisoned. It seems certain that the man who made the threat is in this room.'

'Gliddon,' a voice said. Snewin had divested himself of the white smock and red nightcap, and now appeared as his customary respectable self.

'Yes. This letter, and others he had received, were signed with the name of James Gliddon, a man who bore a grudge against Lord Acrise which went back nearly half a century. Gliddon became a profes-

sional smuggler and crook. He would now be in his late sixties.'

'But dammit man, this Gliddon's not here.' That was the General, who took off his wig and beard. 'Lot of tomfoolery.'

In a shamefaced way the other members of the Santa Claus Club removed their facial trappings. Marley took off his chains and the lady discarded her cloak of tinsel.

Quarles said, 'Isn't he here? But Lord Acrise is dead.'

Snewin coughed. 'Excuse me, sir, but would it be possible for my colleagues from our local dramatic society to retire?'

'Everybody must stay in this room until the police arrive,' Quarles said grimly. 'The problem, as you will all realize, is how the poison was administered. All of us ate the same food, drank the same wine. I sat next to Lord Acrise, and I watched as closely as possible to make sure of this. After dinner some of you smoked cigars or cigarettes, but not Lord Acrise.'

'Just a moment.' It was Roddy Davis who spoke. 'This sounds fantastic, but wasn't it Sherlock Holmes who said that when you'd eliminated all other possibilities, even a fantastic one must be right? Supposing poison in powder form was put on to Acrise's food? Through the pepper pots, say . . .'

Erdington was shaking his head, but Quarles unscrewed both salt and pepper pots and tasted their contents. 'Salt and pepper,' he said briefly. 'Hello, what's this.'

'It's Acrise's napkin,' Endell said. 'What's remarkable about that?'

'It's a napkin, but not the one Acrise used. He wiped his mouth half a dozen times on his napkin, and wiped his greasy fingers on it too, when he'd gnawed a turkey bone. He must certainly have left grease marks on it. But look at this napkin.'

He held it up, and they saw that it was spotless. Quarles said softly, 'The murderer's mistake.'

Quarles turned to Erdington. 'Sir James and I agree that the poison used was probably nitro benzene. This is deadly as a liquid, but it is also poisonous as a vapour—isn't that so?'

Erdington nodded. 'You'll remember the case of the unfortunate young man who used shoe polish containing nitro benzene on damp shoes, put them on and wore them, and was killed by the fumes.'

'Yes. Somebody made sure that Lord Acrise had a napkin that had been soaked in nitro benzene but was dry enough to use. The same person substituted the proper napkin, the one belonging to the restaurant, after Acrise was dead.'

'That means the napkin must still be here,' Davis said.

'It does.'

'Then I vote that we submit to a search!'

'That won't be necessary,' Quarles said. 'Only one person here fulfils all the qualifications of the murderer.'

'James Gliddon?'

'No. Gliddon is almost certainly dead, as I found out when I made enquiries about him. But the murderer is somebody who knew about Acrise's relationship with Gliddon, and tried to be clever by writing those letters to lead us along a wrong track.' He paused. 'Then the murderer is somebody who had the opportunity of coming in here before dinner, and who knew exactly where Acrise would be sitting.'

There was a dead silence in the room.

Quarles said, 'He removed any possible

suspicion from himself, as he thought, by being absent from the dinner table, but he arranged to come in afterwards to exchange the napkins. He probably put the poisoned napkin into the clothes he discarded. As for motive, long-standing hatred might be enough, but he is also somebody who knew that he would benefit handsomely when Acrise died. . . stop him, will you?'

But the General, with a tackle reminiscent of the days when he had been the best wing three-quarter in the country, had already brought to the floor Lord Acrise's secretary, Snewin.

SHERLOCK HOLMES is the most parodied detective in fiction. Nothing startling in that; he's also the most famous. What is startling is how soon the parodists identified their prey and pounced on him.

Luke Sharp (in fact the novelist and editor Robert Barr) is probably—though who knows?—the first: his 'Adventures of Sherlaw Kombs' appeared in the *Idler* in 1892, before the first series of Holmes stories had even finished its run in the *Strand Magazine*. R.C. Lehmann's admirable cycle of stories (eight in all) featuring Picklock Holes ran in *Punch* (August 1893 to January 1894) during the latter half of the *Strand's* printing of the *Memoirs*. In the same month that Lehmann's final parody, 'Picklock's Disappearance', appeared (nice touch: Holes's amanuensis Dr Potson reveals the ghastly truth that it was Holmes himself who dragged Picklock Holes to his doom), Allan Ramsay contributed a one-off burlesque to *The Bohemian* featuring Thinlock Bones. And Holmes wasn't only exercising the minds of English-speaking humorists: on the Continent 'Les Aventures de Loufolk Holmès' by 'Cami' was running in France sometime around 1895.

Since then, the Deluge: Holmlock Shears, Shylock Homes, Hemlock Holmes, Hemlock Jones, Sheerluck Jones, Sheerluck Soames, Shamrock Jolnes, Sherbet Scones—good grief!

And all over the shop, too. If you have the time (an idle year or so) you can find them easily in newspapers, women's magazines, humorous papers, arts and literary journals, from the 1890s to the present day. And it wasn't only in the high-profile periodicals that parodies appeared.

Pick up a musty bound volume of any great public-school magazine in a secondhand bookshop and a pound to a penny somewhere amongst its browning pages you'll find a Tomes story, or a Fones story, or a Groans story. Leaf through ten years' worth of old issues of your local parish magazine piled on the White Elephant stall at the summer fete and if some bright spark hasn't contributed 'The Mystery of the Exploding Marrow' at some time or another it was a dull decade. Holmes parodies were *everywhere* (probably still are): bicycling magazines, cricketing magazines, amateur dramatics newsletters, nature notes, house journals for banks, insurance companies, charities, catering organizations...

It has to be said that many of them—probably most, if the truth be known—are pretty forgettable, especially when the writer over-extended the joke and pitched into a whole cycle of parodies. What might have started out as a labour of love in short order became just a labour, both for reader and writer.

A parody cycle of course is the toughest thing in the world to maintain successfully. August Derleth did it, although his Solar Pons stories are not really parodies, not really pastiches; uniquely, the series stands on its own as an affectionate (and often highly ingenious) tribute to a favourite sleuth. More recently Robert Fish succeeded too, with his entrancing tales of Schlock Homes: at no time did it look as though he was running the joke into the ground.

The longest-running parody cycle of them all has to be the Herlock Sholmes burlesques which Charles Hamilton, as 'Peter Todd', began in the British boys' story-paper, the *Greyfriars' Herald,* in 1915.

Exactly one hundred of the Sleuth from Shaker Street's extraordinary cases were recorded, mostly by 'Peter Todd', sometimes by 'Dr Jotson', on the odd occasion—as here—by 'Herlock Sholmes' himself. They appeared in a number of weekly papers from 1915 to 1925—*Gem*, *Magnet*, *Penny Popular*—with odd bursts in later decades, and although Hamilton wrote a good many of them other hands took a turn as well. The trouble is it's difficult after so many years to identify the non-Hamilton authors.

It's said that George Samways (b. 1895) wrote many of the Sholmes stories of the early-1920s, although in a letter to me he categorically denied it. Other candidates include W.E. Stanton Hope (1889-1961) who, before he became a world-traveller, wrote a good deal for the papers in which Sholmes appeared, and W.L. Catchpole (b. 1900), who certainly contributed quantities of parodies, sketches, and squibs to both *Gem* and *Magnet*. Yet Hope had gone on to better-paying markets by the time Hamilton stopped writing the Sholmes parodies in 1921, and Catchpole didn't really start writing until after the main Sholmes series ended in 1925.

The only thing one can say about 'The Secret in the Pudding Bag' is that it's fine knockabout stuff, but it isn't by Charles Hamilton. I suspect it was a lowly sub-editor earning an honest bob or two on the side.

16

The Secret in the Pudding Bag

(A Story of an Amazing Christmas Mystery recorded by Herlock Sholmes himself)

BEFORE revealing the amazing Secret of the Pudding Bag, I, Herlock Sholmes, detective of Shaker Street, London, desire to explain my action to my readers.

For years my faithful friend, Dr Jotson, who assists me to pay Mrs Spudson's exorbitant rent, had acted as the official recorder of my cases. Never was there a better man. Although a general practitioner, he is an expert on disordered brains. As I have told him many a time, he should be in a mental asylum—as house-surgeon, of course. Yet his great talents have not been wasted altogether in Shaker Street.

But his very devotion to me has one draw-back. He refuses to record any but my astounding successes. And the case of the Pudding Bag can hardly be classified as one. But because of its Christmas flavour the Editor desired it greatly—the story, not the pudding bag.

One day just after I had successfully solved the mystery of the Poisoned Doughnut, in Tooting Bec, I found the Great Man in our consulting-room at Shaker Street, begging Jotson to narrate the tale for the benefit of his readers. Jotson refused.

Therefore, I insisted on recording this amazing case myself.*

For long Dr Jotson had been run-down and depressed. Ever since that day when he left his best pair of silver-plated scissors inside the patient upon whom he had operated for liver trouble, he had not been himself.

For some time I must admit it did not occur to me that there was anything else wrong with poor Jotson save worry for the loss of his patient and the scissors. But shortly before Christmas it was borne on me that something else was amiss.

One night as I sat in my armchair playing Schnoffenstein's Five-Finger Exercise in B Flat on my violin, curious rumbling noises assailed my ear. At first I thought the G string wanted tightening; then it occurred to me that the strange, deep sounds were proceeding from the next room.

I ceased playing. Creeping stealthily towards the bed-room door, my fiddle grasped in my right hand ready for any emergency, I stooped down with the skilled grace of long practice, and applied my ear to the keyhole.

Now I could hear the rumbling clearly. Dr Jotson was talking to himself. Throwing open the door, I stood a tall and, I hope, dignified figure in my purple dressing-gown with the little green birds on the holly branches round the hem.

'Jotson' I cried. 'You are distraught.'

My old friend Jotson, who had been pacing the bed-room, stopped, his hands behind him. There was a startled look on his face, his sandy, walrus moustache drooping guiltily.

*And on pocketing the fee usually awarded to poor Jotson.—Ed.

'Sholmes,' he said, 'you have been listening. What have you heard?'

'Aah.' I said. 'What! Well might I ask you a question. What are you concealing from me, Jotson? What have you behind your back?'

'He, he, he! Only a couple of patches,' replied Jotson, faintly laughing at his own feeble joke. 'Now pray go and resume your amateur vivisection on my guineapigs!'

Candidly, I felt offended, and I left the room. But I resolved to keep my eye on my old and faithful friend for any further symptoms before formally notifying Colney Hatch.

Gradually, as the days sped by, I became more convinced that Jotson was ailing mentally. Several times I heard him mumbling behind closed doors. Occasionally, too, he left the house in the evenings on some pretext or another. But I felt that when Jotson needed my help he would tell me. So I snuffed my cocaine, played my violin, and solved a couple of dozen poison mysteries which had baffled Scotland Yard and the Continental police, and temporarily left Jotson to look after himself.

On Christmas Eve Dr Jotson made one more of his mysterious disappearances. For long I sat before the fire in the consulting-room, casually perusing the evening paper as I smoked my pipe. Outside the snow snowed and the waits waited—I was hard up that Christmas.

Suddenly a paragraph on an inner news page riveted my attention. It was headed: 'Proposed River Trip for Crown Prince', and read: 'The Crown Prince of Schlacca-Splittzen, who arrived this afternoon in London from Paris, has expressed a desire to see the London County Council Hall from the river. He remarked to reporters that his view of this magnificent structure from the railway reminded him of the municipal Torture House in Tchmnomzyte, the capital of his own state of Schlacca-Splittzen, which lies to the south of Russia. The Crown Prince is being carefully guarded by Inspector Pinkeye and three other well-known detectives from Scotland Yard. These precautions are being taken because it is rumoured that the Schlacca-Splittzen Co-operative Society of Anarchists have threatened to drop a bomb into his porridge if he visited Britain's shores.'

As I read this little paragraph a dark suspicion entered my mind, and there I determined that Jotson must be watched.

It was at eleven o'clock on Christmas Eve. Mrs Spudson, her hair in curl-papers, had retired to rest. I damped down the fire, covered the canary's cage, turned the consulting-room lights out, chained up the dog, put out the cat, and left the key under the front doormat for Jotson. Then I went to my room.

I was about to doff my dressing-gown when I heard Jotson enter the house. Slowly he came upstairs, and I heard him switch on the consulting-room light. Leaving my room, I crept along the passage and quickly opened the door of the consulting-room.

As I did so Jotson leaped from the hearth as though stung.

'Great porous plasters!' he gasped. 'What a fright you gave me! For a moment I thought you were the ghost of Old Man Scrooge. You see, I've been attending the recital of the "Christmas Carol." He, he, he!'

The halting words of my old friend and his musical cackle told me he was not speaking the truth.

'Jotson,' I said sternly, 'you've no more been to any recital to-night than I've been to the tax-collector to pay next year's income-tax in advance. Now, tell me. Where have you been?'

As I spoke, my trained eye swept the fire grate. From the flames and ashes which I saw there I deduced that Jotson had been burning something. Quickly I averted my gaze so that he should not know I knew.

My old friend tugged nervously at his moustache.

'It's nothing, really, my dear Sholmes,' he said nervously. 'If I told you, you would only laugh at me. And I hate being laughed at!'

'Nonsense, Jotson!' I said heartily. 'Everyone laughs at you—er—except your patients, of course. And they usually don't last long enough to laugh long.'

This I said in a gentle, bantering tone to cheer Jotson up. To my surprise, it seemed to have the opposite effect, and he stumped out of the room in a huff.

That was the opportunity I wanted. In a moment my nose was in the fender. Quickly I peered about. Before you could say 'forcemeat stuffing' I had found a narrow strip of torn paper bearing some typewritten words. Hearing Jotson's footsteps returning I hastily crammed it in my pocket, and was innocently cracking Brazil nuts with my teeth when he entered the consulting-room to apologise for his former rudeness.

I said nothing about my discovery, but in my bedroom I examined the find carefully. To my stupefaction the typewritten words, which were in English, read as follows:

'. . . this honour. You have been chosen, comrade. See you fail not.'

Ding, dong! Clatter Bang! Ding dong!

The merry Christmas bells were chiming as Jotson and I met at breakfast on the following morning and exchanged greetings.

My eagle eye was quick to notice that Dr Jotson was not himself at breakfast. Quite absent-mindedly he helped me to the larger half of the breakfast kipper, and then gave me the first cup from the coffee-pot, instead of the usual dregs. All my old fears for my poor friend's condition returned with renewed force.

Sitting in my chair, daintily flicking the kipper-bones from the lapel of my mauve dressing-gown, I watched Jotson as he went to the window and tried to entice the friendship of a robin redbreast by means of a fish-head.

'What do you say to a walk round Marylebone Station or the Waxworks, to get an appetite for our Christmas dinner, Jotson!' I remarked casually.

Jotson's walrus moustache gave a perceptible quiver.

'Er—I'm afraid you will have to excuse me, my dear Sholmes!' he stammered. 'A new patient of mine, a dear old lady who is suffering from a temporary attack of suspended vibration of the right bozookum, and wishes me to test her high tension battery to enable her to get 2LO for the Christmas glee singers. I'm afraid—'

'Tut, tut! I said. 'I'll come with you, Jotson.'

'No, my dear Sholmes,' said Jotson very firmly. 'I shouldn't think of taking you to a case like this on Christmas Day. Why don't you take the bus up to the Zoological Gardens, or, if you prefer it, remain in front of the fire cracking a few monkey-nuts yourself?'

I said no more, but I thought a lot. For a time I sat myself in the armchair.

Speedily it became apparent that Jotson was up to some game. It seemed almost impossible to keep track of his movements. He was a slippery as an eel in an old pail. But at last I heard him stealthily take his hat and coat from the peg in the hall and leave the house.

Within a minute I was tracking my old friend down Shaker Street. Dr Jotson had a large brown paper parcel under his right arm. The parcel looked innocent enough. What did that parcel contain? That I was determined to find out.

Poor Jotson was worried. I deduced that from the absent-minded way that he pushed the face of a little boy who asked him for a cigarette-card. Stopping at the corner outside the Goat and Gooseberry Bush, he hesitated a moment, and then leaped on a passing bus. I waited until he had gone inside with his parcel; then I swung myself on the step and darted aloft.

Peering from the bus top, I saw Jotson alight at Charing Cross. I waited a few moments until the bus had started to move again, and then I ran nimbly down the steps. As I did so, with consummate cunning I knocked off the conductor's hat and leaped into the road. As he prepared to stop the bus I swiftly tossed him my own cap, and retrieved his fallen property. Then replacing the peaked, blue cap on my head and gumming a false black moustache to my upper lip, I followed in the track of my old friend.

Once Jotson stopped and looked back. All he saw, apparently, was an attenuated bus-conductor about to turn into a near by chop-house.

Waiting in the shelter of the doorway a

Newnes
FFICES

minute, I emerged and followed him again. As I watched his stocky form stumping down Whitehall towards the Houses of Parliament, a gust of wind blew the paper from under his arm. A white, earthenware pudding basin was revealed, with a cloth over the top of it.

After a vain attempt to retrieve the paper Jotson went on his way, looking uncommonly foolish walking down Whitehall holding that pudding-cloth, with the basin swinging at his side.

At first the sight of that pudding-basin brought a sense of relief to me. Then a horrible thought occurred to me. This was no pudding-basin. It was a bomb! Rapidly I reviewed in my mind the events leading up to this Christmas morning walk. I remembered Jotson's curious mumblings. I remembered the paragraph about the Crown Prince of Schlacca-Splittzen. I called to mind the mysterious message on the scrap of paper I had taken from the fire-grate. With a bomb in that innocent-looking bag, Jotson was on his way to the river to fulfil his dread mission.

My friend strode firmly to the Thames Embankment.

Quite a crowd was lining the parapet.

'What's the excitement?' I heard him ask a low-looking ruffian.

'It's that there Crown Prince of Slaccy-Splittem,' replied the fellow. 'He's just about to land at the jetty.'

Jotson pushed his way through the crowd to the parapet. I kept close at his heels, my heart hammering against my ribs.

With a gasp of dismay I saw Jotson hoist the pudding-basin on to the parapet and give it a gentle shove.

'Stop!' I cried, and thrust my hand forward.

I must have diverted Jotson's aim, for the basin struck against a jutting ledge of the Embankment. There was no time to duck, for I feared the next moment there would be an explosion that would bring about the end of all things as far as we were concerned. To my surprise, however, the basin broke, and out shot a great plum-pudding. It struck a boatman standing on the jetty waiting for the prince's launch right on the back of the neck and burst into fragments, while the onlookers gasped with astonishment. Then when they realised what had happened, a great shout of laughter burst forth. The boatman was annoyed—very! He looked aloft, with a great piece of pudding crowning his head, and passed a few remarks totally unconnected with that 'peace on earth and good will to men' which one associates with the Yuletide season. Then, as the fellow turned to help with the mooring of the prince's launch, I grasped Jotson by the hand and dragged him away.

'You thundering idiot!' I said. 'What do you mean by it all?'

'Sholmes!' cried Jotson. There was both surprise and disappointment in his tone.

And then bit by bit I dragged the story out of Jotson. He knew that Mrs Spudson had made a Christmas pudding and that she would insist on him and me partaking of it at the Christmas dinner.

'Knowing your good nature, Sholmes,' he said, 'I knew that you would have eaten some of it to avoid offending our landlady. You did last year, and what was the consequence? For two days you groaned on the couch with the collywobbles. This year I determined at all costs I would get rid of the Christmas pudding. As a medical man I knew it was positively dangerous, but I didn't want to drag you into the matter, nor did I wish to offend Mrs Spudson. And so I quietly lifted the basin containing the pudding, intending to dispose of it in the first possible way that presented itself. As you know, in desperation I finally toppled it over into the river.'

Then I told him how his rumblings had roused my suspicions, and the finding of the torn piece of typewritten paper had corroborated them.

Now it was Jotson's turn to laugh.

''Pon my word, Sholmes!' he chuckled. 'I didn't know you were so worried about me! You see, a fortnight ago I joined the Marylebone Dramatic Society, and was offered the role of Koffituppe in the play, 'Crown Jewels in Pawn,' by Msmooji, the famous Russian dramatist. Afraid you would laugh at me, I would retire to my bed-room to study my role. Finally, in disgust at my inability to learn the part, I tore it up and threw it on the fire. The typewritten piece of paper you found was a portion of the play.'

'But why on earth didn't you tell me all this before, my dear fellow?' I cried.

'Because,' answered Jotson, 'I should have had to acknowledge failure, and, as you know, no man likes to do that.'

'Ah, well,' I laughed, 'the mystery is solved! And we can safely return to Shaker Street to pull the wish-bone of a turkey without the fear of having to partake of any of the amazing stodgy concoction which Mrs Spudson calls Christmas pudding!'

THE GREAT CHAM of twentieth-century letters? In a mystery anthology? Well, why not? Although a late starter (nearly 40 when his first book was published), Anthony Burgess (real name Anthony Burgess Wilson, b. 1917) has tackled most literary forms over the past thirty years—essays, reviews, editing chores, librettos (not to mention the music to go with them), biographies, histories, critical analyses, books about music, books about books, books about books about books, books about James Joyce.

And fiction. Quantities of fiction. Satirical fiction, science fiction, semi-autobiographical fiction, experimental fiction, pseudonymous fiction (for which he wrote a rave review under his own name, then got thrown off the paper by an irate and humourless editor when twigged), blockbuster-length fiction, novella-length fiction, short fiction. It should come as no great surprise to discover the odd mystery hidden away somewhere amongst his huge, and hugely readable, output—although I'll admit that stumbling across this one was a matter of the purest serendipity.

Having tracked down a copy of the British digest magazine *Suspense* with Julian Symons's 'The Santa Claus Club' in it (and if you haven't read it yet, it's on page 171), I spotted Burgess's name on the contents page.

Was it the same Anthony Burgess? If so, was it a real mystery? If so, and much more to the point (given certain mainstream authors' lamentable conviction that genre fiction's an easy number), was it any good? Yes to the first; yes to the second (a clever, and unusual, con-trick); and absolutely yes to the third. Here is a neat little tale, tellingly told (watch how Burgess perfectly captures his narrator's fed-uppedness through his use of downbeat dialogue), with a decided nip to it.

17

The Great Christmas Train Mystery

ANTHONY BURGESS

THIS story's as true as I'm standing here with this pint in my right hand and my left foot on this bar-rail. It's rails that put me in mind of it. It happened to me when I was a dining-car steward on British Railways a few years back. It happened on Christmas Day.

I suppose you'd regard it as funny when you come to think of it—that people should travel by railway, quite long distances too, on Christmas Day, the same as if it was any other day. But people do it, quite a lot of them. They have their reasons—quite well-dressed people a lot of them are, too—which I suppose they might be willing to tell if you asked them nicely. But really it's none of your business and it's none of mine. Right. Ours not to reason why. Right. You do your job and I'll do mine and no questions asked. Right.

When you come to think of it, there could be a lot of reasons. They could be working, some of them, late on Christmas Eve, and promised to be with their mothers and dads for Christmas Day and no late trains to precisely where they're going on Christmas Eve. Some of them could just have been let out. Nick, hospital, what have you...

There are all sorts of reasons.

But this was the first time I'd ever worked on Christmas Day on the railways, and it all looked a bit weird to me. They looked almost a bit like ghosts, getting on the train at all the different stops, dressed up, hearty, but still like ghosts because, as I saw it, they shouldn't have been there. They should have been at home by the fire, pulling crackers or cracking nuts or putting the turkey in the oven or getting the port out of the sideboard cupboard. As I say, there was something, to my mind at the time, a bit weird about it.

Anyway, there was a nice special Christmas Day lunch laid on that day, though only one sitting as was only proper, because the train was not exactly jampacked as it would have been on an ordinary day, and one sitting could take care of all who wanted lunch easy enough. Right. The menu was all decorated with holly and mistletoe, and there was gravy soup, turkey with stuffing, spuds done three ways, brussels, Christmas pud with brandy sauce. It was all right, nicely done and plenty of it. We started to serve lunch at Reading, and there was quite a number sitting down to it, both in the first class and what is now second, though it used to be third.

The customers were really jolly about it all. It wasn't a bit like what it is on ordinary days—you know, when nobody talks to anybody and they drink their bottled beer like as if it was medicine. Somebody had a box of crackers, which British Railways didn't provide in those days, and soon there were fancy hats and false noses, and streamers floating all over the place, with loud laughter and what not. There was even a bit of mistletoe that somebody had, and festive screams rose high as we rattled over the points. People ordered cocktails and sherry and bottles of claret and sauterne. People with winy voices kept saying, 'Your very good health, steward, and a very merry Christmas to you and yours.'

Then there was port and brandy and cigars for some, and everybody got redder in the face. One old one with a fair pot on him said, in a colonel-sort-of-voice, 'An excellent lunch, steward, really excellent.'

'And excellently served,' said somebody else.

'Hear, hear,' said one young smasher.

'Our compliments to the chef,' said another.

'And a very merry Christmas,' said another.

So I thought, and Bert and young Jack thought, that this was going to be all right. This was going to be real sort of compensation for working on Christmas Day. In my mind's eye I could see five bob tips, ten bob tips, all sorts of tips just flowing in, some of the kinder-hearted ones saying, 'And here's an extra ten bob to buy something for the kids.'

So, all ready for this, we began to take the bills round, saying, just to remind them, 'I hope your lunch was satisfactory, sir,' and 'I trust you enjoyed your lunch, madam.' They all said they did, and this colonel-type kept on saying 'Excellent, excellent,' with a big Corona Corona stuck in his gob.

And here's where the mystery came in. At least it was a mystery at the time, such a big sort of mystery that I really began to think we were all haunted, and very nearly decided to get off for good at the next stop.

Not one tip did we get. Not a sausage. Not a threepenny joey, not a solitary claud. As true as I'm standing here now, not one of those well-fed and, as they themselves put it, highly satisfied passengers, whether first-class or third as it was then, gave as much as a worn-out meg. They'd gorged themselves silly, saying 'Excellent, excellent' and 'Really delightful, steward,' but every ounce of change we put on their plates they scooped right back in their pockets or purses or what have you.

I couldn't believe it, nor could Bert and young Jack. I mean, we were too flabbergasted even to get a bit nasty, which, all things considered, we would have been quite right to get. I just gasped like a fish at them. I even said to the colonel bloke. 'Are you *sure* you enjoyed your lunch, sir?' and he said, 'Excellent, excellent. Really first-class, steward, really first-rate lunch.' And some idiot next to him—idiot I thought then, anyway—said, 'Hear, hear.'

As they made their way back to their compartments, some of them even gave me the old pat on the back with 'Merry Christmas, steward,' and all the rest of it. They must have seen us all looking a bit gloomy, but I suppose they'd put it down to us being far from home and our loved ones and all that load of tripe on Christmas Day, working like blacks instead of watching others guzzle. Anyway, that ungrateful-seeming lot went back to their compartments to snore it off. And when we'd packed everything away and had our own bit to eat, the lot of us just sat about, gloomy as you-know-what, wondering about it all.

'I just can't understand it,' said young Jack. He was near to crying, that poor young lad was, and I couldn't really blame him.

'Mystery, that's what it is,' said Bert. 'I never known anything like it.'

'Like as though everybody's haunted,' I said. That had been in my mind all day.

Anyway, tea-time came along and we only had one customer. He was a big, tall sort of a bloke who didn't look a bit Christmassy. He ordered a pot of tea, just that. When he asked how much, I said a bob. And he gave a bob, just that. But I was past caring. He went back to his compartment, then five minutes later he was back again, asking for another pot of tea. He knew it was a bob now, and a bob he gave, just that. As I say, I was past caring. He went back to his compartment again, and blow me if he wasn't back five minutes later asking for another pot of tea.

'You seem to like our tea,' I said, bitter.

'Yes,' he said, 'I like your tea. It's a nice pot of tea. It's worth a bob,' he said. He saw me looking a bit gloomy, so he made himself a bit more comfortable behind his pot of tea and said, 'Not been too good a day for you lot, has it?'

'I don't quite understand what you mean,' I said, trying not to look interested.

'Come off it,' he said. 'All that lot saying what a good time had been had by all, mistletoe in the dining-car and what-not, and not one penny piece in tips from the whole lot put together.'

'What about it?' I said.

'I'm on duty,' said this bloke. 'I get my expenses, see, but that doesn't cover tips. I'm on duty, and I've been asking some of the passengers about it all. They were a bit surprised to find out that you didn't get what you should have got.'

'Surprised, were they?' I said.

'Yes. And would you like to know why you didn't? Would you like to know what happened?'

He seemed a bit too eager to tell me all about it—there was a bit too much relish

about him, as you might say. So I said, 'It's up to you whether you tell me or not.'

'Right,' he said. And he leaned back more comfortable, his hands over his belly. 'I've missed her now,' he said. 'I've been after her all over Christmas. She was a bit too quick. She got off just before I got on. We'll get her, though, never fear, never have any fear about that, matey. She goes under various names—Mrs Mervin, the Hon. Dora Goffin, Fast Lizzie, and various others more. She's a very good-looking woman, and very well-spoken.'

'Well,' I said, 'What about it?'

'She's been up and down the train all morning, I gather. She was on other trains yesterday and the day before. She goes up to the passengers and she says, ever so polite and well-off, "Don't you think it would be ever so nice and ever so jolly an idea if we gave a little present to the dining-car staff? After all, it is Christmas, isn't it, and they do work ever so hard, don't they?'

He said all this in a refined sort of voice, a kind of squeak, like taking the Mickey out of somebody speaking well-off. It began to dawn on me then what had happened.

'Yes,' said this copper-in-disguise, 'that's what happened.' He spoke in his ordinary voice again, quite common. 'I don't know how much she got away with, but it must have been a nice little bit. People are always generous round about Christmas. I suppose she got off at Reading. Anyway, we'll get her yet. But that doesn't help you much, does it?' He looked at me in a pitying sort of way and said, 'Fetch us another pot of that tea. If you don't mind,' he added politely.

When I brought it, he was ready with his bob. But he looked at me sort of pitying again and said, 'Here. Just to show you that a heart of gold beats beneath this rough exterior, here's a tanner. That comes out of my own pocket, mind, not expenses. Don't forget to share it with the others.'

I could have thrown it in his face, but it doesn't do to be impolite to a copper. Besides, it was Christmas Day. Peace on earth and all that tripe.

Never mind.

THERE ARE three major strikes against James Powell (b. 1932): (1) he's very funny, (2) he writes short stories, (3) his short stories are mystery-oriented. What could be worse?

Frankly, not a lot. Received wisdom, out of the thin-lipped, pursed mouths of flinty-eyed publishers' accountants, has it that (1) humour doesn't sell (Wodehouse excepted; he's an irritating aberration), (2) short stories don't sell, and (3) publishing a volume of humorous *mystery* short stories is the only sure-fire way to the bankruptcy court there is. You could issue a book entitled *On the Fifty-Three Distinct Regional Variations In the Bomongo Sub-Dialect* and it'd be a hot one; you could push out a twenty-eight volume set on Cuban cooking and Book Club buyers'd be fighting with axes for the reprint rights. Publish a volume of funny detective stories and (so the theory goes) as far as the book-buying public are concerned it'd be akin to serving up rare topside of beef at a vegan Thanksgiving.

Well, I don't know about that. All I know is, *I'd* buy it. Like a shot. And especially if it was by James Powell.

Powell is not just funny, he's hilarious. He makes me guffaw out loud. I once read a Powell story in *Ellery Queen* on a Tube journey from Baker Street to West Hampstead and nearly cleared the compartment. They thought I was either a subway crazy or having a fit. I think what probably shook them most was that I was laughing helplessly at a story in a *mystery* magazine, and you just don't snort like a horse and howl like a jackass when you're reading a *mystery* story.

But that's the point. James Powell is funny—very, very funny—but he still manages, just about, to keep within the mystery tradition. There are still problems to be solved, wacky as those problems often are; there are still good guys and villains, even though the good guys are sometimes numbskulls and nincompoops, the villains really rather interesting when you get right down to it.

My favourite types of Powell stories are those where he takes a traditional fairy tale or a patently infantile situation and gives it a good shaking. Such as this absurd—and actually, towards the end, almost nail-biting—offering featuring murder and mayhem in a place where you would least expect it.

So come with us now, dear reader, to the most magical land there ever was... come with us to the Toyworks beneath the North Pole—only don't read this story with a full glass in your hand...

18

The Plot Against Santa Claus

JAMES POWELL

RORY BIGTOES, Santa's Security Chief, was tall for an elf, measuring almost seven inches from the curly tips of his shoes to the top of his fedora. But he had to stride to keep abreast of Garth Hardnoggin, the quick little Director General of the Toy-works, as they hurried, beards streaming back over their shoulders, through the racket and bustle of Shop Number 5, one of the many vaulted caverns honeycombing the undiscovered island beneath the Polar icecap.

Director General Hardnoggin wasn't pleased. He slapped his megaphone, the symbol of his office (for as a member of the Board he spoke directly to Santa Claus), against his thigh. 'A bomb in the Board Room on Christmas Eve!' he muttered with angry disbelief.

'I'll admit that Security doesn't look good,' said Bigtoes.

Hardnoggin gave a snort and stopped at a construction site for Dick and Jane Doll dollhouses. Elf carpenters and painters were hard at work, pipes in their jaws and beards tucked into their belts. A foreman darted over to show Hardnoggin the wall-paper samples for the dining room.

'See this unit, Bigtoes?' said Hardnoggin, 'Split-level ranch type. Wall-to-wall carpeting. Breakfast nook. Your choice of Early American or French Provincial furnishings. They said I couldn't build it for the price. But I did. And how did I do it?'

'Cardboard,' said a passing elf, an old carpenter with a plank over his shoulder.

'And what's wrong with cardboard? Good substantial cardboard for the interior walls!' shouted the Director General striding off again. 'Let them bellyache, Bigtoes. I'm not out to win any popularity contests. But I do my job. Let's see you do yours. Find Dirk Crouchback and find him fast.'

At the automotive section the new Lazaretto sports cars (1/32 scale) were coming off the assembly line. Hardnoggin stopped to slam one of the car doors. 'You left out the *kachunk*,' he told an elf engineer in white cover-alls.

'Nobody gets a tin door to go *kachunk*,' said the engineer.

'Detroit does. So can we,' said Hardnoggin, moving on. 'You think I don't miss the good old days, Bigtoes?' he said. 'I was a spinner. And a damn good one. Nobody made a top that could spin as long and smooth as Garth Hardnoggin's.'

'I was a jacksmith myself,' said Bigtoes. Satisfying work, building each jack-in-the-box from the ground up, carpentering the box, rigging the spring mechanism, making the funny head, spreading each careful coat of paint.

'How many could you make in a week?' asked Director General Hardnoggin.

'Three, with overtime,' said Security Chief Bigtoes.

Hardnoggin nodded. 'And how many children had empty stockings on Christmas morning because we couldn't handcraft enough stuff to go around? That's where your Ghengis Khans, your Hitlers, and your Stalins come from, Bigtoes—children who through no fault of their own didn't get any toys for Christmas. So Santa had to make a policy decision: quality or quantity? He opted for quantity.'

Crouchback, at that time one of Santa's right-hand elves, had blamed the decision on Hardnoggin's sinister influence. By way of protest he had placed a bomb in the new plastic machine. The explosion had coated three elves with a thick layer of plastic which had to be chipped off with hammers and chisels. Of course they lost their beards. Santa, who was particularly sensitive about beards, sentenced Crouchback to two years in the cooler, as the elves called it. This meant he was assigned to a refrigerator (one in Ottawa, Canada, as it happened) with the responsibility of turning the light on and off as the door was opened or closed.

But after a month Crouchback had failed to answer the daily roll call which Security made by means of a two way intercom system. He had fled the refrigerator and become a renegade elf. Then suddenly, three years later, Crouchback had reappeared at the North Pole, a shadowy fugitive figure, editor of a clandestine newspaper, *The Midnight Elf*, which made violent attacks on Director General Hardnoggin and his policies. More recently, Crouchback had become the leader of SHAFT—Santa's Helpers Against Flimsy Toys—an organization of dissident groups including the Anti-plastic League, the Sons and Daughters of the Good Old Days, the Ban the Toy-Bomb people and the Hippie Elves for Peace . . .

'Santa opted for quantity,' repeated Hardnoggin. 'And I carried out his decision. Just between the two of us it hasn't always been easy.' Hardnoggin waved his megaphone at the Pacification and Rehabilitation Section where thousands of toy bacteriological warfare kits (JiffyPox) were being converted to civilian use (The Freckle Machine). After years of pondering Santa had finally ordered a halt to war-toy production. His decision was considered a victory for SHAFT and a defeat for Hardnoggin.

'Unilateral disarmament is a mistake, Bigtoes,' said Hardnoggin grimly as they passed through a door marked *Santa's Executive Helpers Only* and into the carpeted world of the front office. 'Mark my words, right now the tanks and planes are rolling off the assembly lines at Acme Toy and into the department stores.' (Acme Toy, the international consortium of toymakers, was the elves' greatest bugbear.) 'So the rich kids will have war toys, while the poor kids won't even have a popgun. That's not democratic.'

Bigtoes stopped at a door marked *Security*. Hardnoggin strode on without slackening his pace. 'Sticks-and-Stones session at five o'clock,' he said over his shoulder. 'Don't be late. And do your job. Find Crouchback!'

Dejected, Bigtoes slumped down at his desk, receiving a sympathetic smile from Charity Nosegay, his little blonde blue-eyed secretary. Charity was a recent acquisition and Bigtoes had intended to make a play for her once the Sticks-and-Stones paperwork was out of the way. (Security had to prepare a report for Santa on each alleged naughty boy and girl.) Now that play would have to wait.

Bigtoes sighed. Security looked bad. Bigtoes had even been warned. The night before, a battered and broken elf had crawled into his office, gasped, 'He's going to kill Santa,' and died. It was Darby Shortribs who had once been a brilliant doll designer. But then one day he had decided that if war toys encouraged little boys to become soldiers when they grew up, then dolls encouraged little girls to become mothers, contributing to overpopulation. So Shortribs had joined SHAFT and risen to membership on its Central Committee.

The trail of Shortribs' blood had led to the Quality Control lab and the Endurance Machine which simulated the brutal punishment, the bashing, crushing, and kicking that a toy receives at the hands of a four-year-old (or two two-year-olds). A hell of a way for an elf to die!

After Shortribs' warning, Bigtoes had alerted his Security elves and sent a flying squad after Crouchback. But the SHAFT leader had disappeared. The next morning a bomb had exploded in the Board Room.

On the top of Bigtoes' desk were the remains of that bomb. Small enough to fit into an elf's briefcase, it had been placed under the Board Room table, just at Santa's feet. If Owen Brassbottom, Santa's Traffic Manager, hadn't chosen just that moment to usher the jolly old man into the Map Room to pinpoint the spot where, with the permission and blessing of the Strategic Air Command, Santa's sleigh and reindeer were to penetrate the DEW Line, there wouldn't have been much left of Santa from the waist down. Seconds before the bomb went off, Director General Hardnoggin had been called from the room to take a private phone call. Fergus Bandylegs, Vice-President of Santa Enterprises, Inc., had just gone down to the other end of the table to discuss something with Tom Thumbskin, Santa's Creative Head, and escaped the blast. But Thumbskin had to be sent to the hospital with a concussion when his chair—the elves sat on high chairs with ladders up the side like those used by life-guards—was knocked over backward by the explosion.

All this was important, for the room had been searched before the meeting and found safe. So the bomb must have been brought in by a member of the Board. It certainly hadn't been Traffic Manager Brassbottom who had saved Santa, and probably not Thumbskin. That left Director General Hardnoggin and Vice-President Bandylegs...

'Any luck checking out that personal phone call Hardnoggin received just before the bomb went off?' asked Bigtoes.

Charity shook her golden locks.

'The switchboard operator fainted right after she took the call. She's still out cold.'

Leaving the Toyworks, Bigtoes walked quickly down a corridor lined with expensive boutiques and fashionable restaurants. On one wall of Mademoiselle Fanny's Salon of Haute Couture some SHAFT elf had written: *Santa, Si! Hardnoggin, No!* On one wall of the Hotel St. Nicholas some Hardnoggin backer had written: *Support Your Local Director General!* Bigtoes was no philosopher and the social unrest that was racking the North Pole confused him. Once, in disguise, he had attended a SHAFT rally in The Underwood, that vast and forbidding cavern of phosphorescent stinkhorn and hanging roots. Gathered beneath an immense picture of Santa were hippie elves with their beards tied in outlandish knots, matron-lady elves in sensible shoes, tweedy elves and green-collar elves.

Crouchback himself had made a surprise appearance, coming out of hiding to deliver his now famous 'Plastic Lives!' speech. 'Hardnoggin says plastic is inanimate. But I say that plastic lives! Plastic infects all it touches and spreads like crab grass in the innocent souls of little children. Plastic toys make plastic girls and boys!' Crouchback drew himself up to his full six inches. 'I say: quality—quality now!' The crowd roared his words back at him. The meeting closed with all the elves joining hands and singing 'We shall Overcome.' It had been a moving experience...

As he expected, Bigtoes found Bandylegs at the Hotel St Nicholas bar, staring morosely down into a thimble-mug of ale. Fergus Bandylegs was a dapper, fast-talking elf with a chestnut beard which he scented with lavender. As Vice-President of Santa Enterprises, Inc., he was in charge of financing the entire Toyworks operation by arranging for Santa to appear in advertising campaigns, by collecting royalties on the use of the jolly old man's name, and by leasing Santa suits to department stores.

Bandylegs ordered a drink for the Security Chief. Their friendship went back to Rory Bigtoes' jacksmith days when Bandylegs had been a master sledwright. 'These are topsy-turvy times, Rory,' said Bandylegs. 'First there's that bomb and now Santa's turned down the Jolly Roger cigarette account. For years now they've had this ad campaign showing Santa slipping a carton of Jolly Rogers into Christmas stockings. But not any more. "Smoking may be hazardous to your health," says Santa.'

'Santa knows best,' said Bigtoes.

'Granted,' said Bandylegs. 'But counting television residuals, that's a cool two million sugar plums thrown out the window.' (At the current rate of exchange there are 4.27 sugar plums to the U.S. dollar.) 'Hardnoggin's already on my back to make up the loss. Nothing must interfere with his grand plan for automating the Toyworks. So it's off to Madison Avenue again. Sure I'll stay at the Plaza and eat at the Chambord, but I'll still get homesick.'

The Vice-President smiled sadly. 'Do you know what I used to do? There's this guy who stands outside Grand Central Station selling those little mechanical men you wind up and they march around. I used to march around with them. It made me feel better somehow. But now they remind me of Hardnoggin. He's a machine, Rory, and he wants to make all of us into machines.'

'What about the bomb?' asked Bigtoes.

Bandylegs shrugged. 'Acme Toy, I suppose.'

Bigtoes shook his head. Acme Toy hadn't slipped an elf spy into the North Pole for months. 'What about Crouchback?'

'No,' said Bandylegs firmly. 'I'll level with you, Rory. I had a get-together with Crouchback just last week. He wanted to get my thoughts on the quality-versus-quantity question and on the future of the Toyworks. Maybe I'm wrong, but I got the impression that a top-level shake-up is in the works with Crouchback slated to become the new Director General. In any event I found him a very perceptive and understanding elf.'

Bandylegs smiled and went on, 'Darby Shortribs was there, prattling on against dolls. As I left, Crouchback shook my hand and whispered, "Every movement needs its lunatic fringe, Bandylegs. Shortribs is ours".' Bandylegs lowered his voice. 'I'm tired of the grown-up ratrace, Rory. I want to get back to the sled shed and make Blue Streaks and High Flyers again. I'll never get there with Hardnoggin and his modern ideas at the helm.'

Bigtoes pulled at his beard. It was common knowledge that Crouchback had an elf spy on the Board. The reports on the meetings in *The Midnight Elf* were just too complete. Was it his friend Bandylegs? But would Bandylegs try to kill Santa?

That brought Bigtoes back to Hardnoggin again. But cautiously. As Security Chief, Bigtoes had to be objective. Yet he yearned to prove Hardnoggin the villain. This, as he knew, was because of the beautiful Carlotta Peachfuzz, beloved by children all around the world. As the voice of the Peachy Pippin Doll, Carlotta was the most envied female at the North Pole, next to Mrs Santa. Girl elves followed her glamorous exploits in the press. Male elves had Peachy Pippin Dolls propped beside their beds so they could fall asleep with Carlotta's sultry voice saying: 'Hello, I'm your talking Peachy Pippin Doll. I love you. I love you. I love you . . .'

But once it had just been Rory and Carlotta, Carlotta and Rory—until the day Bigtoes had introduced her to Hardnoggin. 'You have a beautiful voice, Miss Peachfuzz,' the Director General had said. 'Have you ever considered being in the talkies?' So Carlotta had dropped Bigtoes for Hardnoggin and risen to stardom in the talking-doll industry. But her liaison with Director General Hardnoggin had become so notorious that a dutiful Santa—with Mrs Santa present—had had to read the riot act about executive hanky-panky. Hardnoggin had broken off the relationship. Disgruntled, Carlotta had become active with SHAFT, only to leave after a violent argument with Shortribs over his anti-doll position.

Today Bigtoes couldn't care less about Carlotta. But he still had that old score to settle with the Director General.

Leaving the fashionable section behind, Bigtoes turned down Apple Alley, a residential corridor of modest, old-fashioned houses with thatched roofs and carved beams. Here the mushrooms were in full bloom—the stropharia, inocybe, and chanterelle—dotting the corridor with indigo, vermilion, and many yellows. Elf householders were out troweling in their gardens. Elf wives gossiped over hedges of gypsy pholiota. Somewhere an old elf was singing one of the ancient work songs, accompanying himself on a concertina. Until Director General Hardnoggin discovered that it slowed down production, the elves had always sung while they worked, beating out the time with their hammers; now the foremen passed out song sheets and led them in song twice a day. But it wasn't the same thing.

Elf gardeners looked up, took their pipes from their mouths, and watched Bigtoes pass. They regarded all front-office people with suspicion—even this big elf with the candy-stripe rosette of the Order of Santa, First Class, in his buttonhole.

Bigtoes had won the decoration many years ago when he was a young Security elf, still wet behind his pointed ears. Somehow on that fateful day, Billy Roy Scoggins, President of Acme Toy, had found the secret entrance to the North Pole and appeared suddenly in parka and snowshoes, demanding to see Santa Claus. Santa arrived, jolly and smiling, surrounded by Bigtoes and the other Security elves. Scoggins announced he had a proposition 'from one hard-headed businessman to another.'

Pointing out the foolishness of competition, the intruder had offered Santa a king's ransom to come in with Acme Toy. 'Ho, ho, ho,' boomed Santa with jovial firmness, 'that isn't Santa's way.' Scoggins—perhaps it was the 'ho, ho, ho' that did it—turned purple and threw a punch that floored the jolly old man. Security sprang into action.

Four elves had died as Scoggins flayed at them, a snowshoe in one hand and a rolled up copy of *The Wall Street Journal* in the other. But Bigtoes had crawled up the outside of Scoggins' pantleg. It had taken him twelve karate chops to break the intruder's kneecap and send him crashing to the ground like a stricken tree. To this day the President of Acme Toy walks with a cane and curses Rory Bigtoes whenever it rains.

As Bigtoes passed a tavern—The Bowling Green, with a huge horse mushroom shading the door—someone inside banged down a thimble-mug and shouted the famous elf toast: 'My Santa, right or wrong! May he always be right, but right or wrong, my Santa!' Bigtoes sighed. Life should be so simple for elves. They all loved Santa—what did it matter that he used blueing when he washed his beard, or liked to sleep late, or hit the martinis a bit too hard—and they all wanted to do what was best for good little girls and boys. But here the agreement ended. Here the split between Hardnoggin and Crouchback—between the Establishment and the revolutionary—took over.

Beyond the tavern was a crossroads, the left corridor leading to the immense storage areas for completed toys, the right corridor to The Underwood. Bigtoes continued straight and was soon entering that intersection of corridors called Pumpkin Corners, the North Pole's bohemian quarter. Here, until his disappearance, the SHAFT leader Crouchback had lived with relative impunity, protected by the inhabitants. For this was SHAFT country. A special edition of *The Midnight Elf* was already on the streets denying that SHAFT was involved in the assassination attempt on Santa. A love-bead vendor, his beard tied in a sheepshank, had *Hardnoggin Is a Dwarf* written across the side of his pushcart. *Make love, not plastic* declared the wall of The Electric Carrot, a popular discotheque and hippie hangout.

The Electric Carrot was crowded with elves dancing the latest craze, the Scalywag. Until recently, dancing hadn't been popular with elves. They kept stepping on their beards. The hippie knots effectively eliminated that stumbling block.

Buck Withers, leader of the Hippie Elves for Peace, was sitting in a corner wearing a *Santa Is Love* button. Bigtoes had once dropped a first-offense drug charge against Withers and three other elves caught nibbling on morning-glory seeds. 'Where's Crouchback, Buck?' said Bigtoes.

'Like who's asking?' said Withers. 'The head of Hardnoggin's Gestapo?'

'A friend,' said Bigtoes.

'Friend, like when the news broke about Shortribs, he says "I'm next, Buck." Better fled than dead, and he split for parts unknown.'

'It looks bad, Buck.'

'Listen, friend,' said Withers, 'SHAFT's the wave of the future. Like Santa's already come over to our side on the disarmament thing. What do we need with bombs? That's a bad scene, friend. Violence isn't SHAFT's bag.'

As Bigtoes left The Electric Carrot a voice said, 'I wonder, my dear sir, if you could help an unfortunate elf.' Bigtoes turned to find a tattered derelict in a filthy button-down shirt and greasy gray-flannel suit. His beard was matted with twigs and straw.

'Hello, Baldwin,' said Bigtoes. Baldwin Redpate had once been the head of Santa's Shipping Department. Then came the Slugger Nolan Official Baseball Mitt Scandal. The mitt had been a big item one year, much requested in letters to Santa. Through some gigantic snafu in Shipping, thousands of inflatable rubber ducks had been sent out instead. For months afterward, Santa received letters from indignant little boys, and though each one cut him like a knife he never reproached Redpate. But Redpate knew he had failed Santa. He brooded, had attacks of silent crying and finally took to drink, falling so much under the spell of bee wine that Hardnoggin had to insist he resign.

'Rory, you're just the elf I'm looking for,' said Redpate. 'Have you ever seen an elf skulking? Well, I have.'

Bigtoes was interested. Elves were straightforward creatures. They didn't skulk.

'Last night I woke up in a cold sweat and saw strange things, Rory,' said Redpate. 'Comings and goings, lights, skulking.' Large tears rolled down Redpate's cheeks. 'You see, I get these nightmares, Rory. Thousands of inflatable rubber ducks come marching across my body and their eyes are Santa's eyes when someone's let him down.' He leaned toward Bigtoes confidentially. 'I may be a washout. Occasionally I may even drink too much. But I don't skulk!' Redpate began to cry again.

His tears looked endless. Bigtoes was due at the Sticks-and-Stones session. He slipped Redpate ten sugar plums. 'Got to go, Baldwin.'

Redpate dabbed at the tears with the dusty end of his beard. 'When you see Santa, ask him to think kindly of old Baldy Redpate,' he sniffed and headed straight for The Good Gray Goose, the tavern across the street—making a beeline for the bee wine, as the elves would say. But then he turned. 'Strange goings-on,' he called. 'Storeroom Number 14, Unit 24, Row 58. Skulking.'

'Hardnoggin's phone call was from Carlotta Peachfuzz,' said Charity, looking lovelier than ever. 'The switchboard operator is a big Carlotta fan. She fainted when she recognized her voice. The thrill was just too much.'

Interesting. In spite of Santa's orders, were Carlotta and Hardnoggin back together on the sly? If so, had they conspired on the bomb attempt? Or had it really been Carlotta's voice? Carlotta Peachfuzz impersonations were a dime a dozen.

'Get me the switchboard operator,' said Bigtoes and returned to stuffing Sticks-and-Stones reports into his briefcase.

'No luck,' said Charity, putting down the phone. 'She just took another call and fainted again.'

Vice-President Bandylegs looked quite pleased with himself and threw Bigtoes a wink. 'Don't be surprised when I cut out of Sticks-and-Stones early, Rory,' he smiled. 'An affair of the heart. All of a sudden the old Bandylegs charm has come through again.' He nodded down the hall at Hardnoggin, waiting impatiently at the Projection Room door. 'When the cat's away, the mice will play.'

The Projection Room was built like a movie theater. 'Come over here beside Santa, Rory, my boy,' boomed the jolly old man. So Bigtoes scrambled up into a tiny seat hooked over the back of the seat on Santa's left. On Bigtoes' left sat Traffic Manager Brassbottom, Vice-President Bandylegs, and Director General Hardnoggin. In this way Mrs Santa, at the portable bar against the wall, could send Santa's martinis to him down an assembly line of elves.

Confident that no one would dare to try anything with Santa's Security Chief present, Bigtoes listened to the Traffic Manager, a red-lipped elf with a straw-colored beard, talk enthusiastically about the television coverage planned for Santa's trip. This year, live and in color via satellite, the North Pole would see Santa's arrival at each stop on his journey. Santa's first martini was passed from Hardnoggin to Bandylegs to Brassbottom to Bigtoes. The Security Chief grasped the stem of the glass in both hands and, avoiding the heady gin fumes as best he could, passed it to Santa.

'All right,' said Santa, taking his first sip, 'let's roll 'em, starting with the worst.'

The lights dimmed. A film appeared on the screen. 'Waldo Rogers, age five,' said Bigtoes. 'Mistreatment of pets, eight demerits.' (The film showed a smirking little boy pulling a cat's tail.) 'Not coming when he's called, ten demerits.' (The film showed Waldo's mother at the screen door, shouting.) 'Also, as an indication of his general bad behavior, he gets his mother to buy Sugar Gizmos but he won't eat them.

He just wants the box-tops.' (The camera panned a pantry shelf crowded with opened Sugar Gizmo boxes.) The elves clucked disapprovingly.

'Waldo Rogers certainly isn't Santa's idea of a nice little boy,' said Santa. 'What do you think, Mother?' Mrs Santa agreed.

'Sticks-and-Stones then?' asked Hardnoggin hopefully.

But the jolly old man hesitated. 'Santa always likes to check the list twice before deciding,' he said.

Hardnoggin groaned. Santa was always bollixing up his production schedules by going easy on bad little girls and boys.

A new film began. 'Next on the list,' said Bigtoes, 'is Nancy Ruth Ashley, age four and a half. . .'

Two hours and seven martinis later, Santa's jolly laughter and Mrs Santa's giggles filled the room. 'She's a little dickens, that one,' chuckled Santa as they watched a six-year-old fill her father's custom-made shoes with molasses, 'but Santa will find a little something for her.' Hardnoggin groaned. That was the end of the list and so far no one had been given Sticks-and-Stones. They rolled the film on Waldo Rogers again. 'Santa understands some cats like having their tails pulled,' chuckled Santa as he drained his glass. 'And what the heck are Sugar Gizmos?'

Bandylegs, who had just excused himself from the meeting, paused on his way up the aisle. 'They're a delicious blend of toasted oats and corn,' he shouted, 'with an energy-packed coating of sparkling sugar. As a matter of fact, Santa, the Gizmo people are thinking of featuring you in their new advertising campaign. It would be a great selling point if I could say that Santa had given a little boy Sticks-and-Stones because he wouldn't eat his Sugar Gizmos.'

'Here now, Fergy,' said the jolly old man, 'you know that isn't Santa's way.'

Bandylegs left, muttering to himself.

'Santa,' protested Hardnoggin as the jolly old man passed his glass down the line for a refill, 'let's be realistic. If we can't draw the line at Waldo Rogers, where can we?'

Santa reflected for a moment. 'Suppose Santa let you make the decision, Garth, my boy. What would little Waldo Rogers find in his stocking on Christmas morning?'

Hardnoggin hesitated. Then he said, 'Sticks-and-Stones.'

Santa looked disappointed. 'So be it,' he said.

The lights dimmed again as they continued their review of the list. Santa's eighth martini came down the line from elf to elf. As Bigtoes passed it to Santa, the fumes caught him—the smell of gin and something else. Bitter almonds. He struck the glass from Santa's hand.

Silent and dimly lit, Storeroom Number 14 seemed an immense, dull suburb of split-level, ranch-type Dick and Jane Doll doll-houses. Bigtoes stepped into the papier-mâché shrubbery fronting Unit 24, Row 58 as an elf watchman on a bicycle pedaled by singing 'Colossal Carlotta,' a current hit song. Bigtoes hoped he hadn't made a mistake by refraining from picking Hardnoggin up.

Bandylegs had left before the cyanide was put in the glass. Mrs Santa, of course, was above suspicion. So that left Director General Hardnoggin and Traffic Manager Brassbottom. But why would Brassbottom first save Santa from the bomb only to poison him later? So that left Hardnoggin.

Bigtoes had been eager to act on this logic, perhaps too eager. He wanted no one to say that Santa's Security Chief had let personal feelings color his judgment. Bigtoes would be fair.

Hardnoggin had insisted that Crouchback was the villain. All right, he would bring Crouchback in for questioning. After all, Santa was now safe, napping under a heavy guard in preparation for his all-night trip. Hardnoggin—if *he* was the villain—could do him no harm for the present.

As Bigtoes crept up the fabric lawn on all fours, the front door of the dollhouse opened and a shadowy figure came down the walk. It paused at the street, looked this way and that, then disappeared into the darkness. Redpate had been right about the skulking. But it wasn't Crouchback—Bigtoes was sure of that.

The Security Chief climbed in through a dining-room window. In the living room were three elves, one on the couch, one in an easy chair, and, behind the bar, Dirk Crouchback, a distinguished-looking elf with a salt-and-pepper beard and graying temples. The leader of SHAFT poured himself a drink and turned. 'Welcome to my little ménage-à-trois, Rory Bigtoes,' he said with a surprised smile. The two other elves turned out to be Dick and Jane dolls.

'I'm taking you in, Crouchback,' said the Security Chief.

The revolutionary came out from behind the bar pushing a .55mm. howitzer (1/32 scale) with his foot. 'I'm sorry about this,' he said. 'As you know we are opposed to the use of violence. But I'd rather not fall into Hardnoggin's hands just now. Sit over there by Jane.' Bigtoes obeyed. At that short range the howitzer's plastic shell could be fatal to an elf.

Crouchback sat down on the arm of Dick's easy chair. 'Yes,' he said, 'Hardnoggin's days are numbered. But as the incidents of last night and today illustrate, the Old Order dies hard. I'd rather not be one of its victims.'

Crouchback paused and took a drink. 'Look at this room, Bigtoes. This is Hardnoggin's world. Wall-to-wall carpeting. Breakfast nooks. Cheap materials. Shoddy workmanship.' He picked up an end table and dropped it on the floor. Two of the legs broke. 'Plastic,' said Crouchback contemptuously, flinging the table through the plastic television set. 'It's the whole middle-class, bourgeois, suburban scene.' Crouchback put the heel of his hand on Dick's jaw and pushed the doll over. 'Is this vapid plastic nonentity the kind of grownup we want little boys and girls to become?'

'No,' said Bigtoes. 'But what's your alternative?'

'Close down the Toyworks for a few years,' said Crouchback earnestly. 'Relearn our ancient heritage of handcrafted toys. We owe it to millions of little boys and girls as yet unborn!'

'All very idealistic,' said Bigtoes, 'but—'

'Practical, Bigtoes. And down to earth,' said the SHAFT leader, tapping his head. 'The plan's all here.'

'But what about Acme Toy?' protested Bigtoes. 'The rich kids would still get presents and the poor kids wouldn't.'

Crouchback smiled. 'I can't go into the details now. But my plan includes the elimination of Acme Toy.'

'Suppose you could,' said Bigtoes. 'We still couldn't handcraft enough toys to keep pace with the population explosion.'

'Not at first,' said Crouchback. 'But suppose population growth was not allowed to exceed our rate of toy production?' He tapped his head again.

'But good grief,' said Bigtoes, 'closing down the Toyworks means millions of children with empty stockings on Christmas. Who could be that cruel?'

'Cruel?' exclaimed Crouchback. 'Bigtoes, do you know how a grownup cooks a live lobster? Some drop it into boiling water. But others say, "How cruel!" They drop it in cold water and then bring the water to a boil slowly. No, Bigtoes, we have to bite the bullet. Granted there'll be no Christmas toys for a few years. But we'd fill children's stockings with literature explaining what's going on and with discussion-group outlines so they can get together and talk up the importance of sacrificing their Christmas toys today so the children of the future can have quality handcrafted toys. They'll understand.'

Before Bigtoes could protest again, Crouchback got to his feet. 'Now that I've given you some food for thought I have to go,' he said. 'That closet should hold you until I make my escape.'

Bigtoes was in the closet for more than an hour. The door proved stronger than he had expected. Then he remembered Hardnoggin's cardboard interior walls and karate-chopped his way through the back of the closet and out into the kitchen.

Security headquarters was a flurry of excitement as Bigtoes strode in the door. 'They just caught Hardnoggin trying to put a bomb on Santa's sleigh,' said Charity, her voice shaking.

Bigtoes passed through to the Interrogation Room where Hardnoggin, gray and haggard, sat with his wrists between his knees. The Security elves hadn't handled him gently. One eye was swollen, his beard was in disarray, and there was a dent in his megaphone. 'It was a Christmas present for that little beast, Waldo Rogers,' shouted Hardnoggin.

'A bomb?' said Bigtoes.

'It was supposed to be a little fire engine,' shouted the Director General, 'with a bell that goes clang-clang!' Hardnoggin struggled to control himself. 'I just couldn't be responsible for that little monster finding nothing in his stocking but sticks-and-stones. But a busy man hasn't time for last-minute shopping. I got a—a friend to pick something out for me.'

'Who?' said Bigtoes.

Hardnoggin hung his head. 'I demand to be taken to Santa Claus,' he said. But Santa, under guard, had already left his apartment for the formal departure ceremony.

Bigtoes ordered Hardnoggin detained and hurried to meet Santa at the elevator. He would have enjoyed shouting up at the jolly old man that Hardnoggin was the culprit. But of course that just didn't hold water. Hardnoggin was too smart to believe he could just walk up and put a bomb on Santa's sleigh. Or—now that Bigtoes thought about it—to finger himself so obviously by waiting until Bandylegs had left the Sticks-and-Stones session before poisoning Santa's glass.

The villain now seemed to be the beautiful and glamorous Carlotta Peachfuzz. Here's the way it figured: Carlotta phones Hardnoggin just before the bomb goes off in the Board Room, thus making him a prime suspect; Carlotta makes a rendezvous with Bandylegs that causes him to leave Sticks-and-Stones, thus again making Hardnoggin Suspect Number One; then when

THE BOSS

Bigtoes fails to pick up the Director General, Carlotta talks him into giving little Waldo Rogers a present that turns out to be a bomb. Her object? To frame Hardnoggin for the murder or attempted murder of Santa. Her elf spy? Traffic Manager Brassbottom. It all worked out—or seemed to. . .

Bigtoes met Santa at the elevator surrounded by a dozen Security elves. The jolly old eyes were bloodshot, his smile slightly strained. 'Easy does it, Billy,' said Santa to Billy Brisket, the Security elf at the elevator controls. 'Santa's a bit hungover.'

Bigtoes moved to the rear of the elevator. So it was Brassbottom who had planted the bomb and then deliberately taken Santa out of the room. So it was Brassbottom who had poisoned the martini with cyanide, knowing that Bigtoes would detect the smell. And it was Carlotta who had gift-wrapped the bomb. All to frame Hardnoggin. And yet. . . Bigtoes sighed at his own confusion. And yet a dying Shortribs had said that someone was going to kill Santa.

As the elevator eased up into the interior of the Polar icecap, Bigtoes focused his mind on Shortribs. Suppose the dead elf had stumbled on your well-laid plan to kill Santa. Suppose you botched Shortribs' murder and therefore knew that Security had been alerted. What would you do? Stage three fake attempts on Santa's life to provide Security with a culprit, hoping to get Security to drop its guard? Possibly. But the bomb in the Board Room could have killed Santa. Why not just do it that way?

The elevator reached the surface and the first floor of the Control Tower building which was ingeniously camouflaged as an icy crag. But suppose, thought Bigtoes, it was important that you kill Santa in a certain way—say, with half the North Pole looking on?

More Security elves were waiting when the elevator doors opened. Bigtoes moved quickly among them, urging the utmost vigilance. Then Santa and his party stepped out onto the frozen runway to be greeted by thousands of cheering elves. Hippie elves from Pumpkin Corners, green-collar elves from the Toyworks, young elves and old had all gathered there to wish the jolly old man godspeed.

Santa's smile broadened and he waved to the crowd. Then everybody stood at attention and doffed their hats as the massed bands of the Mushroom Fanciers Association, Wade Snoot conducting, broke into 'Santa Claus Is Coming to Town.' When the music reached its stirring conclusion, Santa, escorted by a flying wedge of Security elves, made his way through the exuberant crowd and toward his sleigh.

Bigtoes' eyes kept darting everywhere, searching for a happy face that might mask a homicidal intent. His heart almost stopped when Santa paused to accept a bouquet from an elf child who stuttered through a tribute in verse to the jolly old man. It almost stopped again when Santa leaned over the Security cordon to speak to some elf in the crowd. A pat on the head from Santa and even Roger Chinwhiskers, leader of the Sons and Daughters of the Good Old Days, grinned and admitted that perhaps the world wasn't going to hell in a handbasket. A kind word from Santa and Baldwin Redpate tearfully announced—as he did every year at that time—that he was off the bee wine for good.

After what seemed an eternity to Bigtoes, they reached the sleigh. Santa got on board, gave one last wave to the crowd, and called to his eight tiny reindeer, one by one, by name. The reindeer leaned against the harness and the sleigh, with Security elves trotting alongside, and slid forward on the ice. Then four of the reindeer were air-borne. Then the other four. At last the sleigh itself left the ground. Santa gained altitude, circled the runway once, and was gone. But they heard him exclaim, ere he drove out of sight: ''Happy Christmas to all, and to all a good night!'

The crowd dispersed quickly. Only Bigtoes remained on the wind-swept runway. He walked back and forth, head down, kicking at the snow. Santa's departure had gone off without a hitch. Had the Security Chief been wrong about the frame-up? Had Hardnoggin been trying to kill Santa after all? Bigtoes went over the three attempts again. The bomb in the Board Room. The poison. The bomb on the sleigh.

Suddenly Bigtoes broke into a run.

He had remembered Brassbottom's pretext for taking Santa into the Map Room.

Taking the steps three at a time, Bigtoes burst into the Control Room. Crouchback was standing over the remains of the radio equipment with a monkey wrench in his hand. 'Too late, Bigtoes,' he said triumphantly. 'Santa's as good as dead.'

Bigtoes grabbed the phone and ordered the operator to put through an emergency call to the Strategic Air Command in Denver, Colorado. But the telephone cable had been cut. 'Baby Polar bears like to teethe on it,' said the operator.

Santa Claus was doomed. There was no way to call him back or to warn the Americans.

Crouchback smiled. 'In eleven minutes Santa will pass over the DEW Line. But at the wrong place, thanks to Traffic Manager Brassbottom. The American ground-to-air missiles will make short work of him.'

'But why?' demanded Bigtoes.

'Nothing destroys a dissident movement like a modest success or two,' said Crouchback. 'Ever since Santa came out for unilateral disarmament, I've felt SHAFT coming apart in my hands. So I had to act. I've nothing against Santa personally, borgeois sentimentalist that he is. But his death will be a great step forward in our task of forming better children for a better world. What do you think will happen when Santa is shot down by American missiles?'

Bigtoes shaded his eyes. His voice was thick with emotion. 'Every good little boy and girl in the world will be up in arms. A Children's Crusade against the United States.'

'And with the Americans disposed of, what nation will become the dominant force in the world?' said Crouchback.

'So that's it—you're a Marxist-Leninist elf!' shouted Bigtoes.

'No!' said Crouchback sharply. 'But I'll use the Russians to achieve a better world. Who else could eliminate Acme Toy? Who else could limit world population to our rate of toy production? And they have agreed to that in writing, Bigtoes. Oh, I know the Russians are grownups too and just as corrupt as the rest of the grownups. But once the kids have had the plastic flushed out of their systems and are back on quality hand-crafted toys, I, Dirk Crouchback, the New Santa Claus, with the beautiful and beloved Carlotta Peachfuzz at my side as the New Mrs. Santa, will handle the Russians.'

'What about Brassbottom?' asked Bigtoes contemptuously.

'Brassbottom will be Assistant New Santa,' said Crouchback quickly, annoyed at the interruption. 'Yes,' he continued, 'the New Santa Claus will speak to the children of the world and tell them one thing: Don't trust anyone over thirty inches tall. And that will be the dawning of a new era full of happy laughing children, where grownups will be irrelevant and just wither away!'

'You're mad, Crouchback. I'm taking you in,' said Bigtoes.

'I'll offer no resistance,' said Crouchback. 'But five minutes after Santa fails to appear at his first pit stop, a special edition of *The Midnight Elf* will hit the streets announcing that he has been the victim of a conspiracy between Hardnoggin and the CIA. The same mob of angry elves that breaks into Security headquarters to tear Hardnoggin limb from limb will also free Dirk Crouchback and proclaim him their new leader. I've laid the groundwork well. A knowing smile here, an innuendo there, and now many elves inside SHAFT and out believe that on his return Santa intended to make me Director General.'

Crouchback smiled. 'Ironically enough, I'd never have learned to be so devious if you Security people hadn't fouled up your own plans and assigned me to a refrigerator in the Russian Embassy in Ottawa. Ever since they found a CIA listening device in their smoked sturgeon, the Russians had been keeping a sharp eye open. They nabbed me almost at once and flew me to Moscow in a diplomatic pouch. When they thought they had me brainwashed, they trained me in deviousness and other grownup revolutionary techniques. They thought they could use me, Bigtoes. But Dirk Crouchback is going to use them!'

Bigtoes wasn't listening. Crouchback had just given him an idea—one chance in a thousand of saving Santa. He dived for the phone.

'We're in luck,' said Charity, handing Bigtoes a file. 'His name is Colin Tanglefoot, a stuffer in the Teddy Bear Section. Sentenced to a year in the cooler for setting another stuffer's beard on fire. Assigned to a refrigerator in the DEW Line station at Moose Landing. Sparks has got him on the intercom.'

Bigtoes took the microphone. 'Tanglefoot, this is Bigtoes,' he said.

'Big deal,' said a grumpy voice with a head cold.

'Listen, Tanglefoot,' said Bigtoes, 'in less than seven minutes Santa will be flying right over where you are. Warn the grownups not to shoot him down.'

'Tough,' said Tanglefoot petulantly. 'You know, old Santa gave yours truly a pretty raw deal.'

'Six minutes, Tanglefoot.'

'Listen,' said Tanglefoot. 'Old Valentine Woody is ho-ho-hoing around with that "jollier than thou" attitude of his, see? So as a joke I tamp my pipe with the tip of his beard. It went up like a Christmas tree.'

'Tanglefoot—'

'Yours truly threw the bucket of water that saved his life,' said Tanglefoot. 'I should have got a medal.'

'You'll get your medal!' shouted Bigtoes. 'Just save Santa.'

Tanglefoot sneezed four times. 'Okay,' he said at last. 'Do or die for Santa. I know the guy on duty—Myron Smith. He's always in here raiding the cold cuts. But he's not the kind that would believe a six-inch elf with a head cold.'

'Let me talk to him then,' said Bigtoes. 'But move—you've got only four minutes.'

Tanglefoot signed off. Would the tiny elf win his race against the clock and avoid the fate of most elves who revealed themselves to grownups—being flattened with the first object that came to hand? And if he did, what would Bigtoes say to Smith? Grownups—suspicious, short of imagination, afraid—grownups were difficult enough to reason with under ideal circumstances. But what could you say to a grownup with his head stuck in a refrigerator?

An enormous squawk came out of the intercom, toppling Sparks over backward in his chair. 'Hello there, Myron,' said Bigtoes as calmly as he could. 'My name is Rory Bigtoes. I'm one of Santa's little helpers.'

Silence. The hostile silence of a grownup thinking. 'Yeah? Yeah?' said Smith at last. 'How do I know this isn't some Commie trick? You bug our icebox, you plant a little pinko squirt to feed me some garbage about Santa coming over and then, whammo, you slip the big one by us, nuclear warhead and all, winging its way into Heartland, U.S.A.'

'Myron,' pleaded Bigtoes, 'we're talking about Santa Claus, the one who always brought you and the other good little boys and girls toys at Christmas.'

'What's he done for me lately?' said Smith unpleasantly. 'And hey! I wrote him once asking for a Slugger Nolan Official Baseball Mitt. Do you know what I got?'

'An inflatable rubber duck,' said Bigtoes quickly.

Silence. The profound silence of a thunderstruck grownup. Smith's voice had an amazed belief in it. 'Yeah,' he said. 'Yeah.'

Pit Stop Number One. A December cornfield in Iowa blazing with landing lights. As thousands of elfin eyes watched on their television screens, crews of elves in coveralls changed the runners on Santa's sleigh, packed fresh toys aboard, and chipped the ice from the reindeer antlers. The camera panned to one side where Santa stood out of the wind, sipping on a hot buttered rum. As the camera dollied in on him, the jolly old man, his beard and eyebrows caked with frost, his cheeks as red as apples, broke into a ho-ho-ho and raised his glass in a toast.

Sitting before the television at Security headquarters, a smiling Director General Hardnoggin raised his thimble-mug of ale. 'My Santa, right or wrong,' he said.

Security Chief Bigtoes raised his glass. He wanted to think of a new toast. Crouchback was under guard and Carlotta and Brassbottom had fled to the Underwood. But he wanted to remind the Director General that SHAFT and the desire for something better still remained. Was automation the answer? Would machines finally free the elves to handcraft toys again? Bigtoes didn't know. He did know that times were changing. They would never be the same. He raised his glass, but the right words escaped him and he missed his turn.

Charity Nosegay raised her glass. 'Yes, Virginia,' she said, using the popular abbreviation for another elf toast; 'yes, Virginia, there is a Santa Claus.'

Hardnoggin turned and looked at her with a smile. 'You have a beautiful voice, Miss Nosegay,' he said. 'Have you ever considered being in the talkies?'

— Afterword —

Biggles's Apple Snowballs

AFTER all that felony and foul play, murder, mayhem and malfeasance, let us end with—food. And why not? It's Christmas, after all.

Prowl through the pages of a hundred years' worth of detective novels and short stories and there ought to be something seasonal to tempt the palate. Nero Wolfe, now—he was a gourmet; anything from him? And Robert Parker's Spenser has a habit of whipping together tasty little snacks when the pace slackens. But nothing springs immediately to mind. The trouble is, at Christmas (as we've seen) dire things sometimes happen even in the best-regulated circles, and food tends to be given a low priority at times of crisis.

In Cyril Hare's *An English Murder* Christmas Dinner at Warbeck Hall was a bad-tempered affair which ended with cyanide in the champagne. And festive fare isn't mentioned at all by the house-party guests in *Hercule Poirot's Christmas.* Hardly surprising, I suppose; the host had had his throat cut on Christmas Eve. Mind you, for year after year Sexton Blake (the detective who out-Holmesed Holmes in almost every particular) cleverly managed it so that he sat down to Christmas dinner only after whatever knotty problem he was presented with had been well and truly disentangled, although—after a strenuous bout with Zenith the Albino, say, or the Red Vulture, or the Crime Minister—he was singularly unadventurous in the food line: either goose or turkey with all the trimmings, a flaming plum pudding, and trifle to follow.

The gorge rises. No, something simple is required. Better, something simple yet oddball. And better still, something from an offbeat source.

Luckily, I stumbled across a recipe not too long ago—by someone who certainly wrote mystery stories but who's far better known in quite another field.

Captain W. E. Johns (1893-1968) wasn't really a captain but a Flying-Officer, a touch lower in the ranking system. But one can forgive a great storyteller such mild deceit. And Johns was a *great* storyteller, make no mistake about it, despite nowadays being dumped on from a great height by trendy sociologists and librarians who should know better as a racist, sexist, warmongering jingoist. Acutally, he was a humanist and anti-imperialist whose view was that most of the world's woes may be placed squarely at the door of the land-grabbing white man. He vigorously campaigned for sexual equality, was an anti-appeaser, and his message to his readers, in book after book, was: Put not your trust in politicians, generals, those in authority; inevitably, they will betray you. All in all, not a bad philosophy.

Johns was a machine-gunner at Gallipoli and there saw enough carnage to last him nine lifetimes; he transferred to the Royal Flying Corps, was shot down in 1918, and then made a nuisance of himself escaping from various POW camps. His first book *Mossyface,* an adult thriller published under a pseudonym, was issued in the exceedingly scarce *Weekly Telegraph Novels* series in the early 1920s (later reprinted by Mellifont, a cheap paperback firm, in 1932). After that Johns wrote more adult thrillers then concentrated on turning out two or three books a year featuring his flying-ace hero James Bigglesworth. He wrote over a hundred Biggles novels and short-story collections; over 160 books in all, including thrillers, detective novels, buccaneering yarns, and technical flying manuals.

Johns was an excellent journalist and a very fine, and courageous, editor; during the 1930s he was at the helm of two of the most popular flying magazines of the day, until the government had him kicked out of the editor's chair because of his vitriolic attacks on them over the betrayal of Czechoslovakia at Munich and his muscular anti-appeasement line.

He was also a keen gardener who for ten years (from 1934 to 1944) wrote a delightful column for Theo. A. Stephens' splendid little magazine *My Garden.* This took the form of a monthly diary describing the trials and tribulations of the amateur gardener.

Christmas of 1939 was a particularly vexing period. A neighbour was getting uppity about one of Johns's noble Scotch firs, and he was also having problems with the Customs, who had impounded a parcel of bulbs from California. There were shortages everywhere, his handyman had joined the army, petty rules and regulations were doing bad things to his blood pressure. Still, the gloom was not entirely unrelieved:

There is something extremely satisfying about harvesting one's own produce. This year, for the simple reason that there was no one else to do it, I have had to dry and store the root crops and the fruit, so I dole them out to the household with a sparing hand. I suppose it is a deep-rooted instinct that makes people always pick the big ones, whether it be peaches or potatoes.

Which reminds me, here is a recipe for a war-time winter sweet which, apart from being cheap, has the advantage of requiring neither sugar nor cream; it is a good way of using up windfall apples. I've often made it, so can recommend it.

Weigh 1½ lbs of quick cooking apples—the sort that soon go to a white pulp. Peel, core and quarter (small quarters). Place in saucepan with *just* enough water to prevent burning, and the strained juice of half a lemon. Cook to a pulp. Turn into a large basin and beat to make sure that there are no lumps. Well stir in one small tin of *sweetened* condensed milk with one whisked egg. Return to saucepan, and cook over low heat, stirring, for a few minutes—until it begins to thicken. Turn into glass goblets, and serve cold. Serves six.

To be honest, Johns didn't call his recipe 'Biggles' Apple Snowballs', I did. He called it 'Apple Snow', but what's in a name? As W. C. Fields once nearly said, 'It'll taste just as well.'

Indeed. Certainly tastier than cold Christmas pud for the umpteenth time. And I can vouch for that.

Acknowledgements

Every effort has been made to contact the owners of all the copyrighted stories, and grateful thanks are extended to the copyright holders for allowing them to be reprinted. If any necessary acknowledgements have been omitted, the editor and publisher hope that the copyright holders concerned will accept their apologies in advance.

'A Problem in White' by Nicholas Blake/C. Day Lewis. Copyright © 1949. Reprinted by permission of A.D. Peters & Co. Ltd.

'Detective's Day Off' by John Dickson Carr. Copyright © 1957. Reprinted by permission of David Higham Associates Ltd. and Harold Ober Associates Inc.

'The Three Travellers' by Edward D. Hoch. Copyright © 1976. Reprinted by permission of the author.

'Murder in Store' by Peter Lovesey. Copyright © 1985. Reprinted by permission of John Farquharson Ltd.

'Waxworks' by Ethel Lina White. Copyright © 1930. Reprinted by permission of Laurence Pollinger Ltd on behalf of the Estate of Ethel Lina White.

'Serenade to a Killer' by Joseph Commings. Copyright © 1957. Reprinted by permission of the author.

'No Room at the Inn' by Bill Pronzini. Copyright © 1988.

'Santa-San Solves It' by James Melville. Copyright © 1988.

'Sister Bessie' by Cyril Hare. Copyright © 1949, 1959. Reprinted by permission of A.P. Watt Ltd on behalf of the Revd C.P. Gordon Clark.

'Murder Under the Mistletoe' by Margery Allingham. Copyright © P. & M. Youngman Carter Ltd 1963. Reprinted by permission of Curtis Brown Ltd, London.

'The Santa Claus Club' by Julian Symons. Copyright © 1960, 1965. Reprinted by permission of Curtis Brown Ltd, London.

'The Plot Against Santa Claus' by James Powell. Copyright © 1971. Reprinted by permission of the author and the author's agents, Scott Meredith Literary Agency, Inc, 845 Third Avenue, New York, NY 10022, USA.

Special thanks and acknowledgements to the following: Bob Adey (not least for letting me prowl through his loft); Ed Hoch (for his usual friendly help); Bob Sampson and Walker Martin (for their sleuthing amongst the browned and brittle pages of old pulp magazines); Bill Pronzini and Barry Pike (for both suggesting superb stories, which I subsequently couldn't use—well, you tried); A.J. Flavell, Assistant Librarian of that most civilized of repositories, the Bodleian; the old firm of Bill Lofts and Derek Adley; the Revd Charles Gordon Clark; Sarah Cartledge of *Woman's Own*; G.R. Samways, Eric Fayne, John Cooper, Maurice Hall, Fr Francis Hertzberg and Mary Cadogan; and, not least, Robyn Sisman (for one very good reason best known to herself).

Sources

The stories in this collection originally appeared as follows:

Margery Allingham
'Murder Under the Mistletoe': *Ellery Queen's Mystery Magazine* (US), January 1963.

Robert Arthur
'A Present for Christmas': *Detective Fiction Weekly* (US), 21 January 1939.

Nicholas Blake
'A Problem in White': as 'The Snow Line', *Strand Magazine*, February 1949. As 'A Study in White', *Queen's Awards*, 4th Series (1949).

Anthony Burgess
'The Great Christmas Train Mystery': *Suspense*, December 1960.

John Dickson Carr
'Detective's Day Off': *Weekend*, 25/29 December 1957.

Joseph Commings
'Serenade to a Killer': *Mystery Digest* (US), July 1957.

Cyril Hare
'Sister Bessie': *Evening Standard*, 23 December 1949. *The Best Short Stories of Cyril Hare* (1959).

Edward D. Hoch
'The Three Travellers': *Ellery Queen's Mystery Magazine* (US), January 1976 (as by 'R.L. Stevens').

Peter Lovesey
'Murder in Store': *Woman's Own*, 21/28 December 1985.

James Powell
'The Plot Against Santa Claus': *Ellery Queen's Mystery Magazine* (US), January 1971.

Will Scott
'Christmas Train': *Passing Show*, 23 December 1933.

'Herlock Sholmes'
'The Secret in the Pudding Bag': *Penny Popular*, 27 December 1924.

Julian Symons
'The Santa Claus Club': *Suspense*, December 1960. *Francis Quarles Investigates* (1965).

'Peter Todd'
'Herlock Sholmes's Christmas Case': *Magnet*, 3 December 1916.

Edgar Wallace
'Stuffing': *John Bull Xmas Annual,* December 1926.

Ethel Lina White
'Waxworks': *Pearson's Magazine*, December 1930.

James Melville's *Santa-San Solves It* and Bill Pronzini's *No Room at the Inn* were written especially for this collection, and now appear in print for the first time.

A PROBLEM IN WHITE. The solution to Nicholas Blake's puzzle-story is printed overleaf. DON'T turn the page until you've read the story or unless, having read it you can't stand the suspense any longer.

Solution to
A Problem in White

THE Inspector arrested the Guard for the wilful murder of Arthur J. Kilmington.

Kilmington's pocket had been picked by Inez Blake, when she pretended to faint at 8:25, and his gold watch was at once passed by her to her accomplice, Macdonald.

Now Kilmington was constantly consulting his watch. It is inconceivable, if he was not killed till after 9 p.m., that he should not have missed the watch and made a scene. This point was clinched by the first-class passenger, who deposed that a man, answering to the description of Kilmington, had asked him the time at 8:50: if it had really been Kilmington, he would certainly, before inquiring the time of anyone else, have first tried to consult his own watch, found it was gone, and reported the theft. The fact that Kilmington neither reported the loss to the Guard, nor returned to his original compartment to look for the watch, proves he must have been murdered before he became aware of the loss, i.e. shortly after he left the compartment at 8:27. But the Guard claimed to have spoken to Kilmington at 9 p.m. Therefore the Guard was lying. And why should he lie, except to create an alibi for himself? This is Clue A.

The Guard claimed to have talked with Kilmington at 9 p.m. Now, at 8:55 the blizzard had diminished to a light snowfall, which soon afterwards ceased. When Stansfield discovered the body, it was buried under snow. Therefore Kilmington must have been murdered while the blizzard was still raging, i.e. some time before 9 p.m. Therefore the Guard was lying when he said Kilmington was alive at 9 p.m. This is Clue B.

Henry Stansfield, who was investigating on behalf of the Cosmopolitan Insurance Company the loss of the Countess of Axminster's emeralds, reconstructed the crime as follows:

Motive. The Guard's wife had been gravely ill before Christmas: then, just about the time of the train robbery, he had got her the best surgeon in Glasgow and put her in a nursing home (evidence of engine-driver: Clue C): a Guard's pay does not usually run to such expensive treatment; it seemed likely, therefore, that the man, driven desperate by his wife's need, had agreed to take part in the robbery in return for a substantial bribe. What part did he play? During the investigation, the Guard had stated that he had left his van for five minutes, while the train was climbing the last section of Shap Bank, and on his return found the mail-bags missing. But Kilmington, who was travelling on this train, had found the Guard's van locked at this point, and now (evidence of Mrs Grant: Clue D) declared his intention of reporting the Guard. The latter knew that Kilmington's report would contradict his own evidence and thus convict him of complicity in the crime, since he had locked the van for a few minutes to throw out the mail-bags himself, and pretended to Kilmington that he had been asleep (evidence of K.) when the latter knocked at the door. So Kilmington had to be silenced.

Stansfield already had Percy Dukes under suspicion as the organiser of the robbery. During the journey, Dukes gave himself away three times. First, although it had not been mentioned in the papers, he betrayed knowledge of the point on the line where the bags had been thrown out. Second, though the loss of the emeralds had been also kept out of the Press, Dukes knew it was an emerald *necklace* which had been stolen; Stansfield had laid a trap for him by calling it a bracelet, but later in conversation Dukes referred to the 'necklace'. Third, his great discomposure at the (false) statement by Stansfield that the emeralds were worth £25,000 was the reaction of a criminal who believes he has been badly gypped by the fence to whom he has sold them.

Dukes was now planning a second train robbery, and meant to compel the Guard to act as accomplice again. Inez Blake's evidence (Clue E) of hearing him say "You're going to help us again, chum," etc., clearly pointed to the Guard's complicity in the previous robbery; it was almost certainly the Guard to whom she had heard Dukes say this, for only a railway servant would have known about the existence of a platelayers' hut up the line, and made an appointment to meet Dukes there; moreover, to anyone *but* a railway servant Dukes could have talked about his plans for the next robbery on the train itself, without either of them incurring suspicion should they be seen talking together.

Method. At 8:27 Kilmington goes into the Guard's van. He threatens to report the Guard, though he is quite unaware of the dire consequences this would entail for the latter. The Guard, probably on the pretext of showing him the route to the village, gets Kilmington out of the train, walks him away from the lighted area, stuns him (the bruise was a light one and did not reveal itself to Stansfield's brief examination of the body), carries him to the spot where Stansfield found the body, packs mouth and nostrils tight with snow. Then, instead of leaving well alone, the Guard decides to create an alibi for himself. He takes his victim's hat, returns to the train, puts on his own dark, off-duty overcoat, finds a solitary passenger asleep, masquerades as Kilmington inquiring the time, and strengthens the impression by saying he'd walk to the village if the relief engine did not turn up in five minutes, then returns to the body and throws down the hat beside it (Stansfield found the hat only lightly covered with snow, as compared with the body: Clue F). Moreover, the passenger noticed that the inquirer was wearing blue trousers (Clue G); the Guard's regulation suit was blue; Duke's suit was grey, Macdonald's a loud check—therefore the masquerader could not have been either of them.

The time is now 8:55. The Guard decides

to reinforce his alibi by going to intercept the returning fireman. He takes a short cut from the body to the platelayers' hut. The track he now makes, compared with the beaten trail towards the village, is much more lightly filled in with snow when Stansfield finds it (Clue H); therefore it must have been made some little time after the murder, and could not incriminate Percy Dukes. The Guard meets the fireman just after 8:55.

They walk back to the train. The Guard is taken aside by Dukes, who has gone out for his 'airing,' and the conversation overheard by Inez Blake takes place. The Guard tells Dukes he will meet him presently in the platelayers' hut; this is vaguely aimed to incriminate Dukes, should the murder by any chance be discovered, for Dukes would find it difficult to explain why he should have sat alone in a cold hut for half an hour just around the time when Kilmington was presumably murdered only 150 yards away.

The Guard now goes along to the engine and stays there chatting with the crew for some forty minutes. His alibi is thus established for the period from 8:55 to 9:40 p.m. His plan might well have succeeded but for three unlucky factors he could not possibly have taken into account—Stansfield's presence on the train, the blizzard stopping soon after 9 p.m., and the theft of Arthur J. Kilmington's watch.